DIRECT ACTION

ALSO BY JOHN WEISMAN

FICTION

Jack in the Box: A Shadow War Thriller
SOAR: A Black Ops Novel

The Rogue Warrior series
(with Richard Marcinko)
Detachment Bravo
Echo Platoon
SEAL Force Alpha
Option Delta
Designation Gold
Task Force Blue
Green Team
Red Cell

Blood Cries
Watchdogs
Evidence

NONFICTION

Rogue Warrior (with Richard Marcinko)
Shadow Warrior (with Felix Rodriguez)

ANTHOLOGIES

The Best American Mystery Stories of 1997 (edited by Robert B. Parker)
Unusual Suspects (edited by James Grady)

DIRECT ACTION

A Covert War Thriller

JOHN WEISMAN

wm

WILLIAM MORROW
An Imprint of HarperCollins*Publishers*

HarperCollins books may be purchased for educational, business, or sales promotional use. For information please write: Special Markets Department, HarperCollins Publishers, 10 East 53rd Street, New York, NY 10022.

FIRST EDITION

Designed by Katy Riegel

Printed on acid-free paper

Library of Congress Cataloging-in-Publication Data

Weisman, John.
    Direct action : a covert war thriller / by John Weisman.—1st ed.
      p. cm.
    ISBN 0-06-075751-5 (acid-free paper)
    1. Terrorism—Prevention—Fiction.   2. Intelligence officers—Fiction.   3. Military intelligence—Fiction.   4. Undercover operations—Fiction.   I. Title.

PS3573.E399D57   2005

813'.54—dc22   2005040009

05 06 07 08 09 WBC/RRD 10 9 8 7 6 5 4 3 2 1

For Mimi Crocker
and
For Lieutenant Colonel Richard Campbell, USMC (Ret.)

CAREER GUIDANCE 101:
Big ops, big risks
Small ops, small risks
No ops, no risks.
—Hand-lettered sign posted outside a cubicle
in the CTC (Counterterrorist Center)
at CIA headquarters, spring 2003

CONTENTS

DIRECT ACTION

LANGLEY, VIRGINIA

1

ON 21 SEPTEMBER 1995, AT 11:47 A.M., five senior officers from the Central Intelligence Agency's Directorate of Operations—the CIA's clandestine service—quietly gathered in room 4D-627A, one of the sensitive compartmentalized information facilities colloquially known as bubble rooms, on the fourth floor of the headquarters building at Langley, Virginia. The Agency was still reeling from the February 1994 arrest of Aldrich Hazen Ames. Ames, an alcoholic, money-hungry wreck of a career case officer, had betrayed dozens of America's most valuable Russian agents to the KGB, resulting in their arrests and executions. He had also handed over many of CIA's technical tradecraft secrets and the identities of American undercover operatives.

Two of the clandestine officers at the meeting had been tasked with writing a Top Secret/Codeword damage assessment of the Ames debacle, a preliminary draft of which, at their peril, they were now sharing with three of their most trusted colleagues.

The assessment was grim. One had, it said, to assume that CIA had been completely penetrated because of Ames's treason. The Agency, therefore, was now transparent. Not only to the opposition, which still included Moscow, but to all of Moscow's current clients, including Libya, Syria, Sudan, Iraq, and—equally if not more critical—to the transnational terrorist organizations supported by those states. Transparency meant that the entire structure of the Directorate of Operations had to be considered as compromised; that every operation, every agent, every case officer was known to the opposition and its allies.

The only way to ensure that the clandestine service could survive in the coming years, the seniormost of the report writers suggested to his colleagues, would be to build a whole new and totally sterile spy organization inside CIA—a *covert* clandestine service within the *overt* clandestine service. But such a utopian solution, all five knew, would be impossible to achieve. The current director of central intelligence, John M. Deutch, would never allow it. Deutch, a tall, bumbling, angular, bookish MIT professor of chemistry who had served as undersecretary of defense, had been sent over from the Pentagon the previous May to clean CIA's post-Ames house. Instead of selecting savvy advisers to help ease his way into Langley's unique culture, the new director—himself a neophyte in matters of spycraft—brought with him as his closest aides two individuals neither of whom had any operational intelligence experience.

Deutch's executive director was Nora Slatkin, a presidential-appointee assistant secretary of the Navy. His deputy and right arm was George John Tenet, an NSC staffer who'd toiled on Capitol Hill for Senator David Boren among others. It didn't take more than a few weeks for the great majority of seasoned intelligence professionals of CIA's clandestine service, the Directorate of Operations or DO, to detest all three. The situation was made even worse when Deutch appointed David Cohen, a DI (Directorate of Intelligence) reports officer, to head the DO. Cohen, the corridor gossip went, absolutely *detested* spying and those who did it.

So no one was surprised that it took only a few months for Deutch and his associates to promulgate a series of orders that, in effect, prevented CIA's clandestine service from . . . spying. Under the new rules of engagement, every agent who had a criminal record, or was suspected of human rights violations, or who might be involved in any kind of criminal or terrorist activity, was to be jettisoned. Dumped. Ditched. Discarded. Their agent networks were to be disassembled.

By the 21 September meeting, more than half of CIA's foreign agents had been struck from the rolls and their names erased from BigPond, CIA's computer database run by Nora Slatkin's administrative division. More than fifty productive agent networks in Europe, the Middle East, South America, and Asia were summarily disbanded. Unable to recruit the sorts of unsavory but productive individuals it had targeted in the past, American intelligence quickly found itself going deaf, dumb, and blind. After the BigPond debacle, the old hands started referring to Slatkin as "Tora-Tora" Nora.

And voting with their feet. By summer's end of 1995, more than 240 experienced case officers—40 percent of those with more than fifteen years of field experience—had resigned or taken early retirement. The Agency's Counterterrorism Center (CTC) had been eviscerated, with many of its physical and technical assets either eliminated altogether or handed over to other agencies, including CIA's detested rival, the Federal Bureau of Investigation. CTC operations at Rhine-Main airport, Frankfurt, where its European crisis-management "crash team" was forward-deployed, was shut down completely.

It wasn't long before it was proudly announced during a closed-door session of the House Permanent Select Committee on Intelligence (HPSCI) that the new CIA leadership was saving more than $3.6 billion annually by closing nine CIA stations in sub-Saharan Africa and CIA's bases[1] in half a dozen Western European cities. The rationale was that with the Cold War over, America didn't need to keep tabs on Soviet agents anymore and the Agency outposts in such places as Düsseldorf, Barcelona, Marseille, and Milan were superfluous.

Alan Martin, CIA's assistant deputy director for collection, couldn't get an appointment with Deutch or his deputy, George Tenet. So he finally corralled one of Tenet's growing army of special assistants in the cafeteria.

---

[1]A CIA base is a small intelligence operation that functions as a satellite to the main intelligence-gathering unit, the CIA station, which is normally quartered in an embassy or in some cases a consulate general. The CIA station in Germany, for example, is physically located within the U.S. embassy in Berlin. There were, at one point, CIA bases in Frankfurt, Düsseldorf, Hamburg, and Munich. All were closed between 1995 and 2000.

He explained that the bases could be used to keep an eye on the growing number of Islamist radicals living in Germany, Spain, France, and Italy.

Martin was greeted with a blank stare. *Islamist radicals?* Who the hell cared about Islamist radicals living in Düsseldorf? We are into saving money here. Get with the program, Al, he was told, or get lost.

But that wasn't the worst part. The worst part was the tectonic shift taking place in the quality of the DO's people. The situation wasn't new: under previous directors William Webster and Robert M. Gates, DO had been forced to accept within its ranks analysts, reports officers, and secretaries, few of whom had either the inclination or the ability to spot, assess, and recruit agents to spy for America. The prissy Gates even had a politically correct term for it: *cross-fertilization.*

Now, under Deutch, Slatkin, Tenet, and Cohen, the vacuum left by the loss of experienced case officers was being filled by a growing torrent of unskilled, naive, risk-averse individuals who had no field experience. None whatsoever. Zip. Zilch. Zero. Analysts had already been appointed as chiefs of station in Tel Aviv, Riyadh, Nairobi, and Lisbon. A reports officer was running Warsaw. A former secretary with only six months of training had been made station chief in Kiev. *Kiev,* with Ukraine's vast store of Soviet-era nuclear weapons. Jeezus, it was like appointing a hospital's chief file clerk to head its neurosurgical team.

12:26 P.M. The five men in 4D-627A had more than a hundred years of combined intelligence work under their belts. Among them, there wasn't a region anywhere on the globe that they weren't familiar with.

Until Deutch had replaced him with a reports officer, Bronco—for Bronislaw—Panitz had been CIA's assistant deputy director for operations. Panitz had served in Eastern Europe. He'd been chief in Budapest and Singapore, come back to run Agency operations in Western Europe, then gone out again, this time to Madrid. At fifty-five, Bronco still had the imposing build of an NFL fullback. He worked out in Langley's gym four days a week, pumping iron and playing the same kind of full-contact, half-court basketball he'd first learned on the streets of Manhattan's Yorkville neighborhood as a teenager.

Antony Wyman currently ran CIA's much-reduced Counterterrorism Center. But the corridor gossip said he was about to be eased out, replaced by someone who'd be more compliant to the new director's wishes. Wyman was known as "tony Tony" because he was a complete and devoted Anglophile. His MA (history, honors) was from Cambridge. He wore bespoke chalk-striped London-tailored suits, loud Turnbull & Asser shirts, even louder T&A ties, and bench-made brown suede shoes from John Lobb. A gold-rimmed monocle customarily hung on a black silk ribbon around his neck, and a silk foulard square perpetually drooped from his breast pocket.

But Tony Wyman was no more a foppish dandy than the Scarlet Pimpernel. He'd served as chief in London, where he'd helped MI5 and MI6 put a dent in IRA terrorism, and in Rome, where he'd pressed SISMI, the Italian military intelligence service, to dismember the Red Brigades piece by piece. After Rome, tony Tony had been assigned by DCI William Casey to destroy the Abu Nidal Organization. The ANO had just killed five Americans during simultaneous December 27, 1985, attacks on TWA and El Al passengers at international airports in Rome and Vienna, and Casey wanted to put them out of business.

"You do what you have to, Tony," Casey had bellowed, spewing tuna salad as he spoke. He dropped the half-eaten sandwich onto its plate and slapped his cluttered desk for emphasis. "I want that rotten son of a bitch's head on a pike right next to our front gate. So don't you let me down."

Tony Tony had brushed the director's food from his *strié* velvet vest and gone to work. By the middle of 1987, a series of Wyman-devised covert-action programs had turned Abu Nidal into a paranoid psychotic. That November, he machine-gunned a hundred and sixty of his own people. Two weeks later, the terrorist chief ordered a hundred and seventy of ANO's Libyan-based operatives killed. By the end of the year, he'd tortured and murdered more than four hundred of his closest associates because Wyman's covert-action program had convinced Abu Nidal they might be leaking information to CIA. By 1988, the ANO ceased to be a serious threat.

Charles Hoskinson, the oldest officer at the meeting, was a lifelong Arabist. Short and round-faced, with longish, wispy white hair and neutral gray eyes set off by old-fashioned tortoiseshell, round-framed spectacles, Hoskinson presented a lot more of Bob Cratchit than he did James Bond. But his string of achievements was nothing short of remarkable.

In 1972, as Damascus chief of station—Hoskinson's first COS posting—he managed to recruit the brother of the Syrian ███████████

██

██

██

██

██

compromising poses ████████████████████████████████

██. Henry Kissinger during the 1973 October War. Then he ████████████████

████████████████████████████.

As chief in Beirut during the bloody Lebanese Civil War, Hoskinson maintained a clandestine backchannel relationship with the PLO that had included chaperoning Ali Hassan Salameh, Black September's chief of operations, the architect of the Munich Olympics massacre, and a CIA developmental, on a 1977 honeymoon vacation to Hawaii with his new Lebanese wife, the former Miss Universe Georgina Rizak. Hoskinson even tried to teach Salameh how to scuba dive, but discovered that the man who'd cold-bloodedly ordered the deaths of so many hundreds got claustrophobic and panicked underwater.

In Cairo, where he'd served from 1978 through 1981, Hoskinson was not only responsible for helping to guide Egyptian president Anwar el-Sadat through the negotiations that had resulted in the Camp David peace treaty, but he also convinced Sadat that it was in Egypt's long-term interests to throw the Soviets out—something Sadat did mere weeks before his October 13, 1981, assassination.

Hoskinson, however, had been sidelined. It happened after the thirty-plus-year veteran refused to terminate MJPLUMBER, a Palestinian agent who'd been involved in the 1987 attempted assassination of the Israeli ambassador to Spain. Sure, PLUMBER had murdered Israelis in the past, and he'd probably do so again if given the chance. But these days he was one of the PA's highest-ranking West Bank security officials. PLUMBER, however, had always had a weakness, a predilection for little boys. It was a vulnerability that had made him an ideal (and successful) candidate for recruitment by Giles T. PRENDERGAST, one of Hoskinson's case officers, in the mid-1980s.

Hoskinson was convinced Arafat was going to cheat on Oslo. And PLUMBER, who didn't like the way Arafat was skimming millions without sharing the loot, would divulge how the chairman planned to do it, since he was now a trusted member of Arafat's inner circle.

But Deutch's troika wanted no part of MJPLUMBER. "I get everything I need from the Israelis," Deutch had reportedly growled. "I don't want some senator complaining that we hire buggering pedophile assassins as agents."

Hoskinson wasn't about to tell the DCI that you don't *hire* an agent, you *recruit* him, because the distinction would have been lost. Despite his entreaties, PLUMBER was cut loose, and CIA was denied its only unilateral access to Arafat's clique. When Charlie went to CIA's inspector general and filed a formal protest, Deutch's people went ballistic. The DCI summoned Hoskinson to his office and flat-out ordered him to retire. When Hoskinson refused, Deutch loosed his attack dogs to hasten the decision.

Ten days ago, Hoskinson had been forced to become a hall walker after Tora-Tora Nora's deputy had him evicted from his office. Undeterred, he'd set up shop in the cafeteria and used the extension of a friendly Near East division desk officer to receive messages. But one of the troika's spies had ratted him out.

This very morning, Tenet's toad of an assistant had appeared in the cafeteria with a note instructing Hoskinson to appear forthwith for a psychological exam. Obviously, since Hoskinson hadn't obeyed Deutch's every command, he was mentally unstable. An old friend who had access to Deutch's office suite warned Charlie the DCI was going to terminate him with cause.

Hoskinson had spent thirty-four years and three months at CIA. He loved the place and what it stood for, and he was damned if he was going to let Deutch and his people destroy it. Stan Turner, Bobby Gates, and Bill Webster had been bad enough. But Deutch, *Jeezus H. Keerist*. Hoskinson looked at Tony Wyman. "Goddamnit, Tony—it's time to get off our asses."

P█████████████,[2] the case officer who'd been tasked to write the majority of the Ames report, blinked. "I agree, Charlie. But what course do we take? I think we should sleep on it. Reconvene tomorrow with some ideas."

"Some of us already know what we have to do, STIGGINS," Hoskinson growled. Even in the bubble room he used the undercover officer's Agency pseudonym, Edward C. STIGGINS. "Ed, you made the perfect suggestion yourself an hour and a half ago. Sleeping on it won't change anything. There's only one element that has to be changed."

"Which is," Wyman continued, "that instead of building a new DO on the inside, we do it on the outside—and we make a lot of money in the process."

Alan Martin's knuckles rapped the table. "Take the DO private. Brilliant."

"A two-level organization." Wyman polished his monocle. "Level one: overt. A privately held corporation. Commercial and industrial risk and threat assessment, crisis management, and security counseling. Big market. Believe me, I've been approached." He looked at Panitz. "We're talking revenue in the mid-seven figures our first year."

Bronco Panitz caught the look between Hoskinson and tony Tony. *They'd been plotting this for some time now.*

Wyman shot his French cuffs to display antique five-dollar gold-piece cuff links. "Level two: covert. We target the areas where the DO is blind—Middle East, Southwest Asia, Africa, et cetera, and then we sell our product—twenty-four-karat stuff—back to Langley. For a stiff fee, of course."

"And Langley will pay," Hoskinson said. "Because it's a Potemkin Village these days."

"He's right," Alan Martin grumbled. "There's virtually no human product coming in. It's all liaison and technical."

---

[2]This officer, who retired on ███████ 200█, spent his entire career working undercover. He was listed as a senior Foreign Service officer (rank of career minister) of the Department of State when he left government service. Later that same day, at a private ceremony on Langley's seventh floor, ███████████ was awarded CIA's Intelligence Star for Valor, the Agency's third highest award, as well as the gold medallion signifying more than thirty years of service. Since ██████'s retirement was covert, both awards currently sit in a safe at CIA headquarters.

"Recruiting won't be a problem, believe me," Tony Wyman said. "Deutch is pushing the best people out. I've got commitments from more than a dozen of our colleagues."

Alan Martin had to admit it was brilliant. In order to save the Directorate of Operations from self-destructing, Hoskinson and Tony were suggesting they run the same sort of covert action they'd used successfully in the past against the Soviet Union, China, Iran, and dozens of other nations, political parties, and terrorist groups. But instead of providing information that would destabilize, they'd pass on the intelligence CIA was currently incapable of gathering for itself.

STIGGINS frowned. "Deutch won't like it."

"Deutch won't ever know." When STIGGINS started to object, Bronco Panitz said, "Christ, David Cohen's always contracting annuitants for odd jobs. As well as farming out work to half a dozen consultants."

It was true. Retirees currently ran one-man CIA stations in five sub-Saharan African nations on a contract basis. In the NE bureau, there were two acting branch chiefs who were actually employees of private risk-assessment firms. One had resigned from CIA in 1994, the other in 1995. But because they had current clearances and polygraphs, they'd been hired back—in their old slots no less—because CIA had so few experienced case officers available with real street experience in the region. The two, who'd retired at the GS-14 level and earned roughly $86,000 a year, were now costing the American taxpayer $1,250 per day each, plus benefits: $325,000 a year.

"You'll need a network at headquarters, Tony." Alan Martin's expression grew intense. "Access agents, penetration agents, agents of influence, and most important, *moles*. You know how it is on the seventh floor. It's all about job security. If you don't have a handle on what the seventh floor is thinking, sooner or later they'll scapegoat you."

Tony Wyman fixed the monocle into his right eye and stared first at STIGGINS, then swiveled oh . . . so . . . slowly toward Martin, then panned back again to STIGGINS. He released his facial muscles. The monocle fell. "And your point is . . ."

Alan Martin got the message. "STIGGINS and Martin. It sounds like a vaudeville act."

Tony Wyman grinned. "It sounds more like the 4D-627 Network to me."

By 2:30 P.M. they'd reached a consensus. An hour and a half later, Antony Wyman, Bronco Panitz, and Charles Hoskinson had started the paperwork for their retirements. When Tony's secretary asked what he planned to do, he said he and a couple of friends were going to open a private security firm.

"What are you going to call it? Wyman and Associates?"

"Wyman and Associates. Has a nice ring to it, m'dear, but perish the thought. Far too . . . *égoïste pour moi*. We are calling ourselves . . . the 4627 Company."

EREZ CROSSING

2

SASS RODRIGUEZ SHIFTED IN THE DRIVER'S SEAT of the armored Chevy Suburban and panned his Oakleys through the thick, bulletproof windshield of the big silver FAV.[3] "Perfect day for the beach, huh, McGee?"

"You're right, Sass-man. It's beer weather." Jim McGee was riding shotgun. His dark eyes flicked up toward the clear blue sky. He sighed, ran his fingers through close-cropped, prematurely gray hair, then rapped scarred knuckles on the thick glass of the permanently sealed, two-inch-

---

[3]Fully armored vehicle. FAVs are six-ton Chevy Suburbans whose glass can withstand repeated AK-47 rounds, whose body armor plating is impervious to RPG fire, and whose undercarriages have been structurally reinforced to withstand many types of improvised explosive devices (IEDs).

thick side window. "All that draft Carlsberg and all that beautiful Israeli booty and we'll be stuck in this sardine can all day."

"You volunteered to waste your time, Jimbo," Sass said. "Not my prob."

"You're right—stupid me." McGee scanned the knot of vehicles in front of them as Sass eased forward past the first line of scarred concrete Jersey barriers leading to one of the checkpoint funnels. "Time to check in." The FAV halted abruptly as a cluster of nervous-looking Israeli soldiers in full combat gear signaled Sass to stop. Then, using the muzzles of their rifles to give instructions, they shifted half a dozen cars aside, pulled a white Citroën with four young Arabs from the line, yanked the Palestinians out of the car, and proned them facedown in the dust.

McGee unlatched the microphone from the radio bolted to the console, pressed the transmit button, and said, "Tel Aviv Base, Lima-One. Pulling into Erez checkpoint."

There was a six-second pause. Then the radio crackled: "Lima-One, Tel Aviv. Position confirmed."

"What would we do without GPS?" Sass scratched his ear and swiveled toward the third man in the FAV. "Think we'll get held up today, Skip?"

"Nah." Skip O'Toole tapped his earpiece, squelched the volume on the walkie-talkie, held his hand over the microphone clipped to the collar of his 5.11 tactical vest, and leaned forward. "It's been quiet since the holidays." He pointed toward the Citroën. Two of the four passengers were being flexi-cuffed, arms pinioned tightly behind their backs, Israeli M-16s pointed at their heads. "See how mellow the Is are today? They ain't kicking anybody. They ain't shooting anybody. Just poking 'em a little— enough to rile 'em but not enough to set 'em off." O'Toole was smaller framed than the other two—a wiry little red-haired bundle of energy who ate like a horse and ran marathons when he wasn't chasing what he liked to call long-haired dictionaries.

But then O'Toole was a SEAL, a West Coaster out of SEAL Five who'd been forward-based in Guam. He was twenty-nine, and he'd loved the Teams. But even Froggish camaraderie wasn't enough to prevent him from leaving the Navy after his third hitch to hire on at DynCorp. Hell, O'Toole had two ex-wives, three kids, and a Stateside girlfriend to support, something that was impossible to do on a petty officer second class's salary. At DynCorp he brought down a hundred grand per year plus expenses, more than twice what he made in the Navy, and just about all of it tax-free.

Sass and McGee were older and both former Special Forces. Sass had retired as a sergeant first class out of Fort Campbell after twenty-five years of soldiering. McGee, who was the shift leader, was an E-7, too. But he'd spent nine years on the far side of the fence with Delta. Plus, he spoke three-minus Arabic and kitchen Pashto. Rumor had it McGee spent time in Afghanistan as a part of a hunter-killer element of combined CIA/Delta shooters. Gossip was he'd spent eight months pursuing UBL and the AQL, which was how Pentagon memo writers referred to Usama Bin Laden and the al-Qa'ida leadership.

Last time he was back in Virginia on a week's home leave, Sass heard whispers that McGee's final Delta assignment was a joint U.S./British op in Iraq: he'd been a squad leader for one of the Coalition's preinvasion insertion groups—the sneak-and-peekers who spent two weeks clandestinely designating targets just prior to D-day. RUMINT, which is how they referred to urinal gossip at the DynCorp cafeteria, had it McGee'd spent nine days in Baghdad setting up phone taps and positioning laser target designators.

But that's all it was—rumor. Because McGee never said anything about Afghanistan, or Iraq. He was pretty closemouthed. About himself in general, and about his time with the Unit, as he called it, in particular. "Been places and done things," is all he'd ever say, in an accent that was tinged with North Carolina but originally could have been from just about anywhere between Miami and Detroit except New England.

Sass Rodriguez wasn't closemouthed. He was a professional Texan from San Antonio—hence Sass, call-sign shorthand for Tex-sass. And he had an opinion about everything. Sometimes two or three opinions, all voiced in a lackadaisical Paul Rodriguez Tex-Mex drawl that McGee, O'Toole, and the rest of the DynCorp crew swore got thicker with the addition of any significant quantities of beer. Sass had been in Afghanistan, too. The big, barrel-chested blankethead worked the mountains with the Northern Alliance—Sheikh Massoud's boys—on horseback and shot himself a lot of Taliban. The CENTCOM commander—General Tommy Franks himself—had pinned a Bronze Star with combat "V" on Sass's blouse. Sass carried a picture of that event in his wallet.

O'Toole's arm stretched between Sass and McGee. "There's our escort," he snorted derisively.

McGee shifted the M4's collapsible stock, which was resting against the snuff can in the cargo pocket of his tan Royal Robbins trousers, and snugged it between the glove compartment and the door trim. He plucked the instant-focusing field glasses from the console and held them to his eyes. A hundred yards beyond the Israeli side of the crossing, two dirty, mud-encrusted black Subarus with dinged quarter panels, bald tires, and Palestinian Authority plates sat idling, thick, noxious-looking exhaust farting from the rusted tailpipes. Half a dozen sloppily uniformed Palestinian gunsels cradling banana-clipped AKs were leaning up against the cars, sandaled feet idly pawing at the dust.

McGee examined their faces up close and personal. Then he dropped the binocs back where they belonged, swiveled and glanced back through the Suburban's rear clamshell doors to make sure the second embassy FAV, the one containing the junior-grade consular officer and driven by Jonny Kieffer, the fourth man in today's detail, was positioned where it should be. Jonny caught McGee's eye through the tinted glass and threw him an A-OK wave. McGee gave Jonny an upturned thumb.

It was a visual pun. In Arab culture, the upturned thumb wasn't the good-to-go sign. It meant "up your ass."

McGee turned back, shifting his body so the Sig-Sauer P-229 that rested just behind his right hip didn't get between him and the seat back. Today was a milk run. They'd hightail past the Israeli-controlled industrial zone on the Gaza side of the checkpoint, then drive straight through Beit Hanoun to Gaza City.

McGee caught himself up. Driving straight through anywhere in Gaza was an oxymoron. The roads—and he used the term loosely—had been ruined by neglect and war. There were axle-snapping potholes and huge gouges made by tank and armored personnel carrier tracks. Palestinian drivers were worse than Beirutis—huge trucks belching black clouds of noxious fumes would cut through intersections without pausing for oncoming traffic. And there were other hazards, too: donkey carts, bicycles, and the deerlike Palestinian kids who paid no heed to the anarchic traffic but sprinted between cars willy-nilly and more than occasionally got themselves smacked like Bambi.

Well, they'd creep and crawl past Beit Hanoun, then weave their way off the garbage-strewn main road to a dusty municipal office next door to the crumbling Red Crescent headquarters on El-Nasser Street, where the consular kid was interviewing some Palestinian honor student about a Fulbright. The route was highlighted on the clear plastic cover of the map McGee'd tossed up on the dashboard.

It was all bullshit of course. Smoke and mirrors. Cover for action. The consular kid was a wet-behind-the-ears Agency case officer. And the honor student was some nineteen-year-old Fatah rock-chucker who was going to be cold-pitched. In English, of course, because the spook didn't speak much Arabic past *min fadlak* and *shukran*. The whole episode was going to be an exercise in futility.

So the only real development to take place this morning was that another Tel Aviv CIA case officer's identity was going to be blown to the Palestinian Authority—not that the PA had had any doubts in the first place about who was Agency and who wasn't. It was laughable. No, it was pitiful. The whole goddamn situation was textbook absurdity.

And it wasn't the people. There were a few good folks at CIA. Hard workers. Risk takers. McGee had operated with some of them in Afghanistan. But the leadership sucked. There was no leadership at CIA these days. CIA had devolved into a huge, unwieldy, risk-averse, molasses-slow bureaucracy. Just like McGee's beloved Army, CIA was controlled by managers, apparatchiks, and bean counters. The Warriors all took early retirement.

That's the way things went in Afghanistan back in 2001. For the first few weeks, the war was executed by black-ops Warriors and unconventional forces. Then Washington declared victory, the staff pukes took over, and the paper started flying. Among the first directives: all Special Forces were henceforth to reassume military grooming standards. That meant no more beards or native garb. It also meant that hundreds of SF personnel became obvious targets because they were no longer able to blend into the indigenous woodwork. The casualty rate went up. But the two-star who issued the order didn't give a damn. He had an MA in public administration, he lived in Tampa, and by God, he was going to make those hairy-assed SF mavericks over there con*form*.

Same sort of numbskull thinking was going on at CIA these days. And the situation wasn't going to change, either. Not in McGee's lifetime. McGee plucked a Styrofoam cup from the dashboard cup holder, spat tobacco juice into it, then used the rim to wipe his lower lip. He cocked his head in the direction of the Palestinian escort. "Y'know, you can tell from how professional they look they were trained by da Company."

"Nasty, nasty." O'Toole stifled a giggle as McGee replaced the cup. But it was true. As a part of Director of Central Intelligence George Tenet's plan for cooperation between Israelis and Palestinians, CIA had trained more than a thousand members of Yasser Arafat's security forces in everything from sniping and close-quarters combat to bomb disposal, defensive driving, interrogation, threat assessment, and counterintelligence.

The two guys who headed what the Palestinians called their Preventive Security Services, Jabril Rajoub and Mohammad Dahlan, were even flown as honored guests to Langley, where they were ushered into the DCI's seventh-floor private dining room. Rajoub and Dahlan ate lamb tenderloin, *haricots verts,* and garlic mashed potatoes on bone china emblazoned with the DCI's seal. They toasted the latest road map to Middle East peace with Opus One drunk from Baccarat stemware. After the second of these lunches went right according to plan, Tenet even allowed a few of the PSS's upper-echelon trainees to be brought to the holy of holies: Camp Peary, the Agency's clandestine facility outside Williamsburg, Virginia, for a few hours of instruction.

Lesser mortals were flown to ISOLATION TROPIC, the huge CIA explosives-and-mayhem school at Harvey Point, North Carolina, or to clandestine sites in South Carolina, Georgia, Arkansas, Louisiana, and Florida, where they received training from retired case officers and paramilitary contract employees. Everyone from the senior instructors at the Farm to the grizzled ex–Special Forces sergeants in Ocala agreed the Palestinians were excellent students—and DCI Tenet issued commendations to all involved. Then, when those excellent students returned to the West Bank and Gaza, instead of using what they'd learned to muzzle Hamas, Islamic Jihad, and the Al Aqsa Martyrs Brigades, the PSS officers promptly turned every bit of their new tradecraft skills against the Israelis.

Sass could see U.S.-financed Beretta pistols tucked ostentatiously into the Palestinians' waistbands. The youngsters reminded him of the neighborhood gangbangers of his childhood. Out of habit he shook the M4 carbine in its custom roof rack to make sure it was properly secured. "This is a cluster fuck waiting to happen," he said adamantly.

"Orders is orders," O'Toole said. But Sass was right and everybody knew it. The embassy's rules of engagement specified that all American diplomatic convoys had to provide twenty-four-hour notice of the precise time and specific route to the Palestinian Authority. Automatic weapons were to be unloaded and kept out of sight.

So far as Jim McGee's DynCorp crew was concerned, the only thing the embassy was doing by giving out their route and insisting on dangerous ROEs was providing aid, comfort, and intelligence to the enemy. And diplomatic milk run or not, McGee insisted that all of his people maintain what he called Condition Orange. That meant weapons loaded, rounds chambered, safeties on, no matter what the State Department rules might be. If crap hit fan, it wasn't going to be McGee's people who came home in body bags.

It wasn't that he'd taken sides, either. It was a matter of operational security pure and simple.

McGee'd been in Israel just over six months now. And being a former Delta trooper, he hadn't needed more than a few days to evaluate the situation on the ground pretty damn thoroughly. But even a novice could have seen the Palestinian security apparatus was completely penetrated by the same terrorist elements the PA was pledged by treaty to eliminate.

Worse, the situation in Gaza was deteriorating by the day. Each of Gaza's separate regions was under nominal control of one of the Palestinian Authority's local Palestinian Resistance Committees. In point of fact, the entire Strip was run by a crime syndicate headed by a Bedouin clan led by one Jamal Semal-Duma, a fifty-year-old drug and weapons smuggler who lived in Rafah, the city that straddles the Gaza–Egypt border. Not that anyone at the embassy cared. The only thing the cookie pushers at the embassy seemed to care about was the process. The talking. The back-and-forth.

It didn't take a genius to understand that the Palestinians were bringing more and more heavy weapons into Gaza. You didn't have to be a rocket scientist to see that sooner or later they'd manage to smuggle a chemical or biological bomb—or worse, the makings of a dirty nuke—into the Territories, or into Tel Aviv. Tel Aviv, where the top-five list of targets included the U.S. embassy.

But those facts, inescapable to McGee, never seemed to cross the embassy's radar. Nor did the nebulous but still unquestionable link between the Palestinian terror organizations and al-Qa'ida, or the similar liaison between the Palestinian militants and Hezbollah, which was a creation of Seppah-e Pasdaran, Iran's Islamic Revolutionary Guard Corps. Or the ultimate unthinkable: a marriage of convenience between Tehran and al-Qa'ida. But not according to AMEMBASSY Tel Aviv. The way McGee saw it, the first thing they handed out to new arrivals from Washington was a set of blinders. So far as McGee was concerned, the call letters for AMEMBASSY Tel Aviv should be SNE—for "see no evil."

3

MCGEE'D SPENT HIS FIRST WEEK and a half in Israel reacquainting himself with the country. He called a few of his old contacts from an Israeli special forces unit with which he'd once cross-trained and listened to their assessments of the current situation. He sat in the security office and read a thick sheaf of reports. He listened as a political officer briefed him on the Embassy's rules of engagement. And he spent five days traveling through the Gaza Strip with a PSS liaison security officer.

The Palestinian was careful to keep McGee away from the Palestinian Authority's weapons factories and the arms caches run by Hamas and the Al Aqsa Martyrs Brigades, as well as the tunnels under Rafah through which the PA smuggled weapons, explosives, and drugs. But McGee had had enough intelligence training at Delta to be able to observe discreetly. And he knew what to look for. And although he'd betrayed no hint of it to the PSS liaison, he spoke Arabic well enough to understand that the PA officer was telling everyone they met to keep their mouths shut in front of the American.

And when he and his team assumed their duties, it didn't take McGee long to realize American officials who traveled outside the Green Line[4] were being observed and targeted. Security vulnerabilities were being probed every time the embassy ran a convoy into Gaza or the Territories. And what with all the heavy weapons and who-knows-what-else being brought through the tunnels from Egypt, McGee was convinced it was only a matter of time until there was a significant attack on American diplomatic interests in the Jewish state.

McGee had gone to the embassy's regional security officer to make his feelings known. The RSO, both a realist and a professional, agreed with everything McGee said. But the bottom line was that at embassies—especially at this particular embassy—political considerations just about always won out over security realities. It was, the RSO said ruefully, all about appearances.

Unlike those in Kabul and Baghdad, for example, Tel Aviv's armored Suburbans were not equipped with the sorts of black-box variable-frequency oscillators that would remotely detonate roadside bombs at distances of 200 meters or more. The ambassador didn't mind the VFOs masquerading as TV satellite dishes that were mounted on the embassy's exterior. Approach within 250 meters of AMEMBASSY Tel Aviv with a remote-controlled car bomb in your car or on your body and you'd simply self-destruct long before you'd get anywhere near the building.

But he'd forbidden the RSO to equip any of the embassy security vehicles with similar devices. Forbade because it was ambassadorial doctrine that outfitting Tel Aviv's FAVs with such markedly proactive devices might incense the Palestinian Authority. Not equipped, the RSO explained, because the ambassador said VFOs would indicate the United States believed the PA to be thoroughly riddled through with bomb-planting terrorists.

The fact that the Palestinian Authority *was* in point of fact thoroughly riddled through with bomb-planting terrorists didn't seem to make a whit of difference. Frankly, McGee was dismayed at what passed for diplomacy these days.

But then, McGee didn't get a vote. Because Sergeant First Class James Edward McGee, United States Army (Retired) was a civilian contractor. A

---

[4]The 1949 armistice line separating Israel from the occupied territories.

hired gun. A merc. He was one of two shift leaders for a sixteen-man Dyn-Corp detachment that worked out of the Tel Aviv embassy's Regional Security Office. His formal job description entailed augmenting State's overextended Diplomatic Security Service agents by providing protective details for diplomats as they pursued their jobs, and furnishing visiting VIPs with competent American watchdogs.

In fact, things went a lot further than that. Sure, McGee and his people were bodyguards and chauffeurs. But they were also occasional nurse-maids, part-time guardian angels, and sometimes even confidants. In return, DynCorp paid them $375 a day, seven days a week, plus generous per diem and living expenses.

In McGee's case, there was also additional income from the Other Job. The job McGee could never talk about. Not to his DynCorp coworkers, not to the ex-wife back in North Carolina who received all of his Army pension and half his DynCorp salary, not even to anyone from the embassy. The spooky job, which was the real reason he'd elbowed his way onto this morning's trip.

At eleven last night, he'd received a phone call on the special cell phone. To all appearances, it was a wrong number. Except it wasn't a wrong number. It was a call-out signal from Shafiq Tubaisi, one of the Palestinian gunsels leaning on the dirty Subarus.

McGee'd spotted Tubaisi within his first couple of trips to Gaza. The kid wore American clothing—real Levi's, which were prohibitively expensive in Gaza, and Ralph Lauren–branded shirts. Turned out they'd been sent by distant relatives living in Dearborn, Michigan. Just about the first words out of Shafiq's mouth were that someday he wanted to visit the United States. It was an opening line McGee could have driven an Abrams tank through.

He asked about Shafiq's family—and picked up on the fact that the kid's father, a pharmacist, was sick and tired of paying kickbacks to the PA and Hamas. He asked his control officer to have the FBI check on Shafiq's Michigan relatives and was encouraged to find out the Tubaisis were not on any of the homeland security watch lists. McGee began by giving Shafiq little presents. Books of photographs. CDs. DVDs. It took a couple of months, but he finally came over the border solo and pitched the kid.

Shafiq took the hook. McGee set it. He played the kid like a fish, reeled him in, and dropped him in the creel. One reason it went so smoothly, McGee believed, was that it wasn't a one-way street. For example, the first thing McGee did after Shafiq proved his bona fides by supplying McGee with a list of all the cell-phone numbers and call signs used by the top leaders of Hamas and the Al Aqsa Martyrs Brigades, was to pull strings so the kid's brother got a visa allowing him to visit the relatives in America, and a couple of hundred bucks from the black-ops slush fund to help with expenses.

Recruit the whole clan, not just one man—that was the couplet McGee'd learned in Afghanistan from his CIA paramilitary colleagues. Obviously, the same poetry worked in Gaza. So, McGee's operational skills as a spy—albeit limited—were paying off. He was about to recruit his first unilateral agent in Gaza. Three weeks ago McGee had received POA—provisional operational authority—to take Shafiq to the next level. He was ordered to formalize the relationship—give the kid a wad of cash and schedule a polygraph so the agent recruitment process could be completed. And start to apply real pressure. McGee's bosses wanted him to start developing actionable intelligence.

A Rome-based polygrapher was dispatched to flutter the kid just after Labor Day. But then things began to unravel. Shafiq missed the appointment for the polygraph—and the box man had scheduled only twenty-four hours on the ground. Christ, it would be a month, maybe more, before the test could be rescheduled. Shafiq blew off the next meeting and it was almost the end of the month before McGee saw him again.

Only to be disappointed: the kid came up dry on the al-Qa'ida front. There was no evidence of al-Qa'ida, he insisted. No foreigners in Gaza.

"What about Arabs?" McGee asked.

"There are always Arabs," Shafiq answered. "Egyptians. *Bedou.* But none of the al-Qa'ida—the ones from Yemen or Saudi Arabia. I have not seen them."

McGee began to think he was getting the runaround. But he pressed on, tasking Shafiq to track down the rumors about personnel from the Islamic Revolutionary Guard Corps—Iran's Seppah-e Pasdaran.

The subject was obviously touchy because Shafiq had gotten nervous the moment McGee said the magic words. Shafiq hemmed and hawed as only Palestinians under pressure can hem and haw. Finally, after an excruciating series of serpentine wavering, flip-flops, vacillations, and equivocations, he whispered that he thought yes, maybe, perhaps, it was possibly possible the Seppah might have a man in Gaza.

McGee's antenna focused. "What makes you think that?"

"This one man, he came maybe two weeks ago or so, Mr. Jim."

McGee nodded. Inside, he was seething. Why the blankety-blank had Shafiq waited so long to tell him. McGee controlled his emotions and his breathing. He waited for the Palestinian to continue.

Shafiq took his time. He lit a cigarette. Inhaled deeply. Blew smoke out through both nostrils and his mouth simultaneously. Finally, he took the cigarette out of his mouth. "This one man, he's different. He moves around constantly. He has his own bodyguards—some are Lebanese from their accents; others speak in a dialect I do not know—and we're not allowed to bring weapons into his compounds."

"Compounds?"

"He moves every day and every night. Often twice. They say that sometimes he dresses as a woman."

"Have you seen him like that with your own eyes?"

Shafiq's own eyes focused on the ceiling.

"Shafiq—"

The Palestinian dropped his gaze to the floor of the dusty three-room flat just south of the Erez industrial zone McGee used as a safe house and drew a circle with the toe of his shoe. "I saw him only once, Mr. Jim. Only once."

"Where?"

Shafiq flicked the half-smoked cigarette onto the floor, ground it out, pulled a pack of Marlboros and a Bic from his shirt pocket, lighted a new one, and exhaled noisily. "In Gaza City. Coming out of a house on Mustafa Hafez Street behind the Islamic University." The Palestinian found something else on the floor to focus on. "I was assigned to guard the end of the street for three days," he mumbled. "That's why I couldn't make the last meeting."

McGee's tone hardened. "You didn't tell me."

The kid's eyes finally shifted past McGee's face. "You didn't ask."

"All right, Shafiq," McGee nodded. "Go on."

"I saw him when he came through the gate and got into the car."

"What does he look like?"

"It was dark. The windows of the car had curtains."

"Then how do you know it was him?"

Shafiq shrugged. McGee edged his chair closer to Shafiq's and stared coldly at the Palestinian. Quickly, Shafiq looked away. It was a cultural thing with Arabs. They detested being stared at; scrutinized. McGee knew it and was instinctively using body language to keep his agent off balance. It was, he'd discovered, an effective way of asserting control. McGee waited the kid out. Finally, Shafiq said, "I did see him, Mr. Jim."

"*Feyn*—where?"

"On Mustafa Hafez Street when I was a part of the security detail. I did see him get into the car."

"And?"

"He is shorter than you with dark hair."

That wasn't much help. "His face—round? Long? Square?"

Shafiq thought about it. "Round. But angular. A prominent nose, but not too big. Heavy eyebrows—like one big eyebrow."

"Beard?" Most of the Seppah had facial hair.

"No." Shafiq rubbed his index finger back and forth under his nose as if stifling a sneeze. "But a mustache like Saddam Hussein."

"How did he dress?"

"Dark trousers, white shirt with no collar, I think. Dark leather jacket."

The guy dressed more like a Hezbollah car bomber from Beirut's southern suburbs than a Seppah operator. McGee mentally tagged him Mr. ML, for Mustached Lebanese.

"Was he armed?"

Shafiq shook his head. "I saw nothing."

McGee scratched his chin. "And why do you think he is *Seppah*?"

"Because they treat him like a god, Mr. Jim."

"They?"

"Everybody."

McGee struggled for the correct Arabic words. They came out of his mouth distorted. "How does said treatment manifest itself?"

The Palestinian looked at McGee, confused.

McGee tried again. "How do you know they treat him like a god?"

Shafiq blew more smoke through his nostrils. "Because I heard when they took him to see the Sheikh Yassin, Yassin kissed both his hands and asked for his blessing."

The self-proclaimed Sheikh Ahmed Yassin was the wheelchair-bound godfather of Hamas. In the past year, the sixtysomething quadriplegic son of a bitch had sent dozens of homicide bombers out to kill hundreds of Israeli women and children.

The guy with the big mustache had to be important. Very important. McGee had read the security files on Yassin and knew the bastard was no hand-kisser.

McGee said nothing, but his mind was working overtime. Immediately he sent a Steg-encrypted message to his boss in Paris about the hand-kissing incident and got a terse message back: Have your agent get us a picture.

McGee set up a clandestine meeting with Shafiq. Obviously, this was potentially a huge development. It was now just before the Jewish New Year—a little over two weeks to Yom Kippur, the holiest day on the Jewish calendar and the thirtieth anniversary of the 1973 October War—exactly to the day, October 6.

If the Seppah was about to make a move in Gaza, that was significant. It confirmed McGee's own suspicions that the reconciliation being backchanneled from Tehran was a diversion. It told him Iran was still attempting to destabilize the region by using terrorist surrogates like this Mr. Mustached Lebanese—and that they conceivably might act on October 6. The Iranians were already involved in Iraq: hundreds of Seppah had crossed the border to take charge of Iraq's Shia majority. If McGee could confirm that the Islamic Revolutionary Guard Corps was simultaneously planning something in Gaza—supporting Hamas, Islamic Jihad, and the Al Aqsa Martyrs Brigades' operations during the Jews' High Holidays—the consequences could be cosmic.

McGee pulled at his right ear. He wished he had the polygraph results so he'd have some indication of whether Shafiq was fabricating or not. But he didn't. He was flying seat-of-the-pants now—hurtling blind through opaque clouds with no sense of up or down because the fucking artificial horizon wasn't functioning. Damnit—he didn't want to pull a John-John. He shot a quick glance at Shafiq, who was talking earnestly with one of the other gunsels. On the one hand, maybe he was being played. But on the other hand, maybe he wasn't. Either way, the clock was ticking.

And Shafiq was coming up with good stuff again. Maybe they were over the hump, whatever the hump might have been.

McGee had war-gamed the session. He'd decided on a direct approach. So he didn't mince words. "You must get me a photograph of this man, Shafiq."

The Palestinian's eyes went wide. "Mr. Jim, Mr. Jim, I cannot," he stammered.

McGee understood the young man's fear. But it didn't matter. McGee needed hard evidence. Paris wanted paper. It was time for Shafiq to deliver.

Shafiq was balky, but McGee insisted. Wore the Palestinian down. He put it to the kid in no-shit Arabic. "I did favors for you—and you keep telling me how much your family owes me. But I ask for nothing. I do more. I pay you—I have your thumbprint on the receipts. And what do I get in return? I get bullshit stories from you about a man in a black leather jacket and a white shirt with no collar who has Lebanese bodyguards and moves around a lot. That's not enough, Shafiq. It's time for you to earn your keep. I don't need rumors about a man from Seppah. I need a photograph. You will get it for me or there will be consequences. You have relatives in the United States. I have friends in high places."

Shafiq hadn't been able to look McGee in the face for the rest of the meeting. And then the kid just plain dropped out of sight. There'd been no contact for more than two weeks. The high holy days between Rosh Hashanah and Yom Kippur had come and gone without incident. There had been a few ripples—some overly ambitious amateur bomb makers had set their explosives off by accident down in southern Gaza. But no Israelis had been killed, there were no suicide attacks inside the Green Line, and—more to the point—the probes of American diplomatic targets seemed to have subsided.

Then the call last night. Today, McGee would get the photograph. Shafiq said so during that brief phone call. Spat out the three-word confirmation sequence twice before he'd hung up. That was why McGee'd pulled rank and assigned himself to the morning milk run.

4

9:56 A.M. The butt of the damn 229 dug into McGee's kidneys. McGee compensated by adjusting his own butt in the seat. Today he'd earn his salary—the contract that paid him six thousand dollars a month. The money was direct-deposited by a small engineering firm in Enid, Oklahoma, into an account in the Northwestern Federal Credit Union of Herndon, Virginia. The credit union in turn sent the funds directly into a bank account in the Cayman Islands.

Six grand a month wasn't a lot of money for putting his life on the line. But then McGee'd never worked for money. The recruiters knew that about him when they'd pitched him to go undercover because they'd already done a psychological profile and they knew just which buttons to push.

Once he'd signed the papers, McGee referred to himself as an IC, or independent contractor. His status was known formally as an A-contract with a GS-12 pay grade. Although he didn't know it, 4627 was charging CIA fifteen hundred a day for McGee's services.

The recruiters showed up about ten days after he'd extracted from

Baghdad. DO spooks. He knew they were for real because they'd been allowed inside the Delta compound, and because they were accompanied by
a tall, thin, bearded guy Jim McGee knew as the Kraut.

The Kraut, whose real name was Bernie Kirchner, was one of the CIA
paramilitaries with whom McGee had served in Afghanistan. The two of
them had been through some tough times. "We shared a shitload of roasted
horse in our three months together," was the way the Kraut put it as they
shook hands. Bernie was visual confirmation of the spooks' bona fides.

Except they weren't exactly from Langley. They said they were retired
CIA and they worked for something called the 4627 Company, which was
handling an Agency outsource contract. That's when McGee understood
this was all about wink-and-nod stuff. Hell, W&N was okay with him.
He'd worked with a few CIA wink-and-nods in Afghanistan. Not a month
ago, some big Washington risk-assessment firm had just sheep-dipped
three of Delta's most senior people to work on a cross-border program in
Iran. Then there was the financial end. Wink-and-nod paid a lot better
money than CIA, where you'd hire on as some GS-9 contractor. Besides,
no one got into the Delta compound unless they were active. Ever since the
Ed Wilson fiasco, there had been safeguards. So these guys could call
themselves whatever they wanted to. McGee would play along.

The lead spook was a tough old bird who called himself Rudy. He was
seventy if he was a day. Rudy told McGee he'd spent his entire career at
CIA doing counterinsurgency. Said he'd started with the Cubans and finished with the Kurds. They played a short round of who-do-you-know, and
Rudy knew them all.

Rudy was missing part of his left index finger. When McGee asked
how it happened, Rudy'd deadpanned, "Moray eel had it for breakfast." He
paused. "I had him for lunch."

McGee knew the real thing when he saw it, and Rudy was it.

The second spook was a thirtysomething youngster dressed in Eurochic
and Levi's who said his name was Tom. Tom had an engaging smile and a
laid-back, surfer-dude attitude. But from the way he moved, the way he
held himself, the way his eyes took everything in without appearing to
even move, McGee understood Tom was a case officer—maybe even one
of the few good ones.

Tom unzipped a black canvas briefcase, brought out a sealed brown envelope, and laid it on the table. Then he spoke to McGee in rapid, flawless Arabic. "Inside this envelope is a nondisclosure form. If you understand what I'm telling you, slide the envelope across the desk—don't lift, just slide—open it, read the form, then sign. After you do, we can tell you why we've come to see you."

"It is my pleasure to do so, sir," McGee answered in Arabic. Then he dropped a big index finger atop the heavy brown paper, drew the envelope to his side of the table, slit the end with the thick sharp blade of his Emerson folder, read the one-page boilerplate agreement, and signed.

They'd wanted to see if he understood Arabic well enough to respond properly. He'd just shown them he did. It also meant the job—whatever it might be—was somewhere in the Middle East.

Well, McGee liked the Middle East, and working for a CIA front company was all right by him. He was thirty-nine, he'd had twenty-two years of Soldiering, and it was time for him to go. Time to make some money for his family. He had an ex-wife and two teenage boys to support, and he was dedicated to them.

Besides, it had been a long ride. He'd begun his Delta selection process just as the Unit was preparing to leave for Somalia. He'd finished his specialized schools—denied area operations, Arab language, State's VIP protection course, safecracking, and other miscellaneous black arts—just as four of Delta's Spanish-language specialists left for Colombia to help track down and kill El Doctor, the notorious Medellín drug cartel boss Pablo Escobar.

He'd spent most of 1994 and 1995 commuting between Jordan, where he instructed the Royal Jordanian Army's elite Black Beret commandos in close-quarters combat and hostage rescue, and Israel, where he trained and then worked with Sayeret Duvdevan, Israel's Special Forces counterterrorist unit.[5] He'd been posted to Beirut under State Department cover to help protect the ambassador right after the 1998 Africa embassy bombings.

---

[5]Sayeret Duvdevan, or Unit 217, is an IDF (Israel Defense Forces) Special Forces unit that specializes in counterterrorist snatch operations. Its members speak Arabic and often pass themselves off as Arabs in order to get close to their targets without being noticed. The history of the unit precedes the creation of the Israeli state. In the 1930s and 1940s, Arab-speaking members of the PALMACH ("crush companies" in Hebrew) operated inside Arab villages to gather intelligence, posed as Arabs in order to smuggle weapons, and mounted clandestine military operations against the British.

McGee's time as a part of a Mistaravim, or undercover Arab-speaking Israeli unit, had given him the skills necessary to operate in Beirut's southern suburbs observing Hezbollah, and in the Bekáa Valley, where he spied on Islamic Revolutionary Guard Corps personnel headquartered in Baalbek.

McGee's familiarity with the Middle East—especially Israel and Lebanon—was what the Langley guys were interested in. It was all very straightforward stuff, Rudy said. "We're talking 'Espionage 101': you keep your eyes open and your mouth shut. Nothing more than you did in Lebanon—except this time you're not reporting to ISA[6] but to us."

Tom checked McGee's signature on the nondis, then provided some background. There was, he said derisively, only one Arabic-speaking case officer currently assigned to Tel Aviv. She worked under embassy cover but her Agency affiliation was known to the Palestinians with whom she liaised. Moreover, the fact that she was a woman compromised her ability to work in Gaza even if her status hadn't been acknowledged. From the way Tom described the situation, McGee understood that things at Tel Aviv station were FUBAR'd.

So, McGee asked, what's the problem?

The problem? Rudy didn't mince words. "CIA is effing eyeless in Gaza. The station chief refuses to recruit agents. That's the problem. Full stop."

The younger guy had shot Rudy a look. But when McGee pressed him, Tom had gone even further. CIA had no unilateral sources in the entire Gaza Strip. No access agents. No penetration agents. Not one single unilateral asset. CIA had trained more than twelve hundred Palestinian security personnel over the past half decade. But between bureaucratic infighting, blockheaded, risk-averse management, and just plain incompetence, Langley hadn't managed to recruit a single one.

And therein lay the rub. All hell was breaking loose in Washington because CIA hadn't had unilateral agents in Iraq before the war. There'd been satellite photos, of course. And signals intercepts by the thousands—so many that No Such Agency's Arab-speaking translators were still working on material from 2001. But all of the human-source intelligence on which

---

[6]Intelligence Support Activity, or ISA, is the former unit designator of the intelligence-gathering component for special operations and black ops. The current designator, ███████████, is classified.

George W. Bush had based his decision to invade Iraq—all of it; every single report—had been supplied either by defectors provided by Iraqi resistance groups or through CIA's liaison relationships with the Brits, the Germans, the Israelis, the Saudis, and the Jordanians.

That dependence on liaison, Tom growled, caused huge problems. When McGee asked how, Tom explained.

"Let's say," he said, "CIA gets a liaison report from MI6. The report says a trusted MI6 agent working in the Middle East has information that Saddam Hussein has developed mobile chemical weapons labs. The info-bit fits CIA's preconceived picture about Saddam's weapons-of-mass-destruction program. But it's uncorroborated. Uncorroborated is unacceptable. But Langley doesn't have any unilateral sources in Iraq. Instead, they e-mail the liaisons: *Anybody out there hear anything about an Iraqi mobile weapons lab program?*

"'We did,' Mossad answers. 'Our military intelligence organization, AMAN, says it's highly probable Saddam has mobile chemical/biological weapons labs moving around the country. We rate AMAN's information source as highly credible.'

"Then CIA goes to the Iraqi defector groups. 'You guys have anybody who knows about weapons laboratories built into tractor trailers?' And the Iraqi National Congress or the Iraqi National Accord, figuring that CIA wants a positive response, tells CIA, 'Sure, we hear about mobile chem/bio weapons labs all the time.'

"CIA says, 'We want to interview a defector with firsthand knowledge.' So INC flies a defector to Washington, where he's interviewed and polygraphed. The defector's polygraph, which shows no deception, is consistent with everything about mobile weapons labs CIA has learned so far.

"But the White House isn't satisfied. The president says, 'I won't go to war unless we've nailed this down one hundred percent.' So CIA goes to its pals in Berlin and asks about mobile weapons labs. BND, the German intelligence agency, tells CIA it interviewed an Iraqi defector pseudonymed CURVEBALL who confirmed that Saddam had mobile labs. He'd even worked on the program.

"Langley insists they want to talk to CURVEBALL. 'Sorry,' say the Krauts. 'You know the rules: he is our unilateral source and we don't compromise sources and methods.'

"No access is generally a no-no," Tom continued. "But in this case, CIA shrugs its institutional shoulders because it doesn't matter: the Agency now has multiple-source corroboration without talking to the BND's source directly. Then Director of Central Intelligence George Tenet briefs the president again. And when Bush asks if Tenet is sure about his info, because the U.S. is going to war based on what CIA has uncovered, Georgie boy says, 'Mr. President, this is a slam dunk.' Three weeks later, a line about mobile biological weapons labs gets inserted into Secretary of State Colin Powell's United Nations speech. When Powell asks Tenet if the information is solid, Tenet says something to the effect of not to worry, we got a triple confirmation. We're talking twenty-four-karat.

"But what CIA *doesn't* know is that London got its information from a unilateral MI6 Israeli agent—a lieutenant colonel working for AMAN. And CIA has no idea that the Brits' agent just happens to be the same guy at AMAN that CIA's Mossad liaison queried. CIA doesn't know because just like BND, MI6 doesn't reveal its sources and methods to liaison agencies. CIA also doesn't realize the defector INC flew to Washington is CURVEBALL—the same guy who told BND about mobile weapons labs.

"Worst of all," Tom said, "CIA can't confirm any of the information because it doesn't have any fucking unilaterals in a position to know about mobile weapons laboratories. Not in Iraq. Not inside the INC. Not in AMAN or Mossad. Not a single fucking agent under unilateral American control anywhere."

The unfortunate result: all of CIA's allegedly high-grade information about weapons of mass destruction, mobile biological warfare laboratories, missiles with chemical warheads, and nuclear-bomb programs was currently unraveling day by day. None of it had been accurate in the first place. It was a colossal humiliation for CIA and DCI Tenet. Worse, the situation was going to become a huge embarrassment for the administration, which was heading into the 2004 election year with a number of independent watchdog commissions tearing chunks of political flesh out of the White House.

And now, Tom said, the same goddamn situation was developing in Gaza. There was huge pressure on the White House to reactivate its Road Map for Peace between the Palestinians and Israel before the 2004 elections. But once again, CIA had no unilateral sources on the ground. And even if they had, the ambassador in Tel Aviv didn't allow CIA to recruit unilaterals from its Israeli and Palestinian liaison relationships.

But McGee, Tom said, could slip in under the radar. He wouldn't come under the ambassador's formal chain of command. He knew what to look for—and how to dig it out without being observed. He knew how to operate in a denied area—how to disappear in plain sight. He'd done it in Lebanon. He'd done it in Baghdad. And compared to Beirut and Baghdad, Gaza was a piece of cake.

McGee'd find a way to gather intelligence on the AQ terrorist cells—if there were in fact AQ terrorist cells. He'd seen how the Seppah operated in Lebanon. He'd be able to tell if they'd set up shop in Gaza. If things went well, he'd even be able to spot potential agents from among the mid- and high-level Palestinian security officials with whom he'd liaise during his official duties. He'd note their vulnerabilities, assess their potential, and pass their names on. After they'd been vetted, he'd recruit them—or pass them on to someone else who would get the job done.

When McGee asked about cover for status, Rudy explained he'd be hired as a part of a DynCorp security contingent for the Tel Aviv embassy. He'd work full-time for DynCorp. In fact, the salary, per diem, and bonuses were his to keep.

"You'll report to me," said Tom. "Encrypted e-mail using steaganography backed up by one-on-one meetings with a control officer. Like Rudy said, this is Espionage 101, Jim. Basic, keep-it-simple-stupid intelligence gathering." He gave McGee an encouraging smile. "C'mon—even you Delta guys can do it."

10:04 A.M. McGee's big Seiko told him they were behind schedule. He squirmed impatiently as a green-bereted Israeli border guard waved the two FAVs through the checkpoint. Sass threaded his way between the barriers, then pulled off to the side of the road behind the two filthy Subarus. As he stopped, McGee reached down, grabbed the M4, opened the door, slid out onto the dusty road, and approached the Palestinians, who were climbing into their cars. "Sabah il-kheer—good morning."

The tallest of the six shifted the thin canvas strap on his AK and peered at McGee through brown-tinted aviator glasses. "*Wenta bi-kheer*—and to you, Mr. Jim." The AK muzzle shifted and McGee moved out of its way. These idiots stood around with their fingers on the weapons' triggers and McGee could see that the AK's safety was in the off position. The Palestinian's eyes noted McGee's wariness and he arced the muzzle of his weapon away from the American's feet. "You are going to the municipality, correct?"

"Yes, Mahmud. Next to the Red Crescent headquarters." McGee's gaze caught Shafiq as he climbed into the shotgun seat of the first Subaru. The Palestinian was working hard to keep from making eye contact. McGee said, "We're late."

The Palestinian officer slung his AK. "*Yalla!* Let's go, then."

McGee turned on his heel and walked back toward the FAVs. Jonny Kieffer had his door cracked. McGee cradled the M4 and put his foot on the running board. "No problems. I'll follow him. You follow me. Let's stay on the radio and keep our eyes open."

"Roger that." Kieffer snapped the door shut and disappeared behind the dark-tinted, inch-thick glass. McGee returned to the silver Suburban, climbed aboard, stowed the M4, fingered the radio earpiece, adjusted the squelch control, slapped the dash, and transmitted: "*Hava na mova,* gentlemen. Let's get on with it."

10:07 A.M. The four-vehicle convoy cleared the industrial zone and headed south. To the east lay Beit Hanoun. Three miles south was Gaza City. The traffic thickened. Sass eased off, putting thirty yards of air between the heavy crash bumper and the Subaru. The dusty, potholed road widened, donkey carts and bicycles crowding the curb lane. Ahead, McGee could make out the first of the huge three-tiered pylons that ran power lines into Gaza City.

As the convoy passed the first of the pylons, the Subaru sped up, opening a hundred-yard space. "Goddamnit." Sass shook his head. "What the hell's he think he's doing." He tromped the accelerator, the big FAV's engine growled, and the Suburban shot forward.

"Stay with him."

Which is when a pair of kids in pajamas shot out from between a donkey cart and a delivery truck and dashed in front of the FAV. McGee shouted, "Holy shit, Sass."

Sass smacked the brakes hard. The big Chevy's nose swerved left as the heavy-duty pads caught the rotors. Then Sass brought the FAV under control. He braked and weaved as a taxi pulled in front of him to make a U-turn, pausing just long enough to shoot a glance back at the two teens who were waving and giving them the finger from the northbound side of the road. "Fucking kids."

McGee tapped the windshield. "Pay attention, will ya?" The Subaru was now easily two hundred yards ahead and McGee was pissed. "C'mon, Sass, do your job—catch up."

Sass started to talk, then caught McGee's expression. McGee wasn't himself this morning. He was testy. Impatient. Edgy. Sass decided not to probe. "Gotcha, boss." Sass accelerated.

They were approaching the Beit Lahiya intersection now and Sass had managed to close the gap by half when something caught McGee's eye. Maybe fifty, sixty yards ahead was a newly patched pothole. It was right in the middle of the southbound traffic lane. It got McGee's attention because it was the only pothole patch he'd seen all day. And it stood out like a sore thumb. A four-by-four foot patch of black asphalt slopped messily into the brown dust of the road surface.

And then McGee saw something else. It was either a thick black wire or maybe a length of flexible electrical conduit that ran from the edge of the patch under a big lorry, across the curb, over the sidewalk, and disappeared under a two-meter-high corrugated metal fence.

The hair on McGee's neck stood straight up. He shouted, "Lima—alert!" into the collar mike, snatched the field glasses, and scanned for threats. That was when McGee saw the mustached man. He was dressed in the same olive-drab shirt and trouser uniform as any minor PSS official. A red-and-white-checked kaffiyeh was draped around his neck, and an AK hung from his left shoulder. But there was something . . . different.

What drew McGee's attention to him was that he was out of position for a security officer. The guy was perched three stories high on a construction scaffolding perhaps a hundred and fifty, two hundred yards down the road, just past the intersection, scanning the U.S. convoy through a pair of binoculars. He held a cell phone in his left hand. McGee focused on him. It was a flip phone and it was open. But the guy in olive drab wasn't holding the phone to his ear: his arm was dangling at his side.

The son of a bitch is looking straight at me, McGee thought.

And then, never moving the binoculars, the man lifted the cell and used his thumb to press the control buttons. It was hard to do with one hand, but he never stopped looking through the field glasses, looking straight into McGee's brain.

That was when McGee understood what was happening.

Oh Mother of God, oh Christ, oh holy shit. "Jam it, Sass—go left—go left—go left!" McGee dropped the binoculars and lunged for the wheel, fighting to get his leg over the console so he could stomp Sass's foot and put pedal to metal.

Then suddenly his existence turned dreamlike and McGee realized that somehow he'd slipped into a parallel universe where everything happened in slow motion. And no matter how hard he tried, McGee just couldn't . . . make . . . things . . . move . . . fast . . . enough.

Sass twisted his head in McGee's direction, mouth wide, a primal scream building in his throat.

McGee never heard him. The Suburban was already disintegrating around the three of them. The worried, confused, childlike expression on the Texan's round face was the last thing McGee saw before the big silver FAV exploded in a huge orange fireball.

HERNDON, VIRGINIA

5

MARILYN JEAN O'CONNOR, Marymount College class of 1994, knew she'd worked at the Central Intelligence Agency for precisely seven years, two months, and eleven days because she was an unusually punctilious record keeper. A GS-9, MJ, as she called herself when she wasn't at work, was a midgrade analyst in the ten-person Counterterrorist Photo Interpretation Group, which was acronymed C-PIG. She and her fellow C-PIGgies spent their days rooting for intelligence truffles in a windowless office facing an interior corridor on the fourth floor of an anonymous, ugly, toad-green glass box of an office building that sat six hundred yards east of Route 28 and 1.3 miles south of the Dulles Toll Road's Exit 10.

Sometimes, as she came and went, MJ felt a little bit like a character out of the movie *Three Days of the Condor*. Actually, she felt like a character out of the novel *Six Days of the Condor,* because being a thorough sort of person, after she'd rented the movie on DVD, she'd gone out and found a copy of that seminally existential work of 1970s espionage fiction. She much preferred the book to the truncated, slick filmic adaptation.

The building in which she worked was, just like the covert CIA office in *Condor,* not identified as a government installation. On the maps at headquarters and in CIA phone books, the place was called Building 213 West, although it was more popularly referred to as Coppermine. What civilians saw as they drove past was a six-story opaque glass-and-steel structure that bore a (bogus) corporate logo that looked little different from the logos of the scores of dot-com slash telecom slash info-com companies that inhabited Northern Virginia's Tyson's-to-Dulles corridor.

It was, so the security types at CIA pronounced, a perfect work of cam-ouflage. A few wags from the DO would from time to time mention that the pneumatic Pentagon-grade traffic barrier at the gate, the triple row of Jersey barriers, and the twenty-four-hour shifts of armed guards toting sub-machine guns in the parking lot might raise an eyebrow or two. But then, given the public's wide acceptance of the Patriot Act and the fact that Capitol Hill tours now included a drive-by of the five Army Patriot missile batteries ringing the complex, perhaps not.

Anyway, just like Ronald Malcolm, *Condor*'s central character, MJ couldn't tell a soul what she actually did for a living.

And just like Malcolm/Condor, MJ had no idea why CIA considered what she did so highly, highly classified. Sensitive? Sure. But MJ's new boss, a covertly retired Very Senior Operative who'd been rehired at CIA in the months following 9/11 as the counterterrorist analysis coordinator, had actually insisted that the members of the C-PIG conduct themselves as if they were stationed on foreign soil. "Hostile territory" were the exact words she used.

Which is why when MJ was on the job, she and her colleagues called one another by pseudonyms. Mark Olshaker, the good-looking, tall, prema-turely gray guy in the cubicle across the way, was known as Julian C. WEATHERALL. She called him Mr. Julian. MJ's pseudonym was Hester P. SUTCLIFFE, and Mark called her Miss Hester. It had taken MJ and her coworkers almost three weeks to get used to their new identities. During the transition, which MJ decided early on was a bureaucratic fusion of sublimely ridiculous and painfully agonizing, they were all ordered by their new supervisor to attach convention cocktail party "My Name Is" peel-and-stick labels bearing the preposterous pseudonyms on their lapels.

Said boss-lady was a petit, autocratic, blue-haired woman in her early seventies who brooked no back talk and wore ivory silk and navy-blue wool no matter what the season. Her peel-and-stick label read

MY NAME IS
PORTIA M. ST. JOHN
ST. JOHN IS PRONOUNCED *SIN*-GIN

"My actual name," she'd said at her first meeting with the newly formed C-PIG and the six other working groups over which she had control, "is need-to-know, and you lot do not have the need." She would be called, she said, Portia M. ST. JOHN, or more simply as Mrs. ST. JOHN. She then enunciated "*Sin*-Gin" twice.

Mrs. ST. JOHN's obsession with secrecy was, she insisted at that same meeting, a matter of life and death. The country was now at war and all the rules had changed. She knew war, she said, because she'd been a teenager during World War II and had come of age in the CIA as a secretary to several chiefs of station during the height of the Cold War. She had, she said, watched as one after another of nation's secrets hemorrhaged through carelessness, neglect, and treason.

Loose lips sink ships, and there would be no bobbing life rafts on her watch. Corridor gossip was henceforth forbidden. There would be no job talk outside the building at any of Herndon's myriad bars and restaurants. The on-site pseudonyms, she reiterated, had been instituted in case the offices were bugged. That way, the staff's real names would remain unknown to the thousands of hostiles intent on stealing America's crown jewels.

Despite the warnings—not to mention the security posters that Mrs. ST. JOHN hung in all the corridors, Marilyn Jean O'Connor often wondered about the need for such analog-generation tradecraft as office pseudonyms. After all, the building's exterior windows were all triple-paned glass with white sound running between the outside two panes, and the secure communications system, the classified computer network, and the unclass telephones were checked daily by technicians from one of the CIA Division of Security's offices. If truth be told, the in-place TECHSEC[7] at C-PIG and the other counterterrorist-related offices that did business from the toad-green glass box on Coppermine Road was newer and far more thorough than what was available at some of the older clandestine CIA satellite buildings that fanned out across a vast swath of Northern Virginia. Only at Coppermine, however, was the personnel's security bar placed so high.

Indeed, Mrs. ST. JOHN affected not only MJ's work environment, but her social life. It was, in a word, constricted. Because of the new regs, Hester P. SUTCLIFFE, spinster, was pretty much confined to dating bachelors whose clearances were either equal to, or higher than, her own. That was a problem, too. Of course Hester (as she thought of herself five and sometimes six days a week) wasn't actually dating these days. She was in mourning over a just-ended long-term relationship with Tom Stafford, a thirty-nine-year-old case officer who worked at the Counterterrorism Center as a troubleshooter. MJ's brain corrected itself. Who *used* to work at CTC.

She was trapped in an emotional maze. The relationship was over—but it wasn't. They'd said it all—but there was a lot left to be said. And then there was the passion. Oh, the passion.

Still, Tom was gone. That was a certainty. He'd quit CIA in January over some dumb flap—refused to elaborate other than to say the people for whom he worked were idiots and he couldn't deal with the place anymore. By April, he'd moved to France and taken a job running the Paris office of the 4627 Company, which MJ understood to be a somewhat shadowy risk-assessment and security consulting firm owned by a bunch of retired CIA supergrades. There was something fishy about it.

Still, she couldn't argue the money. Tom had resigned as a GS-15, step 5. He'd made just over $110,000 a year. The 4627 Company gave him a vice president's title, a $250,000 salary—most of it tax-free—and a €250,000 signing bonus so he could buy an apartment in the fashionable sixteenth arrondissement. Moreover, he was returning to familiar turf. Tom had served at Paris station for almost four years in the mid-1990s and he'd always said he felt more at home in France than he ever did in Washington.

[7]Technical security precautions.

It had been an amiable, if heart-wrenching split. They still talked every three or four days. She'd visited him in Paris in August, staying for a week at his apartment at 17 rue Raynouard and loving every minute of it. She was, in fact, going to Paris tomorrow for a long weekend with him. The keys to rue Raynouard were already in her handbag.

Tom would probably take her to some romantic, candlelit restaurant, buy her champagne, and ask her to come to Paris and move in with him. It had become his mantra. Every time they spoke, Tom pleaded his case.

So far, she'd refused. There were two niggling problems. The first was rooted in her traditional Irish-Catholic upbringing. O'Connors did not quit their jobs and move to Paris to, well, shack up.

When Tom told her she was taking an old-fashioned stance, her answer (in decent brogue) went: "What's your point, laddie?"

Sure she was old-fashioned. Between the parental influence of Assistant Battalion Chief and Mrs. Michael John O'Connor (FDNY, retired) and sixteen years of parochial education, that's how she felt. She was a modern practicing Catholic. She'd always maintained her one-bedroom condo in Rosslyn, even when she and Tom spent most of their time in his Reston town house. It gave her a sense of independence, of security. When—and if—they committed to marriage, she'd give it up.

But that hadn't happened. And it stung. She understood some of his emotional core. He was a case officer—had been for more than seventeen years. And case officers tended to compartmentalize everything in their lives. They had to, because most of the time they lived lies.

There was only a one letter difference between *lives* and *lies*. What a difference that *v* made. It wasn't that Tom lied to her, either. It was that he *compartmentalized* her—as if she were stored in a drawer somewhere in his brain, and when he wasn't out doing what he did, he'd open the drawer and let her out.

There was always a part of him that was, well, a part apart. She'd never sensed the sort of whole-soul commitment she'd always felt marriage deserved. He said he loved her. And he did. She understood that. But whenever she brought up the M-word, he'd shy away. Retreat behind his damnable case officer's emotional bulwarks and raise the drawbridge.

And then he'd resigned from CIA and moved to Paris. Abruptly. And not explained why—at least, not satisfactorily so far as MJ was concerned.

And now he wanted her to give everything up and move to Paris with the possibility that it would all blow up? Sans commitment? *Merci, monsieur, mais non.*

Second, there was the current war on terror in which America was engaged. MJ felt that given the crises that came one after another like aftershocks, she wanted to perform some tangible service that would help the U.S. prevail. Working at C-PIG—despite Mrs. SJ—provided that feeling of commitment.

But the unresolved personal situation left a big hole in her heart. God, how she missed him.

To compensate, she threw herself headlong into her work. What Marilyn Jean and her group did was spend their days perusing news photographs from the dozens of agencies that distributed pictures to newspapers and wire services all across the globe. The analysts would use a series of databases to evaluate the people in the photographs. They would first access the Department of Homeland Security's Terrorist Threat Integration Center database. TTIC, as it was known, held six hundred terabytes of information in its direct-access files, including just over ten thousand photographs of known terrorists.

If TTIC came up dry, MJ would move on to the CIA's BigPond photo database. There, she had access to photographs obtained from identity cards, passport and visa applications, driver's licenses, as well as clandestinely taken surveillance and countersurveillance photographs. There were pictures obtained during case officer and agent debriefings, and footage covertly sluiced from government cameras in half a dozen national capitals across the globe. If something clicked, she'd play with the photograph using a secure program called IdentaBase. IdentaBase was one of CIA's latest VEIL—Virtual Exploitation and Information Leveraging—programs. It allowed MJ not only to access the entire range of national security photographic databases, but its features also included a hugely sophisticated, computerized version of the old police IDenta kits, in which predrawn features—noses, ears, hairlines, face types, and so on—are matched part by part by witnesses.

The result in the old days was a composite drawing of a suspect. VEIL programs went a lot further. MJ could automatically match templated facial characteristics with the TTIC and BigPond photo databases—hundreds of thousands of mug shots and surveillance photos of known or suspected terrorists. Roughly a third of those pictures were new additions to Big-Pond, collected by CIA over the twenty-five post-9/11 months from its stations and bases worldwide. The rest were file photos from half a dozen other agencies—DIA, NSA, FBI, and the National Reconnaissance Office among them—that dated back as far as the 1960s.

The software made its identifications based on 127 separate and distinct points of recognition. Whenever MJ found something in the photographs she believed to be significant, she would flag the photo, print it in high resolution, write a report detailing what she'd found, then pass the package, which was always placed inside an orange-tabbed Top Secret folder, to Mrs. ST. JOHN, who would review it.

If the sin-gin lady thought MJ's work had merit, she would pass it up the chain of command to the Counterterrorist Center's senior analyst, a bookish, long-retired reports officer pseudonymed Percival G. LONG-WOOD, who had also been rehired post-9/11. Percy LONGWOOD worked somewhere in the ever-expanding maze of offices that made up the CTC, which currently took up more than half of the sixth floor of the CIA headquarters main building.

MJ had met him exactly once in the twelve months she'd worked at the C-PIG. He'd come to meet the staff at Coppermine. His first words to her were, "Call me Percy, gorgeous." He was just over five feet tall. He wore a shiny polyester blazer, sported a Ronald Coleman mustache, parted his slicked-down hair in the middle, and he stank of aftershave. When he'd called the next morning on the secure phone and asked her out, she'd had to stifle a huge guffaw.

MJ was bothered by the current level of creative tension at the C-PIG. She found the sin-gin lady's professional views stiflingly inflexible. With the unhappy result that Portia M. ST. JOHN and Hester P. SUTCLIFFE had constantly differing opinions about what the term *significant* meant. To Marilyn Jean O'Connor, significant was whenever a face in a crowd caused the recognition software to hiccup. To Mrs. ST. JOHN, significance only occurred when the recognition software had a 100 percent positive ID—which meant all 127 points that formed the recognition criteria were matched perfectly.

The problem, as MJ had tried to explain, was that setting such an unyieldingly high bar precluded the possibilities of factoring in old-fashioned facial disguises, not to mention the sorts of appearance-changing prosthetic devices that CIA case officers commonly used, as well as more radical transformations, like plastic surgery. But whenever MJ brought the subject up, Mrs. ST. JOHN would remove her wire-frame half-glasses and finger her brooch, a sign that the individual standing before her was dismissed.

Despite the consequences this interpretational schism might have on her career, MJ continually pushed the edge of the analytical envelope. Indeed, if the software as much as twitched, MJ would immediately start the sophisticated IdentaBase program. If IdentaBase hit anything over eighty points, she'd forward the material to Mrs. ST. JOHN. MJ's attitude was better safe than sorry, and if Mrs. SJ didn't like it, to hell with her.

C-PIG's source material was delivered by armed messenger from Langley twice a day. Why the hell Mrs. ST. JOHN insisted on a guy with a gun on the bike was another unfathomable. The photos, after all, were open source. They'd been published in newspapers, magazines, and on the Internet, for chrissakes. In any case, the jpg files were downloaded onto C-PIG's secure computer network, then scanned on ultra-high-resolution twenty-inch flat screens and run through the interpretation group's databases, by region. MJ was responsible for the Middle East and North Africa.

6

8:22 A.M. This particular morning, MJ began by examining a series of Agence France Press pictures chronicling the aftermath of yesterday's nasty attack on a U.S. diplomatic convoy in the Gaza Strip. There were eight photos in the sequence.

MJ shifted the Starbuck's Grande out of the way, clicked on the first thumbnail, and brought it up onto her screen. The photo showed the rear end of a blown-up Suburban SUV. The big vehicle had been completely flipped onto its back by the explosion. MJ could read the license plate clearly. It was a standard Israeli diplomatic plate: black lettering on a white background. *CD* for Corps Diplomatique. The numbers began with 15, which was the Israeli Foreign Ministry designator for the United States, then 833, then 26. The heavy armor plating that covered the gas tank was twisted. One of the clamshell doors hung loose.

In the foreground, a curly-haired Palestinian security man with a bushy gray mustache in an olive-drab uniform glared at the lens. She right-clicked on him and got a hit: he was a major in the Palestinian security forces named Hamid el-Mahmoud. War name: Abu Yunis. Born: Amman, Jordan, 6/16/1960. Admitted to the United States in June 1997 for six months of advanced counterterrorism training. He was wearing a heavy gold watch. MJ zoomed his wrist. It was a Rolex President—a fifteen-thousand-dollar watch on the wrist of a PSS major who made six hundred a month max. MJ shook her head. And the U.S. was paying the PA how much? Forty mil a year. And what did generous Uncle Sam get for its money? It got to put gold Rolexes on Palestinian security officers' wrists.

Behind the wrecked vehicle, a crowd of uniformed Palestinians held back a tide of gawking onlookers, news photographers, and passersby. MJ started the face-recognition software and scanned left to right, clicking on every one of the onlookers, security personnel, and photographers. But there were no more hits, so she double-clicked on the picture and it disappeared.

MJ clicked on the second thumbnail. This was a reverse angle of the first picture. You could see that the entire front axle had been blown off the Suburban. In fact, there was nothing left of the entire front end of the vehicle except charred pieces of twisted metal. MJ got a sudden chill. My God, she thought, there were people riding in that car. Americans. And they're dead.

MJ tried to imagine what terror they'd felt and what pain they'd suffered during the last seconds of their lives, and she found herself tearing up. Funny, she hadn't been affected that way when she'd seen the video on the morning news. But now, staring up close and personal at the skeleton of the Suburban, she was hugely affected.

She wiped her eyes, blew her nose, and got back to work. As in the first photograph, there was a young Palestinian security officer in the foreground. She clicked on his face. Six-tenths of a second later, she learned that his name was Samir Ali, born 4/26/1976 in Jenin, Occupied West Bank; that he was a member of the Preventive Security Services, he had no known aliases, and he had been admitted to the United States on November 14, 1997, for security training. He wasn't wearing a watch.

She moved on, stopping at every one of the other twenty-two full and partial faces in the photograph. There were no more hits. Still, there was something about the picture that bothered her. Something about it was awry. Just . . . not . . . right.

But she couldn't put her finger on whatever it was, so she reduced the photo, brought up the third one, and scanned it. Results were negligible: three of the PSS personnel IDs came up, but there were no hits or anomalies. She went through the rest of the series. Nada.

Next folder on the pen drive was an antiwar demonstration in Cairo. Twenty-five photographs. MJ sighed, craned her neck, and stared at the ceiling. God, she thought, if the public only knew the insanity we go through to protect them.

She was about to open the Cairo thumbnails folder when she remembered the Gaza picture she'd wanted to take a second look at. MJ double-clicked the photo and brought it up onto her screen. She forced her eyes away from the wreckage, isolated the upper right-hand corner of the picture, cropped the area, then enlarged it.

Now she realized what had bothered her subconsciously. What wasn't right. What the anomaly was. Everyone in the photograph—everyone with the exception of Samir Ali, the security man in the foreground who was scowling into the camera—was staring at or reacting to the carnage. There were forty-seven people in the photo. All of them were looking at the Suburban.

Except for the six men in the upper right-hand corner of the photo.

Each of those six was facing in a different direction, and yet, now that she'd blown the photo up and cropped it, she could see they were relationally connected to one another. They were, she understood instinctively, a group. First of all, they dressed similarly. Most of the other onlookers were wearing T-shirts or open-necked short-sleeved sport shirts. These six wore long-sleeved shirts, which hung over their dark trousers. One of the figure's shirts was open, and MJ could make out something dark underneath. She keyed on the area, blew it up, and saw the top edge of what appeared to be either a low-necked T-shirt or the top of a bulletproof vest.

Now her interest was really piqued. She went back to the group shot. They were slightly older than the crowd of gawking teenagers who inhabited most of the photo. Three of the men had beards—the kinds of unkempt beards MJ had seen in pictures taken in Beirut's southern suburbs, Afghanistan, and northern Iraq. Two others had thick, fierce, Saddam Hussein–like mustaches. The last, who was older, darker, and heavier than the others, was clean-shaven. His shirt was tucked into his trousers, which were held up by a wide black belt with a big oval metal buckle.

MJ enlarged the cropped section of the photo another 16 percent. Now she was able to see that five of the six men were carrying weapons—only the clean-shaven individual was not. But they weren't toting the AKs common to most of the Palestinian security personnel. She enlarged one of the guns as much as she could, outlined it, right-clicked, and moved the weapon onto the weapons database icon.

Thirty-nine hundredths of a second later she learned these guys were hefting Heckler & Koch MP7A1s, three-pound, microsize machine pistols that fire a 4.6×30mm round capable of penetrating most body armor. Intrigued, MJ searched the BigPond database and discovered that the weapon was currently issued to some of the retired Special Air Service soldiers employed as bodyguards and drivers by the Saudi Royal family.

MJ had made herself something of a specialist on the Palestinian Authority and she knew for a fact that none of the PSS units carried MP7s. Still, she double-checked the database just to make sure, and BigPond confirmed that the gun was not in use by the PSS.

She checked further and discovered that worldwide sales of the unique, armor-piercing 4.6mm ammunition were restricted to elite military and law enforcement units. Aside from the two-plus dozen of the Saudi crown prince's bodyguards, the MP7 was carried by only two active-duty units: Britain's SAS, which had replaced its mini-mini Uzis with MP7s, and Germany's elite counterterrorist Wehrmacht unit, the Kommando Spezialkräfte or KSK.

By now MJ was totally wired. She enlarged the cropped area once more to see if she could find what the six men were doing—where and how they fit in the particular instant in time frozen in the photograph. She worked as methodically as if she were examining the contents of a petri dish or a lab specimen preserved under the glass slide of a microscope. It took her half an hour or so, but she finally realized what the six men were doing.

They were bodyguards. For a seventh man. A Palestinian security officer from the look of his uniform. That was odd. PSS officers provided security, they didn't receive it.

She hadn't paid much interest to the guy before. But now she lavished her attention on him. Except he wasn't entirely visible. The Palestinian's face was partially obscured by the red-and-white checked kaffiyeh he'd wrapped around his head and shoulders.

Just under two-thirds of his face could be seen. MJ's eyes crinkled. "Not for long, Buster Brown." She brushed her shoulder-length, butterscotch-colored hair out of her eyes, pulled it straight back, and trussed it with a rubber band. Then she took the photo crop, saved it as a separate jpg file, opened her Adobe Photo Shop software, and started playing with the editing tools. This son of a bitch was going to be *hers*.

1:14 P.M. MJ glanced up at the wall clock that was just visible over the top of her cubicle. Christ, Mrs. SJ was going to have a fit. She expected her C-PIGgies to go through a minimum of sixty photographs a day. MJ had scanned only eight. Well, things had taken longer than expected. But there he was, in living color.

MJ examined the face. The guy was about fifty—maybe a couple of years either side. Olive skin. He sported a thick mustache. But the more MJ stared at the mustache, the more she became convinced it was fake. His eyebrows were thin, and the rest of his face didn't support the weight of the huge brush on his upper lip. It was out of balance to the rest of him. She enlarged the picture so she could see everything more clearly.

Several details bothered her. The picture had been taken at midday. Most men shave in the mornings. There were light traces of five-o'clock shadow at the edges of the man's cheeks. But the upper lip area adjacent to his mustache had no discernible hair. That meant it was clean-shaven. But his cheeks weren't. Paying special attention to one area of the face when shaving was, she knew, consistent with wearing a disguise or a prosthetic. She'd seen Tom prepare disguises and that's how he did things.

Okay, let's assume disguise. She played with the software for a while. After half an hour she had composited seven distinct full facials. There was one with mustache; one with Ayatollah-style beard and another with close-cropped Yasser Arafat stubble; one barefaced, one with full head of hair, another one balding, and a final one with shaved head. After MJ finished playing with noses, chins, and cheekbones, she had more than forty images. Then she keyed up the IdentaBase facial recognition database and let it do its magic.

3:26 P.M. This made no sense. No sense at all. None of the more than twoscore composites had caused the recognition software to hiccup.

MJ sighed. Back to the drawing board. She focused on her first composite—the one in which she'd erased the kaffiyeh and reconstructed the left side of his face.

By now, she'd given him a name. She called him Khalil, because that was the name of a Palestinian terrorist in John Le Carré's novel *The Little Drummer Girl,* a book she'd read in college.

Okay, Khalil, MJ posited as she stared, what if you had plastic surgery so the Israelis couldn't identify you?

She blew up the photo, then scanned it as closely as she could to see if Khalil's face bore any signs of cosmetic alteration. When she saw—or at least thought she saw—possible changes, she tried to conjure up what he'd had done to himself.

It took her hours of trial and error, but she finally put together something she was happy with. The Khalil she now stared at certainly was different from the man in the original photograph—and yet he was the same man. She'd made small but significant changes: enlarged his upper lip, reduced the prominence of the cheekbones to make his face slightly more oblong, extended the hairline just a tad lower onto the forehead, and taken the Roman-like hook out of the nose.

6:45 P.M. MJ sent Khalil's image to the IdentaBase software. Six minutes later, she'd gotten the hiccup she was waiting for. The software pulled ninety-two points and a name.

The name was Imad Mugniyah. MJ went white. Imad Mugniyah was the world's second most wanted terrorist. The founder of the Islamic Jihad Organization. The man who'd blown up two American embassies in Lebanon and killed 241 U.S. Marines. The man who had kidnapped and tortured to death CIA's Beirut station chief William Buckley.

She'd once seen one of the CIA's two photographs of Imad Mugniyah—and the guy in that picture, which dated from 1988, looked nothing like either the individual in the Reuters photo or the composite she'd sent to IdentaBase.

And yet there it was in black-and-white: ninety-two points. Holy Mother of God.

Just to make sure, MJ logged onto BigPond and pulled up the original picture. The photo had been obtained in September 1988 by a Hezbollah penetration agent working for a Beirut-based Arabic-speaking case officer named ███████████████.[8] It showed Mugniyah, surrounded by seven of his IJO colleagues, watching CNN's coverage of the aftermath of the July 1988 shoot-down of a civilian Iranian Airbus by the USS *Vincennes*.

There was significance to this. In December 1988, Pan Am's Flight 103 from London to Washington exploded over Lockerbie, Scotland. Among the 259 passengers were five CIA officers, including the son-in-law of the Agency's deputy director for operations and ████████████████,[9] a former Beirut station chief who had come close to killing or capturing Imad Mugniyah twice. Despite the fact that the Libyan intelligence service had ultimately been convicted of bombing Pan Am 103, there were those at CIA—and MJ's boyfriend Tom Stafford was among them—who believed it was the *Vincennes* incident that led to the bombing, that Iran was ultimately responsible, and that Imad Mugniyah was somehow complicit in the atrocity.

MJ printed out the BigPond photo and compared it with her afternoon's work. There was a slight resemblance. Imad Mugniyah had been born sometime in the 1960s: 1962 or 1963 was what came to mind. He'd be in his forties now. Which was more or less the age of the man in the Reuters photograph. But Imad Mugniyah? At the site of a bombing in Gaza? Such things were way above her pay grade.

MJ decided to let Mrs. Sin-Gin handle the problem. She wrote a half-page single-spaced memo, clipped all of the photos together, slipped them into an envelope, which she sealed and then put inside an orange-tabbed folder. At 8:15 P.M., MJ walked the folder down the corridor to Mrs. ST. JOHN's office suite. The outer door was locked and the receptionist had long since left. So she pushed the file through the letter slot in the top of the receptionist's secure documents repository, returned to her own cubicle, removed the hard drive from her classified computer, slid it into the safe that sat adjacent to her desk, put the pen drive with the original photos on top of the hard drive, locked the door, and gave the knob an extra twirl. Mrs. SJ could deal with Imad Mugniyah in the morning.

---

[8]This officer resigned covertly in 1997.

[9]████████████ was a covert-operations officer. His name has never been made public. The star that denotes his death on the memorial wall at CIA headquarters is one of the anonymous stars.

17 OCTOBER 2003
8:03 A.M.

MJ was still shrugging out of her coat when she saw the Mugniyah file on her desk. There were two light green Post-its on top of the file, both hand-lettered in Mrs. SJ's distinctive penmanship. On the first was the single word REJECTED. On the second, *You have a daily quota of analysis to fulfill. Deviation could result in disciplinary action.* MJ tucked the folder under her arm like a football and tore down the corridor toward the chief's suite.

She made it as far as Mrs. SJ's outer office. Sylvia N. HIGGIN-BOTHAM, the chief's special assistant, looked up as MJ barged through the door.

"Is she in?"

Sylvia rose out of her chair and stepped between MJ and Mrs. ST. JOHN's door. "I wouldn't push this one, Hester."

"Why?" MJ slapped the folder on Sylvia's desk. "This has to do with Americans being murdered. Didn't we all hear the president say we won't spare any effort to track down and punish anybody who kills Americans?"

"Hester—don't go there."

"Why the hell not?" MJ stood her ground, fists clenched. "Christ, Sylvia, people died."

"I know. And it stinks." The special assistant flicked her head in the direction of Mrs. ST. JOHN's office. "Who can tell. C'mon, Hester." Sylvia took the file, came around the desk, put her arm around MJ's shoulders, gave her a look that said, *Don't talk in front of the receptionist,* and walked her out of the suite into the corridor, closing the door behind her.

She stopped when they were safely out of range and gave MJ back the file. "All I know," she whispered, "is that Sin-Gin started making phone calls as soon as she saw what you'd done." She inclined her head toward MJ's ear and whispered, "She even called the seventh floor."

"Who?"

"Who knows. She placed the calls herself. So maybe the big boss. Maybe the executive director. Maybe the DDI—maybe even the DDO." Sylvia rolled her eyes. "It doesn't matter who, Hester. But she got a call back. That much I know. And ever since, she's been growling she has to get rid of you. Move you to another division."

"The bitch." MJ shook her head in derision. "I'll grieve. I'll file a grievance over this, Sylvia."

"That would really drive her crazy."

"I'm serious."

"I know." Sylvia took MJ's hands in her own. "But maybe there's a better way."

"Such as?"

"You're scheduled for three vacation days, right? You're leaving tonight. Visiting Tom in Paris. You're not coming back to work until next Wednesday. So, you go—and I'll see what I can do before then."

"Do?"

"If I hint you might grieve, I think I can persuade her not to try to transfer you. Look, Mrs. SJ doesn't like flaps. She won't like the idea of you talking to somebody from the IG's office about the fact that unless a picture has a one-hundred-and-twenty-seven-point match, it can't be sent onward."

MJ shook her head. "What's wrong with her, Syl? What does she do, work for al-Qa'ida?"

"Perish the thought. I think she's just old and set in her ways."

"Makes me wonder if Tom's right."

"About?"

"This place. My job. Everything. How can we wage war when from the seventh floor down, they all keep people like me from doing my job?"

"Go to Paris, Hester. See your fella. Have fun. We'll worry about Mrs. Sin-Gin when you get back."

RUE RAYNOUARD

7

TOM STAFFORD PREFERRED TO SIT at the far corner table in Les Gourmets des Ternes' back room because the restaurant was constantly so jam-packed at lunch that it was just about the only table in the whole place where he could listen to whoever sat next to him without being bombarded by six or seven simultaneous conversations. The small, perpetually crowded bistro was vintage Paris: mix-and-match tables and chairs, paintings and prints stacked erratically on the walls, well-worn leather banquettes, Art Deco light fixtures, dusty fin de siècle mirrors in ornate varnished wood frames, red awnings that covered the sidewalk tables in the spring and summer months, and a ceaseless crescendo of conversation as the two undersize dining rooms filled up after the glass-paneled front doors were unlocked promptly at noon, Mondays through Fridays.

Tom ate lunch at Les Gourmets once a week or so. If he was doing business, he preferred the anonymity of one of Paris's steak-and-frites or moules-and-beer chains like Hippopotamus or Leon's, where there was less chance that DST, the French domestic security agency, had the tables wired. He brought his friends here, where the proprietor, Monsieur Francis Marie, a gray-haired bulldog of a man whom Tom greeted as "Monsieur Francis," always had two bottles waiting on his table: the house Brouilly and a liter bottle of Evian.

Today, Tom was lunching with another Les Gourmets regular. Shahram Shahristani was in his early sixties. As a young man, the Iranian had been an officer of the shah's military intelligence service, rising to the rank of one-star general in the months before the Pahlavi reign came crashing down in the spring of 1979. Shahristani had been peripherally involved in the Iran-Contra scandals of the 1980s. He'd conceived an elaborate shell game that had allowed the CIA to move TOW missiles through Portugal into Tehran in the misguided idea that giving arms to the mullahs would help free American hostages held in Lebanon by Iranian surrogates and their Islamic Revolutionary Guards Corps advisers. Although Shahristani had advised CIA against the ploy, the White House had pursued it anyway—with bad results.

These days, Shahram had a villa in Cap d'Antibes, and pieds-à-terres in London, Paris, and Tel Aviv. His business interests ranged from subcontracts for rebuilding Iraq's postinvasion oil infrastructure to wireless telecommunications systems for the Democratic Republic of Congo. It was rumored he also took retainers from several intelligence agencies, something that didn't surprise Tom Stafford.

After all, Shahristani was an outspoken opponent of Iran's current hard-line regime. He maintained contacts inside Tehran's power structure. And from the amount of inside information to which Shahram had access, he obviously still operated his own agent networks in a spectrum of political organizations and terrorist groups that ran the gamut from al-Qa'ida to the Mujahedin-e Khalq (also known as the MEK, or People's Mujahedin of Iran), an Iraq-based group that carried out attacks against Tehran. He kept abreast of the political developments inside Lebanon's Seppah-financed Hezbollah. He had sources inside Algeria's murderous GIA (*Groupe Islamique Armé*) as well as Palestinian factions that ranged from Arafat's Fatah itself to Hamas and Islamic Jihad.

Shahram first became a source of Tom's in 1993. To be precise, on February 27, the day after terrorists had set off a twelve-hundred-pound bomb in the underground garage of the World Trade Center in New York City, killing six and injuring hundreds.

Initial reaction to the bombing was that it had been perpetrated by a domestic group because the modus operandi resembled the attack that had brought down the Murrah Federal Building in Oklahoma City. Nonetheless, Tom, who was working the CTC's Arab branch desk in Paris, had been scrambled to see if any of his agents had information about the attack. He'd had a late-night coffee with one of his better developmentals, an Iranian émigré named Hosein al-Quraishi, who raised money and ran messages for the Mujahedin-e Khalq.

MEK was a mixed blessing. Originally, the group had supported the overthrow of the shah and the occupation of the American embassy in Tehran, so it had ended up on the United States official list of terrorist organizations. But these days it battled the regime in Tehran, received tacit if clandestine encouragement from the U.S., and was headquartered in the southern Iraqi city of Basra, where it received financial support from Iraqi dictator Saddam Hussein and other opponents of the hard-line mullahs.

Tom had queried al-Quraishi about Iranian involvement in the World Trade Center attack. The bomb, which had been placed in a rented van, had many of the earmarks of a Seppah operation. Hosein had shrugged Tom's questions off, claiming he had no knowledge of such subjects. When Tom pressed hard, he'd finally said, "Perhaps I know someone who can tell you something helpful."

Al-Quraishi made a phone call, and the next afternoon, in the long, narrow bar of the George V Hotel, he introduced Tom to Shahram. The three of them chatted for a quarter of an hour, and then Hosein excused himself, claiming a prior appointment.

Shahram remained, sipping orange juice and chain-smoking Dunhills as he and Tom played a chess game under the pretext of a perfunctory whom-do-you-know-and-how-do-you-know-them dialogue. After an hour and a half, the Iranian unbuttoned the jacket of his bespoke Givenchy suit, adjusted his narrow dark tie, and put both his hands on the table. "You have to understand my motive for seeing you."

Tom looked at Shahristani.

"Your . . . organization has a sorry record," Shahram said. "But that doesn't matter. My motive has to do with Iran."

"Iran?"

"If it weren't for the madman Khomeini, Iran would be a prosperous Western country, edging toward its own form of democracy. Instead, it fosters hate and death under the guise of Shia Islam. The mullahs are devils, and despite your organization's treatment of me, I will do what I have to do to bring them down."

Tom started to say something, then realized that silence was his best ally right now. He watched as the Iranian scanned his face, his eyes probing. Finally, after what seemed to Tom to be an interminable period, Shahristani leaned across the table and stage-whispered, "Have the computer at your headquarters run the name Ramzi Ahmed Yousef, born in 1968 in Pakistan of a Palestinian mother. You will discover there will be records in the New York City for Yousef as having obtained a taxi driver's license."

Jerry von Brünwald, Tom's station chief, had made a sour face when he'd mentioned Shahristani. "The man's a fabricator," von Brünwald said derisively. "A double-dealing, lying son of a bitch. Because of him, I was subpoenaed by a goddamn grand jury in 1987—the Iran-Contra flap. I don't want to see anything with his name attached to it."

Von Brünwald's deputy, Sam Waterman, had been more open-minded. He approved Tom's cable and backchanneled it to an old friend in the administrative division. Waterman's contact passed the information up the chain of command. But Shahristani's name was red-flagged. The Iranian had shown deception in a 1986 polygraph session during which he'd claimed to know the identities of the people who'd kidnapped the American hostages in Beirut. And so, the branch chief at Langley deep-sixed Waterman's cable and its references to Ramzi Yousef.

Undeterred, Waterman himself washed Yousef's name through the database and discovered the terrorist had, in fact, sought political asylum in the United States back in September of 1992. CIA records indicated Yousef had arrived in the company of a Palestinian who was on the Immigration and Naturalization Service's terrorist watch list. The Palestinian was detained. Yousef, although he wasn't carrying any documentation and was traveling on an expired Iraqi passport, was—absurdly, Waterman had said to Tom—granted asylum. And within weeks, Yousef had indeed applied for a New York City hack license.

Even though Shahristani's information panned out, von Brünwald instructed Tom to give the man a wide berth. It was an order the younger man disobeyed. Indeed, so far as Tom Stafford was concerned, Shahram Shahristani's information usually turned out to be on the money. He'd been right about Ramzi Yousef. He'd been right the following year, too, when in March he'd told Tom that the Seppah-e Pasdaran was planning a major attack on Israeli interests in South America. Shahram even told Tom the name of the Iranian who was running the operation: a high-level IRGC official named Feridoun Mehdi-Nezhad. The other major player was Talal Hamiyah, a Lebanese terrorist who'd been involved in the hijacking of TWA Flight 847 and the subsequent murder of U.S. Navy diver Robert Stethem.

Tom forwarded both names to Langley. He never received any response.

Then more than one hundred people were killed on July 18, 1994, when a car bomb exploded outside the Israeli-Argentine Mutual Association in Buenos Aires. Tom recabled Langley, reminding them about Shahristani's heads-up. Once again, his message went unanswered.

To CIA, Shahram Shahristani was persona non grata. For Tom, however, the Iranian became a valued source. Sure, Shahristani had a grudge against Tehran—and sometimes his motives were transparent. Sure, he had a soft spot for Israel, but that was because he'd been trained by Mossad. Besides, Tom had learned how to factor Shahram's prejudices and biases into what the Iranian said. And so far as he could determine, Shahristani had never lied to him.

Today, Tom was at Les Gourmets under protest. He'd seen Shahram less than two weeks ago. They'd spoken about the war in Iraq. Shahristani—as usual—had warned that Tehran was trying to influence Iraq's Shia majority to mount an insurrection against the Americans. He claimed that Iran's Islamic Revolutionary Guard Corps was responsible for the killing of a moderate Shia cleric the previous month. He maintained that the IRGC was not only subsidizing the anti-American newspaper published by a young radical Shia cleric named Moqtada al-Sadr, it was also slipping money to al-

Sadr to finance the cleric's militia, a collection of goons and thugs known as the Al Madhi Army. Tom had nodded politely. He'd heard that song from Shahristani before. Many times over.

Meeting Shahram today meant rearranging everything. Tom had been up for almost two days now. The retired Delta trooper he'd recruited for Tel Aviv had been murdered in Gaza. The initial reports from AMEMBASSY Tel Aviv was that the bombing had been the work of a renegade Palestinian splinter group intended to embarrass Arafat and derail the American road map.

Maybe. But maybe not. McGee had sent an e-mail to Tom's Yahoo mailbox the night of the fourteenth. Attached to the "Hi, how are you" message was a postcard-pretty photo of the Old Jaffa port. Hidden in the picture through steaganography was a short encrypted message telling Tom that within twenty-four hours, McGee would be transmitting a photograph that needed urgent identification and please to stand by.

Now McGee was dead, 4627's Israeli office had lost track of McGee's Palestinian developmental, and Tom couldn't help thinking that by putting McGee in harm's way, he'd been complicit in his death. Then there was MJ. She was due to arrive tomorrow morning. And there was his boss. Antony Wyman had called to say he was stopping over in Paris for a day or so on his way back from Moscow. He wanted a thorough debrief on the Gaza fiasco, which had sent Tom scrambling.

And then last night, just before midnight, Shahram had reached him on the cell phone. "My dear boy, where have you been? I have been trying to contact you for more than a day. I have left messages."

This was not true. On Monday, Shahram had left *one* message—which had been both short and nonspecific. Tom was curt and uncharacteristically frosty. "I am sorry, Shahram. It's been quite busy."

The Iranian hadn't seemed to notice. "I have been away—self-preservation of a sort. But I have an engaging story to tell you," he said. "*Très provocateur.* You will be fascinated. We must meet tomorrow. Must. I will not accept an excuse."

Perhaps it was the fact that Tom genuinely liked Shahram Shahristani. The Iranian had suffered financial losses over the past year that sapped both his monetary and emotional resources, and Tom didn't want Shahram to feel he was letting him down. Or perhaps it was that having spent sixteen years as a case officer, he couldn't resist the temptation of a juicy piece of gossip. But there was something else as well. He'd sensed an urgency to Shahristani's voice that belied the Iranian's chatty tone. So he'd surprised himself by immediately saying yes, then broke another self-imposed rule by accepting the Iranian's suggestion that they rendezvous chez Monsieur Francis Marie at noon.

8

12:14 P.M. Tom watched as Monsieur Marie greeted Shahristani warmly, waited until he'd shed his gloves, then folded the Iranian's dark blue overcoat and burgundy silk scarf over his arm. The *patron*'s son Jeff ushered the Iranian to the rear dining room.

Tom rose, slid out from behind the banquette, and took Shahristani's hands in his own. "Shahram, *bienvenue.*" He and the Iranian kissed each other's cheeks in the Middle Eastern fashion: right, then left, then right again.

The Iranian's hands were cold. Shahram rubbed them together as Tom slid into the banquette, his back against the restaurant's rear wall. "The winter is coming, Thomas," he said, pronouncing Tom's name "To-*mass.*" "My bones begin to ache. I'll have to go south again soon." He smiled fleetingly. "South, like a bird." He gestured past the restaurant's curtained front windows with his head. "Too bad for them, eh?"

"Them" had to be the DST surveillance team that from time to time overtly shadowed Shahristani. Of course the French were interested in knowing with whom the Iranian met. But he'd also been the target of three assassination attempts and the interior minister wanted nothing to happen to Shahram on Chirac's watch. So they'd assigned Shahristani a regular crew, which had been following him so long that Shahram sent their families presents at Christmas.

"Do they actually travel with you, Shahram?"

"No—these poor devils have to stay in Paris. There's another team waiting for me in Antibes when I go back tonight." Tom settled himself on his guest's left. He poured Shahristani a full glass of water from the bottle of Evian, then waited as the Iranian wrapped it in a napkin, took it up, and sipped. Shahram was a prudent man. He was even careful about leaving fingerprints in restaurants. He looked probingly at Tom. "My boy, you look drawn. Is something the matter?"

"It's been a busy couple of days, Shahram."

"Not Gaza, was it? What a mess the other day, eh?"

Tom nodded grimly. "I knew one of the casualties."

"I am sorry." The Iranian set the water glass down. "They weren't 4627 people."

Shahram was eliciting. That was uncharacteristic. The Iranian's habit was to back into the day's business conversation in the slow-paced Middle Eastern fashion after first inquiring solicitously about the details of Tom's own life. Today he was all business. Tom decided to follow Shahram's lead. He poured himself a half glass of the Brouilly and deflected. "No. DynCorp contractors." Tom stopped talking as a waiter unfurled two starched napkins and offered one to him and the other to Shahram. "But I'd known him, peripherally . . . before."

"In your other life."

"My other life. That's an interesting way of putting it."

"What you used to do, my boy, was live in an alternative universe. Everything was nothing, and nothing was everything. It was totally existential. I know this from my own experience." He paused. "And when it was good, there was nothing like it, eh?"

"Agreed, Shahram."

"And now . . ." The Iranian gave Tom a sly look. "You are like me. You take information and you turn it into money—like dross into gold. And you do . . . other things."

Tom examined the bemused expression on his old friend's face. *I won-*

der how much he knows. Shahram had an exceptional talent for sniffing out information. He'd been schooled by Mossad, which in the 1960s and 1970s sent instructors to all of the shah's intelligence agencies.[10] That was why, unlike so many other operatives from his part of the globe, Shahram had never operated in the rigid Soviet style. Instead, he took the more pragmatic and fluid approach to the craft epitomized by the Israelis, the French, and the Brits. A dialogue with him was like a chess game. Tom had to think half a dozen moves ahead to avoid falling into a trap.

Another element of the Iranian's success as a spymaster was his appearance. He didn't look threatening. He was a Persian George Smiley of average height—perhaps five feet eight or so. He kept himself trim by walking no fewer than five miles a day, rain or shine. His olive skin was set off by sparse gray-white hair, which he wore longish, so that it fell over his collar in back. Shahram looked a lot more like the central casting archetype for a semiretired French businessman or bureaucrat's banker than what he was: a talented intelligence operative; the "gray man" who disappeared into a crowd with a pocketful of secrets.

Except for his eyes. There was fire in them. Shahram's eyes betrayed the Iranian's burning dedication to intelligence gathering and his talents for eliciting information and running intricate, convoluted, elaborate—and often profitable—operations. Those passions had served Shahram well when he'd worked for the shah. In the two-plus decades since, they had made him a multimillionaire several times over.

Most of the time, Shahram concealed his eyes behind brown-tinted glasses. Still, every once in a while, when he stared at Tom, his eyes bore right into the younger man's skull—drilled inside his brain, and reminded Tom that Shahram was a world-class player who'd never left the game.

Shahram sipped water. "Your girlfriend arrives tomorrow, doesn't she?"

"Former girlfriend."

"Marilyn Jean. You call her MJ, if I am not mistaken."

Tom nodded.

"Then MJ is not quite former if she's visiting you."

---

[10]In doing so, Mossad also managed to recruit dozens of Iranians, many of whom even now still report to Mossad case officers on a regular basis.

Tom deflected the roundabout elicitation of information about his personal life. "Didn't you mention something about *très provocateur?*"

"I must go south—at least for the weekend." Shahristani smiled paternally as he deflected Tom's direct question. "But if Mademoiselle Marilyn Jean is still here next Tuesday, allow me return in order to buy the two of you dinner."

"That's very kind, Shahram." In point of fact, Tom had no intention of taking MJ to dinner with Shahram Shahristani. The Iranian knew only too well where she worked. More to the point, MJ was subject to a biannual polygraph, and any association with Shahram—a foreign national on CIA's Do Not Contact list who had connections to God knows how many intelligence agencies—could jeopardize her clearance.

Jeopardize? Boy, was that an understatement. Tom waited until Shahram put the water glass down. "Shahram, you said you had a story to tell."

"You are all business today. Preoccupied, I think, about MJ's arrival." Suddenly the Iranian's eyes flicked toward the mirror on the back wall and he started—like a deer flushed from heavy brush.

Tom could feel the chill as the front door opened. Then it subsided. Shahram refocused on him. "Yes?"

"Yes, what?" Tom was confused.

The Iranian raised his palms in mock surrender and began to speak in Arabic. "Yes, I will tell you. It has to do with what happened in Gaza."

Tom focused on Shahram's face. "Gaza."

The Iranian inclined his head and spoke softly. "Yes. The killing of your embassy personnel. I know who did it."

Tom's expression reflected skepticism.

"I know who did it. And why." Shahristani paused to arrange the flatware until it was absolutely symmetrical, then fixed his attention on Tom. "The simple answer—which is what your CIA director currently is telling the president—is that it was Fatah. Arafat was sending a message to the Americans through the Al Aqsa Martyrs Brigades. Reminding them they are targets of opportunity in a hostile environment; transmitting a not-so-subtle signal that Washington should yank Sharon's leash every once in a while."

"The rationale makes sense to me." Sure it made sense. The Americans had allowed Israel to keep Arafat a prisoner in the ruins of his Ramallah headquarters for almost two years now. It was logical that the Palestinian would finally strike back. But Arafat also knew he couldn't break wind these days without half a dozen intelligence agencies catching it on CD-ROM. So if he'd okayed the hit on the American convoy, it had to have been done through winks, nods, and subtle hand signals. Nothing that could be taken to court.

Then Tom looked at Shahram's face. "It wasn't Arafat, was it?"

The Iranian's expression told the story. "No," he said. "This was Tehran's doing, albeit with Arafat's approval and foreknowledge."

"Tehran again." Tom shook his head indulgently. He'd gotten excited over nothing. This lunch was going to be a waste of his time, albeit not his palate. "You always find a way to pin things on Tehran, don't you?"

Shahram's thick eyebrows cocked warily. "When Tehran is guilty."

"And they're guilty now?"

"I will tell you the truth, my friend," Shahristani said, slipping into Farsi-accented English. "All this talk of rapprochement between Washington and Tehran is a facade—every bit of it. A smoke screen constructed by Iran in order to confuse and obscure its real goals and intentions."

Privately, Tom agreed. But he wasn't about to say so. He was there to elicit and absorb whatever Shahram was peddling, finish lunch, make notes, send them on if they warranted forwarding, and get on with his life. He had flowers to buy. He spoke in Arabic. "Do you have specifics, Shahram?"

The Iranian sipped his water. "I do."

Tom waited. Shahram smiled. "You are anxious, Thomas," he said. "Patience, please." Shahram reached inside his jacket, retrieved a gold-trimmed ostrich leather cigarette case, and laid it on the tablecloth. From his trouser pocket came a gold-and-tortoiseshell enamel Dupont lighter. Shahristani opened the case, took a cigarette out, closed the case, and returned it to his breast pocket, then lit the cigarette and put the lighter back where it belonged.

Finally, he exhaled and turned his head in Tom's direction. "One: while Khameini makes noises about cracking down on terrorism, he gave sanctuary to more than eight hundred of al-Qa'ida's fighters after they were displaced from Afghanistan. Two: Tehran allows Ansar-al-Islam safe refuge. Three: the Seppah has infiltrated more than a thousand Islamic Revolutionary Guard Corps personnel into southern Iraq, where they are organizing the most radical Shia elements to fight an insurgency against the Americans."

Tom made a dismissive gesture. "I've heard all this from you before, Shahram. Within the past couple of weeks, in fact."

"And what did you make of it?"

"Nothing more than business as usual for Tehran."

"Perhaps." Shahristani paused as handwritten menus were set in front of them. The Iranian didn't bother looking at his. "Green salad," he said. "And the sole—grilled, please."

Shahristani nodded at the menu. The waiter picked it up and looked over at Tom. "Monsieur Stafford?"

Quickly, Tom ordered a beet salad and an entrecôte *à la moelle*. He wanted to get back to the subject at hand.

"You were saying?"

Shahristani inclined his head closer to Tom's. "Perhaps it is, as you say, business as usual. After all, despite the fact that your government refuses to admit it, Tehran has waged war against the United States for two decades— ever since the Seppah blew up your Beirut embassy in 1983. But I think things are about to get more serious. I believe the Gaza murders were the opening of a new terror campaign. I think Tehran has begun a long-term covert action against Israel and the West—and they are using some new al- lies as well as their old surrogates to do so."

Tom looked at his old friend. It was just like Shahristani to see circles within circles—and Tehran in the middle of it all. "C'mon, Shahram—"

The Iranian's eyes flashed as he exhaled. He slipped into Persian- accented Arabic. "*Listen to me, Tom.* Gaza was a Seppah operation. It was only one of a series of attacks."

"A series."

"Probes and distractions. Like a sidewalk shell game. You understand that Tehran's long-term objective is to knock the West off balance, agreed? To obtain nuclear weapons, agreed? To use those weapons to change the balance of power in the region forever, agreed?"

"Agreed, agreed, agreed, Shahram. But what's your point?"

"It is that short-term, Tehran wants continual destabilization. How better than by a marriage of convenience with al-Qa'ida."

"Go on." Despite Tom's skepticism, Shahram was on solid ground. Tehran was already host to perhaps a hundred of al-Qa'ida's most dangerous senior-level combatants. And the fact that al-Qa'ida was Sunni and Tehran was Shia, or that Iran was Persian and al-Qa'ida was Arab meant little. In the Middle East, the old "the enemy of my enemy is my friend" paradigm still held sway.

"To mark this new alliance, the Seppah will facilitate and help coordinate a major al-Qa'ida strike against the Americans—an attack equal to or bigger than 9/11."

There he goes again. Tom had heard it all before—and he was hugely dubious. "It's easy to talk about an alliance between al-Qa'ida and Tehran. I read about it all the time in the *Telegraph* op-ed pages. It's a constant litany sung by the neocon pundits. But what about proof?"

Shahristani balanced his cigarette on the rim of the ashtray. He took an elegant, gold-cornered Asprey pocket secretary from his jacket pocket and extracted a three-by-five photograph from it.

"This," he said. "This is proof." He slid the photograph across the table.

Tom pulled a pair of reading glasses from his breast pocket and slipped them on. He looked down at what appeared to be a surveillance photo. In the foreground was the blurred hood of a car. Behind the vehicle, two men were walking past a café or bistro with sidewalk tables. One man was slightly in front of the other. Tom looked up, puzzled. "Here." Shahristani handed him a pocket magnifier.

Tom shifted his wine out of the way, laid the photo on the tablecloth, and squinted into the thick glass, playing it back and forth over the photo. Behind the two figures, he saw an awning with writing on it. Squinting, Tom played with the magnifier. "L'Étrier?"

"Justement."

"Is this Paris?"

"Yes." Shahristani drew deeply on his cigarette and nodded. "Rue Lambert in Montmartre."

"Who's the mark?"

"There are two of them. Don't you know?"

Tom shrugged. "Never seen either one before."

"Yes, you have—one of them you know."

Tom pulled the reading glasses off and looked skeptically at Shahristani. "Stop playing games, Shahram."

"They are coming from a meeting at a safe house next door to the bistro." The Iranian stabbed the Dunhill out, leaned over, cupped his hand across the side of his face so what he said couldn't be lip-read from across the room. "I believe the man in front to be a mercenary currently working for al-Qa'ida. He was born a Moroccan, of that much I am reasonably certain, although one of his two or three current passports is French, and was issued in the name of Tariq Ben Said, born Tunis, August of 1958."

"Tariq Ben Said."

"Yes, so let's call him that. What his real name is, who can tell. When he was first brought to my attention about three years ago, he was working freelance."

"By whom?"

"By whom?"

"Who brought him to your attention?"

Shahristani deflected Tom's query. "He is a killer by trade. His instrument of choice is plastique explosive. Clandestine bombs, although I believe the current fashionable term is IED, for improvised explosive device."

"An IED maker?"

"There is nothing improvised about his bombs, Thomas. He is said to have used case studies."

Tom shrugged. "Such as?"

"It sounds perverse, but he bases much of his technique on what the Israelis pioneered."

"Really?"

"Yes. When you look at it coldly, Tom, the Israeli secret services perfected most of the techniques currently used by terrorists. Remotely detonated devices? That's how Mossad got Ali Hassan Salameh, the operations chief of Black September and architect of the 1972 Munich Olympics massacre. Remember? In 1979, Mossad remotely exploded a Volkswagen as Salameh's car passed by on rue Madame Curie in Beirut." Shahram's eyes flicked toward the ceiling. "As I recall, the operation was run by a woman—something something Chambers."[11]

He returned his gaze to Tom. "Exploding cell phones—they pioneered that technique, too, and put it to good use in counterterror operations on the West Bank and even in Europe. Czech plastique—Semtex—molded into everyday items? That tactic, too, was enhanced by Mossad. And now—"

"Shahram," Tom interrupted. "Ben Said—*please*."

"He is more than a bomb maker, Tom. He is an assassin. Others use a knife or a gun. He uses plastic explosive. He has killed hundreds—hundreds. He is a chameleon. His tactics are fluid; he changes his appearance regularly. He has had plastic surgery half a dozen times. He uses"—the Iranian paused as he searched for the right word—"*des prosthétiques*—devices to change his appearance."

"And now?"

"And now he has allied himself with al-Qa'ida." The Iranian set his water glass down. "For money, of course. Tens of millions of Euros. I have been reliably told that the bomber Ben Said was recently seen in the company of this man." The Iranian produced a second photograph and slid it across the table. "Yahia Hamzi. Based in Paris. He imports Moroccan wine—a company with the unlikely name Boissons Maghreb, with a small warehouse near the rue du Congo near the Pantin industrial zone. Hamzi himself is secular, not religious at all. But he is very active in civic affairs out beyond the nineteenth."

Tom examined the photo, which had obviously been duplicated from a passport because a portion of an official seal was visible in the bottom right-hand corner. The clean-shaven man had sharp Arabic features and curly hair—what might almost be described as an Afro. He wore the sort of thick-framed eyeglasses favored by old-fashioned Parisians.

"Hamzi." Tom looked up from the photo. "The nineteenth, you say?"

"Affirmative."

---

[11]Shahristani's memory is on the mark. On January 22, 1979, a Mossad officer using the alias Erica Mary Chambers remotely detonated one hundred kilos of plastique explosives packed into a Volkswagen parked on rue Madame Curie, a heavily traveled street that runs on an east–west axis slightly southeast of the Ras through the heart of West Beirut, just as Ali Hassan Salameh's tan station wagon and its Land Rover chase vehicle passed by on its way from Salameh's apartment on rue Verdun. Salameh and his eight bodyguards were all killed instantly.

It made sense. The nineteenth arrondissement was out near Aubervilliers and Pantin, where there were huge apartment blocks of suburban slums known as *banlieues,* as bad as the worst Chicago, Washington, D.C., or Los Angeles had to offer—filled with North African immigrants. And gangs. Drugs were rampant, killings commonplace. The north end of the nineteenth was a hotbed of Islamist activity. "What's the Iranian angle?"

"Hamzi uses the importing business to launder money for a Salafiya splinter group known as the CIM, for Combatants Islamiques Marocains."

Tom took a sip of his wine. "Don't know of them."

"No one knows of them. The reason is because CIM does not exist. It is a cover name, created by Seppah to throw hunters like you and me off the scent. Just the way Seppah created the Islamic Jihad Organization in Lebanon during the 1980s to fool Western intelligence. CIA treated the IJO as an Iranian-sponsored organization. It wasn't. IJO wasn't Iranian-sponsored; it was a creation entirely molded by Tehran. By the Seppah."

The Seppah again. Tom frowned. Shahristani wasn't making sense. "CIM is a Seppah creation?"

"That is my guess. And therefore Hamzi is a Seppah agent. I believe he is also what you might call Ben Said's banker."

"Might call?"

In response, Shahristani shrugged. Tom decided to take another tack. "You just said Ben Said is al-Qa'ida's man."

"By his own choice. He also takes contracts from Tehran." Shahristani made a face. "You should have dealt with them years ago."

"You have no argument from me about that."

The Iranian nodded. "It appears to me," he said, "that much of the original structure of al-Qa'ida is fractured. Degraded. Dispersed."

Tom had no idea where Shahram was going. But he played along. "Agreed."

"So what do they do? They adapt. They improvise. They metamorphose. They transmogrify."

"You mean they change identity?"

"No, Thomas. I mean that like a pilot fish on a shark, al-Qa'ida attaches itself to an existing organization, uses it for a while, and then moves on. I believe Ben Said, whose real name could be anything, is also a pilot fish. Now he has attached himself to both al-Qa'ida and the Seppah."

"Do the French know about Ben Said?"

"No. They keep an eye on Hamzi from time to time—they think he may be engaged in smuggling. But the name Ben Said is unknown to all of Western intelligence."

Tom's right index finger pulled at the skin below his right eye, indicating that he was dubious.

Shahristani continued unfazed. "Ask the Israelis. They know there is a bomber out there with a unique talent. They just have no idea who he is."

"How unique?"

"You know how hard it is to build a miniature explosive device."

"Of course." It was true. For all the current hysteria about bombs, Tom knew it was incredibly difficult to make a sophisticated explosive device that was simultaneously powerful and small. Sure, you could use dynamite, C4, RDX, or nitro in a car bomb. But none of those could be miniaturized. You could make a shoe bomb out of Semtex. But there wasn't a lot of Semtex around these days. Vaclav Havel, God bless him, had quickly destroyed most of the Soviet-era Czechoslovak stocks after he'd become president of the Czech Republic. Besides, what Semtex there was could be detected by the latest generation of explosives-detection sniffers. To be able to create a truly undetectable, miniature IED—that was something. Tom was intrigued. "Has this Ben Said done it?"

The Iranian dismissed Tom's question with a flick of his hand. "No one knows who he is. No one fit the pieces together." Shahristani lit a fresh Dunhill and gave Tom a Cheshire cat smirk. "Except me."

Tom was going to have to wait for his answer. He focused on Shahristani. "Go on."

The Iranian exhaled smoke through his nose. "Ben Said's legend began in August of 1978. He was not even twenty, as best I can tell. But it was his bomb design that assassinated the Englishman Lord Louis Mountbatten by blowing up his fishing boat at Mullaghmore in County Sligo. He taught the Lebanese how to perfect car bombs, making them twice as lethal. He has worked with the Chechens. And with Islamists. The sneakers worn by Richard Reid, the British Islamist shoe bomber who frequented the Finsbury Park mosque in London, were of Ben Said's design."

"But Reid's shoe bomb didn't work."

"That was because of time constraints. Al-Qa'ida insisted on using prototypes. The fusing hadn't been perfected. If they'd waited six more weeks, Reid wouldn't have needed matches or a lighter. He would have yanked on one of his shoelaces and the plane would have been brought down."

The Iranian knocked the ash off his cigarette. "For the Chechens, he is rumored to have designed explosives so small Black Widows can wear them onto aircraft."

"How does he get them past security?"

"I am told he has reformulated Semtex into something twice as powerful and absolutely undetectable. It is time-consuming, dangerous, and he can make only small batches. But with this new formula, he can make bombs the size and shape of tampons. The fuse is self-contained. The bomber goes to the rearmost lavatory, removes the weapon from her privates, sets the fuse, and flushes the IED down the toilet. It's impossible to retrieve and at cruising altitude the explosion is capable of blowing the tail off the aircraft."

"Incredible."

"In 2001, a Wahabist imam in Saudi Arabia paid Ben Said a million dollars to reconfigure the exploding vests used by Palestinian suicide bombers, making them smaller and lighter—and thus less identifiable and more deadly. The French have been on his case since 1995, when Ben Said was hired by GIA—Groupe Islamique Armé. He provided GIA with three bombs, which Algerian Islamists set off in the Paris metro. DST has a thick file. The British, too. And Israel. But no one has ever been able to pinpoint him."

"So whoever he is, he is a shadow."

Shahristani nodded in agreement. "A ghost, a wraith." He indicated the photograph lying on the tablecloth. "It's altogether possible you are looking at the only surveillance picture of Ben Said that exists."

Tom squinted at the picture. Ben Said was the taller of the two men. He didn't look like your typical Hollywood assassin. No muscular build, chiseled profile, or catlike bearing. What Tom saw was a slightly pudgy, clean-shaven man of about forty or so with a square face and a full head of longish dark hair combed straight back. His double-breasted sport coat was open and flapping as he walked, revealing dark trousers held up by a wide belt with an oversize oval buckle. "Who took this? Is it from a credible source?"

"Thomas, *please*." Shahristani gave him a sly smile. "Sources and methods, dear boy." He paused, then stared into Tom's eyes. "I took the picture, Thomas. And verified who was in it."

"How?"

"I discovered Ben Said's safe house."

"When did you do this, Shahram?"

"Just over two months ago. In August."

Tom turned his attention back to the photograph. Two steps behind Ben Said was a shorter, older man, also clean-shaven, with a round face, a prominent, Roman-like nose, and gray hair.

"Who's the number two?"

"Don't you know?"

"Shahram—"

The Iranian's expression was grim. "It is Imad Mugniyah, Thomas. Imad Mugniyah. After Usama Bin Laden, the world's most wanted terrorist. The man with a twenty-five-million-dollar bounty on his head."

9

"WHAT?" TOM WAS INCREDULOUS. "Impossible." There were only two surveillance photographs of Imad Mugniyah in existence. Tom had copies of both, and this guy was not the man in those pictures. Tom had pinned one of the Mugniyah pictures to the wall of his cubicle at CTC so he could stare at it every single day he went to work. He tapped the photo. "This isn't Imad Mugniyah."

"It is. He, too, has had plastic surgery."

That was news. "When?"

"Most recently, two years ago."

"We heard nothing about it—not a whisper."

"Why would you?" Shahristani said dismissively. "You have no agents in the Seppah. You have penetrated no one into Hezbollah—in fact, your CIA officers are still forbidden to operate in West Beirut. *Forbidden*—it is insanity. And you have no agents inside the Palestinian terror networks, either."

"That's because I work for a private company."

"You know what I'm saying." The Iranian's dark eyes flashed at Tom. "I am telling you the truth. Imad Mugniyah himself killed your three Americans. There were three kilos of Ben Said's precious new plastique— virtually his entire supply from what I can tell—planted on the motorcade route and detonated using a cell phone. The explosives were sent by Tariq Ben Said on an Air France flight from Paris."

"Impossible."

"Not impossible. I told you: Ben Said has been working for years to fabricate a form of plastique that gives off no scent. He's obviously done it, because the explosive was shipped right under the Israelis' noses, using a European mule. The plastique was concealed in a suitcase on the September tenth Air France flight to Tel Aviv. That same day, Imad Mugniyah took a train to Rome. The next day he flew Alitalia to Cairo, and he slipped through the Rafah tunnels on the twelfth." The Iranian saw Tom's incredulous expression and made a dismissive gesture. "Ben Said himself arrived in Israel the last week of September—just before the Jewish holidays."

"From where?"

"Paris."

"Israel is a hard target, Shahram. Why would Ben Said risk exposing himself?"

"The stakes were very high, Thomas. There was a lot of money involved. Ben Said's presence was Imad Mugniyah's way of proving to Arafat that Iran and al-Qa'ida are willing to put aside religious differences in order to wage jihad against Israel and the West."

"Why do they need Arafat?"

"Because Arafat has something both Imad Mugniyah and Tariq Ben Said lack: he has an organization that enjoys diplomatic status and is favorably received in the European capitals." Shahristani made a sour face. "The Europeans are fools. No—worse. They are petit bourgeois who want to keep their thirty-hour work weeks, their full pensions, their government subsidies, and their full bellies, and if paying off terrorists helps them, then so be it." He rapped his knuckles on the tablecloth. "Europe's comfortable lifestyle makes it blind to the truth."

"The truth?"

"That Arafat has never stopped employing terror." Shahristani sipped Evian. "PLO emissaries travel with immunity. How do you think Arafat ships the millions he's skimmed from the Palestinian aid packages? He used the PA's diplomatic pouch. Now Imad Mugniyah and Tariq Ben Said need those same diplomatic pouches to move their supplies around Europe—even into America."

"And the Gaza hits?"

Shahristani frowned. "I don't understand."

"Motive?"

"I'm not sure," Shahristani said, far too quickly. "Imad Mugniyah's presence in Gaza was close-hold. He had his own security—his Hezbollah guards from Lebanon, and two men from Seppah."

Shahram had changed the subject. It was classic tradecraft, indicating reticence, or deception. Tom decided to press the issue. "*Motive, Shahram . . .*"

Shahristani lit another cigarette, took a long drag, and let his silence do the talking.

Tom tried another tack. "So, we knew nothing?"

"Nothing. You were blind." Shahristani shook his head. "And so were the Israelis—until it was far too late."

"What do you mean?"

"Twice in the last three months, the Israelis uncovered Ben Said's untraceable explosives. But they didn't realize the implications."

"What? How?"

"This past August, there was an explosion in a second-story room at the Nablus Road Hotel in East Jerusalem. When the authorities arrived they found a tourist—a German citizen of Arabic descent named Heinrich Azouz—who'd blown both arms and a good part of his face off. Obviously, Azouz had been building a bomb and he'd set off the explosives by accident. Shin Bet checked Azouz's records. He'd traveled from Frankfurt the previous day on Lufthansa. Shin Bet assumed—incorrectly—that he'd been supplied with explosives domestically. When the Shin Bet lab did its forensics on the residue, they identified it as Semtex—assumed it was from the Fatah stocks. Ben Said's formula prints just like Semtex. It employs virtually identical tagants. So that's what they saw: Semtex. Just like the stuff the Al Aqsa Martyrs Brigades uses. They never did any follow-up analysis. Never sent the explosives to their security people. Never reverse-engineered the explosives and put samples through any of their detection devices."

"But?"

The Iranian paid no attention to Tom's interruption. "Last month, a French citizen named Malik Suleiman, whose papers identified him as the London correspondent for a Paris-based Arab literary magazine, suicide-bombed a Tel Aviv nightclub. When the Israelis checked, they discovered that the magazine Suleiman worked for existed only on paper. There was a phone number, and a letter-drop address. But no offices—and more to the point, no magazines. Suleiman was traveling with a British woman named Dianne Lamb. Lamb was in the nightclub's lavatory when Suleiman blew himself up. Shin Bet learned they were involved romantically and believed he'd had second thoughts about killing her. Since both of them had just visited the West Bank—Ramallah, to be exact—the Israelis assumed Suleiman received the explosives there, because once again the residue printed as Semtex. Shin Bet was wrong. Suleiman, too, was using Ben Said's materials. In fact, the woman had unknowingly carried them all the way from Heathrow concealed in a portable radio—something the Israelis finally realized only after they'd fully interrogated Lamb." Shahram's eyes flashed behind his glasses. "These were disposables, Thomas. Azouz, Suleiman, Lamb—all of them."

Instinctively, Tom understood. Ben Said had been probing his adversaries' weaknesses. The KGB had done the same thing during the Cold War. They'd send a disposable and see how far he got. Then they'd make adjustments and send another. Then a third and fourth, if necessary. The Sovs were never worried about losing people. Christ, they'd lost tens of millions during wars and purges. What were the lives of a few dozen agents? And now, it seemed, al-Qa'ida had adopted the tactic, too. Just like the Soviets, al-Qa'ida didn't worry about losing agents.

Now Tom saw the Gaza bombing in a new light: it wasn't an operation in and of itself. It was a penetration exercise: Ben Said had been testing the limits. Seeing how far he could go before being discovered. Watching what the Israelis did—how they reacted. If bells and whistles had gone off, he'd have known they'd discovered his new plastique formula.

But there had been neither bell nor whistle. In fact, Tom had called 4627's Tel Aviv office the minute he'd heard the radio bulletin about the Gaza bombing. Reuven Ayalon, the retired Mossad combatant who ran the one-man 4627 base out of his house in Herzlyia, had trolled his sources.

Thirteen hours later, he'd telephoned Tom to report that despite Palestinian attempts to pollute the Gaza crime scene, Shin Bet had managed to obtain a trace amount of residue from the explosive that had blown up the embassy Suburban. The sample had printed as Semtex.

But there had to be more. If the two incidents had indeed been penetration exercises, what was Ben Said trying to penetrate? Israeli security? Possibly. But al-Qa'ida might just as easily have larger targets in mind. Western Europe. The United States.

"You know why?" Shahram asked.

"Why what?"

"Why Ben Said was in Israel."

"Of course I do. He was testing to see how far he could go before his weapons were discovered."

"You are wrong."

"No, I'm not."

"You are thinking too logically, Thomas." Shahram slipped into French. "Ben Said was using Israel as a testing ground to perfect weapons that would be used this winter against the West. Against America. Against Britain. Against France."

"Impossible." Tom was incredulous.

"Not impossible. Just as Hitler once tested his war-making capabilities in Spain, so was"—Shahristani looked around then continued in a whisper—"Ben Said using Israel as a laboratory for clandestine weapons of mass destruction that will be targeted at the West."

"Why in heaven's name would he do that?"

"Because he *could,* Tom. Because what makes headlines in Paris or London gets hardly a mention if it carries a Tel Aviv dateline."

"That's awfully far-fetched, Shahram."

"Perhaps." The Iranian went back to Arabic. "But there you have it." He sipped water. "More to the point, you have Imad Mugniyah and Tariq Ben Said in the same photograph. That is something, Tom. That is something."

Well, Shahram was right about that. *If,* that is. If the information was good—if it was twenty-four-karat stuff. Even the prospect set Tom's pulse throbbing. Quickly, he took a gulp of wine to mask his excitement. "Shahram, how long have you had this information confirmed?"

"Six days."

Jeezus, that was an eternity. "Why didn't you call me immediately?"

"Because," Shahristani said, "I wanted to verify things to my own satisfaction before I wasted anyone's time."

"And did you?"

The Iranian's face was oblique. "I am satisfied with what I know."

Tom had one final base to cover. "Did you contact our embassy?"

The Iranian nodded.

"When?"

"A short while after I'd confirmed my information."

He was being evasive. He was trying to deflect. Tom wondered why. "I need specifics, Shahram."

Shahristani paused. He scanned the mirror behind Tom. "I phoned."

"When?"

"Yesterday morning."

"Reaction?"

Shahristani fell silent as a salad was placed in front of him. He glanced at Tom to make sure the American had concealed the photographs, which he already had.

When the waiter withdrew, Tom repeated the question. In response, Shahristani merely shrugged. Tom pressed him. "You gave no specifics?"

"You know how careful I am on the telephone, Thomas."

Shahram was both prudent and circumspect on the telephone. Tom tapped his shirt pocket where he'd slipped the photos. "Who has seen these photos, Shahram?"

"Not so many people." Shahristani read the expression on Tom's face. "You and I, Tom, and the people who first passed the information on to me."

"And whomever you talked to at the embassy."

Shahristani shrugged. "I never got past your former employer's gatekeeper."

"Who was?"

The Iranian shrugged the question off. "Still, I can see why Langley would be . . . reticent. Langley completely bungled all the preinvasion intelligence on Iraq. Ever since, it has badly misjudged the situation on the ground there. Then there's the global war on terror. CIA's operational resources are stretched thinner than a crêpe. Don't you think Tehran and al-Qa'ida understand that if there's a major terror campaign this winter, there's a good chance Langley will implode under the operational stress?"

Tom Stafford's expression never changed. But Shahram was practicing tradecraft again. Shifting the subject. He was evading, deflecting, sidestepping. It was a common technique when agents didn't want to fabricate outright, but were reluctant to continue about a specific matter. Shahram was a canny individual. He'd shifted subjects by telling the truth: CIA had long suffered operational stress fractures. In its present state, Langley was incapable of fighting the multifronted war it was being asked—no, *ordered*—to fight.

The Iranian leaned forward. "The doves have taken over CIA's analytic side. They're all globalists these days—Europhiles. The last thing anyone at CIA wants to know is that Tehran—which Langley's National Intelligence Estimates have long maintained wants a dialogue with the West—is about to ally itself with an assassin working for al-Qa'ida."

Shahristani took his fork, stabbed at the salad, and waved the forkful of greens in Tom's direction. "But that's what's happened. Gaza was a joint Seppah–al-Qa'ida job. Imad Mugniyah and Tariq Ben Said are working together, and CIA covers its eyes and plugs its ears. Full stop, Thomas. End of story."

Tom wasn't about to let Shahram off the hook. "The embassy, Shahram. What happened when you called the embassy?"

"Imad Mugniyah and Tariq Ben Said in the same photograph, Tom." The Iranian filled his mouth, chewed, swallowed, then laid the fork tines-down on the rim of his plate. "I see your face. You know I'm right."

2:12 P.M. "Let's walk the lunch off." Shahram shrugged into his overcoat, draped the long scarf around his neck in the European fashion, and pulled on his gloves while Tom said his good-byes to Monsieur Marie and Jeff then grabbed his own coat from the antique rack next to the front window.

The two men emerged through the narrow glass-paned door into a gray Paris afternoon. Tom glanced up at fast-moving slate-colored clouds that threatened rain and hunched his shoulders against the bone-chilling wind. Shahram didn't seem to notice. He gave an offhand wave to the two DST agents sitting in a haze of cigarette smoke inside a silver Peugeot parked across the street.

"You have your shadows with you today."

"They were waiting for me at the airport this morning."

"Oh? Any reason?" Tom remembered the urgency in Shahram's tone the previous night. And at lunch, his demeanor had been both intense and unsettled, anomalous behavior for the Iranian.

Once again, Shahristani deflected the question. "Henri and Jean-Claude. Good kids. Henri's the one behind the wheel. He has twins."

Tom caught a quick glimpse of the pair. They *were* kids, too—twentysomethings who wore mustaches so they'd look older—dressed in the wide-lapel, double-breasted retro chalk-stripe suits that were just now coming back into fashion. A couple of baby-faced gumshoes trying to look like Humphrey Bogart in *The Maltese Falcon*.

But they were no doubt well trained. DST's Paris agents were some of the best operators in the world when it came to surveillance. In fact, CIA insisted that case officers heading for Paris take the denied-area-operations course—the same six-week course designed for spooks going to Moscow and Beijing. That was because DST was better equipped, more sophisticated, and much more highly motivated than the Soviets or the Chinese had ever been.

"Come." Shahram put his right arm through Tom's left and steered the younger man by the elbow along the busy sidewalk toward the Place des Ternes. Shahram pointed past the garish facade and rolled-up red awning of Hippopotamus, a branch of the American cum Parisian steak-and-frites chain that sat on the far side of the Faubourg du St. Honoré. "We'll walk as far as Étoile. We'll take our lives in our hands and cross above ground, then go down Victor Hugo as far as Boutique 22. I will buy you a cigar and myself a carton of cigarettes. Then I will go straight home for a nap and you will be free to write your report."

Tom's mind was racing. He didn't want a cigar or a twenty-minute stroll. He wanted to go straight back to the five-story, nineteenth-century town house at 223 rue du Faubourg St. Honoré that was 4627's European headquarters, scan the picture Shahram had given him into the computer, and start the process of verifying the Iranian's claims. If Shahram's information proved valid, Tom wanted to move the information about Imad Mugniyah and Tariq Ben Said *right now*. And the explosives. Air France flights to Tel Aviv were subject to extraordinary security measures. If Ben

Said's new formula for plastique could escape detection at de Gaulle, it truly was invisible.

The threat was unprecedented. In the 1990s, Ramzi Yousef, who'd been responsible for the 1993 World Trade Center bombing, had devised a plan to blow up a dozen American airliners at the same time. If Ben Said's plastique was undetectable, al-Qa'ida could bring down God knows how many flights simultaneously.

Tom said, "Hold on just a sec, Shahram." He reached into his pocket, took the cell phone, and punched a number into it. "Tony, it's Tom. Where are you?" He paused. "Can you get away? Meet me back in the office in"—he looked over at Shahristani and shrugged—"fifteen minutes. It's critical."

Shahristani said, "Half an hour, Tom—we must walk farther."

Tom didn't want any delay. Because what he'd just learned was more than critical. It was personal. Personal, because Tom felt he owed something to Jim McGee. Jim McGee, the disposable who'd volunteered to put his butt on the line without backup and paid the price. McGee's murder deserved to be avenged—and in a timely fashion.

He looked into the Iranian's sad eyes and sighed. This was Shahram, and certain . . . proprieties had to be observed. It was all about tradition, and respect. So he said, "I'll see you in half an hour, Tony," shut the phone down, slipped it back into his coat, and allowed himself to be guided by the older man.

They marched in slow, deliberate lockstep toward the square. As the two of them ambled past the entrance to the huge Brasserie Lorraine, which took up most of the northeastern side of the irregularly shaped *place,* Tom suddenly caught the scent of the sea wafting past his nose. He glanced over at the brasserie. Crates filled with oysters, shrimp, crabs, and lobsters all packed in ice and cradled by seaweed were piled against the restaurant's wall. One of the brasserie's countermen was shucking large, green-tinged Marennes and placing them on a three-tiered server.

Shahram gestured with his head toward the stacks of shellfish. "The best oysters in Paris, Thomas. Have you ever eaten here?"

"Twice. The food was okay."

" 'Okay,' he says." Shahram laughed and tweaked Tom's elbow, pulling himself closer to avoid a pair of overeager tourists weighed down by video cameras and carrying huge, partially unfolded Michelin maps. "You *are* preoccupied, dear boy."

Tom grunted. His attention was focused on the steel-and-glass display cases that held Belons, Marennes, and Creuses arranged artfully by size and displayed on shaved ice. You could order them by the piece or by *la douzaine* and eat them on the spot. They were delicious.

Suddenly, from somewhere behind him, Tom heard shouting.

Instinctively, he turned toward the sound. "What the—"

The Iranian's grip on his elbow tightened. Shahram pushed him rudely, almost knocking him to the ground.

Tom staggered, but caught his balance. Shahram fell up against him. The Iranian uttered a huge wheeze and gasped, "Tho-*mas*?"

As Tom reacted, the old man's knees went out from under him and he sagged to the ground.

"Shahram?" Tom tried to catch his friend under his arms. But Shahram was already deadweight.

It was a goddamn heart attack. Shahram slipped to the sidewalk. He collapsed face forward. Tom tried to roll him onto his back, but couldn't. He screamed, "Somebody get a doctor, a doctor—quickly!"

Tom lifted Shahram's head. He saw that the Iranian's eyes had rolled back. He reached around, unbuttoned Shahram's coat, and loosened the scarf. "C'mon, c'mon—a doctor!"

He felt Shahram's neck, but sensed no pulse. He pressed his cheek against Shahram's chest to listen for a heartbeat. Nothing. He was about to start CPR when suddenly an arm was thrown around his neck, he was yanked backward, wrestled across the sidewalk, spun rudely onto all fours, and kicked in the ribs hard enough to lift him clear off the pavement.

He landed badly, his trouser knees shredding on the rough concrete. He tried to claw his way back to Shahram, but got a chop to the throat and an elbow to the side of his head for his troubles.

Tom saw stars. Everything went out of focus. He fought the pain, struggled to his feet, half collapsed, then regained his balance. He tried to scream that Shahram had suffered a heart attack, but all that came out of his throat was a gurgle.

He saw he'd been attacked by one of Shahram's DST shadows. The youngster was already on his knees, unbuttoning Shahram's jacket and shirt. But when he looked down, all he said was, *"Merde."*

Where was the other agent? As Tom looked around in panic, he saw the second DST man, a gun in one hand, a radio in the other, dashing across the boulevard, heading north, toward Avenue de Wagram.

And then he saw the dark stain spreading onto Shahram's shirt. The DST agent moved the Iranian's left arm upward, and Tom saw where he'd been wounded—shot or stabbed just under the armpit.

He edged forward. "Please . . ." The DST agent gave Tom a long and dirty look. But he finally gestured as if to say, *C'mon,* and Tom crawled over to his friend.

Shahram's eyes were open. But they were already clouded. Tom lifted the old man off the cold concrete and cradled his head in his lap. He looked down at his left hand. It was wet—covered with blood. He wiped the hand on his jacket.

Tom began to see spots in front of his eyes. The world started to turn black and white. Tom hyperventilated, fighting to remain conscious. From somewhere in the distance, he could hear the raucous hee-hawing of sirens approaching. It had begun to drizzle. He hunched over, to protect his friend from the raindrops, and regained control over his own body. Carefully, he brushed hair away from the Iranian's forehead. Then he slipped his hand over Shahram's face and tenderly closed his eyes.

10

MJ USED ONE OF THE FOUR KEYS on her Arc de Triomphe souvenir key chain to open the heavy wood door that led into the courtyard hidden behind the gray stone facade of the six-story apartment building. She held the door open with her shoulder, shifted her huge purse, which had slipped off her shoulder, back where it belonged, and muscled her carry-on through the opening. Carefully, she leaned against the door to press it closed, then rolled the suitcase across the flagstones to a second door, which led into the small foyer just past the concierge's apartment, where the antique elevator shaft ascended up through the stairwell.

She watched as the cagelike *ascenseur* descended. MJ was more than a little upset. More than a little? Hell—she was fuming. The day had begun with Mrs. Sin-Gin. It had ended with a horrendous flight. The plane was full—every single seat occupied. There were long stretches of turbulence that kept everyone buckled in, nervous, and claustrophobic. Worst of all, her seat back hadn't reclined, not at all. And so she'd been condemned to sit straight up, the seat in front of her barely six inches from her nose, for the entire eight hours.

Her arrival at de Gaulle was no better. The passport control lines had been endless—only one surly agent on duty for the hundreds of bedraggled travelers from half a dozen flights that had touched down simultaneously. Her bag? It was the last one on the carousel, *naturellement*. Worst of all, Tom had been supposed to meet her, but he hadn't. Instead, as she disembarked she'd been paged, then handed a message.

Something's come up, it read tersely. *See you at the apartment.* He hadn't even bothered to dictate his name or say he was sorry.

And so, instead of a comfortable ride in Tom's Jaguar, she'd rolled her suitcase to the Air France ticket counter, paid her ten euros, waited inside the dank terminal for almost thirty minutes, then climbed aboard a boxy red, white, and blue bus with thirty other loners and sat, getting more and more depressed by the minute, as the steamy-windowed vehicle lumbered through the chill drizzle first to Porte Maillot, then on to Étoile. There, she'd stood in the rain listening to her hair frizz, enduring another fifteen minutes of hell until she was finally able to snag a cab for the seven-minute ride to rue Raynouard.

MJ wrestled the sliding gate open, smacked the elevator door with her suitcase, and emerged into darkness. She fumbled around until she found the *minuterie* switch and pressed it, relieved when the corridor lit up. She pulled her bag out of the elevator and allowed the narrow door to swing closed. She turned to her left and was halfway down the hallway when she stopped, said, "Goddamn French elevators," let go of the suitcase, trudged back the way she'd come, yanked the stupid French door open so she could slam the stupid open-it-yourself French gate shut so all the other damn French could use the damn French elevator.

Of course the lights went out just as she'd let the elevator door hiss closed. She cursed under her breath, found the *minuterie* button, pressed it, and, soggy sneakers squeaking on the marble floor, finally made her way to the end of the hallway, let herself in, and double-locked the metal door behind her.

She turned on the lights and looked around. Nothing had changed. She walked to the window and looked across the rooftops toward the Eiffel Tower, whose crown disappeared in the morning mist. At least *that* was still here. MJ stared for perhaps half a minute, finding the sight hugely therapeutic. Then she turned away and rolled her suitcase into the bedroom.

Propped on the pillow was a huge shopping bag from Louis Vuitton, to which was taped an envelope on which was written *Marilyn Jean*. She opened the envelope. There was a card inside. It was from Tom. It said, *I love you all the world, MJ.*

From the shopping bag she removed a heavy rectangular Vuitton box, tied with brown-and-gold ribbon. She untied the bow and took the cover off the box. Inside, under a layer of perfectly folded tissue paper, sat a brown backpack, trimmed in leather, with gold hardware and patterned with Vuitton's trademark interlocking golden *LV*s. It was absolutely gorgeous. She examined the bag minutely. Minibackpacks were all the rage in Washington. She'd get incredible use out of it. How wonderful. How exotic. And how expensive.

Carefully, MJ replaced the backpack in its box and set it aside. She set her suitcase on the bed and unzipped it so she could unpack her toilet kit. In order of preference, she wanted a long hot shower, a cup of fresh-brewed coffee, and—despite the fantastic backpack—a detailed damn explanation from *him*.

It being the day from hell, however, she soon discovered that the hot water lasted only a miserly six minutes, and that Tom was clean out of coffee. But being MJ, which meant she was resourceful, she adapted. By 10:15, the new backpack slung over her shoulder, she'd reconnoitered the cluster of stores around the Place de Costa Rica and bought enough essentials to last them the weekend. By noon, when she heard Tom's key in the door, she was enjoying her third mug of perfect café au lait and her second, sinful *pain au chocolat.*

"Tom, what a wonderful, wonderful gift. It was perfect because I had the most awful—oh, my *God.*" He looked as if he'd been in a brawl. His shirt was askew. His trousers were ripped at the knees. His jacket had stains all over the front.

Before she could say another word, he held up his hand like a traffic cop, dropped his overcoat onto the floor, and lurched for the kitchen, pulling his jacket off as he went. He ran water onto his hands and, heedless that his clothes were getting soaked, scrubbed messily at his face, neck, and hair. He fumbled blindly until he found a kitchen towel and wiped himself dry. He finally turned around and saw her standing in the doorway. He draped the towel on the sink and ran a hand through his hair to get it out of his eyes. "I'm sorry, love. It's been a bear of a night. Pour me about three fingers of cognac, will you? I'm going to get out of these clothes and climb into a shower."

3:45 P.M. They were lying on the bed, covered by a thick duvet. He'd stood under the shower for nearly a quarter hour while she busied herself, not wanting to pry. He'd finally emerged, a towel wrapped around his middle, clutching the empty cognac glass. He appeared so ingenuously vulnerable in that instant that MJ was able to picture him as a little boy.

His knees were scraped raw and bright red. The scabs were going to be enormous. She noted that the whole right side of his rib cage was bruised—a mottled mélange of purple, yellow, and sickly green that stretched from his chest to his waist. When she asked what had happened, he said someone had kicked him by mistake.

He'd padded into the living room, refilled his glass from the bottle on the oval, Art Deco rolling brass-and-glass bar, and downed it in a single gulp.

"Was it that bad?"

"Worse." He'd poured a third shot, drunk it, then gone and collapsed on the bed. She'd lain down next to him and caressed his shoulder. Half an hour later they'd made love.

He snuggled close and kissed the back of her neck. "I'm sorry, love."

She rolled over and stared into his eyes. "For what?"

"I never even asked how you are."

"You were preoccupied."

"I'm not preoccupied now."

Except he was. She could see it. His face was a mask. His eyes were cold—murderous. The veins on his forehead were throbbing. She'd never seen him like this. MJ decided to take the easy way out. "I'm fine. And I love my backpack."

He kissed her. "They're all the rage here." He paused and looked into her eyes. "Sure you're okay?"

"I don't want to bother you. We have so little time . . ."

His expression softened. He kissed her. "MJ . . ."

She pulled herself up, reached for the shirt she'd draped over the bedpost, and shrugged into it. "Well, if you really want to know, it's been a horrible week for me, too."

He'd surmised as much. "Mrs. Sin-Gin again?"

"I'm not sure how much longer I can take it. It's almost as if she doesn't want me to do my job."

He grunted. "You know you always have someplace to go."

She looked over at him. "No, Tom, I'm serious." She bit her lower lip. "Can I show you something?"

"Always."

"But it's just for you, Tom. Your eyes only. Not to share." She waited for him to say something.

When he didn't, she said, "I'm serious."

Finally, he said, "My eyes only, MJ."

"Okay." MJ wrapped herself in the shirt more tightly, slipped out of the bed, and padded into the living room. Thirty seconds later she was back, a manila envelope clasped to her bosom. "I spent a whole day on this—for nothing." She flipped the sealed envelope onto his lap. "She refused even to look at it."

He pulled a small pocketknife out of the top drawer of the bedside table, used it to slit the top flap, and extracted a dozen photographs. He examined the first three. "Gaza—the embassy Suburban."

She nodded. "I was just trying to be creative. You know—think outside the box. Oh, Tom, it's so hard to work when the person you're working for doesn't have the faintest idea about—"

And then she saw his face, and realized he hadn't heard a word she'd said. He was zoning.

She curled around his shoulder to see what he was looking at. It was the blowup of the six bodyguards. "What is it? What's wrong?"

He let the photo drop onto the duvet. "MJ," he said, his face as somber as she'd ever seen it, "tell me exactly what you were doing. Exactly, and why. And then tell me what the reaction was at Langley. Down to the tiniest detail."

HERZLYIA

11

AIR FRANCE 1620 ARRIVED HALF AN HOUR LATE. As the plane emerged from the opaque wall of cloud cover, MJ pressed her nose against the window listening to the whine as the pilot extended his flaps and descended quickly over an Israeli coast lit brilliant orange red by the setting sun. She'd expected . . . well, she hadn't known what to expect. Camels and tents maybe, or some sort of Mediterranean Lower East Side. Certainly not the seawall of high-rises and glass-and-steel skyscrapers that looked a lot more Miami than her mind's eye picture of Tel Aviv. Then the plane banked sharply over scrub-covered hills, descended rapidly, and landed. They rode a jam-packed shuttle bus to the terminal, passed without incident through passport control, claimed their baggage, then fought their way through the crowd into the bustling terminal itself.

Tom guided her through double doors, then steered her around a squad of soldiers, M-16s slung over their shoulders, along a wide swath of sidewalk that smelled of diesel fumes, sweat, and smoke. At the far end of the terminal they bumped their wheeled suitcases over the curb and scampered across three lanes of fast-moving traffic to a small asphalt island on the far side of the roadway. There, in a clearly marked no-parking zone, sat a white Jeep Cherokee trimmed in gold.

The driver saw them coming. He extracted himself from the vehicle, strode toward them, threw his arms around Tom, and kissed him thrice in the Arab fashion. "*Ahlan,* Tom," he said. "*Ahlan wahsalan.* Welcome back to Israel, my friend."

"Reuven. Good to see you." Tom put his hand on MJ's back and propelled her forward. "Reuven, this is my friend MJ."

The Israeli's eyes scanned her professionally and his expression left no doubt he'd sensed her shock. He took her hand and kissed it in the European fashion. She couldn't help but notice that he favored a lot of sweet and slightly citrus-scented cologne.

He slowly withdrew his lips from her hand but never let it go. "I am Reuven Ayalon." The Israeli smiled warmly, his dark eyes locked with hers. His accent was unmistakably French. "You are most welcome to Israel, beautiful MJ."

She blushed. The intensity of his gaze was making her uneasy. "Thank you," she stammered. MJ couldn't help but stare back at him. He was a fascinating picture; almost a caricature. Tall and dark, but soft around the middle, he was dressed entirely in black: black silk shirt open halfway down his chest, baggy black trousers, and shiny black tasseled loafers. His coal-black hair was, on second glance, a perfectly coiffed and hugely expensive hairpiece, which was balanced below by the same sort of well-manicured mustache and triangular goatee favored by Saudi royalty. Around Reuven's neck hung a heavy-linked gold chain. His left wrist held a thick gold Rolex whose bezel was implanted with diamonds at the three-, six-, nine-, and twelve-o'clock positions. On Reuven's right wrist was an oversize diamond-accented gold ID bracelet with Hebrew lettering.

Tom opened the rear door for her and helped her in as Reuven tossed their suitcases in the back and slammed the cargo door shut. Tom eased into the shotgun seat and cinched his seat belt. "I know Reuven from

Paris," he explained. "He was with the Israeli embassy. We covered some of the same ground. Now he works for 4627."

"Uh-huh." It wasn't what MJ wanted to hear. The fact that she was in Israel was bad enough. Israel wasn't on the itinerary Mrs. SJ required her to file before she'd left Coppermine. And now she'd met an Israeli foreign intelligence officer. It didn't matter that he was retired, either. In fact, just sitting in his car was enough of a no-no to jeopardize her Top Secret clearance.

Tom swiveled. "Hey . . . just relax and enjoy the scenery. You're gonna love this place." It was as if he'd read her mind.

And of course he was right. What's done is done, is what her father always said. Besides, this was all her own doing. Her clearance was already in jeopardy—hadn't she removed the Gaza photographs from the office? Hadn't she brought them for Tom to see? Hadn't—her reverie was shattered as Reuven Ayalon slammed the Jeep into gear, smacked pedal to metal, and fishtailed toward the airport exit, cutting off a huge bus without a second thought or any hint of a glance at the rearview mirror.

The Israeli raced past a security checkpoint manned by khaki-clad troops and in a matter of seconds the Jeep was on a modernistic four-lane highway bordered by cotton fields and orange groves. The Jeep flew west into the disappearing light, Reuven signaling with his horn and weaving in and out of the thick evening traffic as if he were drunk-driving the Daytona 500. MJ glanced at the dash. Mother of God, he was doing 155 kilometers an hour. Instinctively, she reached over her right shoulder for the seat belt. There was no seat belt.

They hurtled through a long underpass and came out under Tel Aviv. Reuven passed a police car on the right, veered into an exit lane, and steered the Jeep onto another freeway. MJ saw a solid wall of brake lights ahead. The gridlock didn't faze Reuven, who steered the Jeep onto the narrow shoulder of the road, leaned on the horn, and just kept going. When the Jeep skidded on some loose gravel, fishtailed, and almost hit the guardrail, she actually screamed. When Tom caught a glimpse of her horrified expression, he laughed out loud.

5:55 P.M. Reuven Ayalon sped north along the Herzlyia beachfront, swerved right, and accelerated into a narrow side street past a sign that bore the words KEDOSHAI HASHOAH. Two hundred feet later he pulled up onto the garage apron of a walled three-story villa. A foot-square antique tile set into the wall next to the mail slot was emblazoned with the number 71 and Hebrew lettering.

Reuven switched off the lights and set the parking brake. "Home sweet home."

Tom looked confused. "I thought you told me you'd made us reservations."

"I did," the Israeli said. "At the Ayalon Hilton. You get your own suite."

"We don't want to put you out."

"Out? Me? I welcome the company. Ever since Leah died, I've become *un reclus.*" He turned toward MJ. "A bit of a hermit. You know she was killed in a homicide bombing last year."

"Tom told me. I'm so sorry."

He nodded. "Thank you. It was why when Tom asked me to join his firm I couldn't say no." Reuven opened the Jeep's rear gate, yanked MJ's suitcase onto the concrete, and extended the handle. "So you're staying here—I don't accept arguments. My boys are both married. They have their own lives. Believe me, I crave adult company." He waited as Tom retrieved his own suitcase. "Look—for the last ten days or so, I've begun asking the dogs for investment advice. What worries me is that they're starting to make sense."

To the sound of muffled barking, Reuven led the way to a tall, wide, eggplant-colored metal gate. He punched a code into the keypad that sat at eye level, waited until the gate lock buzzed, then nudged it with his shoulder. "*Bou*—come. Follow me."

He led the way. MJ was impressed. The thick, razor-wire-topped wall was covered in bougainvillea and wild roses. The pathway from the gate to the front door was made of textured stones and bordered in ground cover. There were palm trees and lemon trees and Roman columns all lit by accent lights. A millstone, also beautifully illuminated, rested against the far end of the garden wall. To its right, near a huge dining table protected by a tent-like covering, sat a terra-cotta urn that had to be six feet high. MJ was entranced. "This is breathtaking, Reuven."

"Thank you. Believe me, I didn't do anything. It was all Leah." The Israeli pushed open the ornate wooden front door, and they made their way into a marble-floored foyer. To their left was a wide marble staircase. MJ could see what looked like a living room up the half-dozen steps. At the top of the steps, two huge black Bouviers des Flandres poked their square muzzles around the wall, Totem-pole fashion. They saw the strangers and barked.

"*Sheket, klavim.*" Reuven gathered Tom and MJ in his arms and squeezed them close to him. He machine-gunned Hebrew at the dogs, who trotted down the stairs and sniffed the visitors.

"Let them smell your hands, MJ," Reuven instructed. "Tom they'll remember."

And indeed, the smaller of the two Bouviers was already standing on its hind legs, forepaws on Tom's shoulders, licking his face.

Tom laughed and ruffled the dog's ears. "This is Cleo, right?"

"Of course. Your girlfriend." Reuven made a clicking sound and the dogs sat obediently. He turned to MJ. "Cleo likes to sleep with Tom when he visits." He looked at Tom reprovingly. "Not that he visits very often. The big male is named Bilbo."

Cleo nudged Tom, herding him up against a wall until he scratched behind her ears then transferred his attention to her rump, grinning when her stump of a tail vibrated with pleasure. "How're the boys?"

Reuven extracted a treat from his pocket and tossed it at Bilbo, who caught it midair. "Like I said, married. They have their families and big success in business. In the summer, they go to Turkey on the weekends. In the winter, Switzerland to ski." He glanced at Tom. "Take your bags upstairs— you know where to go—and then come down. I'll open a bottle of wine. We can sit outside and catch up, and I'll cook us some dinner later."

10:35 P.M. MJ sat on the wide marble balcony, her feet propped on the low wall, and stared westward toward the high-rise buildings that rimmed the coast road. The clouds had blown out to sea and the night was brilliant— the moon huge and golden. At 8:30, Reuven had cooked a simple dinner of omelets filled with onions, goat cheese, and wonderful Russian sausage, along with green salad and an extraordinary red wine. They ate outside, and it was chilly enough for MJ to run upstairs for a sweater.

Now she drained the glass of mellow red, padded inside to the kitchen, and poured herself another two fingers' worth. She stared at the label. It was unintelligible—entirely in Hebrew. Well, that made sense because the wine was Israeli. Reuven had said it was a Merlot—he'd called it a Kfira Merlot to be precise. Well, this Israeli Kfira Merlot was as good as any she'd ever tasted. Cleo at her side, she headed back to the balcony. She'd already had three glasses tonight and she was slightly tipsy.

She sat, sipped, then let her head loll back against the chair while her left hand played with the Bouvier's rough coat. There'd be time tomorrow to call the office and explain the fact that she wasn't going to be back for a few more days. But that would be tomorrow. Tonight, she was content to sit and stare into space while Tom and Reuven jabbered at each other in a bewildering mixture of Arabic and French with an English word thrown in every now and then. She guessed they were talking about the materials she'd brought to Paris. So what? No one at Coppermine cared enough to give her work a second thought. Tom had found it valuable enough to bring it here.

He was a complex man, was Tom. So different. He'd grown up overseas. His mother had died of cancer when Tom was ten. His father, who'd never remarried, worked for the State Department. They'd lived in France, and Belgium, and Germany, and Morocco, and Tunisia, and Italy. By the time Tom was fifteen, he spoke three languages fluently and "got along," as he put it, in what he'd called kitchen Arabic.

He'd been educated in a series of French, German, and Swiss boarding schools, and finally at St. Paul's and Dartmouth. She'd grown up on Long Island and gone to parochial schools. Tom had skied at Gstaad and climbed the Matterhorn. She'd summered on Long Beach, learned to eat steamed clams at Lundy's in Sheepshead Bay, and ridden the Ferris wheel at Coney Island. Tom's idea of fun was skiing downhill or riding his motorcycle at some obscene speed. She'd ridden with him—twice. After the first episode, her fingers had taken half an hour to unclench. And yet, when she curled up with the *New York Times* crossword puzzle, he'd sit and watch her noodle the words, and tease that they'd make love as soon as she finished—which she always did.

They were so different. And yet so good together. Opposites do attract. Because, underneath it all, they weren't that opposite. They were both pretty conservative. They both loved their country. For both of them, their lives revolved around public service, something that had been inculcated into them by their parents.

Even MJ's father, who was hugely protective of her, had been charmed and impressed with Tom. MJ had been nervous about bringing Tom home. She'd finally been browbeaten into doing it only the previous Thanksgiving.

Sitting in the Great Neck living room after the turkey, and the two kinds of dressing, and the mash (which is what they called the potatoes in the house of O'Connor)—after the overcooked vegetables, the three kinds of home-baked pie, and the Folgers brewed in an old-fashioned Farberware percolator, Michael O'Connor poured Tom a healthy tumbler of twelve-year-old Jameson and, as the grandkids squalled and played, took the younger man aside and asked what he was doing to dismember al-Qa'ida and defeat Islamist terror against the West.

"I went to seventy-eight funerals, Tom," Michael O'Connor growled. "Seventy-eight funerals and seventy-eight wakes. And then I had to stop, because there were no more tears in me. Just rage, Tom. White-hot, searing rage."

Tom had looked her father square in the face and said, "I'm going to bring as many of them as I can to justice to avenge the people you lost at the WTC, Chief O'Connor. And believe me, when I can't do that where I'm working now, I'll do it somewhere else."

"God bless you, then," Michael John O'Connor had said, and then he'd looked over at his daughter. "Marilyn Jean, the man's a keeper," he'd shouted above the din, bringing silence to the room and a blush to her cheeks. "Always welcome in my house he is."

She hadn't understood the significance of Tom's remark back then. Later, she'd realized it was the first hint that he'd been talking to Tony Wyman about leaving CIA, taking over the Paris office of 4627, and turning their lives—and their relationship—upside down.

She looked up as she heard Tom's distinctive laugh. It was good to see him laugh. Those last months at CTC had been hell for him. From the little he'd said, the director had thrown money and people into counterterrorism willy-nilly. There had been no plan. There had been no thought. Tom fought for a comprehensive strategy instead of the Band-Aid approach ordered by the seventh floor. He'd been overruled, and then when he'd protested to his superiors, he'd been increasingly shut out of the decision-making process.

Of course he had. At George Tenet's CIA, dissent was not allowed. Hadn't she learned that only a few days ago.

Oh boy, had she ever. MJ drained the glass, stood up, wobbled just a little, and looked down at the two men, smoking cigars and conversing in the garden below. "G'night all," she mumbled, her voice slurring from the effects of the wine. "I'm going to bed."

From below, Tom waved offhandedly. "I'll be up soon." He tapped his cigar on the edge of the ashtray that sat between him and Reuven and swiveled toward the Israeli.

Reuven waited until MJ disappeared from the balcony. The guest room faced the street. There was no way for her to eavesdrop—and besides, he and Tom habitually talked business either in Arabic or French and she spoke neither.

He topped off the Napoleon cognac in the crystal bell glass sitting at his own elbow, did the same for Tom's, then picked up his cigar, stuck it in his mouth, puffed on it, exhaled a perfect smoke ring that hung in the cool air for almost five seconds. "Ah," Reuven said. "The perfect combination: a Romeo and Julieta Churchill, and Paul Giraud's twenty-year-old cognac from Caves Auge. *Merci mille fois,* Tom. *Shukran. Todah rabbah. Chein-chein.* Thank you." He saluted the American with his glass then sipped.

He set the cognac down, stroked his beard, and spoke in French. "There is no news on Shafiq, McGee's Palestinian. He has disappeared. My guess is he's dead. And the body already in pieces in the Mediterranean. If he was a double, then he was a loose end. And they don't like loose ends any more than we do. But I'll stay on the case. I know someone who knows someone who can sniff around the family—see if they've been paid off."

"Good. And the plastique?"

"I will check in the morning. I can't believe *Shabak*[12] didn't run anything more than a swab test—at the very least a spectrograph to check the tagants. But if what you say turns out to be correct, Tom, then sooner or later we're going to have to hunt him down, this Ben Said. He cannot be permitted to continue."

---

[12]Israeli term for Shin Bet.

"I understand." Even though he did understand, Tom still felt a little out of his depth. He was a capable case officer. Which meant he had honed all the talents necessary to spot, assess, develop, and recruit agents to spy on behalf of the United States. He'd had successful tours in Egypt, France, Sudan, and Dubai. In that last post, he'd actually recruited an agent who had access to one of the bankers who helped funnel al-Qa'ida money in and out of the Emirates. Later, as a branch chief at the Counterterrorism Center, he'd specialized in identifying the links between certain members of the Saudi royal family and the private charities that through monetary sleight of hand bankrolled Islamist terrorists around the globe. But when it came to dealing with terrorists—really *dealing* with them, as in eliminating them—Tom was ill-equipped.

Reuven was different. Before going to Mossad, he'd served in Sayeret Mat'kal, the Israeli Defense Force's most elite special-operations unit. A Moroccan-born Jew who'd emigrated to Israel as an eleven-year-old in 1956, Reuven spoke native Arabic, as well as fluent French, German, Turkish, and passable Farsi. As a soldier, he had penetrated terrorist camps in Syria and Jordan, identifying, stalking, and single-handedly killing more than half a dozen of Israel's most wanted enemies. As Mossad chief in Ankara—his final posting—he had helped the Turks eliminate a score of Kurdistan Workers Party (PKK) terrorists who had allied themselves with radical Islamist groups and helped attack Jewish targets in Turkey.

In April 1988, as a senior-level Mossad officer, Reuven spent nineteen harrowing days performing advance reconnaissance on PLO operations chief Abu Jihad's home in the Tunis suburb of Sidi Bou Said. Working solo, under Lebanese cover, he flew to Tunisia. There, he researched and mapped the infiltration and exfiltration routes to be used by the Sayeret Mat'kal shooters who on the night of April 15–16, would execute the man who'd helped form Black September and was responsible for hundreds of Israeli deaths. Six weeks later, Reuven was presented Israel's second highest award for valor, the Ott Ha'Oz, for his bravery and initiative.

It wasn't his only award. On June 8, 1992, as Mossad's deputy station chief in Paris, Reuven had led a quickly mounted operation to kill Atif B'sisou, the acting head of Fatah's intelligence organization, as B'sisou drove his brand-new Mercedes SUV through Paris on the way to the Marseille–Tunis ferry.

B'sisou's last-minute schedule changes were betrayed to Mossad's Paris station by Mahmoud Yassin, a Tunis-based midranking PLO intelligence official. Reuven had recruited Yassin in 1990 when the Palestinian brought his wife to Paris for medical treatment. So when Atif B'sisou called Tunis from Frankfurt to tell his office he was going to stop over a day in Paris, Yassin immediately burst-transmitted the news to his Mossad control officer. By the time Atif arrived in Paris midafternoon on June 8 and checked into the Méridien Montparnasse under an assumed name, Reuven was ready and waiting.

Atif was kept under constant surveillance. He was tracked as he and his Paris station chief, S██████ R██████,[13] drove to dinner at the Montparnasse branch of Hippopotamus, the steak-and-frites chain, in R██████'s yellow Volkswagen Beetle convertible. And just after 1 A.M., when the VW pulled up under the Méridien's low-slung marquee, Reuven had watched from two hundred yards away through night-vision binoculars as two of his young paramilitary officers slung B'sisou across the hood of a Volkswagen Beetle, pumped three 9mm bullets into his head from a Browning High Power concealed in a backpack, and vanished into the Méridien's cat-acomblike garage.

Six weeks later, in the Mossad headquarters building that sits across the main highway from the Tel Aviv Country Club, Reuven had been presented with Mossad's Israel Prize, given only to those few combatants who lead the most successful and high-risk operations.

Tom could claim no similar background. As a case officer trainee, he'd had a total of three weeks of paramilitary training. He'd jumped out of a plane—from twelve hundred feet. He'd taken a one-week course in land navigation skills. He'd been given the basic explosives course in North Carolina. And he'd had the Agency's weapons familiarity courses on pistols, rifles, and automatic weapons. But all of that had been before three

---

[13]S██████ R██████, who formerly worked for PLO intelligence chief Abu Iyad as a PLO mole for an international broadcast network in Beirut in the 1980s, was recruited as a penetration agent by R██████ B██████, a CIA case officer at Paris station, in 1988. When B██████ left Paris, R██████ was handed over to a case officer who spoke neither Arabic nor French. Disillusioned by the new case officer's lack of sophistication and street smarts, R██████, over a period of a year, disengaged himself from all involvement with CIA. Currently, he is a successful Paris-based businessman whose associates have no idea about his intelligence background.

years of Arabic language training and his first posting, to the consulate in Cairo. He hadn't touched a weapon in more than a decade.

Indeed, like most of the case officers of his generation, Tom Stafford had never served in the military. His old boss in Paris, Sam Waterman, was a former Marine who'd served in Vietnam. So had the CEO of the 4627 Company, Antony Wyman. And of course there was Rudy—the paramilitary veteran with whom Tom had recruited Jim McGee. Rudy was a Navy veteran who'd seen combat in Vietnam, too.

And it wasn't that Tom felt incapable of violence. Two deaths in less than three days had taken their emotional toll on him. There was a newfound fury in Tom's gut—MJ's father had called it white heat and the phrase stuck with him—that burned for revenge. It was simply that CIA had never trained him in the way Israel had trained Reuven. Sure, CIA engaged in what was euphemistically and neutrally termed *direct action*. But direct action—DA, as it was usually called—was the rare exception to the hard-and-fast rule: thou shalt not kill thy country's enemies without a Lethal Finding signed by the president, and a ton of paperwork.

He'd never thought much about it before, but now he realized that the whole goddamn American intelligence community was built around strictures—thousands upon thousands of thou-shalt-nots. There was Executive Order 12333, which prohibited the Agency from carrying out political assassinations. There were still Clinton-era rules of engagement in force that prevented case officers from pursuing Russian targets. There were Kafkaesque guidelines governing the development and recruiting of agents. And there was an ever-expanding catalog of preposterous controls, absurd limitations, and cartoonish constraints imposed by the dithering, idiotic dilettantes of the congressional intelligence oversight committees.

Even now, when, in the midst of the global war on terror, the Agency needed more flexibility, nimbleness, and lethality than ever, the numbskulls up on Capitol Hill were trying to add new layers of management to CIA's already top-heavy bureaucracy and dummkopf rules that would, in effect, add hundreds of hours of case officer record keeping for every new agent spotted, assessed, developed, recruited, and run.

That's what had made such sense about the 4627 Company: 4627 was built like OSS during World War II. It was lean. It relied on inventiveness and ingenuity. It was mission-driven. At 4627, Tom's marching orders could be reduced to one biblically simple commandment: "thou shalt not fail."

Like the old Mossad. The way Tom saw it, Mossad had historically operated under two succinct rules of engagement. The first was "thou shalt have no limits" and the second was "thou shalt not get caught."

Even now, more than two years after 9/11, the American intelligence community leadership was still refusing to think that way. But changing CIA's modus operandi was like turning a supertanker around. You couldn't do it overnight. Not without the right personnel. And CIA just didn't have enough experienced old hands to do the human intelligence gathering, fight the global war on terror, and supply the military with the kind of actionable intelligence it needed to fight the two-front war in Iraq and Afghanistan.

Indeed, limits, constrictions, and lack of competent personnel were three of the reasons Langley was forced to subcontract such a sizable chunk of CIA's historic responsibilities to outside firms these days. Some independent contractors, or ICs, provided security for CIA case officers in Iraq and Afghanistan. Others provided CIA with language-capable interrogators and translators to accompany the junior case officers who'd been pushed through training without the ability to speak anything except Gringo.

And then there were the black-ops ICs. International Alternatives, one of 4627's main K Street competitors, for example, was currently running a covert program for Langley and DOD, sending sheep-dipped Delta operators into Iran with teams from the Mujahedin-e Khalq (the People's Mujahedin of Iran, or MEK), a group listed by the State Department as a terrorist organization, in the hope of providing eyes-on information about Iran's nuclear weapons development program. And a precious few ICs, firms like 4627, were paid extravagantly to covertly collect, interpret, analyze, and then disseminate the holy of holies, intelligence product itself, to Langley.

Intelligence product because CIA lacked the capabilities to fulfill many of its obligations these days. CIA was peopled with so many layers of managerial deadwood it simply did not have enough qualified personnel to get the job done. And then there was the deniability angle. In the politically correct world of the twenty-four-hour news cycle, outsourcing gave CIA deniability. That was because the Agency's major ICs, firms like 4627, were, in point of fact, cutouts.

ICs operated in the black. More to the point, private contractors were under no obligation to inform the House and Senate intelligence committees about what they did—and to whom. There was huge potential for abuse, of course. Not at 4627, where Tony Wyman, Charlie Hoskinson, and Bronco Panitz maintained a strong chain of command. But other ICs weren't so well run. Tom had already heard gossip about abuses in Iraq and Afghanistan.

And what if something did go wrong—what if Tom mucked up? Well, as Tony had said more than once, the bottom line is that 4627 and all its people were disposables. He had said as much to Tom the day he'd recruited him. "We can't afford to screw up," is what Tony said. "Because unlike your time at Langley, we work out here without a net. Just like the guys in *Mission: Impossible,* 'The secretary will deny any knowledge . . .' You know how the mantra goes."

Which was one reason the thought of hunting and killing made Tom Stafford just a little uncomfortable. *Well, he didn't have to like it.*

Besides, they weren't anywhere near the direct-action stage yet. "There's a lot to nail down before the hunting season opens, Reuven." Tom took a long pull on the cigar. "First things first. Check with Shin Bet on the explosives—see if they'll run supplemental tests for you. And Shin Bet is holding two prisoners I want to interrogate. The ones Shahram told me about. The guy from Jerusalem—the one with no hands. Then the bomber from Tel Aviv. Set it up for me first thing in the morning."

"First thing in the morning?" Reuven drained the cognac and poured himself another. "First thing in the morning, my friend, I am going to drive you and your lady friend to Jerusalem so she can walk through the Old City and feel some of the magic of this country—and tell her not to worry about the Intifada because she'll be a lot safer in Jerusalem than she would be in much of Washington, D.C. Then we'll drive back to Tel Aviv so I can take the two of you to a great fish restaurant in Jaffa for lunch. After lunch, we go up the coast to the Roman ruins in Caesarea. And for dinner, I have a friend from Shayetet 13—the Israeli SEALs—who opened the best restaurant in Herzlyia."

"Reuven—"

The Israeli's hand went up like a traffic cop's. He cocked his head toward the second floor of the house. "Look," he said in Arabic, "Imad

Mugniyah is long gone. Zip-zip through the Rafah tunnels to Egypt, and from there, who knows where—maybe Tehran, maybe back to Beirut. Ben Said no doubt used the same route, although now that I have a name and a picture, maybe I can pick up a scent." He shot the American a look that preempted any objections "That's that, Tom. So, tomorrow we go sight-seeing. The whole day. Tuesday afternoon, your friend, she goes on a plane back to Washington, full of stories about her wonderful surprise trip to the Holy Land."

The Israeli knocked an inch and a half of ash off his cigar. "Frankly, I think you should propose."

Reuven saw the shocked expression on Tom's face and cocked his head in the American's direction. "What's the problem? You love this woman, right?"

"For sure, Reuven."

"So in Tel Aviv I know a place you can find an engagement ring for her. He's a diamond merchant. I served with him overseas. He has only the best. And I can get you a great price."

"Reuven—"

"Look, I'm thinking only professionally. Engaged. That would give her real—how do you Americans say it—cover for status for being here." He laughed. "Cover for status. Perfect."

"Marriage isn't a game, Reuven."

"I'm not playing games. You love this woman, right?"

"Yes, I do."

"So do the right thing. Don't make trouble for her—marry her, Tom." The Israeli's face clouded over. "If I had it to do all over again, I'd marry Leah five years earlier than I did. That would have given us five more years, Tom. We had thirty-six years together. I can tell you now it wasn't enough."

"I'm sorry, Reuven."

"Believe me, Tom, I am sorrier than you. So give your MJ a good time, buy her a ring, then put her on the plane home. No business, Tom. Not a hint of it. After she's safely away, ecstatic with a diamond she can show all her colleagues—that's when we do business. Then—I'll arrange for you to debrief the scum who came here so they could kill women and children. Then we can start the hunt."

12

IT WAS THE SMELL, more than anything, that had made Tom uneasy; an ineffable but palpable mélange of disinfectant, urine, sweat, must, and fear. The result of this assault on his senses—and this took place even though Tom knew intellectually he was just a visitor here—was a huge and totally unexpected psychological tsunami. It sucked Tom into an emotional undertow that combined apprehension, anxiety, and, as much as he tried to fight against it, complete and utter heart-palpitating dread. He couldn't help himself. Dread was . . . just in the air.

They'd left at nine. Reuven had taken the coast road. Just north of Udim, opposite a Toys "R" Us superstore that would have done justice to the Paramus Mall, he'd swerved off the highway, drove down the exit ramp, and continued north on a dusty track that ran parallel to the highway.

Two kilometers on, he'd made a sharp turn onto a potholed, single-lane road bordered on both sides by denuded cotton fields. There would be only one interview today. Reuven told Tom that Heinrich Azouz, the Jerusalem bomber, had died of his wounds. But he'd pulled enough strings to get Tom granted permission to interrogate Dianne Lamb. It was a one-shot deal.

They'd driven due east, followed the browntop as it turned north then east again, crossed the tracks of the main Tel Aviv–Haifa rail line, and continued another three kilometers past brick factories, concrete plants, and quarries until they intersected a four-lane blacktop road so new that the center line hadn't been painted yet. Tom caught glimpses, but he was focused on the work at hand.

Reuven turned north. Tom looked up. The highway was bordered by cypress groves. About three-quarters of a kilometer north of the intersection, Reuven turned onto an unmarked gravel road bulldozed into the wall of trees. He headed west, toward the sea. For the first half kilometer, the road ascended. Then it crested and dipped. As they descended, the tree line opened slightly and Tom saw an old British fort in the distance. It was a squat, square three-story affair built of thick Jerusalem stone, with crenellated watchtowers that looked like old-fashioned chess pieces at each corner.

Reuven pulled up at a rudimentary roadblock manned by half a dozen troops armed with M-16s. Tom glanced into the woods and was surprised to see four olive-drab Jeeps with pintle-mounted .50-caliber machine guns and three camouflaged APCs close at hand. He waited while Reuven palavered with the guards, then watched as a soldier pulled a twenty-foot length of tire spikes out of the way so they could proceed.

The heavy weapons had gotten Tom's attention, and he scanned carefully as they drove the last half klik to the old fort. In the sixty seconds it took them to do so, he identified five layers of defensive countermeasures: raked cordons sanitaires, surveillance cameras, infrared sensors, K-9 teams, and razor wire. He wondered what he'd missed.

As they pulled onto the small parking lot Reuven turned to him, his face serious. "Listen carefully. This place does not exist. So far as I know, you're the first foreigner ever allowed inside. Point of fact, Tom, I was surprised when they said yes. So treat what you see and hear here accordingly, okay?"

Tom's expression showed that he understood the gravity of what he was being told. "Got it, Reuven. And thank you."

10:12 A.M. In a sterile, windowless interrogation room holding a metal desk and two metal chairs bolted to the concrete floor, he stripped down to his underwear and was given a set of utilitarian olive-drab coveralls and a pair of scuffed black leather boots that looked about half a size too small. He'd even had to hand over his watch, which along with his other personal belongings were sealed into a heavy brown envelope then taken away to be stored in a safe in the commandant's office. The only thing he carried was the handkerchief he'd transferred from his trouser pocket.

When he'd asked why he couldn't keep the watch, he was told the prisoners were allowed no sense of time. It was an integral part of the interrogation process. The cells were lit by artificial light, which could be regulated to disorient and throw their biometric schedules and thinking processes into chaos. Some "days" were eight hours in length; others might last thirty-six.

"We do not use physical abuse," the officer in charge of his visit explained. He was a diminutive man who looked to be in his mid- to late sixties and who spoke to Tom in Kurdish-accented Arabic. The left arm of his olive-drab coveralls was folded neatly and attached by the cuff just below the epaulet. From what Tom could make out, the man's whole left arm had been taken off at the shoulder.

The Israeli introduced himself as Salah and volunteered no further information as to his rank or position. When Tom asked how the prisoners were treated, Salah cocked his head defensively. "There are no stress positions, hooding, or coercion used here."

"Why not? That's how our detainees in Afghanistan and Iraq are being treated."

"Of course." Salah rubbed his pencil-thin mustache with the edge of his right hand. "They are effective techniques in the acquiring of actionable intelligence. Quick results for immediate needs. A slap in the face, a threat, the pit-of-stomach claustrophobia from being hooded sometimes works to jar loose information about an imminent operation. That's fear, my friend. You can extract information by using fear—I believe you Americans teach a technique at Fort Huachuca called 'fear up/fear down.' But fear is short-lived. I prefer dread. Day-in, day-out, marrow-of-the-bone angst is what I want to produce. Our prisoners know we have a reputation for ruthlessness. It doesn't matter whether that reputation is true or not. What matters is the psychological effect it has on them. Let me tell you something, my friend: dread works. Dread works very well."

Tom remembered how he'd felt when they'd come through the gates. The unpleasant sensations that had been prodded by what he'd smelled. "Including sensory exploitation, right?"

A sly smile crossed Salah's face. "How do you mean?"

"What I smelled when we came into the facility. It made me react viscerally."

"Ah, *le parfum pénitentiaire*. It took us months to develop. What did you think?"

"I was impressed. It made me extremely . . . apprehensive."

"You felt dread, correct?"

"Precisely."

"That's why it works. Look—I throw into a cell a man. He's no hardliner, but let's say he was standing close by when two Israeli reservists are attacked, beaten, then thrown out of the second-story window of a Palestinian Authority police station, then stomped to death by the crowd the Palestinian police have assembled below. There is video—a Western camera crew was rolling during the incident, so we have lots of faces but no names. This guy, we think he has names."

"Why?"

"Because in the video he's a part of the crowd. He looks like he knows the people around him—the same animals who tore our soldiers apart limb from limb and then turned to the camera to show off their bloody hands. Either they're his neighbors or he's a part of one of the murderers' extended families. I have to fracture that clan loyalty and get him to name names before Arafat ships the scum with the blood on their hands out to Gaza or Egypt or Syria, where it's harder for us to lay our hands on them. So Shabak noses around until they find him, scoop him up, and bring him to me. Not here. To another place. Things are abrupt, quick. He has no time to think or react. He's yanked into a truck, and the next thing he knows he's smelling what you smelled—and all of a sudden he is afraid. He is very, very afraid. Then he loses his clothes. He's handed dirty, anonymous over-alls that smell of someone else's sweat and urine. He's alone. He's frightened. He's been separated from his family, his village, all his friends. He's pushed into a cell. A very spartan cell. Then I start the disorientation and, more important, the anticipation of dread. A few slaps in the face—*whap-whap*. A cuff or two on the back of the head—*smack-smack*. Then he's left alone to wonder what's coming next. Then I use heat. Followed by cold. Then sleep deprivation. During this time, he's hooded for what he thinks is a day, maybe even two."

"How does he know?"

"Because we designed the hoods so he can see just enough to know when the lights go on and when they go off. Because he can hear the other prisoners being served breakfast or dinner." Salah's eyes narrowed. "His senses tell him what's what."

"And how long are we really talking about?"

"Nine to thirteen hours tops. Sometimes much less."

Tom pursed his lips. Impressive.

Salah continued. "He can hear things but not see anything. He hears someone being taken away. He hears screams—I mean serious. Like fingernails being pulled out, or hot irons burning flesh or electroshock. Sometime later—he has no idea how long—he hears the sound of a body being dragged down the corridor and thrown into the adjacent cell. If he listens very carefully, he can make out excruciating moans. It may all be role-playing or sound effects coming from a compact disc and a very sophisticated speaker system—sophisticated enough to make the walls of his cell rumble if we have to. But my target doesn't know that. All he knows is what his buddies have told him and what he's picked up on the street about how ruthless we are—and what he's just gone through. Believe me, by the time I ask him the first question, he is already putty."

"But what you're talking about *is* ruthless."

"Ruthless works, my friend. You have to be pragmatic. Flexible. You Americans forget you are at war. That's because you think you are eight thousand miles from it, even though you're not. We live in the middle of the battlefield, my friend." Salah pulled a pack of Jordanian cigarettes from his pocket, shook one into his mouth, and lit it with a disposable lighter. "That's how you get actionable intelligence. Stuff you use today, tomorrow, this week."

"But you said you don't use those techniques at Qadima."

"Correct. Here we are interested in the long term. To learn how these people think and why. This woman you came to see—she is no terrorist. We know that. But we want to learn about the man she traveled with. We want to be able to give our security services information that will help them uncover developing capabilities, impending objectives, future trends. And so, we prefer psychological means—yes, we still use light, heat, and cold, sound or the absolute lack of it. But the key is long, intensive, almost psychoanalytic sessions."

"But she's British. What about the British consul? Didn't he demand to see her?"

Salah put his right hand on the edge of the metal desk and exhaled smoke through his nose. "That is not my concern. When those in a position to grant the British consul permission to see this woman do so, she will be moved to another facility." He swiveled toward Tom. "Our goals here are different. Time is of no concern. We want to extract information right down to the subconscious level. To understand what attracted these people to terrorism—to comprehend not only their motives, but get inside their psyches."

"When you say long . . ."

The Israeli switched into French. "Twenty-two, twenty-three hours is common. I have seen interrogations that last more than thirty-two hours— almost a day and a half. And believe me, they are just as hard on the interrogator as they are on the subject."

Tom followed suit, speaking French. "You don't tag-team?"

"It doesn't work if you switch boats in midstream. There has to be a real line of communication developed. Something akin to trust. Like I said, in many ways the process here resembles psychoanalysis. You get inside their heads. You take them back, get them almost fetal, and then bring them forward step-by-step."

Tom understood Salah's modus operandi. The agent recruitment process operated under many of the same precepts. The case officer controls the situation by creating and subsequently encouraging the kind of rapport in which the agent quickly becomes dependent on the case officer. Through the ability to read people, the force of personality, and the exploitation of vulnerabilities, the case officer creates a Potemkin Village relationship in which he or she becomes the agent's best friend, surrogate parent, trusted confessor, and shrink. "Potemkin Village" because it is all an act. The case officer's every emotion is feigned, every response choreographed in order to manipulate, steer, and influence the target in a certain prescribed direction. At the end of the process, which is called "getting close," the target will trust the case officer more than he or she will trust their own husbands or wives, families, or the groups to which they belong.

Indeed, if the case officers are sophisticated enough, and flexible enough, and know enough about the culture, mores, and psychological quirks of the target, they can even run this mind game on individuals whose religious and political beliefs might at first appear to be impenetrable and unshakable. Like members of the Muslim Brotherhood or the Da'wa, for example. Tom had recruited members of both vehemently anti-Western Islamist factions as agents. It hadn't been an overnight process. It had taken more than half a year in one case—that had been a false-flag recruitment—and a local access agent to act as an intermediary in the other. But he had pulled them off.

He looked at the one-armed man who flicked the cigarette from his lips and ground it out with the toe of his boot. This guy knew whereof he spoke.

"Why was I allowed to come here?"

"You are here because Reuven Ayalon vouches for you, and because Reuven has a lot of friends." He gave Tom a sidelong glance. "I was against it at first. It breaks the rhythm, and we're almost finished with her. But I was finally convinced that in the long term your visit will bear valuable fruit for us as well as you."

"Thank you."

"Don't be so quick to thank. Besides, Reuven or no Reuven, you are here because I was told you are able to ask questions exactly the way we do—in Arabic or French that doesn't sound as if it's being spoken by a Yankee Doodle dandy."

The words came out "Yenki Duudul dendi." The Israeli looked at Tom, his face serious. "You speak even your French with a slight Tunisian accent. There is no hint of American in your speech."

"Is that important?"

Salah shook another cigarette out, put it to his lips, and replaced the pack in his pocket. "It is critical. It is important for some of the detainees to believe they have been shipped somewhere that is not Israel. And so there is no Hebrew spoken anywhere in this facility. No English either. Arabic, French, and sometimes Farsi, Russian, or German."

"Isn't that skirting the ethical edge?"

"Ethical? It's not ethical to murder civilians, my friend. I told you: I am against torture. I am against abuse. But I've already been condemned to fight with one sleeve pinned to my shoulder, my friend. I'm not willing to tie my only good hand behind my back, too." Salah withdrew a greenish bandanna from his coveralls, blew his nose loudly, then stuffed the handkerchief back in his back pocket. "So, we can—and we do without apology—hold detainees in solitary confinement for years if we feel it is necessary. Just like the French, incidentally. In fact, a major factor in our high success rate is the complete isolation in which these terrorists are kept. You Americans tend to coddle prisoners—even terrorists. You cave in to human rights organizations. You allow lawyers, family visits, and other amenities. I cannot believe what I saw when I visited high-security facilities in the United States some years ago. Cable television. Gyms. Libraries. It was like sending your criminals to college."

"That was a civilian prison."

"But your so-called white supremacists were incarcerated there alongside rapists and bank robbers. You treat your own terrorists as if they were burglars or carjackers." Salah's hand made a dismissive gesture. "Terrorists are not criminals. They are enemy combatants, and they deserve no coddling. You Americans often ignore the realities. That kind of fuzzy thinking pervades your abilities, especially in this kind of total war." He exhaled smoke through his nose. "Jihad, they call it. All-out effort, remember? Sometimes I think you Americans forget that when you deal with enemy combatants."

"That's not what I hear about the ones being held in Afghanistan and Guantánamo."

"For you, Iraq and Afghanistan are the exceptions to the rule, believe me." Salah pulled on the collar of his sterile coveralls. "Besides, you Americans have very few trained interrogators." His black eyes flashed in Tom's direction. "You had to send more than fifty of your paramilitary people here just after the Kandahar and Baghram facilities were established in Afghanistan because your CIA didn't have any qualified personnel. *Any.* Unbelievable. So we had to teach them the basics, believe me. But it didn't matter, because they all lacked Arabic, not to mention Pashto, or Urdu, or Uzbek. A friend of mine at AMAN[14] told me when the 9/11 attacks occurred, there were less than a hundred Arabic-speaking interrogators in your entire army—and perhaps another hundred and fifty in the reserves. And CIA? It was a joke. At the military interrogation center in Kandahar, not a single CIA officer had sufficient Arabic, Pashto, Urdu, or Farsi to do proper interrogations. And yet the most critical element is the ability to speak in the detainee's native tongue and understand his culture. You cannot do the job using an interpreter."

Well, Salah was right about that. The 4627 Company had more Top Secret–cleared four-plus Uzbek speakers than CIA did these days. In fact, in the spring of 2002, CIA had approached 4627 to recruit, vet, and hire language-capable interrogators for Abu Ghraib prison in Iraq. Langley was offering $2,500 a day plus expenses for ninety-day deployments, and they wanted a minimum of a dozen people. The math was great: 4627's profit on two ninety-day cycles would be $3.2 million—and Langley wanted a minimum of six ninety-day cycles. But Tony Wyman turned the Agency down cold. It was a slippery slope, he said. One bad apple—one case of prisoner abuse in the newspapers—and the firm's credibility worldwide would be jeopardized. Let some other contractor take the money and run.

And yet Tom understood the need. It often took Americans weeks to accomplish what trained native speakers could do in a matter of days because the Americans too often had to rely on interpreters—linguists, they were euphemistically called by the Pentagon. It was like trying to play the old kids' game of telephone. Tom knew it was impossible to recruit an agent using an interpreter. So why the hell did the numbskulls at DOD and Langley believe it would be productive to interrogate hard-core al-Qa'ida militants—Wahabists who were willing to die for their beliefs—that way? It made no sense at all.

Besides, interrogating terrorists was an art as well as a science. The Israelis had perfected it out of necessity. In the United States, until 9/11 at least, terrorism had been largely considered a criminal activity not an act of war. The FBI's techniques for interrogating terrorists were exactly the

---

[14]Abbreviation for Israel's military intelligence organization.

same as they were for interrogating bank robbers or mafiosi. Christ, the Bureau was surveilling potential militants at Washington, D.C.'s Massachusetts Avenue mosque the same way they'd taped comings and goings at the old Soviet embassy on Sixteenth Street. Sure, they had audio as well as video from bugs planted inside the Mosque and adjacent grounds. But rumor was, translation lag time at SIOP[15] was about nine months.

In the military, interrogator trainees at Fort Huachuca were still using Cold War scenarios. The only change was that instead of calling the role-players Boris, they were calling them Muhammad. At CIA, the subject of prisoner interrogation still took up less than six hours of the basic intelligence operations course taken by trainees at the Farm. Didn't *anybody* Get It? Tom zipped the coveralls up to his throat. "Will there be a transcript available to me?"

"We will give you a DVD—full audio and video, as well as a transcript, in Microsoft Word format." He watched as the American sat on the edge of the straight-backed chair and pulled on the scuffed black leather boots. "Obviously, you will not possess these materials unilaterally."

"I understand." Tom yanked the laces secure and tied them in a double bow. "How long can I have with her?"

"As much time as you need. But I don't think you'll need a lot of time."

"Why is that?"

"I believe we were pretty thorough. Reuven has made the interrogation transcripts available, yes?"

"He has—except for the summary and several pages that were redacted."

"That was because I wanted you to come to your own conclusions. Afterward, we'll compare notes. You will give me your evaluation of the situation, and I will give you mine."

"That's fair."

"Thank you." Salah spat the cigarette from his lips and ground it out against the floor. "Remember: you'll interrogate the woman in French, please."

---

[15]The FBI's Special Intelligence Operations Center, located in the J. Edgar Hoover Building on Ninth Street and Pennsylvania Avenue in Washington, D.C., is the nerve center for its current counterterrorism activities.

"Will do." Tom looked at Salah. "I could even use a Marseille accent if you think it would be effective." The accent was something he'd worked on as he created the persona he'd use during the interrogation.

The Israeli cocked his head in Tom's direction with newfound respect. "Yes," he said. "It is a good idea."

"Then I'm ready."

Salah examined Tom up and down. Tom started for the door, but Salah cut him off. "Wait—" The Israeli slapped the file folder he was carrying onto the chair, rummaged through the drawer of the steel desk, pulled out a wrinkled olive-drab barracks cap, shook it energetically, then slapped it against Tom's upper arm. "Here—put this on," he said brusquely. "You have an American-style haircut."

13

10:26 A.M. Tom pulled the cap on and followed the Israeli. They walked down a long corridor, turned right, descended a flight of stairs, and turned left, entering another ominous, dimly lit corridor lined with heavy gray steel doors.

Interesting. The room where Tom had changed clothes had a concrete floor. So did the corridor. The steps he'd just descended were also concrete, with steel edges. But the floor in this corridor was covered in inch-thick, hard rubber—like the nonslip pads sometimes used in restaurant kitchens. Their footfalls made no noise whatsoever.

Tom worked to keep his emotions under control. It was difficult. He had actually run agents who were terrorists. His first had been a courier for Al Jihad—a handover on his first overseas tour when he'd worked under consular cover in Cairo. There'd been a car bomber in Sudan—a worker bee in the Muslim Brotherhood who was occasionally loaned out to al-Qa'ida. And of course there was Rashid in Paris. Rashid had what—half a dozen Israeli scalps on his belt. But this was different. He'd never inter-rogated a jailed terrorist before, never got up close and personal.

More pertinent: Tom had had only three days in which to prepare for this one-shot deal. That was like having no time at all. Prior to agent meet-ings, you often went back over months and months of reports, memorizing the tiniest details, so that if there were contradictions or fabrications, your internal b.s. detector sounded and they could be identified, highlighted, and probed. You asked your developmentals the same question twenty different ways, perpetually searching for minute inconsistencies or tiny discrepan-cies, because one word could make the difference between success and failure; between a unilateral asset and a double agent; between that agent's life and their death.

That's why the bloody recruitment process took so long. Tom shook his head. God—the damn 9/11 Commission was already leaking stories about putting more CIA agents, as they often incorrectly called them, on the street. Either the commission was made up of ignoramuses, or they'd all seen too much TV or read too much Tom Clancy.

The way they talked, all you had to do was hire someone, give him or her six months of training, and *poof,* presto change-o, a full-grown case officer—Smiley out of the head of Zeus. It didn't work that way. It could take years to learn the ropes, even if you were talented. You needed men-toring. There wasn't a day that Tom didn't silently thank Sam Waterman for taking the time to inculcate the dark arts of tradecraft into him.

The commission acted as if you could stroll into a bar in London's Shepherd's Market, spot a suspicious-looking Yemenite Arab sipping a bourbon daiquiri, sidle up next to him, have a ten-minute conversation, and all of a sudden said Arab tells you precisely where Saddam Hussein has cached his weapons of mass destruction, or in precisely which cave in Tora Bora Usama Bin Laden is currently hanging his kaffiyeh.

Jeezus. Didn't anybody realize it doesn't work that way? First of all, for every ten pitches you make, you strike out nine times. In Cairo, Tom had botched his first attempt to recruit an agent. He'd pitched an Egyptian Army major attached to the Mukhabarat el-Khabeya (military intelligence service) whom he'd cultivated for more than six months. The officer had looked at him as if he were crazy, stood up, and said, "Do not ever try to contact me again or I will have you arrested." Recruiting was a risk-intensive business. And when you did finally snare a target, the information you received most of the time was piecemeal—a fragment of a puzzle, not the whole thing.

Didn't people understand that HUMINT—for HUMan INTelligence gathering—was like paleontology? You probed and you dug and you prodded and you excavated for what seemed like forever. And then, after an excruciatingly and often interminable period of time, you might—if you're smart, and talented, and above all lucky—you might discover a tiny intelligence fossil that is, perhaps, a single part of a much-larger life-form. And yet from this microscopic shard—which may, by the way, have been planted by an evil archaeologist working for one of your adversaries—Congress and the 9/11 Commission, and, for that matter, the misguided and ill-informed American public insist it is not only possible to divine what sort of creature the fossil could have come from, but also tell you exactly where the entire skeleton of the creature can be found.

In real life, the recruitment process could take months of careful gumshoeing to make sure the opposition wasn't screwing with you. In the field, you had to watch your emotions so you didn't get sucked in. In the field, enthusiasm was the enemy of thoroughness. You developed a mental sonar that was never turned off. That's what had killed McGee. He lacked the sensors to realize he was developing a double. Or a dangle. Or a provocateur. Or an assassin. Achieving that highly developed defensive awareness took years.

It looked easy in the movies. Or in fiction. But in real life, becoming a productive, streetwise case officer doesn't happen overnight. And spotting, assessing, developing, and then recruiting a single agent is a laborious, time-intensive, painstaking process. Charlie Hoskinson, who'd recruited the ███ of the Syrian president, said it had taken him the better part of his three-year-tour in Damascus to do so. Bronco Panitz, who was 4627's CEO, had been promoted to the Senior Intelligence Service on the strength of two Soviet recruitments, a process that had taken him more than four years on two continents—only to lose them both to Aldrich Ames.

So when the 9/11 Commission or the fools on the House or Senate intelligence oversight committees wrote reports with prose that read *it is im-*

perative for CIA to increase its human intelligence capabilities immediately, Tom and the rest of his fellow intelligence professionals had to laugh. George Tenet—a disaster as DCI—had boldly told Congress that the DO wouldn't be up to speed for another five years. Everyone at Langley who had an ounce of sense knew Tenet grossly understated the case to make himself look better. The evidence? Tom's own curriculum vitae belied the DCI's assertion.

Tom had spent seventeen years and seven months at CIA. He'd entered training just after Labor Day of 1985, recruited straight out of Dartmouth College. In late March 1986, he'd been assigned to headquarters—spending seven months at NE Division as a desk officer trainee to learn the bureaucratic ropes. During that time, he managed to take a number of the advanced tradecraft courses offered in Washington: lock-picking, secure communications, and the "guerrilla driving course" out in West Virginia at Bill Scott Raceway, where he learned how to run roadblocks and make bootlegger's and J-turns. Then it had been a year at the Foreign Service Institute's language school in Rosslyn, Virginia, followed by nineteen months in Tunis, in FSI's immersion Arabic program.

Tom's first overseas tour hadn't commenced until June 1989, when he began work under consular cover at the Cairo embassy. And even then he was a greenhorn with no field experience. And little chance of receiving much in the immediate future.

His chief in Cairo, John ███████████, was a prissy, non-Arab speaker who'd spent eighteen years as a reports officer before being brought into the Directorate of Operations under DCI Robert Gates's "crossfertilization" program that larded DO with inexperienced analysts, academic reports officers, and secretaries—all in the name of EEO diversification. A GS-15 on his second (and final) go-round for promotion to the Senior Intelligence Service, ████████ got so fidgety when the subject of recruitments was brought up he was known around the embassy as Twitch. The situation wasn't improved by Tom's immediate superior, a chronic alcoholic named McWhirter who signed out to interview developmentals but actually spent his afternoons sipping vodkas on the rocks in the bar of the Méridien.

No one in Cairo showed any inclination to mentor the first-time case officer. So Tom sat in his teller's cage and stamped visas, learned as much about Cairo as he could, worked hard to improve his conversational Arabic, and pursued his spycraft through trial and error—mostly, he realized later, through error.

In point of fact, Tom didn't receive any decent mentoring until after he'd arrived in Paris in July 1992. There, the deputy chief, Sam Waterman, took the youngster under his wing. He taught Tom how to go black—slip out from under DST surveillance—by exploiting the seams in the French domestic security agency's rigidly defined regional areas of coverage. He allowed Tom the freedom to occasionally push the edge of the envelope when it came to recruiting and running agents with less-than-squeaky-clean backgrounds. And perhaps most important, he'd forced Tom to spend long hours working on his reporting and interrogation skills.

Waterman had schoolmarmishly insisted that Tom spend every bit of his spare time—and there wasn't a lot of it—reading old reports so that he'd have absorbed all the background he needed for his agent handovers. Long before Tom met his first handover, he'd memorized three years of reporting about the man. Waterman had grilled him on the material before he'd allowed the handover to proceed. The interrogation hadn't been pleasant, either.

It didn't stop there. Under Waterman's incessant tutelage, Tom wrote and then rewrote every report half a dozen times—sometimes more. Waterman was merciless. "You're not providing any frigging details, Tom." Waterman would pound the desk. He was a big man and he knew how to use his size to intimidate "You were in a restaurant. What did it look like? What were the surroundings? Was there any sign of DST? Your developmental was ten minutes late. Why? Did his explanation satisfy you? Was he hiding something? What did your developmental wear? Was he wearing anything he hadn't worn before? What about new jewelry? How did he appear to you? What emotional traits did he display? What did his body language tell you? Did he show any of the physical signs of deception or guilt? Dry mouth? Was his face pale? Did you see any throbbing in the vein on his neck or the backs of his hands? Was his voice steady? What were his feet doing while the two of you were speaking? I don't see any frigging hints about any of those reactions in your reporting."

Now he'd had a mere three days to prepare—to construct a scenario, develop a persona, get all his physical and mental ducks in the proverbial row. Not enough time. Not by far, given the stakes. But it was all the time there was.

He'd followed Reuven's advice to the letter. Popped the question at six Monday morning. By eight that night, MJ was sporting a magnificent two-point-three-carat diamond set off by two quarter-carat baguettes, all in a regal but simple platinum setting. She couldn't stop looking at the damn thing and smiling.

Tuesday afternoon, Reuven had used his connections to put MJ on the overbooked Air France flight to Paris—bumped to first class. She'd spend the night at rue Raynouard, get the rest of her stuff, then continue on to Washington Thursday. The radiant look on her face as she went through the departure gate was ample evidence that Tom had indeed provided her with perfect cover for status.

While he was at Ben Gurion with MJ, Reuven had obtained copies of the pertinent debriefs. They were in Hebrew, of course, and so he'd had to translate while Tom made his own notes. It had taken the better part of two days to go through the hundreds of pages of transcripts. Then he and Reuven worked on interrogation scenarios. They'd gone for almost twenty hours straight. Reuven had finally insisted that Tom get enough rest so he'd be sharp the next day.

The next day—today. Today was what Sam Waterman used to call "showtime."

10:31 A.M. Salah stopped in front of a gray steel door with a full length sealed pin hinge. He opened the file and displayed the cover page for Tom to see. Attached to the Hebrew typing was a full-face–slash-profile mug shot of a dark-haired woman. She was plain as a sparrow. Not physically unattractive, but exceedingly ordinary. Not like Malik. Tom had seen pictures of Malik. He was an Islamic Tom Cruise.

"She's waiting for you in there." Salah flipped the file closed, turned to Tom, and nodded for him to enter. "Rap twice on the door," he said in French. "I will come for you."

"Agreed."

Tom sneaked a quick look at the inside of his left wrist. His pulse was racing. He paused and stared at the gray door, taking a couple of seconds to clear his mind of all extraneous information, focus his concentration on the interrogation, and slow his respiration. *Show nothing. Give away nothing. Display nothing.*

And yet . . . there was so damn much to remember—so many details, factoids, info-bits. Pieces of a puzzle in a pile on a table. And you had to assemble them blindfolded. With the clock running. And lives at stake. The task was staggering. Daunting. Overwhelming.

And all in a day's work. He put his hand on the heavy steel handle, pushed it downward, and pulled the thick door toward him.

Her name was Dianne Lamb. She was twenty-seven years old. She had been extremely easy to crack. At least that's what the transcripts indicated. It had bothered him at first that she was a woman, because that fact indicated that the bad guys were taking things to a whole new level. In fact, not only was she a woman, but she was an educated woman—a modern, educated Western woman. This was not somebody who acted in order to secure the twenty-five-thousand-dollar onetime payment for homicide bombers from the Saudi royals (money washed through Wahabist charities), the twenty-five-thousand-dollar homicide-bomber payments Saddam Hussein skimmed off the UN's Oil for Food Program or the blood money Arafat paid through a series of middlemen.

Dianne Lamb was a graduate of Cambridge, with a respectable second in French literature. She worked as a copy editor for the BBC's book-publishing division, where she specialized at nitpicking typos and misprints in BBC's profitable cook-book series. Twenty-seven years old, she lived a spinster's life in the chic northern London neighborhood of Islington, where she shared a tiny two-bedroom flat with a forty-five-year-old bookkeeper who worked three floors below her at the Beeb. She hadn't dated much. There'd been one serious and devastating relationship at Cambridge, and nothing since. Her family was upper middle class and professional. They lived in Surrey. Her father, Nigel, was a vice president at an international banking house who commuted to an office in the City every day. Her mother, Stephanie, who'd been born in France but brought to the UK as a three-year-old, did volunteer work at the local hospital. Neither, according to the intelligence reporting, was connected either financially or ideologically with any Islamist terrorist movement or anything that might even come close.

Nine months ago, in January, Dianne met Malik Suleiman. He was the Sorbonne-educated London-based correspondent for *Al Arabia,* which he'd described to her as a small Paris-based Arab-language weekly. He was tall, good-looking, and secular.

They'd met at a bar in Knightsbridge and quickly become involved. In March, he took her to Paris for a long weekend. They'd traveled on the Chunnel train, stayed at the George V, and spent their time in two-star restaurants and exclusive clubs. Malik obviously came from a wealthy family. In July and August, they returned to Paris for two more long week-ends. Again, they stayed at the George V. And then, in September, Malik invited Dianne to visit the Holy Land with him. He said the magazine wanted a piece from him on how ordinary Israelis were coping with the In-tifada. Once again, he would pay all the expenses. Think of it, he'd said, as an engagement trip. Once they'd returned, they'd visit his parents in Mo-rocco and break the good news.

It was an offer she couldn't refuse. But two days after he'd booked their flights, Malik's publisher demanded he fly to Paris and undertake a special interview. It took some jiggling, but Malik was able to fix things. Dianne would fly directly from London. He'd take the train to Paris, do the interview, drop the tape off at the magazine, then catch the first available flight and meet her at the Tel Aviv Hilton.

But there was a problem. Because Malik was jumping from point to point, he wanted to take only carry-on luggage. Dianne had a big suitcase. Could she take a few things for him—so he'd have enough clothes for their week in Israel and the West Bank? And also his portable radio and some other personal effects?

Of course she could. And so, she flew to Israel on a Monday—the British Air flight. She took a cab from Ben Gurion and checked into the Hilton.

The room was perfect: on the eighth floor, with a broad ocean view.

Malik arrived Wednesday evening from Paris, with his rolling leather carry-on and a present for her: a fabulous Louis Vuitton backpack. It was his apology for being tardy.

They made love twice. Afterward, Malik took the radio from her bag and turned it on so he could listen to BBC World News. He was, she'd told the interrogators, a real news freak—had been for as long as she'd known him.

When the radio didn't work, he'd checked the batteries and discovered they were dead. So he'd sent her out to buy fresh ones at the newsstand in the lobby while he unpacked.

They'd traveled all over, Malik making lots of notes and taking lots of digital photographs for his article. They visited Jaffa and walked all around Tel Aviv. They took a bus all the way to Haifa and Acre. They visited Tiberias and swam in the Sea of Galilee. They stayed in a beachfront hotel in Netanya and wandered past the tourist restaurants. They spent two days in Jerusalem, staying at the American Colony Hotel, an old Arab palace on the Nablus Road. On the second day, the hotel concierge hired an Arab taxi for them and they drove through the occupied territories to visit Jericho, and then Ramallah.

In Ramallah, in a restaurant, they'd met by chance a PLO security officer who'd invited them to see evidence of how badly the Palestinians were being treated by the Israelis. He'd taken them to the Fatah offices and played a video: a long montage of photographs showing dead Palestinian children, all murdered, he said, by criminal Israeli settlers. Dianne admitted Malik had spent some time alone with the Palestinian while she looked at the video.

After one more night in Jerusalem, they took a cab to Tel Aviv and reregistered at the Hilton. They ate dinner in the room, then made love. Afterward, Malik suggested they go nightclubbing. They started at Montana, a crowded beer bar on the northern edge of Old Tel Aviv. From there, they went on to a number of clubs, working their way south, toward the Hilton. Then Malik suggested they try to get into what he called the hottest club in Tel Aviv: Michael's Pub. It was on the waterfront, a block and a half from the American embassy.

They'd taken a cab. They were sufficiently fashionable to be allowed through the rope line after Dianne's backpack was checked by the security guard. They'd found a table near the dance floor, ordered a couple of whiskey sours and a plate of *mezze,* and gotten up to dance. They'd danced two dances, and Dianne excused herself to go to the loo. That's where she was when Malik blew himself up.

10:31 A.M. *Showtime.* Tom stepped through the doorway. His face a neutral mask, he reached behind himself and pulled on the handle until he heard the heavy bolt snap shut.

14

10:31 A.M. The interrogation room was bare and palpably cool—at least fifteen degrees cooler than the corridor. There was something else in evidence, too: the faint but unmistakable scent of Salah's *parfum pénitentiaire*.

She was tiny—fragile as a soft-boned baby chick and obviously as vulnerable. Not more than five two or five three. She stood, fists clenched, behind a metal table. She had the sort of delicately featured yet hugely plain face that made her look ten years older than her actual age. Her appearance certainly wasn't helped by the shapeless gray prison shift and dirty tennis shoes with no laces.

She looked at Tom with wide-eyed apprehension. Under his relentless gaze, her right hand jerked upward in order to smooth down her uncombed, short, mouse-brown hair. She was largely unsuccessful. An absurd, recalcitrant cowlick completed her hapless and wretched appearance.

Her body language read *exhausted* written in capital letters, but her brown eyes were clear, even—Tom found this surprising—piercing.

Equally promising, she displayed neither the zombie look, the loony's smile, or the thousand-yard stare. Salah had done well. He'd wrung her dry, yet been careful not to break her into unusable emotional shards.

Tom slipped into character and kept his voice neutral but commanding. *"Assieds-toi."* It was the way you told a dog or a naughty child to sit.

She slipped demurely onto a straight-backed chair that was bolted to the concrete. She looked like a schoolgirl: knees pressed together under her shift, ankles locked. She raised her hands from her lap and clasped them together, interlocking her fingers as if she were about to play the old nursery game. "This is the church, this is the steeple, open the doors and see all the people."

Tom allowed himself a quick scan of the room. The cameras had to be behind him. And the microphones? There were probably three or four of them, spread out so nothing would be missed.

He looked down at her. *"Parle-moi de Mal-ik,"* he said, speaking in a slow, almost pedantic Marseillaise accent. "Tell me everything the two of you did on that first"—he punched the word—"*wonderful* trip to Paris last March."

She cocked her head as a child would do and looked up at him for fifteen, perhaps twenty seconds. He could see the gears engaging. She was trying to figure out what he wanted, where he was going.

He gave her nothing. "Paris. Last March."

Finally, a single tear formed in the corner of her right eye. When it had built up enough mass, it rolled down her cheek and plopped from her chin onto the front of her shift. "Oh, Malik," she said. "Poor, silly, romantic Malik. I loved him so."

She started to blubber and tugged at the sleeve of her shift so she could wipe her nose. Then she caught herself and stopped, muffling a huge sob.

"Here. Use this." Reaching into the pocket of his coveralls, Tom played with the fresh, starched handkerchief he'd brought until it released what he'd hidden inside its opaque folds. He extracted the hankie, shook it out, advanced, reached over the chair that had been placed for him, and dropped it onto the surface of the table.

She picked it up. It was an oversize gentleman's handkerchief made of French linen. It had hand-rolled edges and it smelled ever so faintly of Givenchy Gentleman. Tom knew Malik had used the same cologne. And just like Salah, he understood sensory triggers can often help interrogators prime the pump, so to speak, when they're dealing with emotionally frail personalities.

He watched her body language. He silently counted the seconds—one thousand one, one thousand two, one thousand three—until the emotional tidal wave washed over her.

Fire in the hole! She held the handkerchief to her face and silent-screamed, caught her breath, silent-screamed again, and collapsed on the tabletop, her arms splayed out around her head.

He waited until the dry-heaving finally abated. "Dianne," he said. "Dianne, we have to talk."

Her shoulders pumped up and down. She pressed the handkerchief to her face like a talisman. "Have to talk."

"Paris. The George V. Malik."

She swallowed hard. "We took the Friday train from Waterloo. We . . . we'd . . . ." She bit her lips, then wiped at her nose, which was wet.

Tom said nothing. There were perhaps eight, nine, ten seconds of silence. And then she inhaled deeply to get herself under control, wiped her nose with her sleeve, and began again. "We'd decided to take the day off. We met on the platform. I'd come from my flat by subway." Her French was perfectly enunciated and unmistakably upper-crust British in its inflection. She sounded somewhat like the late and unlamented Princess Di—the same nasal, stiff-upper-lip Sloane Ranger tone.

"Where is your flat?"

She held the handkerchief to her face and inhaled deeply. "I live in Islington. On Gerrard Road—just above the canal." She looked at him strangely. "I've been over this material before."

Tom ignored her. "Of which canal do you speak?"

Her eyes were eloquent. They said, *You absolute shit. You are doing this for no reason at all other than you can.* But still, she responded to his question. "The Grand Union."

"How long is the walk from your flat to the Metro stop?" He purposely misspoke.

She gave him a reproving glance. "We call it the Underground in Britain."

Tom rephrased the question.

"About four blocks."

"And you carried your baggage the whole distance?"

"I had a carry-on. I could wheel it."

"And the train took you directly to Waterloo Station?"

"I had to change once—at Euston."

"What underground did you travel?"

"The Northern Line."

"The whole time?"

"The whole time."

Tom adjusted the straight-backed chair on his side of the table, then dropped onto it. "And you met Malik at Waterloo."

She put the handkerchief to her face and inhaled again. "Yes."

"Who arrived first?"

"I did."

"Where did you meet?"

"There is a board, showing all the departing trains."

"Yes?"

"We met in front of it."

"When did you buy your tickets?"

"Malik had bought them."

"When?"

"I don't know. He had them when he arrived."

"So you went directly to the train?"

"Yes."

"Where did you sit?"

"In first class."

Tom nodded. What he'd just done was to pose a series of neutral "control questions," in order to gauge her physical reactions under nonthreatening conditions. She'd responded as he'd hoped she would: breathing even, eye contact steady and nonevasive, and hand-and-foot movement minimal.

He was taking her back to the Paris trips for another reason. The Israelis had been interested in her relationship with Malik because they were deconstructing the bombing. Reverse-engineering everything leading up to the event so they could see where the chinks were, and how they could be closed.

Tom had his own ideas about Malik. The obvious thing was that he'd recruited her as a mule, to carry the explosives. Virtually all agent recruitments are based on four behavioral elements: ego, money, sex, or ideology. EMSI, pronounced "emcee," was the abbreviation they taught at the Farm. Dianne's was a classic sex recruitment. The scenario with plain-Jane targets usually followed similar patterns: a taste of the good life—a few bottles of the bubbly, followed shortly by a romantic French dinner, followed thereafter by a healthy bout of the old in-and-out at a stylish bachelor flat. Tom's eyes scanned the prisoner, read her body language, demeanor, and aura. She was an open book. One great, sweaty orgasm and she'd be wrapped around Malik's little finger forever.

"How did you meet Malik?"

"It was an accident."

"An accident."

"I was having a drink with a friend. We'd been to Beauchamp Street. The sales, you know—the January sales? And we'd stopped at this pub for a glass of wine."

"Which pub?"

"The Bunch of Grapes. It's on Brompton Road."

"Who were you with?"

"Deirdre. Deirdre Ludlow. We'd gone to school together. Known one another since we were eight." Dianne gave Tom a wistful look. "She was always the pretty one. I was always the bright one."

"You say you'd been shopping?"

"We'd been in and out of stores for at least two hours."

"And?"

"Malik spilled a glass of champagne all over my arm."

Tom thought, I wonder where he spotted her. It was obvious to him that Malik had been trolling. Knightsbridge during the January sales was the perfect place to target young women. It was all becoming clear now: the plain wren with her beautiful friend. But what was it Malik had seen? What scent had Dianne thrown off that the predator knew she was the weak one?

Tom already knew the answer. All Malik had had to do was look at the two of them. That was hint enough if he was the pro Tom believed he'd been. He'd probably spotted Dianne by appearance alone. Her clothes were expensive but frumpy. Salah had displayed them to Tom. The labels came from the best shops in Knightsbridge. So having spotted her, Malik had watched from afar and assessed. She wore no engagement or wedding ring. Her beverage of choice? Safe white wine. He'd confirm his first impressions by reading her body language. She was no type A personality. No alpha bitch. She obviously did as she was told, something he was able to confirm by the manner in which she constantly deferred to her better-looking companion. There was more: her eyes always downcast. That meant she was probably submissive.

The recruitment planets aligned, Malik stalked until the time was right. Then he pounced, utilizing an inventive but not unexpected form of cold pitch. "You said Malik spilled his drink on you."

"Yes, and he was so apologetic. He bought us a bottle of champagne. He ran outside and found a flower seller and bought me roses. He was just so . . . effusive."

"How long was it before you went to bed with him?"

Her cheeks grew red. "That night," she said. Her eyes fell and she focused on the table in front of her. "He asked if he could take me to dinner as a way of apologizing. He took me to Che, on St. James's Street."

"And?"

"Che," she said earnestly. "One reads about the people who go there. You have to book weeks ahead. But Malik didn't. We took a cab to St. James's and strolled in as if he owned the place. The manager, who was as pretty as any movie star, kissed him on the lips, gave him a big hug, took us right up the escalator, and gave us the best table in the house."

"And?"

"And?" She looked at him as if he were an idiot. "What do you think? We had champagne. And dinner with wine. He was charming and delightful and extremely attentive. We were sitting next to one another on a banquette. We started holding hands. And then all of a sudden, just before they brought coffee and cognac, he started rubbing the top of my thigh, and then he . . . he, well you know, put his hand underneath my skirt. No one had ever done anything that . . . risky before. It made me tremendously excited." She looked at Tom. "He leaned over and kissed me—a passionate kiss, I can assure you. He told me I excited him. That I excited him. And that I could, you know, feel him to see. And I did. And he was." Another huge tear rolled from the corner of her eye down her cheek and dropped plop off her chin.

"Oh, my God. It was the first time in my life I'd ever caused that reaction on a man that good-looking and that sophisticated and that attentive." She looked at Tom coldly. "Of course I went to bed with him that night. I'd have done anything he wanted me to."

Yes, it was a classic sex recruitment. Absolutely textbook. The KGB had used the technique successfully for years. Ravens and Swallows, they'd called them. Soviet Swallows were particularly effective against young Marine embassy security guards. Tom remembered one, Clayton Lonetree, a Moscow embassy security guard who'd actually stolen secrets for his Soviet lover.

During Tom's Paris tour, Er Bu, the Chinese intelligence service, employed a Raven—Beijing actually called them Cormorants—to successfully seduce a female CIA case officer at Paris station. The case officer had simultaneously been having an affair with the station chief, and so the whole untidy mess had been covered up. Currently, the female officer served under diplomatic cover at United Nations headquarters in New York, where her Chinese lover was posted as a diplomat. Go figure.

In the last few months, he'd read about another Swallow—a double agent—who'd seduced not one but two FBI counterintelligence special agents and kept the simultaneous relationships going for more than a decade while the G-men leaked secret after secret during pillow talk. Oh, yes: sex was an integral part of basic spycraft. Part of the EMSI system. An effective way to exploit your target's vulnerabilities to your advantage.

Besides, Dianne Lamb was prime target material. She was plain. She radiated prim. She was sexually starved and was hungry for a relationship with a man. And of course those qualities made her both vulnerable and valuable.

Valuable, hell: she was worth her weight in gold. A proper Brit from a family of Tories, she would set off none of the alarms that Malik would. Not at Heathrow. Not at de Gaulle. Not even in Tel Aviv. She was the perfect candidate to become Malik's mule and carry Ben Said's explosive to Tel Aviv. And if that worked, they'd no doubt send her on another trip—a one-way magic carpet ride with one of the assassin's bombs packed in her suitcase. Given the range of cell phones these days, Ben Said could set it off from virtually anywhere.

That was the obvious scenario—the one that made the most sense. And if Tom hadn't known a little bit about Tariq Ben Said, he might have pursued things no further. But it was plain to Tom while going over Dianne's interrogation transcripts that the Israelis had never probed beyond the obvious. They'd had a problem to solve: How did Malik get the explosives into the country?

The obvious answer was that he'd used Dianne to carry them. But what if Dianne hadn't been the mule. What if she'd been recruited to play another role: the role of suicide bomber.

That thought had occurred to Tom when Reuven, reading from the pages of Hebrew transcript, said in passing that Malik had given Dianne a backpack—the damn thing had been totally destroyed in the explosion. From the lack of fragments, forensics indicated that was where the bomb had been hidden. It wasn't just any backpack, either. It was a Louis Vuitton Montsouris, which cost about a thousand dollars these days, given the euro's rapid rise against the dollar and the French VAT. Tom knew how much Vuitton backpacks cost because he'd purchased one for MJ not even a week ago.

Malik had bought a *Montsouris* for Dianne, too. But he'd lied about where he'd gotten it. That's what had Tom concerned.

15

12:56 P.M. "Tell me again about the backpack."

She blinked. Her eyes shifted up and to the left, a sign that she was probably going to tell the truth. "It was beautiful. I saw it in the window of the Vuitton store—the one at the corner of avenue George V and the Champs-Élysées—on our first trip. It was on display. I made some comment to Malik—you know, that it was the sort of thing I'd always wanted, but never had the nerve to buy for myself, and that was that. And then, when he arrived in August, he was carrying it with him, and he gave it to me."

"The last night—the night of the bombing—did Malik suggest that you take the backpack?"

"No—I loved it. Loved the way people admired it. I carried it everywhere. I stored the camera in it, and my makeup, and our street maps. It was very handy."

"When Malik brought the backpack from Paris, how was it wrapped?"

"He carried it in a big Vuitton shopping bag."

"And inside the bag?"

"I told you last time we covered this ground." She shrugged. "Inside the shopping bag was the backpack. Malik bought it at the duty-free."

That was what had struck Tom as odd. First, there was no Vuitton duty-free shop at de Gaulle. And second, Vuitton wrapped its backpacks like the treasures they were. They put them inside sturdy cardboard boxes and protected them with tissue paper.

The Israeli assumption was that Malik slipped the bomb into the backpack and set it off when Dianne went to the bathroom. The interrogation verified that he'd had the opportunity to do so before they'd left the hotel, even though her debriefings indicated that Dianne had not seen Malik slip something into her backpack, nor had he asked her to carry any of his belongings that night. Nor had the security guard at Mike's seen anything suspicious when Dianne and Malik entered the club.

Tom had his own ideas. Shahram had emphasized that Tariq was always pushing the envelope when it came to explosives. Like Richard Reid's sneaker bombs. What had Shahram said? Al-Qa'ida had pushed Ben Said to use a prototype fusing and detonator. If they'd waited, Reid would have brought the aircraft down.

Tom focused on Dianne. "Did he say that?"

"Yes."

"Said he bought it at the duty-free."

"Yes."

Now Tom abruptly shifted gears. "Which of Malik's friends did you see in Paris on the March trip?"

She paused. "March? None. We spent all our time alone together."

"And in July?"

"Malik had some sort of business to do. I visited the Louvre while he met with his editor."

"That was the only time you were apart?"

She thought about Tom's question for about ten seconds. "No."

"Tell me."

"He went out one morning. To buy a newspaper, he said. Something they didn't have at the kiosk in the hotel."

"How long was he gone?"

She paused. "About forty-five minutes."

"And?"

"I asked him where he'd been. He told me he'd run into an old friend and they'd stopped for a cup of coffee."

"And the friend's name?"

"I didn't ask."

Tom nodded. But his mind was racing. "Now let's fast-forward to August."

"We were by ourselves, except one evening we had a drink with Malik's editor from *Al Arabia*."

"What was his name?"

"Talal Massoud."

"Describe him."

"He's—" She brought herself up short. "I've been over this material many times before, you know."

"Not with me," Tom said. He'd saved this part for last. "Describe him, please."

"Average. Your height—maybe a bit taller. Overweight. Thick black hair, very curly—" She ran her hand from her brow across the top of her head. "Dark eyes."

It wasn't much of a description and Tom said so.

"He was pretty nondescript."

"Dressed how?"

"Cheap white shirt open at the neck. It was so thin you could see the singlet underneath. Light-colored suit coat and trousers—tannish. And brown loafers."

"Did he wear jewelry or a watch?"

"Not that I remember. He wore some kind of plastic disposable watch."

"Glasses?"

"Oh, yes. Heavy black-framed glasses with tinted lenses." She paused and looked up at the ceiling. It was a sign she was remembering a detail. "The lenses were rose-colored."

"Did he use them to read the menu?"

"He didn't read the menu. He ordered off the top of his head."

"Did he carry a cell phone?"

"I think there was one clipped to his belt."

"Did Talal take any calls?"

"Not until just before he left."

"How was his French?"

"Good, I guess, since he lives there."

"You guess?"

"He spoke to me in English, and to Malik in Arabic. He spoke to the waiters in Arabic, too."

"And the phone call?"

"Arabic."

"You met where?"

"A Lebanese restaurant in the seventeenth."

"What was its name?"

She frowned. "I don't recall."

"Where is it?"

"About a block from the Villiers metro stop."

"How did you get there?"

"From George V, by metro. We changed at Étoile."

"Describe the restaurant."

"It's nothing special to look at."

"Don't be nonspecific, Dianne. You edit cookbooks. You deal with this sort of material every day."

She shot Tom a sharp look. "There were Formica tables and white tablecloths—the inexpensive kind. They used paper napkins. It was nothing special. There were posters—Lebanese tourist posters—on the walls. No unique decor; no style. It was just another neighborhood place. We went there because Malik said *Al Arabia*'s offices were nearby. The restaurant sits at the intersection of boulevard Courcelles and boulevard Malesherbes. There were tables on an enclosed veranda adjacent to the sidewalk—the kind of thing you can enclose during the winter. The main dining room was raised off street level by two or three steps. I can't really recall."

"And the editor? What direction did he come from?"

"He was waiting for us."

Tom nodded. "Where did he sit? Where did you sit?"

"He and Malik sat next to one another. They sat with their backs to the sidewalk. I sat facing the intersection."

"And behind you?"

"There was a wall—a divider, really, about four feet high. Malik said he wanted me to have the view."

Tom was familiar with the intersection and there wasn't much of a view. Not that it wasn't good tradecraft. With their backs to the sidewalk, a lip-reader in a surveillance vehicle wouldn't be able to follow Malik's conversation with Talal. And with the wall behind Dianne, eavesdropping would be nigh on impossible from over her shoulder without being very obvious about it. "What did you talk about?"

"It was small talk mostly. Talal asked a lot of questions about me. About my family, and my job, where I'd gone to college, where I lived in London—that sort of stuff."

"Did he know London?"

"I'm not sure. He said he came to London occasionally."

"Did he say why?"

"He mentioned he had a friend in Finsbury."

Tom blinked. Mentioning Finsbury had been a tactical error on Talal's part. *Finsbury* was a trigger word. The Finsbury Park mosque in a northern London neighborhood was riddled with al-Qa'ida sympathizers.

Dianne seemed to be unaware of its significance. "Did that mean anything to you?"

Hands clasped, she said, "No."

Her tone told him the Israelis had probed the area and come up empty. He decided to leave the subject. "How long did you spend with him?"

"Talal? About an hour. We had some *mezze*—it was quite spectacular, actually—and a half bottle of Moroccan wine. Talal and Malik talked business for about a quarter hour. Then he got a call on his cell phone. He paid the bill, excused himself, and left us to ourselves."

There were no inconsistencies or contradictions from the interrogation transcripts. She had seen nothing passed between Malik and Talal. Tom was convinced she was telling him the truth as best she could remember it.

It was time to wind things up. Time to play out the hunch that had smacked him upside the head when he'd read about the Vuitton backpack. Tom slid his hand into the pocket of the coveralls and felt for the first of the three photographs he'd concealed in the handkerchief. The one he'd decided to show her first had one of its corners folded back so he could identify it by feel.

He slid the small black-and-white rectangle with Imad Mugniyah's likeness across the table. "Do you recognize this man?"

Dianne squinted down at the small picture. "No."

"Are you sure?"

"Absolutely. I've never seen him in my life."

Tom picked up the photo of Imad Mugniyah, stuck it back in his pocket, and replaced it with the second picture, which he'd cropped from Shahram Shahristani's surveillance photo of Tariq Ben Said. "What about him?"

She pulled the image across the table. "No."

He retrieved Ben Said and pulled a third photo from his pocket—it was a crop of Yahia Hamzi's passport picture. Reuven had made sure to remove the stamp in the bottom corner so its origin would be obscured.

She glanced at the photo then looked over at Tom. "That's Talal Massoud—Malik's editor at *Al Arabia*. His hair is longer, his face is a little bit rounder, and he's wearing different glasses. But it's Talal."

Tom reclaimed the picture and returned it to his coveralls, fighting to keep his composure so that he'd give off no hint of the excitement he felt. The pulse racing in his temples, he stared at her coolly and spoke in laconic Marseillaise. "Thank you, Dianne. We're done."

He rose, walked to the door, and rapped twice sharply on the cold metal. The pieces of the puzzle were coming together and it was time that he and Reuven called Tony Wyman on the secure phone and laid things out.

They—whoever they were—had been worried enough about Jim McGee to murder him. Blew up the Suburban and killed Jim and two others because they believed McGee knew something he shouldn't have known: that Imad Mugniyah was in Gaza.

Except McGee *hadn't* known it was Mugniyah. All he knew was that there was a mysterious individual who moved frequently and who was protected by an imported crew of bodyguards, some of whom were Hezbollah, others possibly Iranians—the Seppah.

Those revelations hadn't killed McGee. What had set the ambush in motion was Shafiq Tubaisi's offhand comment that Sheikh Ahmed Yassin, the godfather of Hamas, had kissed the man's hands. *Yassin kissed both his hands and asked for his blessing.*

That was what Shafiq told McGee. Tom had read it in McGee's penultimate message. He'd understood the significance of the act, even if McGee hadn't. Which was why he'd tasked McGee to order Shafiq to get a picture.

Because of that tasking, McGee was dead—and so was Shafiq. They were dead because somewhere, in somebody's head, an operational clock was ticking. And the bad guys out there, the ones President Bush had so accurately termed the evildoers—accurate because Tom knew that was precisely how the Koran referred to criminals, murderers, and assassins— were about to stage a major hit.

The evildoers were gearing up for something big. Something spectacular. The evildoers' version of shock and awe.

There was, Tom understood all too well, a particular rhythm—a cadence if you will—to megaterror. Megaterror is not impetuous, seat-of-the-pants stuff. It is well planned, highly organized, and above all disciplined. The bad guys plot, probe, and test. They take months performing target assessments in order to weed out the harder-to-strike targets in favor of the softer ones. This very week in New York, Boston, Washington, D.C.; Orlando, and Miami, there are al-Qa'ida sleepers posing as tourists. They visit Universal Studios, Capitol Hill, Faneuil Hall, or South Beach and take thousands of digital photographs, which are passed on to al-Qa'ida analysts who pore over them in order to identify security flaws.

Other sleepers—just like Ramzi Yousef in 1992—find jobs as taxi drivers or commercial messengers. What better way to learn the ebbs and flows of a city and uncover its vulnerabilities? Still others find work on the hundreds of minimum-wage crews who spend their nights scrubbing office-building bathrooms and waxing corporate headquarters' lobbies and corridors. When's the last time anyone paid much attention to the anonymous peons who clean Citigroup's offices at night? Or Merrill Lynch's? Or GM's? Yet what better way to discover the best places to preposition blocks of C4 or Semtex; to disable the elevators; to cause the largest number of casualties.

Still other sleepers gauge first-responder reaction time by phoning in bogus threats and videoing the results. Tom knew that for the past ninety days, there had been a precipitous rise in the number of false alarms in New York, Paris, London, and Madrid. That told him that at least one of those cities had been targeted.

They were probing the airports, too. A three-week-old memo from 4627's Washington office reported that al-Qa'ida was currently identifying chinks and weak spots in domestic U.S. airline security by sending easily identifiable Muslims on cross-country flights with orders to act suspiciously and thus identify the federal air marshals on the flight. Other, less noticeable sleepers were photographing the incidents with cell-phone cams. The air marshals' faces went into an al-Qa'ida database. Interpol reports from Brussels indicated similar occurrences on domestic flights all over Europe. But no one had any inkling what al-Qa'ida was planning— with or without Tehran's help, with or without Fatah's diplomatic pouches.

That was why the megaterror process often took years to identify and target, why it was so hard to go proactive. The first al-Qa'ida reconnaissance of U.S. embassies in Africa that resulted in the 1998 attacks in Kenya and Tanzania took place in 1993. The planning for the October 2000 suicide bombing of the USS *Cole* began four years earlier. Plotting for 9/11 also began in 1996, more than half a decade before the attacks on the World Trade Center and the Pentagon, when Khalid Sheikh Mohammad first suggested training terrorists to fly hijacked aircraft into buildings in the U.S.

But in each case, the pace accelerated inexorably in the period running up to the attack itself. There was always a palpable quickening of tempo. Intensified message traffic, multiple probes and/or dry runs, and increased target assessments always—*always*—indicated that al-Qa'ida had started its countdown.

The Big Question, as the pundits always said on those long-winded Washington talk shows, was: Countdown to what? To that, Tom hadn't an answer.

But then, neither did CIA. CIA was dysfunctional these days. That's why the Company, as it was sometimes called, was currently reduced to hiring private firms like 4627 to gather human-source intelligence on its behalf. And 4627 was hiring people like Jim McGee because CIA was incapable of completing the mission it had been created to do. CIA was in a shambles. The Agency was clueless.

Of course Tom hadn't a clue either. But he knew a lot more than CIA did.

• Tom knew that Imad Mugniyah and Tariq Ben Said had been on-site when Jim McGee was killed in Gaza. CIA, in the person of Mrs. Portia M. ST. JOHN, had rejected that possibility out of hand.

• Tom knew that Ben Said the master bombmaker was about to perfect a new, sophisticated, and undetectable remote detonator for his IEDs. CIA had no inkling Tariq Ben Said even existed.

• And finally, Tom understood that if he could OODA-loop[16] Ben Said, he could disorient the assassin, disrupt his plans, and neutralize him before he killed anyone else.

The heavy steel door in front of his nose opened outward and Tom stepped ecstatically onto the rubber pad of the corridor, where Salah was waiting for him, a reproachful look on his face. Obviously, Salah was kicking himself for not having Tom shake his handkerchief out before he'd been allowed to bring it into the interrogation room.

Tom was sweating heavily. He looked down at his hands. They were shaking. And as quickly as it had come on, his excitement was replaced by a sudden gnawing pain in the pit of his gut. That spasm reinforced Tom's gloomy acknowledgment that even though he understood the clock was ticking, he had absolutely no idea how much time was left before the attack would occur.

Tom had always been told knowledge was power. If that was true, and given all he knew right now, why did he feel as helpless as a drowning man?

---

[16]The OODA-loop—observe, orient, decide, and act—was a product of John Boyd, the fighter pilot–philosopher. It was Boyd who first realized that it wasn't the pilots with the best physical dexterity who won dogfights, but the pilots who got inside their opponents' OODA loops by thinking clearer, faster, and more decisively.

16

6:35 P.M. Tom looked around Reuven's garden, the Bouviers stretched out, snoring, at his feet, the lanterns providing soft light as dusk settled over Herzlyia. He felt a lot better and guessed that the surroundings had a lot to do with the fact that his earlier spasm of panic and helplessness had largely subsided. Reuven's housekeeper had set out a huge earthenware bowl of fresh figs for them. Reuven had augmented the fragrant fruit with a large slab of Morbier and a chunk of *saucisson de Lyon sec* on a white Limoges platter.

Now the Israeli emerged from the kitchen and made his way down the marble steps carrying a 1960s-vintage Chemex and a round cork trivet. He set the trivet on the table and poured Nescafé into three mugs emblazoned with the CIA seal.

Three mugs because Tom and Reuven weren't alone. They'd been joined by a third man. Amos Aricha was a former assistant director of Shin Bet. Aricha was a lifelong counterterrorist who had commanded the agency's selected targeting task force. His job: arresting or eliminating the individuals who built the explosive vests and car bombs and the master-minds who dispatched homicide bombers against Israeli civilians. These days, he said, he was a partner in a private company that trained security personnel and did risk assessments. He gave Tom his business card. On it was engraved a bird of prey in flight. Below, in Hebrew, was his old task force's motto, adapted from the old American TV show *Hill Street Blues*. It read, *Let's Do It to Them Before They Do It to Us.*

But doing it to them was becoming more and more difficult, what with the media's bias against Israel and the pressure to wage politically correct warfare against enemies who didn't give a damn about humane rules of en-gagement. "I feel like a whatchamacallit sal-o-mon swimming upstream." Aricha dropped heavily onto a chair. "And believe me, kiddo, I seen sal-o-mon. I've done my share of white-water rafting all around your wild, wild west."

Amos had gone through basic training with Reuven. They'd both served in Sayeret Mat'kal, and after active duty they'd done their *meluim*[17] in the same unit. Which meant the two men had known each other virtually since they'd been teenagers. Tom sneaked a look at the interaction between the Israelis. Their easy relationship—the inside jokes, the back-and-forth bantering, the way they dealt with each other—made him envious. He was a Foreign Service brat. He'd grown up in seven different countries and had attended sixteen different schools before he'd settled down at Dartmouth for four straight years in the same place.

Afterward, at CIA, he'd resumed his peripatetic lifestyle with three- and four-year tours. He hadn't ever lived in one place long enough to make the sorts of friends one keeps for a lifetime. Until he'd returned to Paris.

Aricha reached across the table for the small earthenware pitcher of milk and poured some into his coffee. He was, Tom had to admit, an unlikely-looking manhunter. A big-boned man in his late sixties with a shock of curly white hair tied back into a 1960s-style ponytail, Aricha wore faded Levi's cinched by a tooled rodeo belt with a silver-and-turquoise buckle the size of a horseshoe, topped by a matching denim shirt whose mother-of-

[17]Annual reserve duty.

pearl–topped snaps were open halfway down his hairy chest. His sleeves were rolled up past the elbows to display muscular, suntanned arms and a gold Rolex on his left wrist. The ragged cuffs of his jeans fell onto scuffed brown sharkskin Tony Lama cowboy boots. All he lacked, Tom thought, was the Colt Peacemaker on his hip and the tin star on his chest.

"My boy," Aricha said to Tom in thickly accented English, "you have what we call *balagan gadol*—a big problem—and so do we."

It all made such perfect sense in hindsight. On the way back from the prison, Tom had called his office and had one of his people check on whether there had been multiple sales of Vuitton Montsouris backpacks in August 2003. It took less than two hours for the results to come in from Paris. Malik and Dianne had met with his "editor" on Saturday, August 15. On Monday the eighteenth, twelve Vuitton backpacks—the entire stock in Vuitton's Champs-Élysées store—had been ordered by telephone. A commercial messenger had picked them up, paying in cash. There was no record of where they'd been delivered.

But there was a signature from the messenger on the receipt. Using the secure phone at Reuven's office, Tom had called one of 4627's Parisian gumshoes and had him wash the name through the police computer. By four o'clock Tel Aviv time, the private investigator had the name of the messenger service and verified the delivery address: Boissons Maghreb. By 4:30, 4627's Paris office had used one of its technical employees to set up a phone tap and begun the slightly more intricate arrangements to intercept Yahia Hamzi's cell-phone transmissions. There was no jumping through hoops to satisfy a station chief, no waiting for ambassadorial approval, no back-and-forth with Langley.

More to the point, Tom understood there'd been no explosives in the radio Dianne Lamb had brought from London at Malik's request. Malik had carried the bomb. Tariq Ben Said had somehow incorporated the plastique into the lining of the Vuitton backpack and done it in a way that still allowed the explosive to have the same lethal effect as a shaped charge.

God, how sophisticated things had become. When Tom had gone through case officer training in the 1980s, IEDs were relatively simple. You had your pipe bombs. You had your car bombs. You had your Molotov cocktails. You had your basic explosives: PETN, RDX, dynamite, or plastique—C3, C4, or Semtex. There were homemade mortars (the IRA favored those) and there were the occasional remotely detonated devices used by the ETA Basque separatists against the Spanish. But they were the exceptions to the rule.

Nope. In the 1980s, IEDs were all pretty basic, keep-it-simple-stupid bombs. Tom, for example, had been taught to make a cone charge powerful enough to blast through three inches of armor plate using a wine bottle and a one-pound block of C4. Today, he'd need less than a quarter of that amount. Today, it was all miniature devices and remote control. Explosives were now so concentrated that you could build a bomb powerful enough to bring down a 747 and conceal it in a tennis shoe. You could set off an IED planted in a car on a street in Haifa by making a cell-phone call from a café on the rue du Midi in Brussels. And you could—if you were Tariq Ben Said—create a totally unidentifiable bomb capable of killing sixteen and wounding scores more by transmogrifying the lining of a Louis Vuitton backpack into a weapon of mass destruction. The stuff was frigging invisible. Malik Suleiman had carried the goddamn backpack right past the baggage inspectors at de Gaulle and subsequently slipped it through Israel's vaunted security systems. What would happen when he brought it through U.S. airports, whose ineffective TSA (Transportation Security Administration) personnel were known derogatorily as "thousands standing around"?

Tom popped a chunk of sausage into his mouth. "Which brings me to point number two. Why did Malik ask Dianne Lamb to bring his radio in her suitcase? After all, the explosives were in the backpack."

"There was a radio involved in the Jerusalem explosion." Aricha sipped his coffee. "So there's got to be a reason." He set the mug on the table. "But let me tell you, I still talk to Shin Bet. And their forensics people have been over the goddamn thing top to whatchamacallit bottom. They haven't found anything. There were never any explosives concealed in either one of the radios."

"These people never do anything without a reason." Reuven picked up his mug and sipped. "There had to be explosives somewhere."

"No there didn't, goddamnit—" Tom almost choked on his sausage. "Don't you see, Reuven?"

"See what?"

"It's always been the assumption that Dianne unwittingly carried the explosives."

Amos nodded. "That's the pattern. The Irish woman flying from Heathrow, the—"

"I know about all those cases. But there was no trace of explosives in anything Dianne brought from London."

"So far. We also know the man you call Ben Said and we call Bomber-X—he had to make small whatchamacallit batches of a new formula."

That Aricha knew Ben Said's formula was made in small quantities was surprising because Tom hadn't mentioned that fact to Reuven, or anyone else. He decided to elicit. "Are you sure, Amos?"

Tom caught a flicker of motion in the Shin Bet man's eyes. And then Amos deflected the question. "It's not impossible there were explosives in the radio as well as the backpack."

Tom decided not to follow up the elicitation. It would be too obvious. So he deflected back. "What's the point?"

Aricha looked at Tom. "The point is, one plus one equals two. Two radios. Two bombs. The point is that this Ben Said has come up with a new way of targeting Israel."

"Hold it." Tom scampered from the patio up to the living room, where he'd left his interrogation notes. He flipped through the sheets until he found what he wanted and charged back downstairs. "The batteries were dead, Amos. The radio batteries were dead."

The Israeli shrugged. "So, *nu?*"

"Don't you see? They weren't dead—they were something else. Dummies. Containers for some critical element of his bomb. Malik sent Dianne to buy new batteries. He got her out of the room while he did whatever he had to do. Removed whatever was concealed in the batteries. There had to be something in the batteries."

Amos frowned. "When you go through security at Heathrow," he said, "especially when it's a Tel Aviv flight, they make you turn on all your electronic devices. No exceptions. They would have done the same at de Gaulle, or Dulles, or wherever. That's the standard practice these days."

"But Malik's radio was in Dianne's suitcase, not her hand luggage," Tom said. "It would never have been inspected. Not in Europe. In Europe, you can lock your luggage. Only in the U.S. is luggage for the hold hand-inspected."

"This has nothing to do with the U.S. He was trying to launch attacks here in Israel."

Tom ignored the Shin Bet man. "There had to be something concealed in the batteries. I think Dianne carried detonators. They spent all their time together on the August trip. But in July, Malik was by himself twice in three days. Once for a meeting with his editor—who we know works with Ben Said. And once for a meeting with 'an old friend' whom he met while buying a newspaper. My guess is that Malik picked the detonators up in Paris on the previous trip."

Reuven shrugged. "What's your point?"

"My point is that maybe they were Ben Said's prototype detonators. We can't discount that, can we?"

Amos gave Tom a dismissive stare. "Prototype-schmotype. I don't think it makes much difference at this point."

"I do. I think we've been focusing on the wrong target. We're thinking inside the box. We're no better than Langley."

He got blank stares from the two Israelis. "Look," he said, gulping some coffee to wash the sausage down. "There's this old shaggy-dog story about a guy who goes through a diamond-mine gate every night for a week with a wheelbarrow full of dirt. The security guard sifts the dirt. He searches the guy—even puts on rubber gloves and does a body-cavity search. Nothing. Bubkes. The guard never finds a thing. After two weeks of this, he pulls the fellow aside. 'Look,' he says, 'I know you're stealing diamonds. I just can't figure out how you're doing it.' And the fellow looks at the guard and says, 'Since this is my last day on this job, I'll tell you what I've been doing. I've been stealing wheelbarrows.'"

"That's supposed to be funny?" Amos shrugged. "What's the point?"

"Let me put it another way."

"Maybe you'd better, because you're confusing me good."

"We've all been trying to analyze the situation so we can solve the Ben Said problem, right?"

"Of course." Aricha set his coffee down. "The goal must be to stop or prevent the megaterror he is planning to commit on Israeli soil."

"That's always been the assumption."

"But you also contend, Tom, that the ambush ten days ago in Gaza in which three American embassy employees were killed, and the two bombings—Heinrich Azouz, the German national in the Nablus Road Hotel, and Malik Suleiman at Mike's Bar in Tel Aviv—are all related equally to the planning for this megaterror."

"I do."

Aricha cracked his knuckles. "I can tell you for sure Shin Bet doesn't see it."

"See what?"

"The relationship. In the first incident, the bomb went off prematurely while Azouz was affixing the detonator. That's what you call operator error. We were able to prove conclusively that the explosion was caused by static electricity. End of story. In the second, a survivor swears he heard Malik, the perpetrator, exclaim, *'Allah akbar!'* just before the explosion went off. We are convinced he detonated the bomb after having second thoughts about killing his girlfriend. No operator error, no static. Full stop. And the Gaza incident was Arafat's way of sending a signal to the Bush administration to back off its support of Sharon."

Aricha rapped scarred knuckles on the tabletop. "I accept that incidents one and two are related. I accept your theory that the man you call Ben Said and we refer to as Bomber-X is working on a new form of undetectable explosive. I accept that he was a participant in the Gaza incident, by which I mean he supplied the plastique and was on-site for its detonation so he could watch firsthand its effects. But that's the extent of it, Tom. Gaza is a whole other whatchamacallit—kettle from fish. Full stop again. End of story, kiddo."

Tom said, "Wheelbarrows, Amos. Think wheelbarrows."

The Israeli scratched his head. "Reuven, what's with these wheelbarrows?"

Reuven toyed with the heavy gold chain around his neck. "Pay attention, Grandfather," he said in Hebrew. "Maybe even you will learn something from the youngster."

Tom caught the look that passed between the old soldiers. He swiveled toward Aricha. "You're basing your conclusions on two common threads: the explosives, and the fact that there's a plan to wage megaterror against Israel sometime in the near term."

"Because those are the logical conclusions to draw from what we know about the events. We look at what happened, and we draw conclusions from our experience. We rely on"—he fought for the word in English—"empirical logic."

"Precisely." Tom noted the look of confusion on Aricha's face. "But, Amos, too often, when we analyze a problem, we begin the process by formulating our conclusions. I think that's what happened in Shin Bet."

"You say we start with conclusions? I think not." Aricha folded his arms on his chest. "Shabak started with explosions."

It was a defensive position. Tom extended his legs, shifting his own body into a nonthreatening attitude. He softened his tone. "I'm not talking about you personally. It's a problem that's endemic to the whole intelligence community—you, us, everybody." He paused as he caught the confused look on the Israeli's face. "A natural mistake, if you will. In this case, Amos, the conclusion Shin Bet drew—and it's a perfectly logical one to reach—is that two of the three incidents are directly related to explosives and evidence of a mega-attack on Israel in the near future." He looked at Aricha. "Am I correct in the way I characterized the situation?"

The Shin Bet man's head bobbed up and down. "On the money."

"What I'm saying is that if that's how you see things, then all of your analysis—all the evidence—tends to support that predetermined conclusion—this is all about megaterror directed at Israel."

Aricha frowned at Reuven. "Again he thinks our evidence is wrong."

"No." Tom began again. "Your evidence is accurate. But I think by focusing on the *literal* substance of the problem—the evidence, the arguments pro and con, the conclusions—we're missing the point. We all missed the point. That's what I mean by wheelbarrows, Amos. The security guard reached a logical conclusion: since it was a diamond mine, the guy had to be stealing diamonds. That was a logical assumption, right?"

"From a diamond mine you don't steal rubies. Yes—logical."

"But incorrect. Bad analysis. If the guard had approached the problem with an open mind—if he hadn't boxed himself in by not considering any other conclusion than 'diamonds are being stolen,' he might have included the possibility that something else was being taken. Like wheelbarrows."

Tom watched as Aricha stroked his chin. Warily, the Israeli said, "Go on."

"We've been focusing on explosives for use in attacks against Israel. I think these people solved the explosives problem a long time ago. I think Ben Said has a formula that worked—until now. Why now? Because now we can all start devising countermeasures." He paused, gratified to see Amos nodding in agreement. "I think what Ben Said's been working on since August . . . is *detonators*." Tom took another swallow of coffee. "Jerusalem—the German Arab. He blew himself up arming the detonator, right?"

"Yes."

"And Malik. What was he doing? He was attaching the detonator to the bomb, or arming it, or something. Because the idea was for him to go to the restroom and detonate the device remotely. He was going to be a lucky survivor. Dianne was going to take the fall."

Aricha cut one of the figs in half, speared a piece, and put it in his mouth. "So how did the device go off prematurely, kiddo?"

"It could have been a faulty detonator," Tom said. "It also could have been the embassy—set off by one of the variable-frequency oscillators mounted on the embassy building."

"Mike's is two hundred and five meters from the northwest corner of the embassy," Reuven said. "I paced it off yesterday."

Aricha frowned. "Wouldn't they know that? These people do target assessments, Reuven."

"It's common knowledge the ambassador has forbidden VFOs on embassy vehicles, Amos," Tom continued. "The embassy's devices have been camouflaged to look like TV satellite dishes. No different than hundreds of others."

"Go on."

"But I decided the explosion wasn't set off by the embassy devices. It was Malik's carelessness. Or, the detonator was faulty. Possibly the remote—maybe there's something awry in the circuitry. I don't know— I'm not an explosives expert. Which brought me to the third incident: Gaza. It was an anomaly."

Aricha frowned. "Anomaly?"

"There was something about Gaza that didn't fit. I can accept that our man was killed because of the information about Imad Mugniyah. I think that's pretty clear. But it doesn't explain Ben Said's presence."

Amos cocked his head in Tom's direction. "A meeting with Arafat perhaps."

"Unlikely. Ben Said likes his anonymity. His pattern all along has been to work through middlemen. No: I believe he was here because he was fine-tuning his detonators. Two of them had failed. He came here so he could make adjustments—do the last-minute work before he puts his latest generation of IEDs into play—against the West, not against Israel."

Now it was Reuven who shook his head. "He came to Israel to perfect detonators? Tom, that's preposterous."

"No, it's not." Tom was insistent. "Shahram Shahristani said as much to me last week and it totally went out of my head until now. Shahram claimed Ben Said was using Israel as his weapons lab—his test kitchen. I thought he'd gone off the deep end. But he was on the money. Spot on."

Amos Aricha looked skeptically at Tom. "Used Israel to perfect his explosive devices."

"And his detonators."

"Whatever. So, what's the reason this man, who knows that if we laid hands on him he'd never get out of prison, and who knows that we have, shall I say, an extremely effective internal security apparatus—and yet still he chooses to bless us with his presence? Why is that, kiddo, since you seem to be so knowledgeable in this area?"

Tom paid no attention to Aricha's sarcasm. "Ben Said was testing his weapons here in Israel because he could."

Aricha scowled at Reuven Ayalon. "The kid's crazy," he said in Hebrew. Then he looked at Tom. "Listen, kiddo—"

"Amos," Tom interrupted, "let me posit that Ben Said is working on detonators, not explosives. Okay, so he wants to make tests—not in a lab, but under real-life conditions. Two detonators have exploded prematurely. So he wants to do some reverse engineering. See which of the steps caused the problems. He needs volunteers to assemble bombs. He won't tell them that it could be dangerous work, that they could get killed. He doesn't say, 'If the detonators don't blow up in your face, then you get to use the bombs.' He gives them instructions and turns them loose. If the detonators fail, too bad—one or two people are killed and it's back to the drawing board."

As Tom caught his breath he saw Amos Aricha give Reuven a "this guy is nuts" look. Undeterred, Tom pressed on. "Okay—what better place than Israel, or the West Bank, or Gaza, where there are hundreds of willing guinea pigs to build bombs to use against Israeli targets. Plus this: if he did his real-life testing in Paris, or London, or Madrid, or Washington, or any-where else," Tom said, "it would make waves."

Aricha interrupted him. "What about Iraq or Afghanistan?"

"I thought about that," Tom said. "In Iraq and Afghanistan, the situation is too uncontrolled, too chaotic. In Israel, you have a unique societal situation. The country is basically stable, but there's also an environment in which terror organizations exist—Hamas, the Al Aqsa Martyrs Brigades, Fatah. Plus, there's the media factor. If Ben Said tried this in Europe there'd be headlines. Governments would ratchet up the threat levels. An explosion in Israel—even if it kills someone—is a one-day story." He looked at the Shin Bet man. "Sorry, Amos, but it's true."

"Living with terrorism is an everyday fact of life here." The Israeli nodded in mournful agreement. "We even came up with a word for it—*ha'matzav*—the situation."

"So—can you check to see whether there were any bombings between the last week of September and the October fifteenth explosion in Gaza?"

"I certainly don't recall any." Aricha extracted a cell phone from his shirt pocket, punched a number into it, machine-gunned ten seconds of rapid Hebrew. He tucked the cell phone between his shoulder and neck, cut himself some Morbier, sliced a thin piece of sausage, and set it atop the cheese. But before he could eat, he set it on the table, grabbed the phone, and listened intently for about half a minute, pausing only to grunt in monosyllables from time to time.

Finally, the Shin Bet man turned off the phone. He ate the cheese and sausage and washed it down with a swallow of coffee. "It was a quiet holiday season—we stopped about sixteen, seventeen individuals before they made it across the Green Line."

"What were they carrying?"

"The usual," Amos said. "Explosive vests filled with nails and bolts and nuts and screws dipped in rat poison."

"And the detonation devices?"

"Batteries and a push button."

"No remotes? No cell phones attached just in case the perps had second thoughts?"

"No."

"Can you ask anyone about remote detonations, Amos?"

Aricha gave Tom a jaundiced look. But he retrieved the cell phone and made another call.

6:55 P.M. Amos Aricha laid the cell phone on the table. "Just as I remembered, gentlemen," he said. "No homicide bombings during the holidays." He looked at Tom. "And not a single vest attached to a cell phone—or other electronic device."

Tom shook his head. "It doesn't make sense."

"What doesn't?"

"Ben Said's presence. I don't believe he'd put himself at risk for more than two weeks just to watch the Gaza operation."

"Wheelbarrows, Tom." Reuven Ayalon slapped the tabletop.

"Huh?"

"Wheelbarrows. Amos, what about explosions in the Territories? In Gaza and the Territories?"

"I told you: none."

Hadn't McGee written something about Gaza explosions during the holidays in one of his memos? "Explosions, Amos," Tom interrupted. "We're not talking about attacks, just explosions. Unexplained explosions. Accidents."

Amos Aricha got Tom's meaning. "Fine-tuning?"

"Exactly."

The Shin Bet man's eyes narrowed. "I'll check."

They had the answer sixteen minutes later. There had been four incidents during the High Holidays. All had occurred in a remote section of southwestern Gaza that was under the control of the Bedouin Semal-Duma clan. Amos blinked and cupped his hand over the phone. "Shabak was inactive in that part of the Strip because things had been quiet." Moreover, Amos reported, the Palestinian Authority, which routinely claimed such explosions were Israeli assassinations—targeted killings—had raised no protests, even though a total of eleven individuals had been killed—a significant number of Palestinian fatalities.

"Press coverage?"

"Minimal. The incidents were reported in the news roundup of what happens in the Territories."

Tom gave Aricha an "I told you so" look. "Anything else, Amos?"

"By the time the Army arrived, the locations had been hosed down, swept, totally cleaned out, and the bodies removed."

Tom asked, "By Fatah?"

Aricha shook his head. "No. Mohammad Dahlan's people were nowhere to be seen." Then he realized what he'd just said. The Shin Bet man smacked his own forehead hard. *"Tembel,"*[18] he said. "I'm a whatchamacallit, a dumbkin."

Tom turned to Reuven Ayalon. "Fine-tuning. Exactly. Amos's information supports what Shahram told me." He looked at his colleague. "I think we have to move."

"Paris." Reuven nodded in agreement.

"Paris," Tom echoed. Yes. Paris was the key. Paris was where Shahram had photographed Imad Mugniyah and Tariq Ben Said together. Paris was the base of Ben Said's support network coordinator, Yahia Hamzi.

Tom glanced at his watch. It was just after noon in Washington. Plenty of time for tony Tony to assemble a crash team and get them on the evening flight to Paris. He pushed his chair away from the table and stood. "You'll have to excuse me, Amos—I've got to make a few calls."

"To whom?" Reuven's expression displayed uncharacteristic concern. "What's going on?"

"I'll explain later." The plan had come to Tom in an epiphany. It was complicated; it was risky, but it might work. And he wasn't about to say anything in front of Amos Aricha. "I'll tell you later. I'm going to call Washington. I want them to send us a crash team."

The Israeli shook his head. "Not yet."

"Why? For what I'm contemplating, we'll need lots of backup. Eight, ten people at least. There's communications, transport, security, counter-surveillance—"

"Tom, grab hold from yourself." The Israeli looked at his old comrade in arms almost apologetically. "That's the Americans for you, Amos."

"Always calling in the whatchamacallit—the cavalry." Amos laughed.

Tom scowled. Reuven didn't even know what he was thinking and already he was criticizing. "What's your problem?"

---

[18]Hebrew for dummkopf.

"Less is sometimes more," Reuven said. "I'm a big believer in thinking small."

"We're going to need support," Tom said adamantly.

"Don't fly off the handle yet. We have our locals. There are half a dozen freelancers under contract we can call on. I still have a few friends left in the City of Light—people who know how to get things done without making ripples. Whatever it is you want to do, we can handle everything right out of the 4627 office. Believe me, boychik, two of us can make more progress—and do it a lot more unobtrusively—than a bunch of outsiders."

"But—"

Amos Aricha broke in. "When you were in Paris, how many case officers at your station?"

"About three dozen."

"Mossad had two—Reuven and another who's now dead, God rest his soul. And they did pretty damn good. I think better than you most of the time."

Tom's voice displayed impatience. "What's your point, Amos?"

"That Reuven's right: sometimes less is more, my boy."

"We go to Paris," Reuven said. "We work on whatever it is you want to do. Without attracting a lot of attention. You can always add people, Tom. It's harder to take them out of the picture once they're on-site. The bigger the crowd, the more attention you attract."

When Tom thought about it, Reuven was making sense. "But we tell Washington what we're doing, right? Keep Tony Wyman and Charlie Hoskinson informed."

"Of course." Reuven smiled. "Every step of the way. Despite how my friend here dresses, we're not all cowboys in Israel."

ST. DENIS

17

TOM'S BREATHING WAS SHALLOW as he pressed the *minuterie* button on the ground floor then sprinted up the first flight of worn marble stairs. The safe house—safe apartment, really—was a *troisième étage* (fourth floor) walk-up located about a hundred yards north of the gridlocked six-lane *périphérique* highway that encircled greater Paris. The 4627 Company had six safe houses in Paris—one more than CIA. But then, 4627 probably had more use for them than Langley did these days. This one was located in a run-down, anonymous working-class district favored by foreign workers and transients.

The five-story building on a one-way street had sagging, weather-beaten shutters and a crumbly stone facade. It was a relic from the mid-1920s, and had it been located inside the beltway, even in the less-than-chic nineteenth or twentieth arrondissements, it would have been worth a pretty penny. But in Clichy, one of Paris's more unfashionable *communes périphériques,* it was just another dump, similar to scores of identical buildings sandwiched in the rough triangle between two decrepit cemeteries and the perpetually bustling beltway.

Tom had left rue Raynouard just before six to run an SDR, or surveillance detection route. It was a set, timed course that would allow him to spot any adversaries. The first leg had taken him as far east as the Île St. Louis, the second into the warren of narrow streets off the rue des Halles, and the third as far north as Pigalle. Once he was confident no one was following—had he sensed he was being tracked, he would have broken off the route, returned to rue Raynouard, and rescheduled his rendezvous—he dropped into the metro at Abbesses, changed trains three times, and finally emerged at Porte de Clichy shortly after 7:30.

There, he tucked his leather briefcase under his arm, braved the fast-moving rush-hour traffic on boulevard Berthier, traversed the pocked concrete of the pedestrian bridge atop *périphérique,* then stopped to linger over a *café crème,* a *petit pain,* and a grease-spattered copy of *Le Matin* at a no-name café on the corner of the rue 8 Mai 1945 that was so run-down it looked like an exterior set from the old Jean Servais movie *Rififi.* The coffee was weak and the bread was full of air but the interlude allowed Tom to countersurveil both people and vehicles for a quarter hour without appearing obvious.

Confident that he was clean, he dropped three euros' worth of small change into the saucer, tore the check in two, and strolled up the boulevard Victor Hugo, walking against the traffic. Just past the Cimetière Parisien des Batignolles, he bolted across the four clogged lanes and jogged toward the oncoming cars in rue Fouquet. At the northern end of the street, he dodged the spray from a street-washing truck, crossed the wet pavement, and punched a four-number combination into the keypad next to the graffiti-sprayed entry door of number 38.

Forty-six-twenty-seven had safe houses in better neighborhoods, but Reuven had insisted on using this particular one because he wanted to fly well below DST's radar. The French were damn good—and highly proprietary about foreigners running snatch operations on native French soil. In fact, DST usually became downright inhospitable when folks using aliases and false documents entered the country for nefarious purposes, as Reuven had just done.

Tom had flown on his own passport, of course—he'd arrived on the twenty-seventh and taken a cab directly from de Gaulle to rue Raynouard. He dropped his suitcase and went straight to the office. There, he made half a dozen phone calls on the secure office line. Starting the next morning, he'd resumed a normal schedule. He telephoned MJ once or twice a day, listened to her complain about Mrs. ST. JOHN, and pleaded with her to hold on and not do anything precipitous, just for a few more weeks. He trolled his sources. He checked with his contact at DST, who claimed there'd been no progress on Shahram Shahristani's murder. He visited Les Gourmets des Ternes and commiserated with Monsieur Marie and Jeff about the Iranian. He made certain to cause no ripples.

But Tom also took precautions. His internal sonar told him he was being pinged, and even though the origin of these pings was indistinct and the identities of those doing the pinging unknown, he began zigzagging. He modified his daily routine so that his routes and agenda were unpredictable. He began to run cleaning routes. He placed intrusion devices at rue Raynouard (such precautions were always used at the 4627 offices) and had one of the company's local contractors monitor his phone lines. On Thursday, he had one of the firm's gumshoes run a countersurveillance pattern as he walked from his apartment to the 4627 offices. The results were inconclusive.

By the weekend, he was chomping at the bit. He wanted to move, to act, to *get things under way*. But it wasn't time yet.

So much of intelligence work entailed watching and waiting. You spent days and days countersurveilling dead drops, letter boxes, and signal sites to see if the opposition had targeted them. You sometimes endured long breaks between agent meetings so as not to arouse suspicion. You spent weeks and weeks crafting SDRs and cleaning routes that might be used only once. You sometimes spent months creating the rabbit holes that allowed you to disappear in plain sight, should the situation warrant.

And you planned. Oh, did you plan. You always had a primary plan, a fallback plan, and a fallback for the fallback. Unlike Hollywood's version of spycraft, where bravado and seat-of-the-pants improvisation commonly ruled, there was virtually nothing in real-world tradecraft that wasn't scripted, vetted, and evaluated before the go-ahead was given. In Paris, Sam Waterman had spent hours with Tom helping him design rabbit holes; taking him through the fallback procedures for agent meetings; walking him through the intricacies of spycraft. Teaching him—forcing him actually—to be patient.

But Sam wasn't available. He'd been pushed out. He'd been sent home persona non grata after the Baranov flap in Moscow, then exiled to one of CIA's Northern Virginia satellite offices. He'd just vanished from everyone's radar screens. After Sam took early retirement, Tom left a series of messages at his Rosslyn apartment. But Waterman had never returned the calls. And then last year, Sam had been involved in some nastiness with another Paris station alumnus, Michael O'Neill. O'Neill had gone postal and killed some senator on SSCI. After that, a memo had come down from the seventh floor advising all DO personnel that Waterman was completely out of bounds. Off-limits. DO NOT CONTACT.

Tom had followed orders. But he knew what Sam would say. Sam would say, "Stick with the plan, Harry." Harrison W. AINSWORTH was Tom's CIA pseudonym, and Sam habitually called his young officers by pseudonym, even inside the station.

Okay. Now the plan was to wait for Reuven Ayalon. So that's what Tom had done. But he didn't like it. Not one bit.

Tom was forced to wait because the Israeli took a much more circuitous route to Clichy. He had his reasons. First, he was on DST's watch list. The French domestic security agency hadn't forgotten that Reuven was the prime suspect for engineering a 1992 assassination under their very Gallic noses right in the middle of a busy Montparnasse thoroughfare filled with tourists. Second, and in Reuven's mind more important, he had places to go, people to see, and equipment to obtain.

So, on Tuesday, October 28, dressed as a flight engineer and carrying nothing more than a black leather attaché case, Reuven flew on a charter flight from Tel Aviv to Istanbul. Just before touchdown, he changed clothes in the cockpit and exited with the rest of the passengers. Upon leaving the airport, he ran a six-hour cleaning route to ensure that he wasn't being tracked by al-Qa'ida's Turkish cells, or MIT,[19] the Turkish intelligence and security service. Once he felt secure, he used a pay phone to call the commercial attaché at the Israeli embassy. Ninety minutes later, the attaché brush-passed Reuven the keys to a safe house in the Sirkeci district near the train station. There, Reuven changed clothes, hairpieces, and identities.

Then, using a cell phone with a prepaid SIM card he'd brought from Tel Aviv, he dialed a number in the Üsküdar section of the city and left a short innocuous message after the beep. Then he reset the intrusion devices and left the safe house to run another cleaning route. The Turks were competent, and Reuven wasn't about to take chances.

Six hours later, wearing the skullcap of a devout Muslim, Reuven made contact with one of his former agents in a café in the city's bustling Fatih neighborhood on the western side of the peninsula. Sipping thick sweet coffee from tiny cups, the two men spoke in Turkish, their heads inclined toward each other, their lips barely moving.

The meeting lasted less than seven minutes. The agent departed first, disappearing into the crowded street, heading toward Askaray. Reuven sipped his coffee then called for another, countersurveilling the other tables and the passersby for any hint he was being tracked. Half an hour later, he, too, left and made his way back to the safe house by a roundabout route.

Wednesday morning, his Israeli passport along with several other forms of identification concealed in the lining of his attaché, Reuven walked past the jammed fast-food joints, bookstores, and electronics shops toward the Istanbul train station. About halfway there, he sensed surveillance. But he displayed no outward sign of concern. He went in the main entrance, walked straight to one of the ticket counters, and bought a second-class fare to the town of Saray.

Attaché case in hand, Reuven headed for the jam-packed public restroom. Inside, he bypassed the stinking urinals and the open-stall, hole-in-the-floor toilets, slipped half a dozen small coins into the attendant's palm, and was passed through into the first-class section. There, in a stall smelling of disinfectant, he stripped off his gray shirt and black trousers, quickly turned them inside out, and pulled them back on. He was now

---

[19]The abbreviation stands for Milli Istihbarat Teskilati.

dressed in a blue shirt and brown pants. He pulled the black skin off his briefcase and flushed it down the toilet. Underneath, it was utilitarian brown Samsonite. He pulled the toupee off and stuffed it into the case. In less than a minute, he'd changed his silhouette, his physical appearance, and his coloration.

Reuven exited the stall. He walked out of the lavatory, cut through a crowded passageway, slipped out the side entrance to the station, flagged down a cab that had just dropped off a trio of tourists, and ordered the driver to take him to the Egyptian spice bazaar in the Eminönü port district. There, Reuven disappeared into the crowded, narrow streets for an hour-long cleaning route.

Once his instincts told him he was in the clear, the Israeli found another taxi and took it to the airport. Just inside the terminal, he went into a restroom and slipped the toupee back on, so he and his passport picture would be identical. Then he bought a round-trip ticket to Frankfurt, paying with an American Express platinum card, and made his way through immigration control to the departure lounge. Reuven's passport and papers identified him as a French businessman named Jean-Pierre Bertrand.

"Jean-Pierre Bertrand" exited the Rhine-Main airport and caught an express train to the small, bourgeois city of Koblenz, some fifty miles north. There, he checked into the Holiday Inn, made a phone call to one of his longtime local contacts, then napped for two hours. At seven, he called a cab that drove him to a fish restaurant called Loup de Mer, where he had a piece of grilled plaice, a radish salad, and a mediocre half bottle of Pfaltz. When he'd finished, he paid the bill, left the restaurant, and walked around into the alley. It was deserted. Reuven bent down, reached behind the garbage cans next to Loup de Mer's service entrance, and extracted a small, rectangular package. Then he quickly made his way back to the hotel. He slipped the wrapped package into his attaché.

Thursday, still using the Bertrand alias, Reuven rented a big, fast BMW 5000 series from Hertz. He drove west at breakneck speed down the Moselle Valley to Trier and crossed the border into Luxembourg, then France. From Thionville he drove south to Metz, a small industrial city in Lorraine. He parked in a municipal lot and spent an hour shopping, first for a suitcase and a dopp-kit, which he stored in the BMW's trunk, and then clothes—slacks, a black blazer with silver buttons, two shirts, two sets of underwear and socks—as well as an old-fashioned double-edged razor and some other sundry toilet items. Everything was packed carefully in the suitcase. Then Reuven got into the BMW and drove four blocks to the Hotel Cathédrale. He gave the car keys to the doorman and watched as a bellboy carried the suitcase to the registration desk.

Once inside his room, Reuven removed the matchbook sewing kit from the nightstand drawer. From the toilet articles he'd bought, he thumbed a double-edged razor blade from its holder. First he removed all the tags from the items he'd bought. Then he used the blade to carefully slit the lining of the inside breast pocket of the blazer. An hour or so later, he'd created a second, hidden pocket behind the original one.

At seven the next morning, Reuven checked out, paying cash. He wound his way out of town, found the A31 highway. A31 intersected with the toll road that led to Dijon, roughly two hundred kilometers to the southwest. Reuven arrived in Mustard City shortly after 8:30, turned the car in, walked to the railroad station, bought a ticket on Friday's 8:30 TGV[20] to Paris, and hoisted the suitcase and attaché into one of the daily coin lockers.

For two hours he played tourist. He ambled through the Beaux Arts museum in the Palais des Ducs, admiring the Manets, the Courbets, and the Old Masters. He wandered down the rue de la Préfecture to the Notre Dame church, then walked behind the thirteenth-century Gothic masterpiece to Dijon's historic old marketplace. He ate a simple lunch of escargots, steak, frites, and green salad all washed down by a half-liter *pichet* of vibrant, young Côtes de Beaune at a crowded bistro in the market.

At 3:30, he visited a series of working-class bars, smoking Gauloises and sipping rouge de table until he spotted the targets he was looking for. Over the next four hours, the Israeli picked a total of four pockets at half a dozen bars. Less than an hour after he'd scored his final wallet, he was riding the TGV to Paris. The dozen or so items he'd removed from the stolen wallets were secure inside his hidden blazer pocket.

He arrived just after ten Friday night. By eleven, he'd opened the triple

[20]*Train à grande vitesse* (fast train).

locks on the safe-house door, checked the clandestine intrusion devices to make sure no one had made surreptitious entry, poured himself two fingers of Napoleon cognac, then stood under the shower for fifteen minutes until the hot water ran out. He dried off, then wrapped the oversize bath sheet around himself like a toga.

Thus clad, he opened the package he'd retrieved in Koblenz. It contained a sterile Glock model 26 semiautomatic minipistol with a pair of extended, threaded barrels and a second firing pin in a small plastic baggie. Wrapped separately were a short cylindrical suppressor, two ten-round magazines, and a box holding fifty 147-grain subsonic frangible hollow-point bullets in 9mm Luger, similarly untraceable.

Mossad and other Israeli black-ops units were known to employ Beretta single-action .22-caliber pistols. CIA historically favored Browning High Power 9mms. In 1992, Reuven had used a Browning to assassinate the PLO's intelligence chief Atif B'sisou. And indeed Reuven's choice of weapon created some initial confusion over the identities of the perpetrators because the Mossad combatant had had the foresight to use an agent of influence who made sure DST knew B'sisou was suspected by CIA, which had recruited him in 1983, of being a double agent.

Reuven understood that the 4627 organization followed CIA's ground rules: it did not approve of its personnel carrying weapons except in the most extreme of circumstances. It was, the Israeli thought, a naive policy, especially in the largely hostile post-9/11 world. In Israel, Reuven went armed all the time. And for years, he'd made sure that he always had access to weapons when he was overseas, even if he didn't carry them on a daily basis. The pistol and its accoutrements ensured that Paris would not be an exception.

Besides, the Glock itself gave him an added layer of deniability—both with the authorities and with his current employer—should the need to use it arise. Glocks were favored these days by many black-operations units, including Brits, Americans, Egyptians, and Jordanians. The pistol and its accoutrements went into a safe concealed in the parquet flooring beneath an Oriental carpet.

Saturday morning, Reuven awoke at six. By seven, he had pulled the stolen ID cards out of his blazer pocket, switched on the computer and the color laser printer, found the lamination kit and plugged it in, then spent the next thirty hours crafting a series of new identities for himself and Tom.

18

8:03 A.M. Tom rapped on the wood door.

It opened and a stranger peered out *"Bonjour, monsieur. Entrez, s'il vous plaît."*

"Jeezus." Reuven was a bloody chameleon. The man had totally changed his appearance. The beard was gone and the mustache trimmed down to a narrow line that ran a quarter-inch above his upper lip. There was none of the heavy jewelry—only a thin gold chain from which dangled a small golden cross. The bouffant black hairpiece had been exchanged for a short-cropped brown toupee that gave Reuven a decidedly Gallic yet surprisingly Levantine appearance. He might be French, he might be Lebanese.

Tom stepped into the bright foyer, where he noticed that even Reuven's eyes were different. They were no longer dark brown but a greenish hazel—much brighter. Even his heavy eyebrows had been trimmed back. In fact, the whole shape of Reuven's face seemed to have changed. He watched as the Israeli smiled broadly. *Of course it had:* Reuven was using a set of dental prosthetics.

"So—are you ready?" The Israeli was all business.

"Let's do it." Tom shed his clothes and climbed into a black T-shirt, then shrugged into a set of dark blue coveralls with white reflective strips identical to what Reuven was wearing. They were the same as the ones worn by EUREC/GECIR technicians—the crews who serviced Paris's traffic signals and street lighting.

"Hoist your sleeve." Tom rolled up his left cuff over the elbow and displayed the inside of his arm so Reuven could apply an appliqué tattoo like those commonly worn by former French soldiers.

Once the ink was dry, Tom pulled on a pair of rough-soled work boots. He looked over at Reuven. "Paperwork?"

Without comment, Reuven handed Tom a wallet. Tom opened the cheap leather trifold and checked inside. There was a driver's license identifying him as Serge Thénard, as well as a full set of pocket litter for the alias. He flipped through the bundle. There were forty euros, a *carte orange* for the metro, a dog-eared ticket for a 2002 Paris Ste. Germaine football game, half a dozen business cards from various electrical wholesalers, a pair of receipts from an ATM, a union membership card and dues receipt, a Visa card, an honorable discharge card from the French Army, even an old fifty-franc note folded around a *préservatif.*

Tom displayed the condom between thumb and forefinger and gave the Israeli a dirty look. "Funny, Reuven, real funny." He tucked the wallet in the back pocket of his coveralls and paused just long enough to savor the moment.

Savor, because Tom felt a euphoric rush of anticipation and excitement. He was fully charged, totally alive. These were the same larger-than-life emotions he experienced whenever he stood in the door of a plane at twelve thousand feet and then took that first step into the slipstream; the same heady mixture of emotional and physical highs he'd feel the instant he kicked through the starting gate and started the long, inexorable downhill run. He was feeling *the Rush*. And he loved it.

He'd first experienced what he called the Rush as a twelve-year-old when he water-skied up and over a six-foot ramp. The sensation of flying . . . *flying* . . . through the air that way had been the most incredible experience of his young life. Then, when he'd taken sky-diving lessons on his sixteenth birthday, it happened again. Adrenaline, euphoria. An ineffable, exhilarating, physical and emotional high. At St. Paul's, then again at Dartmouth, it was rock-climbing and skiing—downhill and giant slalom. As a member of the Dartmouth ski team, he'd set a course record that had stood for six years.

After college, it was operations that gave him the Rush. Brush passes in hotel corridors, meeting his agents in plain sight in crowded restaurants, or sensing surveillance and slipping into a rabbit hole to go black gave Tom the same physical and emotional highs as jumping out of planes or taking a curve at seventy-plus miles per hour on a downhill course.

He'd gotten the Rush during his training evolution at the Farm, and known in his gut he'd made the right decision in joining CIA. And then, when life in the real world of espionage turned out to be less than he'd imagined—when too many of his bosses were cautious and risk averse, when recruiting agents actually became hazardous to his career, when reports officers and analysts were put in charge of the DO—he'd had to look elsewhere for satisfaction.

That was when he'd discovered motorcycles. During his Paris tour, he'd splurged on a Ducati, which he discovered, much to his delight, was the perfect vehicle on which to run cleaning routes. When he'd been yanked back to headquarters, he'd brought the bike home. He used it to commute to Langley. Hitting a hundred on the George Washington Parkway was the closest thing to the Rush he felt during two and a half years of CTC paper-pushing. He still kept a bike in Paris—a big black BMW 750. He'd pre-positioned it in the tiny courtyard of the safe house four days ago.

Goddamn. *The Rush.* He hadn't thought of the term in months. But as he thought about it now, the Rush was why he'd been so easy for Tony Wyman to recruit. They'd been sitting in the rearmost leather booth at the Palm on Nineteenth Street. Tony had screwed the monocle into his right eye, squinted at the wine list, and ordered a bottle of La Lagune '82. When it had been decanted, poured, and tasted, he'd inclined the rim of his glass in Tom's direction, allowed the monocle to fall onto his vest, and begun his pitch.

You've outgrown the place, he said. *Left it behind. That's because you're one of us. You live for results—to win. You love to steal secrets. I know because that's how I feel—always have, always will. You get the same rush I do when your guy shows up and he's holding paper. You love it when a false-flag recruitment produces a twenty-four-karat nugget. There's nothing like that anymore, is there?* He looked straight into Tom's eyes. *When's the last time you felt like that?*

Tom's expression was neutral. But, of course, Tony was right.

What's going on at stations worldwide? Nothing. Nobody goes out anymore. They're all sitting in goddamn fortresses writing memos. So what are the NOCs doing? They're all using business cover these days. Christ, doesn't Tenet understand that gringo executives and salesmen won't penetrate al-Qa'ida's networks? Why the hell hasn't CIA set up Islamic charity front groups in Germany and France and Holland and Pakistan, in Indonesia and Qatar and Sudan and the UAE and used them to penetrate the Islamists who want to kill us? We should be running our own madrassas, for chrissakes.

You know why. It's because we don't have qualified NOCs. But it's also because it would be very, very risky, and risk-takers don't receive performance bonuses these days. You want to be promoted? You stay on the reservation. You play it safe. You keep your head down. Better to spend your days writing e-mails querying about some arcane matter, or dabbling in the stock market, or buying investment real estate than sticking your neck out to recruit some penetration agent who might be a double. Recruiting's risky, Tom. That's precisely why the crowd on the seventh floor doesn't like it. They weigh every single recruitment these days. "How will it look in the Washington Post*?" That's what they ask. Then they take a pass.* Tony's gray eyes bored into Tom's head. *You see it. All around you. And when you do, you're pissed.*

Tom had sipped his wine and said nothing.

I'm right, Tony had said. *You can't say anything because there's nothing to say. But you know I'm right. Christ—even in Iraq, there are virtually no risk takers. Thirty-day deployments—that's what they're doing now. C'mon, Tom, how many recruitments do you think they're making in thirty days? You know what's happening in Iraq as well as I do. They're spending all their time in the Green Zone, or hunkered down behind concrete barriers at CIA's bases in Mosul, Kirkuk, Basra, or Sulaimaniya.*

Tom's eyes dropped. He'd felt exactly the same way. Too damn many of the people going to Iraq were doing it only to ticket-punch. Get the hazard pay. Make sure the powers that be at Langley checked the appropriate box next to their names so they'd be promoted on schedule. The guys doing the real work—the PMs[21] and the contractors—were treated like peons.

He looked up. Tony was speaking. Tom blinked. Tried to play catch-up.

I saw the writing on the wall, Tony was saying. *So did Charlie and Bronco. We got out. And I can tell you that right now—right at this very second—4627 is doing more human-based intelligence gathering world-wide than you and all of your colleagues at CTC. You come with us, and you'll get the old feeling back, Tom. The same emotional highs and lows. Now, I'm not talking sinecure, Tom. This ain't the Agency. We pay for results—not just for showing up. But we love our work. Oh God, do we ever love our work.* Wyman sipped his wine. He put the big goblet down on the white tablecloth and shot the cuffs of his brightly striped London shirt to display the blue enamel and gold tooling of White House cuff links. *Hunkering down and flying a desk ain't why you joined CIA, Tom.*

Tom drained his wine and waited as Wyman refilled his glass. *Useless.* That was the word that best described the most recent two and a half years of his career. He'd languished at Langley. Skirted depression. Gotten fat on the junk food in the cafeteria. Felt . . . unappreciated.

No more. *The Rush* was back. Tom cast a satisfied, surreptitious look at Reuven's back as the Israeli pulled a pair of latex gloves out of the dispenser box and stuffed them into his coveralls. *God, how incredible it is to be working with a world-class operator again.* Tom pulled his own gloves from the dispenser. Then he picked up one of the six prepaid, disposable cell phones that sat on the nicked porcelain counter and dropped it into a pocket. Finally, he clipped the laminated Eurec photo identity card onto his collar. Without a word of warning, he flipped the condom in Reuven's direction.

The Israeli whirled, snatching the foil-wrapped package out of the air. "Thank you, kind sir. This will be put to good use, believe me."

The guy's still got it. Tom made a dismissive gesture. "C'mon, lover boy, let's get started."

---

[21]The Agency's paramilitary personnel.

19

9:27 A.M. Tom let Reuven off the motorcycle. After the Israeli slid a key into the heavy lock and pulled the narrow reinforced steel door open, Tom wrestled the big bike over the threshold into the warehouse, dropped the kickstand, and switched the motor off.

They'd driven north and east along boulevard Victor Hugo into the industrial zone that took up much of the southern portion of the suburb of St. Denis, which sits due north of the eighteenth arrondissement and the Porte de la Chapelle. But they didn't follow a direct route. Instead, Tom flew between the cars and trucks, backtracking, making random turns, gunning the bike along the railroad tracks that ran through the zone, even occasionally heading the big BMW against traffic on one-way streets to discourage all but the hardiest of followers. So, unless DST was using its aerial assets—which was highly unlikely given the fact that Tom was a relatively low-priority target these days—they reached the 4627 stowage facility clean of surveillance.

The Israeli pulled a small flashlight out of his pocket and shined it on the interior wall until he found the light panel. He opened the box, reached up, and threw the switches that turned the big overhead lights on. It was a cavernous place. Tom could hear birds in the rafters. How they got in without setting off the intrusion devices, Tom had no idea. How they survived, Tom had no idea. But every time he set foot in the warehouse, he could hear birds chirping.

He looked around—there was plenty of room for him to work. It was a good-size facility—sixty meters wide and double that in depth. The ground-floor ceiling was more than thirty feet high, with an industrial staircase along the sidewall leading to an upper-level storage area filled with tools and racks of clothes. The ground floor was cement, which made the warehouse feel cold year-round. In the right rear corner was a walled-off area containing a washroom and an office. Piled against the rear wall were the items he'd need: half a dozen ten-foot-tall scenery bays, holding what looked like prefab modular housing walls, stairways, and exteriors.

Constructing the bays and the units had been Tom's idea. He'd come up with it after his visit to the Delta Force compound the previous spring.

In a matter of hours, Delta could build full-scale models of its targets so that its hostage rescue teams could rehearse their moves to perfection. There was a warehouse inside the Delta compound that was filled with modular walls, doors, stair units, and other assorted building blocks.

Did C Squadron need a second-floor apartment with two bedrooms and one bath, with the hostage held in the tiny galley kitchen whose narrow casement window looked out onto a fire escape? It would take the Delta logistics people less than an hour to fit the proper pieces together so that the entry team could fine-tune its tactical plan. Need to make entry in complete darkness and rehearse using night-vision goggles? There were ceiling pieces that could be fit together to seal out light. Want to make entry just as the sun is going down? There were spotlights hung from a grid so that every condition from dead of night to dawn's early light could be duplicated.

Tom appropriated the concept and modified it so that he and his agents could rehearse their moves before making surreptitious entry to plant a listening device or a miniature camera. He'd assembled two dozen different types of doors, each with a modular locking system, so that he and his people could practice their lock-picking skills. There were dozens of variations: dead bolts and intergrip rim locks, chain locks, mortise locks, tube locks, sprung and unsprung latch-bolt locks, and the old-fashioned crenellated locks used on French doors.

There were double-hung windows sitting in frames so their locks could be jimmied. There were horizontal pivoting windows and vertical pivoters, too, sliding windows, sash windows, louvered windows, and jalousies. There were casement windows so the 4627 people could practice easing the glass panes out of the muntins and sash bars. There were sections of different kinds of wall mounted in frames so that he or his people could practice with the soundproof drills they used to insert audio and video devices from one apartment to the next. He had old-fashioned lath-and-plaster walls you found in European buildings, as well as the more modern Sheetrock-and-foam insulation found in the United States. There were marble wall sections, too, as well as the steel-reinforced walls favored by embassies. All in all, it was a remarkable collection. And untraceable. The building materials had been assembled piece by piece from more than three dozen separate vendors. Parked next to the scenery bays were a pair of hydraulic forklift trucks that could position the heavy elements, which fit together like jigsaw-puzzle pieces.

Even the ownership of the warehouse was untraceable. It had been bought through a series of French front companies and offshore banks. It was one anonymous structure among scores of similar buildings, located in the narrow corridor between the A1 highway that ran due north all the way to Lille and the huge Michelin tire complex. Like the tire plant, the 4627 warehouse straddled the St. Denis–Aubervilliers boundary line. That location was no accident. Tom had planned things that way: he knew that if anything went awry, the St. Denis gendarmerie would defer to the Aubervilliers cops, who would, in turn, wait for their brothers in arms across the boundary line to handle the problem. That was one thing about the French: you could trust their bureaucracy always to remain solidly bureaucratic.

The vehicles parked cheek by jowl against the western wall of the place each had legitimate registrations and owners' certificates for half a dozen separate aliases—aliases that wouldn't disturb police or intelligence trip wires anywhere in Europe. There were more than half a dozen of them: two Renault vans, a Citroën sedan, a big Audi saloon, and a couple of nondescript Fords. There were also a pair of panel trucks—the less dinged-up truck was a boxy van painted French blue with reflective white and orange stripes on the side panels and rear hatches. It bore the EUREC and GECIR logos, and on the sliding door white letters read ÉCLAIRAGE & SIGNALIZA- TION. It looked exactly like the panel trucks driven by traffic-light repair crews. The other was equally unremarkable.

Reuven unlocked the Eurec van. Inside, taped to the equipment locker, was a brown manila envelope. Reuven slit the thick paper seal and ex- tracted a compact disk. He eased out of the truck, went to the office, in- serted the disk in the graphite-gray computer, and waited until it booted up.

Six minutes later, he was back, a sheaf of papers in his right hand. He whistled at Tom, who was scanning the wall sections in the scenery bays. "Take a look," he shouted, waving the target-assessment photos in the American's direction. "Nothing too complicated. We should have the mock-up put together within a couple of hours."

11:14 A.M. Tom went into the office and entered a six-number combination into a large safe that had been lag-bolted into the concrete floor. When he heard the electronic lock release, he punched a second six-number combi- nation, which rendered the thermite explosive charges inside the safe inert. He pulled the double doors open.

From the top shelf of the safe he extracted a gray, injection-molded, HPX high-performance resin-shell Storm Case slightly larger than a com- mercial attaché. He sat the case on the floor, opened the twin combination padlocks then the twin latches, and flipped the waterproof lid up. Inside, protected by black plastic foam, were six pinhole audio/video cameras, each one two and a half inches in length. The battery compartment was just over seven thirty-seconds of an inch in diameter—roughly the same as a cut-down rollerball cartridge. And like a rollerball cartridge, the unit ta- pered into a slender shaft ending with the lens, which was about the same size as the head of a pin. Even so, the field of view was wide-angle, cover- ing more than 106 degrees.

Both audio and video were transmitted to a repeater unit, also in the Storm Case, which amplified the signal before sending it on to the receiver, which could be as much as five miles away. There, the high-resolution dig- ital pictures could be shown on a single television screen—much the same way that multiple security camera images are displayed. Simultaneously, the images were stored on a miniature flash ROM unit for instantaneous playback or transfer into single-frame photographs. The cameras themselves were self-powered by miniature lithium batteries that had a ▮▮▮▮▮▮ hour life. Once activated, they'd transmit ▮▮▮▮▮▮▮▮▮▮[22] months.

Tom closed the Storm Case and carried it over to where Reuven squatted inside the van, rummaging through a tool chest. "You have the drill?"

Without turning, Reuven gave Tom an upturned thumb. "And the paint. And the Spackle. And the tool kit." He reached inside his pocket and brought out a small leather case. "What do you think? I go out with just lock picks?"

Although paint, Spackle, and a sixteen-ounce hammer might appear on the surface to be incongruous with the art of spying, intelligence-gathering tradecraft sometimes requires more than SDRs and cleaning routes, spotting, assessing, developing, and recruiting; polygraphs, rabbit holes, or writing the endless series of postrendezvous reports that disappear into the black hole of Langley. Spying is more than flaps and seals—the art of clandestinely opening other people's mail. It is more than disguise—the ability to change your appearance in plain sight. It is more than microdots and burst transmitters, spy dust, lock-picking, and all the other technically oriented, nimble-fingered sleight-of-hand *arcanum arcanorum* normally associated with the practice of espionage.

Tradecraft is sometimes dependent on nuts-and-bolts basic handyman skills—a lot more *This Old House* or *Trading Spaces* than "Bond—James Bond." Sewing, photography, carpentry, electrical work, auto mechanics, and painting—they're all integral to tradecraft, too.

Indeed, a Russian operation against the State Department's headquarters had provided Tom with an interesting case study in the manual-trades necessities of spycraft.

In 1998, Boris Grumov, a case officer from SVR (the Russian foreign intelligence service) working under embassy cover in Washington, managed to plant an audio transmitter listening device inside a conference room belonging to the Bureau of Oceans and Environmental and Scientific

---

[22]The actual technical specifications for this family of devices, which are currently in use, are classified.

Policy, or OES, on the seventh floor of the Harry S. Truman Building, the two-square-block main State headquarters that sits between Twenty-first and Twenty-third and C and D Streets, Northwest, in Washington, D.C.

In Hollywood movies, bugs are cavalierly applied to the bottoms of tables and chairs or easily screwed into chandeliers or floor lamps. In real life? Not likely, bub.

At the State Department, for example, offices and conference rooms are regularly inspected by Bureau of Diplomatic Security special agents augmented by spit-and-polish U.S. Marines, who look underneath desks, tables, and chairs and inside all the lighting fixtures, make sure that classified materials are properly stored in document safes, and check to see that the removable hard drives from every computer linked to State's classified network have been locked in special safes. Every night. Violations are taken seriously.

So the Russians got erudite. They installed their listening device by planting it inside the chair molding that ran along the perimeter of room 7835.

Talk about a complicated and sophisticated operation. After all, SVR had had to:

• Take photos and measurements of the chair molding so it could be purchased and matched exactly to the molding in 7835.
• Get a paint sample so the paint could be copied, right down to the patina, nicks, and smudges.
• Cut a section of molding out and replace it with the new section containing the listening device.
• Camouflage the seams between the old and the new molding to make them invisible.

And finally, accomplish all the work during the hours when the room was not being used by the OES staff.

Intelligence and law enforcement services maintain huge technical departments and break-and-enter specialists to perform such work. But if time and limited access are factors—which they often are—then much of the work has to be done by the case officer him/herself. In this operation, even though the SVR *resident* (station chief) in the Russians' Washington embassy had a five-man technical section at his disposal, the on-site work at State had to be performed either by Grumov or an American agent because penetrating a team of hostile technicians clandestinely inside HST is exponentially more difficult than getting one hostile case officer with diplomatic immunity through the C Street turnstiles. After all, hostile case officers with diplomatic immunity go through those turnstiles all the time. It made one wonder.

Tom examined the wall section Reuven had attached to the forklift truck. On one side, it was stucco-finish plaster about a quarter of an inch thick, set into lath that was fastened to masonry and sheathed in stone. The opposite surface had crown molding made of poplar wood, behind which was lath and plaster, then another layer of masonry and the common stone sheathing. The total width of the two facing walls was just over sixteen inches.

The Israeli stood with his hands on his hips. "Which one do you want to try first?"

Tom pointed to the stucco. "Back side."

"From the back, you'll want to drill high—into the crown molding."

"Then we'll need a ladder?"

"Of course." Reuven ambled off toward the scenery bay. Thirty seconds later, he was back with a trifolded aluminum multipurpose ladder, the tips of its rails sheathed in soft plastic. "Your wish, Stafford Pasha . . ."

"Let's go, Reuven." Tom was getting impatient.

The Israeli set the ladder down next to Tom, hoisted himself aboard the forklift, and turned on the engine. He reached for the lift control. The wall section rose slowly. Reuven eyeballed the height. "We want three meters. I think that's close. You measure."

Tom pulled a ten-meter cloth tape measure out of the tool kit and clipped it to the pocket of his coveralls. He straightened out the ladder and locked the sections in place. Then he inclined the rails against the wall section, snugged the antislip feet against the concrete, and climbed up until he was able to snag the hook end against the top of the crown molding. He handed the tape measure to Reuven. "Distance?"

The Israeli knelt and squinted. "Eight centimeters short."

He vaulted onto the forklift and eased the wall upward while Tom held on to the ladder, then jumped down and checked the tape. "Only half a centimeter off."

Tom unhooked the tape and let it fall, watching as Reuven caught the end one-handed. "Close enough for government work."

20

11:35 A.M. Tom tightened the elastic band on his protective goggles, leaned forward on the ladder so that he could put pressure on the silent drill, and squeezed the trigger. The bit overrevved and gouged a thumbnail-size hole in the rough plaster surface. "Goddamnit." Tom released the trigger, wiped the bit clean, and prepared to start over.

From below, Reuven looked up. "You're okay. Just take it slow and easy."

"Gotcha." Tom applied pressure cautiously, gauging carefully as the bit revolved ever so slowly. "Okay." He stopped the drill, pressed the tip against the plaster, and eased his finger onto the trigger.

The bit began to turn slowly. Tom put some of his weight behind the drill and watched, satisfied, as the bit eased smoothly into the rough-surfaced plaster. Particles of fine dust floated down onto his coveralls.

Now he increased the speed of the drill, feeling momentary resistance as the bit passed through the plaster and chewed on the lath beneath.

He increased the revolutions. The plaster dust was now joined by tiny wood shavings, which were, in turn, followed by gray masonry dust. Tom pressed harder. The drill bore into the wall. He cocked his head to examine the metric markings on the bit. He'd penetrated just over ten centimeters so far. He'd be coming to the stone sheathing soon—and then it would be time to switch drill bits.

11:39 A.M. Tom pulled the bit out of the wall. He was sweating now, and his arms had begun to ache from holding the drill rock-steady. He hung the drill off the utility belt he'd cinched around his waist, inserted a fiber-optic Snake-Lens Scope into the hole, and depressed the light button. The fiber-optic cable was 2.75 millimeters in diameter—just over a tenth of an inch. It had a close-focusing lens with a fifty-degree field of view. The scope had been designed for SWAT teams so they could peer under doors and into the interiors of locked cars and vans. It was an off-the-shelf model powered by double-A batteries. This one had red-light illumination. But you could get them with bright white, or blue, or even infrared light for clandestine operations. He'd bought the scope out of a police-supply catalog on a whim. It had cost just over three hundred dollars. Now he was glad he'd splurged. He turned the knurled fine-focus knob on the eyepiece until he was satisfied with what he saw, counted the striations, then dead-reckoned how much drilling was left undone.

He was getting close—certainly within an inch and a half of the adjoining wall. He extracted the fiber-optic scope, inserted his measuring rod, and squinted at the markings Reuven had etched on the aluminum as a guide. *Yup—three-point-six centimeters to go.* He retrieved the drill, removed the drill shaft, and replaced it with a long titanium 1mm bit. He double-checked to see that the bit was seated securely and then eased the unit back into the hole.

11:55 A.M. "You're through. Did you feel it?" Reuven was perched on a ladder on the opposite side of the wall.

"Yes." Tom held the drill steady, eased it out, and hung it on his belt. He pulled the minivacuum up and sucked dust out of the hole, then inserted the fiber-optic. "Looks clean."

Now he took the minicamera out of his breast pocket, activated the power, and, using the measuring rod, eased the device into the hole. As he did, he heard Reuven scramble down the ladder. "I'll check the video."

Tom waited until he heard Reuven say, "Okay—go."

"Roger that." He pushed on the rod, eyes focused on the measurements. "One-half centimeter." He felt slight resistance. "See anything?"

"No."

Tom grunted. He applied more pressure, pushing the camera another twenty-five millimeters. "Now?"

"Not yet."

Tom examined the markings on the rod. The lens should have cleared the crown molding by now. He squinted and counted the lines etched on the rod. "You're right, Reuven—I was one centimeter off." Holding the rod steady, Tom pushed.

Too hard. The rod shot forward more than two centimeters—about half an inch.

"I can see very clearly now," Reuven said facetiously.

"I'll bet you can." Tom was pissed. He'd shoved the goddamn camera right through the crown molding. He clambered down the ladder and went around the other side to examine his handiwork. He wasn't impressed. "Jeezus H," he said, hands on his hips. "Let's do it all over again."

12:36 P.M. The entire back of Tom's coveralls was wet with perspiration. The front was covered with dust from the drilling. But he didn't care. He stared at the image on the monitor and grinned. It had taken three attempts, but he'd finally gotten it right. He looked over at Reuven, who gave him an upturned thumb and a mischievous grin. "Am I that big an asshole?"

"You show real promise, Tom. A few more run-throughs and we'll make you into a regular second-story guy."

"Thanks." It might have been easier if Reuven had done the drilling, but Tom had insisted on doing the work himself. "I'm simply a little out of practice is all."

Tom noted the noncommittal expression on Reuven's face. Who was he kidding? The last time Tom worked with silent drills was during the breaking-and-entering refresher he'd taken down at the Farm in 2002 as an excuse to get out of the office. He was on shaky ground here and he knew it.

"If we have to drill from the back, maybe it would be better if you did it."

"Nah." Reuven waved a hand in a dismissive gesture. "You know what Suvorov said."

"Suvorov?"

"Eighteenth-century Russian general. 'Train hard, fight easy.' That was his credo." The Israeli jerked his thumb toward the wall section. "You're getting the feel of it. We've got, what—a week perhaps, before we can move. By the time we do this for real, you'll be fine."

1:58 P.M.
RUE LAMBERT, MONTMARTRE

Tom thought, You have to hand it to the bad guys: they plan well. This frigging street is going to be impossible. Rue Lambert was narrow—barely wide enough for a panel truck. It was short—just over fifty meters in length. It was one-way—dead-ending into another one-way street. It was the kind of street on which people know one another, where the one small bistro served the same customers every day. Where the owner of the corner café knows everyone in the neighborhood by name and keeps a wary eye out for strangers. It was, all in all, a perfect milieu for *counter*surveillance. And a lousy environment in which to do the surveilling.

Oh, it was possible. If you had a crew of sixty. You could run them through as tourists and workers, changing clothes and appearances over a ten-day period. Or if there was enough time to preplan, you could rent a flat—or break into one if the owners were away—and use it as an observation post. But Tom didn't have sixty people, there was nothing for rent— he'd had his French employees check—and no one was on vacation. So there was no choice. They'd have to do this the hard way.

Tom eased the two wheels on the passenger's side of the truck up onto the curb so traffic could pass. He and Reuven had changed into the anonymous sort of coveralls worn by tradesmen and laborers. The old tan Renault with its junk-filled cab and dented, rusty cargo bay didn't rate a second look. Tom and Reuven had changed their appearances. Tom's face was obscured by a thick mustache, and his hair—a wig—was frizzy brown and stuck out from under a knit cap. Reuven wore a neat beard and a full head of short gray hair.

As he parked, Tom angled the Renault so that his side-view mirror caught the entrance of the old house that sat adjacent to the bistro. He'd memorized the angle of Shahram Shahristani's surveillance photograph, and the run-down bistro—L'Étrier was the name on the awning—had to be the place. The awning was rolled back and the tables and chairs had been removed.

Tom eased the door open, pulled a newspaper from between the seats, and extracted himself from the van. He tucked the newspaper under his arm and waited as Reuven opened the passenger-side door. They locked the vehicle, then ambled to the end of the street, toward the café, which was on the southwest corner where rue Lambert dead-ended into rue Nicolet. Tom pushed through the door. The place had the sour smell of stale beer and old cigarette smoke. He dropped onto one of the bar stools that sat facing the smoke-stained window, opened the newspaper, and turned his back to the bar.

Reuven walked across creaking floorboards to where the proprietor stood, cigarette dangling from his lips, his elbow resting on discolored copper, perusing a newspaper. He ordered two glasses of red wine. Tom watched as the man reached down and pulled an unlabeled bottle from the well, drew two smudged glasses off the shelf, gave them a halfhearted wipe-down, then filled them.

"*Merci.*" Reuven dropped coins onto the bar, picked up the glasses, walked over to where Tom was perched, and set them down.

Tom nodded at the Israeli, who drew a pack of cigarettes from the breast pocket of his coveralls, pulled one out, then set the pack on the window shelf. The pack held a wide-angle video lens that transmitted a signal to a digital recorder in the truck. The high-definition images were date- and time-stamped.

The two men sat silently, sipped their wine, and scanned the street. L'Étrier was just emptying out. The bistro occupied the basement and ground floor of a narrow, nineteenth-century four-story house. Above it, according to Tom's research, there were four apartments. To the left of the restaurant was another four-story building of about the same vintage. The ground floor had once held some sort of shop. Now the shop had been gutted and the whole building was in the process of being renovated. Above the shop were six apartments—two to a floor—one of which was Ben Said's safe house. Problem one was separating the intelligence wheat from the intelligence chaff so they'd know which flat to bug.

But for the moment, what Tom and Reuven wanted was to get a sense of rue Lambert's rhythms and pace so they could find ways to adapt themselves to the street and become a part of the environment. Surveillance is one of the most basic yet difficult aspects of intelligence work. It requires long hours, intense concentration, flawless record keeping, and constant focus. A surveillant has to be able to hide in plain sight—much the same way as hunters or snipers camouflage their positions. Indeed, in many ways, surveilling is similar to hunting or sniping. A good hunter, for example, identifies the track used by his prey and sets up an ambush position long enough in advance so that the jungle, or the forest, or the mountain trail returns to its normal condition: the crickets chirp, the birds come and go, the insects resume their normal activities.

It's much the same on a surveillance detail. If you're using an OP[23] to photograph a target, for example, you run a two- or even three-man team, one of whose eyes are looking through a telephoto lens every second of every minute of the day so there is absolutely no chance that the target will show himself and not be noted or photographed. Every single sighting is logged. Every individual entering and exiting the location is logged and photographed. The license plates, make, model, and physical description of every vehicle—cars, taxis, trucks, vans, motorcycles, bicycles, jitneys, rickshaws—that comes into contact with the target location is noted.

If audio surveillance is being conducted from an OP, simple but effective means have to be used to camouflage the listening devices, most of which have been developed by the technical section of the National Security Agency, which use lasers and other technical means to pick up sounds as low as a whisper at ranges up to 250 yards. Sometimes, for example, the surveillance team will use a technique that is commonly used by snipers or

---

[23]Observation post.

countersnipers working in urban environments. The team builds a

██

██

██

██

████████ motionless for long periods of time.

Indeed, fatigue is a critical factor in surveillance operations. It is mind-numbing to stare through a long lens, a pair of binoculars, or a spotting scope for hours on end. Concentration becomes hard to maintain. The mind wanders. Other factors also intrude. In vehicle-based surveillance operations, for example, any motion of the vehicle at all will give the team's position away—something many law enforcement surveillance details find out the hard way. In Hollywood, surveillance is easy. You pull a car into an alley, slink below the dash, and do a Starsky and Hutch sneak-and-peek through the windshield. But that's Hollywood. In real life, operators have to fight through boredom, monotony, and hour-after-hour, day-after-day, week-after-week tedium, but just . . . keep . . . going.

3:46 P.M. Reuven was on his fourth cigarette. Their wineglasses were still a third full. No one had entered or left the safe-house building and the workmen were starting to pack up and close down the ground-floor site for the day.

Tom had just lifted the wine to his lips when the cell phone in his coveralls vibrated. He set the glass down, pulled the phone out, and held it to his ear. *"Allô."*

"C'est Tony. On peut parler?" Tony Wyman sounded stressed.

"Sure," Tom answered in French. "What's up?"

"I've just come in from the home office."

Tom cracked a smile. *"Bienvenue."*

"Stow it. The job's off. Come back to the office. No need to waste your time waiting around where you are."

"You're kidding."

" 'Fraid not." Wyman sighed. Tom could hear the man exhale. He sounded uncharacteristically exhausted—almost as if he'd been beaten. "Get moving—now. We have to talk."

21

"THEY *WHAT*?" Tom looked across the desk at Antony Wyman. Wyman had been flying all day. He hadn't even checked into his hotel, and yet he was impeccably turned out. How the man could do that was something Tom couldn't fathom. "Who shut me down? I'll talk to them. C'mon, Tony—let me talk to whoever it was."

Wyman shook his head. "You know that's impossible."

Tom pulled uncomfortably at his wet shirt collar. "How can they be so stupid?" It had been a rush to get back. He and Reuven had made their way from rue Lambert to the warehouse, changed clothes and IDs, then run a cleaning route to the safe house, where they'd changed clothes and identities once more. Since it was rush hour, Tom used the motorcycle to get to the 4627 offices near the Place des Ternes. It had started to rain just as he'd sped through the Place du Brésil and he'd gotten soaked. He'd been riding alone. Reuven declined Tom's invitation to accompany him, saying there was some trolling to be done and they'd catch up in the morning.

Tom's curt tone reflected his mood. "I was just starting to make some headway, damnit."

"They don't care about headway," Wyman growled. He glanced around the office with the look of a drill sergeant making a white-glove inspection, then he refocused on Tom. "Look, the seventh floor[24] is running scared these days. There are more CYA leaks coming out of Langley than I've ever seen—and I'd be very surprised if a lot of them weren't sanctioned from the top as a way of putting some blue sky between CIA and the administration on these Iraq screwups. As much as I dislike admitting it, politics plays a part in what we do. Sometimes we just have to back off—delay taking action until we can find another way of achieving our goals without making waves."

"You're sounding like one of *them,* Tony." Tom wasn't willing to accept that kind of rationalization—even from someone like Wyman. "Goddamnit, this is too important. I'm onto something big here. Immense."

"I understand. I know the stakes, Tom. More than that—it's personal. These sons of bitches killed Jim McGee and I want their heads on pikes as much as you do. But we're up against a six-hundred-pound gorilla here and its name is bureaucracy. Langley insists on total control, and right now they're yanking at our leash and saying, 'Sit; stay.' Don't forget—we're contractors."

"We're *operators,* and they're idiots." Tom clenched his fists. "Look at how Langley dealt with MJ's stuff."

"When has incompetence ever stopped anyone at Langley from becoming a division chief—or DCI, for that matter?"

"Jeezus, Tony—"

"Look, I'm more pissed than you are." Wyman's palm slapped the desk. "It's absurd: I was told point-blank there is no Tariq Ben Said."

"But—"

"Oh, they admit there's a bomber out there. But they insist that by lay-

---

[24]Langley's seventh floor is the location of the DCI's office suite.

ing low and setting out traplines, the system will find him before he can do any damage."

Wyman caught the incredulous look on Tom's face and cut him off before he could speak. "Don't ask me which system and what traplines, Tom, because I have no more idea what the hell they're talking about than you do. Worse, they take a harder line on Imad Mugniyah. It wasn't Mugniyah. Not in Gaza; and not in the surveillance photographs Shahram took on rue Lambert. The official line is that Mugniyah is somewhere in Lebanon, running Hezbollah's operations against the Israelis and surveilling the American embassy. He is not involved with al-Qa'ida. And he is not partnered with Tariq Ben Said, because there is no Tariq Ben Said. Full stop."

"Why is Langley so unwilling to see what's going on?"

"Like I said, politics." Tony Wyman shook his head. "Headquarters rejects your premise because it contradicts everything they've been telling the president for almost three years now. Accepting the Ben Said–slash–Imad Mugniyah–slash–Arafat–slash–Tehran–slash–al-Qa'ida alliance would mean a direct link between Arafat, UBL, and Tehran."

"So? The president himself has talked about the UBL–Tehran link."

"Ah," Wyman said, "but the Romanoffs at Langley have consistently argued that with the exception of Ansar al-Islam, no such link exists. Worse, tying Mugniyah and Ben Said to Gaza would indicate Arafat's involved—Arafat would be connected to UBL, the Seppah, and Imad Mugniyah. C'mon, Tom—the CIA for years has its money on Arafat and Arafat's Palestinian National Authority. CIA spent hundreds of millions helping the PA create a security apparatus—it was even called the Tenet Plan. CIA spent millions teaching Palestinian security people tradecraft. And what have the Ps done with all that education and all that money? They've become better terrorists is what they've done with it. How the hell can Tenet admit he was so wrong for so long and still not resign? He can't—and so, he and his crowd stick their heads in the sand, leak positive stories to their friends in the media, and tell the White House and the oversight committees everything's great, and they're making real progress on America's global war on terror, and in a mere five years, the clandestine service will be better than ever."

"It's all horse puckey."

"Of course it is. The DO's in a heap of trouble." Wyman's eyes flashed. "Christ, Tom, Ali Atwa, Mugniyah's number two on the TWA 847 hijacking, is wandering around Beirut these days, under real name, and free as a bird. And what has CIA done about it? CIA has done nothing. What has Colin Powell's State Department done? They've done nothing." Wyman paused. "I took a snatch plan to Langley three weeks ago and they turned me down cold. 'State will never agree. The Syrians might get upset.' The *Syrians*? The frigging Syrians are getting paid to ship foreign fighters into Iraq. We should have bombed Damascus the same night we did Baghdad." Wyman played with the monocle hanging around his neck. "Christ, how I wish Casey were still alive."

"You're not the only one." Tom scratched his chin. "Isn't there any way—"

"I spoke to the goddamn ADDO[25] himself on this. He assured me the materials you sent forward were brought to the highest levels."

"So they could be round-filed."

"We have a problem here, Tom. We're dealing with a dysfunctional organism. The WMD groups in Iraq are incapable of handling their jobs and yet they're getting performance bonuses. The chief in Riyadh doesn't speak Arabic, there are no Saudi recruitments, and he got a performance bonus, too. We hired Jim McGee because Langley hadn't recruited a single PA officer in years—but TA got station performance bonuses. A system that pays people bonuses to reward them for failing is entirely broke. But it's the only system we've got right now. Until someone gets rid of Tenet, nothing's going to change."

Tom curled his lower lip. "Thanks, Tony, I needed that."

Wyman's eyes narrowed and his tone grew frosty. "Sarcasm isn't going to help. Bottom line, Tom: Langley insists on handling things their way."

"Which is?"

"To hunker down, stay quiet, and hope all the problems will go away. They won't pay us to uncover Ben Said. And you know as well as I do that these ops are both complicated and costly, and without Langley's funding . . ." He looked at the younger man apologetically. "We're not the government, Tom. There are limits to what we can do unless someone's willing to pay."

[25]Assistant deputy director of operations.

"This sucks."

"Agreed. But unless we can find ourselves a wedge . . ."

Tom crossed his arms. "What about the bombs? The detonators? Ben Said's new explosives? If that isn't a call to action, I don't know what is."

"Action?" Wyman snorted derisively. "The system, Tom, detests action. Trying to get the system to react is like trying to turn a supertanker around."

"What do they want? Another World Trade Center?"

"I think it would take about that much."

Tony was right, of course. Between organizational timidity, political correctness, risk aversion, and lack of strong leadership on the operational level, it was virtually impossible to defeat the jihad Islamists were waging against America and the West. The USG was spending buckets o' cash to—as the State Department's public diplomacy panjandrums kept saying—"win the hearts and minds" of all those hundreds of millions of Muslims living under various forms of dictatorship. "You can't act without listening to the Arab Street," State kept insisting. What crap. Bill Casey said it best: "When you've got 'em by the balls, their hearts and minds will follow."

Tom said, "The Israelis seemed worried enough when I laid it out for them. Maybe they can convince Langley we're on the right track."

"Not these days. There's a problem with Israel these days."

"There seem to be a lot of problems, Tony."

"There *are* a lot of problems, son."

"What's up with Israel?"

Wyman adjusted his right shirt cuff. "We're about to experience a huge hiccup with our Israeli friends. Something to do with Iran policy, classified documents making their way to Mossad via a leak somewhere in the Pentagon. The FBI's gotten into it within the past couple of weeks and Langley is keeping Gelilot[26] at arm's length these days."

"Christ."

"I took some heat over our Israeli associate."

"Reuven?"

---

[26]Gelilot Junction, on the main highway opposite the Tel Aviv Country Club and three kilometers south of Herzlyia, is where Mossad headquarters is located.

"They said they don't like the fact that we have foreign nationals work-ing for us."

Tom was incredulous. "You're kidding."

"I'm serious."

"I love it. Most of our embassies are run by foreign nationals. CIA depends on foreign nationals—liaison relationships. And Langley's upset because we have a retired Mossad officer working for us?"

Tony Wyman played with his monocle. "There are those who insist re-tirement's just another form of cover when it comes to Mossad combatants."

Tom cocked his head toward the window, which was covered with three layers of antisurveillance drapery. "Sam Waterman used to say that all the time about everybody." He paused. "You don't happen to know what Sam's up to?"

"No idea. Saw him about a month ago at the club. He was having lunch with Ed Kane." Wyman shifted in the big leather swivel chair. "Anyway, the seventh floor is unhappy about Reuven Ayalon." He looked at Tom re-assuringly. "But they'll get over it."

"Hope so. Because we've made progress because of Reuven, Tony. You saw the messages from Israel. Reuven and I know who, and we know where. We just don't know when, or what the targets are. That's why I wanted to get inside the safe house."

"Understood." Wyman shifted himself in the chair. "Still . . ."

Tom looked at his boss's face. "What?"

"There's something else. I haven't mentioned it because neither Bronco, Charlie, nor I is sure how to handle things."

The remark was uncharacteristic, and Tom said so.

"We've come to the reluctant conclusion that our contacts at Langley are lying to us. The reluctant conclusion is that they're trying to push us away."

"But why?"

"Ah," Wyman said, "there's the rub. It doesn't make any sense. We've produced incredible product for them over the past twenty months. Char-lie's work in Libya helped result in Qaddafi's decision to end his WMD programs and allow inspections. Bronco's done a lot to repair the rift be-tween the U.S. and Russia. And so far as al-Qa'ida goes, 4627's been re-sponsible for developing the intelligence instrumental in the capture of sixteen top-level AQN[27] operatives. Sure, we butted heads over Iraq—the WMD material. But . . ." His voice trailed off. "It just doesn't make sense."

Tom started to speak, but Wyman cut him off. "Look, this isn't your concern. What does affect both you and Reuven is that Langley won't pay 4627 to follow up on the Gaza murders, even if they were to track to Imad Mugniyah and Ben Said."

"It makes no sense."

"When has absurdity ever been eliminated as a factor when we're talking about the seventh floor?"

Tom looked at his boss. "You think it's coming from the seventh floor?"

"I think the whole seventh floor is running scared. There are four separate reports due out next year from Congress, from the 9/11 Commission, and from CIA's inspector general. Each one will be more devastating to CIA than the last. So how bad do you think it will look when it's revealed that CIA leadership has had to outsource the war on terror because they didn't have the internal resources to develop adequate human-based intelligence to be able to satisfy the administration's demands for answers and results?"

"*That's* why they're shutting me down? Goddamn seventh-floor egos? Frigging executives worried about job security?" Tom was furious. "People are dead, Tony. And there'll be more corpses soon. We know that."

"Langley's beginning to think like an automobile manufacturer."

"How?"

"Let's say carmakers discover a flaw in a vehicle's ignition system that might lead to fires. They estimate it will cost X dollars to fix the problem for the two hundred thousand autos with flaws. If there'll only be Y number of fatalities, and the lawsuit factor is Z, they decide that it will be more cost-efficient to allow the flaw to remain than spend the money to recall every imperfect vehicle."

"That's immoral."

"What's your point? We're in a business that sometimes confronts us with nothing but immoral choices," Wyman said.

He slapped his palm on the desk. "Enough of the thumb-sucking, Tom.

[27]al-Qa'ida Network.

Here's something you can act on: I learned that as of last week, headquarters dumped the whole Imad Mugniyah–slash–Tariq Ben Said mess onto Paris station."

That didn't make sense at all. If Reuven was right—and Tom had no reason to doubt him—Imad Mugniyah had slipped back into the shadows—he was either in Lebanon or Iran. It was Ben Said who'd returned to Paris to put the finishing touches on his backpack IEDs. Tom gave his boss a quizzical look. "I thought you said Langley's opinion was Ben Said doesn't exist."

Wyman gave Tom a jaundiced look. "Strange development, ain't it? We're told it's not Imad Mugniyah in the photos and there is no Ben Said, and now Paris station is ordered to poke around for them."

Tom thought about it. "Very weird."

"Of course it could just be RUMINT. I was having dinner with an old colleague. He said he'd heard some corridor gossip about a meeting in Paris with an Iranian source—couldn't give me a name or any other specifics. The Iranian offered us Imad Mugniyah's head on the proverbial platter. But he wanted the twenty-five-mil reward State's posted. He asked for a down payment of half a million dollars—seed money for baksheesh and payoffs in Tehran was how it was described to me—and the balance of twenty-four mil five hundred thou to be paid on delivery."

"Tony . . ." Tom's antennae went active. "When was that offer made?"

"When . . ." Wyman took a Palm Pilot out of the desk drawer, turned it on, screwed the monocle into his right eye, tapped the screen with the stylus, and peered. "Sometime in mid-October. I was told it was put on the table within a couple of days of the Gaza flap." He looked at Tom. "About the same time you were meeting with your Iranian friend Shahram Shahristani."

"Uh-huh." Tom's mind was kicking into overdrive.

"My contact said RUMINT was the Iranian met with someone from Paris station."

"Do we know who?"

"I thought you'd want to know, so I checked. The name that was floated to me is Adam Margolis."

"Who?"

Wyman squinted at the screen again then let the monocle fall onto his vest. "Margolis. Adam Margolis. He's the deputy to the deputy CT branch chief. A greenhorn. I checked. This is his second tour. First was Guatemala—consular cover. Decent ratings but nothing spectacular."

"Are you sure?"

Wyman's eyes locked coldly onto Tom's. "I said I checked."

When Tony looked at you like that, Tom thought, you could see he was capable of ordering someone's death.

Tom broke off from his boss's lethal stare. "That's odd."

"Why?"

Odd, Tom explained, because Shahram had specifically said he'd telephoned the embassy on October 16—and he'd been deflected. Never made it past the gatekeeper was how Shahram put it.

"Hmm." Tony Wyman pushed back, tilted the big chair, rested his Ballys on the desk mat, and closed his eyes.

After half a minute, Tom grew itchy. "What?"

"But Shahram never denied he went to the embassy."

Tom thought hard about Wyman's query before he answered. "No. In fact, he went evasive when I pressed him."

Wyman put his arms behind his head and interlocked his fingers. "There's something funny going on here." He looked at Tom. "Somebody's trying to run a game on us."

"Who?"

"Maybe the seventh floor. Maybe your friend Shahram. Didn't you say he was down on his luck? Could be he was hoping to score a quick half mil and disappear."

"Isn't Langley smarter than that?"

"Langley," Wyman scoffed, "once paid a Lebanese fifty thousand cash for a map of the Beirut sewer system. The Agency was going to infiltrate a Delta team through the sewers and have them come up next to the house in south Beirut where two Americans were being held hostage."

"So?"

"There are no sewers in Beirut, Tom—except the open sewers in the old Palestinian camps." He paused. "Look—Shahram was smart. He knew Langley's vulnerabilities as well as anyone. And he had a score to settle. He'd been labeled an untouchable. He was out in the cold." Wyman looked at Tom. "Possible?"

"Possible, Tony." Tom sighed. "But I don't think Shahram would run a game on me. He *gave* me the photographs—never mentioned money."

"Okay—here's another scenario. It's the seventh floor. You know how that crowd loves head games. Maybe they're trying to manipulate us to do their work for them but they get away without paying. Hell, for all I know, this Adam Margolis is marking the deck so he gets a promotion and a big performance bonus. Who's doing what here, Tom? Not sure. But someone's trying sleight of hand—and we'd better find out who damn fast, or we're gonna end up holding the short end of the stick."

Wyman's monologue had set Tom's head spinning. Had Shahram played him? Not according to the photographic evidence. Not according to MJ's results on her photo analysis software—and Langley's negative reaction to it. Tom leaned forward and drummed his fingers on the edge of the desk. "I should talk to this Margolis. Maybe I can shake something loose."

Wyman lifted his monocle and examined it, exhaled on the lens, used his silk pocket square as a polishing cloth, then let the instrument fall back onto his lapelled vest. "I agree, Tom. Perhaps you should."

22

SCARF FLAPPING IN THE BREEZE, the collar of his sport coat turned up against the chill in the air, Tom slalomed his way past Place Beauvau, where submachine-gun-toting guards in crisp blue-and-white uniforms manned the ceremonial gates of the Ministry of the Interior. He stopped long enough to admire a pair of old Roman amphorae in the window of a posh antiques store, sprinted across the rue des Saussaies against the light, then pushed through the meandering knots of afternoon window-shoppers crowding the Faubourg's sidewalk.

The day was bracingly cold; the cloudless sky the distinctive shade of azure cum cerulean that makes Paris skies in the fall, well, Paris skies in the fall. The Christmas decorations were already up in the windows of the dozens of haute couture shops crowded *côte-à-côte* on the Faubourg, and the intense woodsy perfume of chestnuts roasting on a charcoal brazier swept suddenly and mercilessly over him as he strode past the rue d'Aguessau, causing his mouth to water involuntarily.

Tom hadn't been to the embassy in months. Indeed, he seldom came to this part of town unless it was to share a bottle of young Bourgueil with his old friend Robert Savoye, who ran Le Griffonnier, a cozy wine bar sandwiched between a pair of shoe-box office buildings on rue des Saussaies opposite the Ministry of the Interior. So he was, if not amazed, then certainly taken aback at the overwhelming amount of security personnel present in this most upscale of Parisian neighborhoods.

Portable barricades lined the south side of the Faubourg, cordoning off both the Palais de l'Élysée and the entrance to the British embassy. The smartly dressed gendarmes in their spiffy caps, red-trimmed tunics, white dress gloves, holstered revolvers, and mirror-polished shoes who normally guarded the French president and the Brit diplomats' front doors had been augmented by dozens of tactical officers in midnight-blue fatigues tucked into jump boots and body armor. The cops had their war faces on. They carried compact FN submachine guns and long rubber truncheons and wore black leather gloves whose knuckles were filled with lead shot. Packets of flexi-cuffs hung from their duty belts. On the side streets, black vans and minibuses held SWAT teams. At the north end of rue d'Aguessau where it dead-ended at the rue de Surène, a huge windowless bus turned into a mobile command center bristling with VHF antennas, a GPS receiver, and a pair of satellite dishes that straddled the narrow street.

He continued past the Versace boutique, crossed the Faubourg, and walked past a cordon of cops who directed him toward a steel barrier funnel that blocked off the entrance to rue Boissy-d'Anglas. A pair of tactical officers stared at him as he approached the barrier.

Tom nodded at them. "Morning."

They nodded back but said nothing.

He continued down the street. On the left stood the service entrance to the grand Hotel Crillon, built as a palace for Louis XV. Marie Antoinette had taken singing lessons there. The hotel entrance stood facing the Place de la Concorde, where she'd been guillotined. On the right was the old Pullman Hotel, which had been rechristened in the 1990s as the Sofitel Faubourg St. Honoré. The Sofitel was where the embassy lodged mid-

and upper-grade diplomat visitors and TDYs. (Supergrades—minister-counselors and career ambassadors—were customarily put up at the Bristol or the Meurice, because as grand exalted pooh-bahs, they rated cars and drivers.)

The bar on the Sofitel's ground floor was exactly 158 paces from the embassy gate. At least that's how many steps it had been when Tom worked at Paris station. Now, where the rear of the embassy looked out on the rue Boissy-d'Anglas, there were barriers and armed cops. Tom was shunted to the Crillon's sidewalk, where he walked past dark stonework and twenty-foot windows, south to the corner. There, at a guard post, two SWAT *flics* checked his ID then allowed him to pass into a mazelike arrangement of steel barriers that blocked avenue Gabriel.

He slalomed past half a dozen submachine-gun–carrying officers, walking parallel to the Champs-Élysées, scanning the small green park to his left. There were tourists of course—a large clump of what appeared to be Indians or Pakistanis followed a guide carrying a ludicrous fluorescent pink parasol. Their tour had been stopped momentarily at the southeast corner barrier so that at the roadblock across the narrow ribbon of blacktop that led to the embassy gate, a black Mercedes could be checked.

Tom paused to watch as two armed men with mirrors inspected the undercarriage, one working each side of the vehicle. Two others popped the trunk lid and the hood and began poking around inside. The passengers were brought out. Each one was patted down and sniffed—no doubt for explosives—by a Malinois on a short leash while the entire performance was videoed by the Japanese. Tom wondered whether the videographer worked for al-Qa'ida. The AQN was known for its painstaking target assessments and contingency planning.

He resumed walking, scanning the park as he made his way to a second barricade. Even though he perceived nothing out of the ordinary, Tom's instincts told him there were DST watchers among the trees and on the benches. It had always been the French agency's practice to surveil the American embassy. And now that the threat level was elevated, they would have increased their vigilance.

Ten yards later, he was stopped by a second pair of tactical officers, who scrutinized his passport, actually holding it up so they could check the picture against his face. He was allowed to pass. But thirty feet on, at the barrier set just yards from the embassy gate itself, he was stopped a third time and his papers checked, this time by one armed police officer and an Inspector Clouseau look-alike in a baggy brown suit.

Tom counted 362 paces from the Sofitel. It was overkill, of course. The entire embassy compound was ringed by Jersey barriers set so that they would keep even the largest of truck bombs a hundred meters—more than a football field's length—from the structure itself. There was no way any car—even an embassy vehicle—could approach the outer security perimeter without being checked thoroughly.

Tom held his passport in his right hand and proceeded through the gate. To his right were the steps of the old embassy entrance. The first time he'd been in Paris—it was the early 1970s—he and his parents had walked off the Place de la Concorde and straight up the steps into the huge embassy foyer. No guards. No barriers. No ID checks. Not, at least, until they'd come to Post Number One, where a Marine sergeant in a starched tan shirt and razor-creased blue trousers asked to see their passports.

Now the old entrance was out-of-bounds. Tom was shunted along a narrow walkway to a gatehouse whose only door was built of heavy steel and dark-tinted bulletproof glass. A metallic voice with a French accent came through the three-inch speaker on the right side of the doorpost. "May I 'elp you?"

"I'm here to see Adam Margolis."

"Do you 'ave an appointment?"

"Yes."

"Your name?"

Tom recited it.

There was a twenty-second pause followed by a dissonant buzzing as the electronic lock on the door disengaged. Tom pulled at it. The damn thing was heavy. He entered a narrow security lock, manned by two French security contractors. They stood inside a bombproof enclosure, behind a chest-high counter and two-inch Plexiglas windows. Six television monitors displayed the area outside the gatehouse.

"Passport, please."

A tray emerged from the counter. Tom dropped the document into it. The security agent inspected it, then turned and marched six steps to a photocopier. He laid the passport on the bed, closed the cover, and pressed a button. He checked to see that the copy was good, then laid the sheet in the tray of a fax machine. As the photocopy transmitted, he picked up an embassy phone book, ran his finger down a page, then dialed an extension and said, "Mr. Margolis, you 'ave a visitor, a Mr. Stafford."

There was a pause. *"Bien sûr, monsieur."* The guard returned the passport to Tom. "Please 'ave a seat. Mr. Margolis will be with you in a few mi-*nute.*"

Tom settled himself on one of the three steel chairs lag-bolted to the wall. The gatehouse counter was U-shaped. Behind and above the desk, hermetically sealed from the gatehouse by another layer of bulletproof glass, was Marine Post Number One. Tom could make out a pair of sergeants looking down at him. He gave them a smile and an offhand wave and got one in return.

To the left and right of the counter were two portals—they were, in fact, metal detector–slash–explosives sniffer units—and ramps that led to steel-and-bombproof glass doors. The one on the left opened onto a ramp leading down to a patio. When Tom had worked at Paris station, the patio, which sat in front of the embassy's west wing housing the USIA library and cultural center, had been a well-kept garden filled with sculptures and stone benches. Now, in their stead, was a makeshift blast wall: a huge blue steel cargo container—the kind you see on oceangoing cargo ships— probably filled top to bottom with sandbags. Behind the container Tom could see that the glass in the big windows of the USIA cultural center had been replaced with thick plastic. The beautiful glass-and-iron French double doors were chained shut.

Under the watchful eye of the two French security guards, Tom panned over to the opposite side of the gatehouse. To the right of the counter was another steel-and-glass door, which opened onto a ramp that ended in what used to be the embassy's courtyard and now was used as a small parking lot. Behind the lot were the wide steps that led to the old formal entrance of the embassy. The steps hadn't been altered. But the entrance itself—which had been in use when Tom had worked there—had been replaced by a pair of utilitarian bombproof doors, in front of which were placed a series of squat, ugly concrete planters—more overkill.

Worse, Tom understood only too well that while these precautions might be perfect so far as the security personnel were concerned, they were an absolute disaster for the intelligence-gathering crew. During Tom's tenure in Paris, there had been dozens of walk-ins who'd come to the embassy and used the gatehouse telephone to ask to speak to an American political officer.

The embassy operators would always shunt those calls to CIA, which kept a small debriefing room off the main entrance, just inside the consular section. The location gave both case officers and walk-ins deniability. The room had audio and video capability, of course—there were even voice-stress detectors wired into the system. It didn't take long to separate wheat from chaff, either. Even a half hour of talk was sufficient to have the person's name and vitals run through the BigPond computer back at Langley. If it became necessary, the walk-in could be taken out through a series of back corridors, which ultimately led to a common wall shared with the British embassy. There, they'd be escorted through a door, walked down a passageway, and deposited at the Brits' service entrance on the Faubourg du St. Honoré. It was all very slick.

Now it was so hard to gain entrance to the embassy that no sane walk-in would dream of risking his hide by going anywhere near AMEMBASSY Paris. There were watchers in the street—Tom had no doubt al-Qa'ida, Tehran, and who knows who else had the embassy under constant surveillance. The bad guys could use teams of taxicabs driven by their agents—there were six cab stands on the Champs and the portions of avenue Gabriel that hadn't been closed down. They could man static positions by renting rooms at the Crillon (UBL had the budget to go first class, if necessary). They could tag-team watchers moving back and forth. It was probable that any walk-in who approached the compound would be photographed.

The heavy, layered security itself was another inhibitor. The French police demanded identification before anyone could get within a hundred yards of the place. Anonymity was impossible to maintain. When Tom had been posted here, walk-ins could make their way to the consulate or speak to a Marine guard, not be forced to go through a local rent-a-cop. Now the Marines were hermetically sealed beyond the gatehouse, there was no exterior telephone available, and unfettered entry to the consulate was impossible. Which left French security personnel as any walk-in's initial contact.

Tom had no doubt that the people behind the gatehouse's U-shaped desk reported to DST. They'd transmitted a photocopy of his passport on the fax before they'd bothered to call Adam Margolis's office. And to whom, pray tell, had the fax been sent? Tom was certain the bloody French would have completed a computer check on him by the time Adam Margolis came down from the station. DST would know he was going to meet with a CIA officer named Margolis.

The whole raison d'être of an embassy—to be able to soak up information that allows your nation to make intelligent foreign policy—had been perverted. From the CIA viewpoint, it was crazy. A majority of all successful agent recruitments began with a walk-in. But the embassy compound and its environs had been turned into a *zone sanitaire* and the obscene level of security made walking in virtually impossible. Indeed, between the barriers, and the watchers, and the ID checks, and the DST informers at the gatehouse counter . . . it was madness. Sheer madness.

23

3:19 P.M. Tom spotted Margolis as the tall, gangling youngster pushed through the embassy's front doors, loped down the stairs, and headed for the gatehouse. Margolis was in his late twenties with longish, dark curly hair. His befuddled, deer-in-the-headlights expression was accentuated by a pair of professorial round tortoiseshell eyeglasses with pink-tinted lenses. He wore a baggy blue pinstripe suit, button-down shirt, rep tie, and rubber-soled maroon-cum-brown leather Rockports, all of which pegged him immediately as a junior-grade American diplomat. Margolis's overall appearance, combined with the awkward gait and pouty lower lip, reminded Tom of the simpleton twit who'd been chief State Department spokesman in the second Clinton administration.

Margolis unlocked the gatehouse door with the pass that dangled around his neck on a long leash and made his way up the ramp, right hand outstretched, to where Tom was standing. "Adam Margolis. Sorry to keep you waiting but it's been a bear of a day."

"Tom Stafford. No problem." Tom looked at the young case officer, waiting for him to say something. When he didn't, Tom said, "Adam, can we go somewhere to talk?"

"Talk?" Margolis blinked uncomfortably as if no one had mentioned to him that Tom might want to actually converse. "What about right here?"

Was he insane? Tom nodded toward the two French security guards. "I'd rather go somewhere a little more private."

"Well, we can't go up to my office." Margolis's head moved birdlike, herky-jerky left, right, up, down. "It's restricted."

Tom felt like rolling his eyes. "It's all right."

The case officer's eyes blinked wildly. "How about the commissary?" He looked over at the French security officer. "I can take him to the commissary, can't I?"

"You will need a pass, Mr. Margolis." The officer reached under the counter and extracted a laminated blue badge with a huge black *V* on it. "You must wear this visibly at all times," he said as he painstakingly annotated the badge's six-digit number in a ledger. He looked over at Tom. "Your passport, please, monsieur."

Tom had no intention of passing through the metal detector. He focused on Margolis's face and winked. "How about we take a walk? I'll buy you a drink up the street."

Blink-blink. Tom could actually hear the gears inside Margolis's head engaging. Then the CIA officer's head cocked in Tom's direction. "Okay. But I have to go back and get a pad and paper."

3:35 P.M. They walked east through the security checkpoints in silence. As they approached the corner of the rue Boissy-d'Anglas, Tom said, "So, how do you like Paris?"

"It's okay," Margolis said. "French are pretty standoffish these days, given the political situation."

"Uh-huh."

"I've had a hard time meeting people."

"How's your French?"

"About a two."

That wasn't anywhere near fluent—it was something akin to high school French.

"Arabic?"

"Here and there." Margolis shrugged. "But I'm a three-plus in Spanish."

That would be helpful . . . in Madrid. Tom shook his head. And this kid was supposed to keep an eye on Islamists?

"Maybe you should take French classes. Or Arabic."

"Why?" Margolis's shoulders heaved once again. "Washington won't pay. And with the euro so high . . ." His voice trailed off. "Was it like that when you were here?"

"Not really." Tom's small trust fund had made it possible for him to augment his meager CIA housing allowance and rent a decent two-bedroom apartment in a high-ceilinged courtyard building just off the rue de Courcelles in the seventeenth. Plus, he'd spoken four-plus French and four-minus Arabic by the time he'd arrived in Paris. "Where do you live?"

"I've got a studio in Cormeilles-en-Parisis."

Tom winced. That was perhaps a thirty-five-minute ride on the sardine-can commuter trains followed by a couple of stops on the metro every morning. Given the fact that walk-ins weren't a possibility these days, how the hell were young officers like Margolis supposed to do their jobs properly—their jobs being to spot, assess, and recruit spies—when they weren't provided with the right tools?

Yes, tools. In this city, a nice apartment in central Paris was a tool of the trade. Because in the style-conscious City of Light, where you lived, how you dressed, and how fluent in French you were all mattered. No self-respecting functionary from the Ministry of Defense was going to take his chicly turned-out wife for cocktails chez Margolis if they had to take two or three metros from their flat in the seventh, then ride the local from Gare St. Lazare twenty-five kilometers northwest to some anonymous suburb, only to sit on a daybed, sip California jug wine, and eat microwaved rumaki bought at the embassy commissary. The French weren't big on white Zinfandel and pizza rolls.

Worse: if the kid worked the normal embassy hours, which was nine to six, how the hell was he supposed to run a two-hour cleaning route, meet with an agent for a couple of hours, then run a second cleaning route, go back to the office and write a report, *then* take a cab all the way home because there were no trains to Cormeilles-en-Parisis at two in the morning?

The problem was ubiquitous. CIA spent billions willy-nilly on technical espionage but counted every penny when it came to setting up their clandestine service personnel in a manner that would allow them to operate effectively. CIA's junior case officers, for example, were regulated by the same draconian rules on housing and expenses as their State Department colleagues. So everyone below the GS-15/FSO-1 level lived on the cheap. Housing was assigned by the number of people and grade. Young Adam Margolis, who was single—the studio apartment was Tom's evidence— was obviously a GS-10 or perhaps an 11. Income? Seventy thousand dollars. It might sound like a lot, but it wasn't enough to do the job in this expensive, cosmopolitan city, where each dollar bought only eighty euro cents—sometimes less.

"Got a car?"

Blink-blink. "I only wish."

"What about a motorcycle?"

The kid looked at him with wounded eyes. "I never learned how to ride."

Margolis was screwed. Full stop, end of story. Because the bottom line, when you crunched the numbers, was that central Paris was a financial impossibility. Therefore, Adam Margolis, American spy, would be forced to live in roughly three hundred square feet of space at a rent that could not exceed four hundred dollars a month and compelled by further economic constraints to commute by public transportation to and from his domicile. And entertainment? Tom guessed the bean counters at Langley had screamed bloody murder the first time the kid spent eighty-five euros taking a developmental to lunch. *Naturellement* young Adam Margolis didn't meet anyone. And just as *naturellement,* therefore, the intelligence product he produced—if he produced any intelligence product at all—was going to be second or third rate at best.

Sure, you could recruit agents on the cheap in Cairo, Dushanbe, or Kinshasa. And Tom had spent his share of time in the City of Light's Lebanese and Algerian restaurants, steakhouse chains, and fast-food cafés. You fit the level of entertainment to the lifestyle and social comfortability of the person you were trying to seduce. But there were times when a bottle of champagne at the George V or a meal at La Butte Chaillot were a necessity— and those cost money. So did a car—or even a motorcycle. Without your own transportation, going black became a lot more complicated. By forcing the kid to exist under such incredibly stupid limitations, Langley was dooming him to failure.

Tom led Margolis back through the maze of barriers, turned the corner onto the rue Boissy-d'Anglas, and headed north. He thought about stopping in the bar of the Sofitel, but marched Margolis past the entrance. He didn't want Margolis running into anyone he knew. Better to take him somewhere he'd never been. Someplace quiet.

3.54 P.M. Tom ushered Margolis through the doorway of Le Griffonnier, walked past the neat bar to one of the small round tables close to the rear staircase, pulled out a chair, and gestured. "Please."

Margolis dropped obediently into the chair and swiveled to take a look around as Tom slid between the marble-topped tables and sat on the tan leather banquette, his back to the wall. "Nice," the kid said. "Nice place."

"Quiet," Tom said. "Private." The proprietor, Robert Savoye, was nowhere to be seen. Neither was Rufus, the friendly wirehaired griffon who'd been retired from hunting because his nose had given out. These days, he lived in the bar and grew fat on snippets of cheese and sausage supplied by willing customers.

"So," Tom said, "what would you like?"

"I've developed a taste for red wine lately," Margolis said, almost guiltily.

"Nothing wrong with that. Had lunch?"

The youngster sighed. "Uh-huh. Commissary."

"Gotcha." Tom nodded. He signaled for the barman, ordered some *saucisson sec,* a selection of cheeses, a plate of sliced tomato, a bowl of baguette slices with butter on the side, and a bottle of Bourgueil—a 1997 Vaumoreau from Pierre-Jacques Druet.

When the man withdrew, Tom said, "So much for red wine." He grinned. "And what vintage are you?"

Margolis gave him a shy smile. "I was accepted into DI in '99. Went in right after grad school."

The light in Tom's brain switched on. The kid was one of Langley's analysts turned case officers. "Where?"

"GW—did my undergraduate work there, too."

"Major?"

"Poly sci. Minor in Spanish lit."

"Why make the choice you did?"

"The truth? Kinda because I was at loose ends. Didn't know what to do. Had no trade, really, although I really enjoy writing analysis. Plus, there was the patriotic thing. My father spent thirty years in the Navy. Retired as an O-6—a captain. My choice made my folks proud."

"Didn't you want to follow in your dad's footsteps?"

"Nope. Or go to State, either. He was an attaché in Chile for three years. I went to school there. I dealt with embassy people a lot. It wasn't something I wanted to do. So the other thing, it just, you know, made sense."

"How are you finding it?"

"I liked the writing part a lot. I was assigned to L.A. Division," Margolis sighed. "Even did one tour in Guatemala. But after 9/11, they came around and sorta kinda ordered a bunch of us to volunteer for DO training at the Farm."

"'Sorta kinda ordered'?"

Margolis leaned across the table. "You know how it was back then. Seventh floor leaked all sorts of stories about how we were gearing up, increasing the operational side—paramilitary and case officers. So they had to have bodies—and I was one of 'em."

"How did you feel about the change of disciplines?"

"Not especially comfortable. But they said it was fast-track." He shrugged. "I got my pseudo—Henry J. NOTKINS—and they put us through the training in eight weeks. Then I worked the desk at L.A. for six months—felt good about that. But then they assigned me to Paris and I went through eight weeks of French-language training. Came over to the embassy"—the kid counted on his fingers—"nine months ago."

"How're you doing?"

"Everything's a lot tougher than I thought. Plus, they make it hard for you to do your work." He leaned in toward Tom conspiratorially. "Most of the time you just sit around the office and read the papers." He sat back. "I bet it wasn't like that when you worked here."

The kid was exhibiting vulnerabilities. How could he? That was one of the first things they teach you in basic—do not reveal. Tom decided to practice a little empathy tradecraft. "You'd be surprised," he snorted. "Even in my day—which wasn't so long ago—you had to fight the system to get anything done. It is worse now, though. I left last winter. Just couldn't deal with the hurdles."

"Know what's the most frustrating thing? It's the word *can't*. It's—" Margolis caught movement reflected in the mirror behind Tom and stopped midthought as the barman approached.

The barman set the food on the table, then showed Tom the Bourgueil. Tom looked at the bottle and nodded. The barman yanked the cork and handed it to Tom, who sniffed appreciatively, then pointed at his companion's glass. "My friend will taste."

Tom watched as Margolis swirled the wine and sniffed it. "Raspberries," the younger man exclaimed. He looked up at the barman. "Framboises. *C'est bon, ça!*" Then he tasted, grinned, and looked at Tom. "That's wonderful. Where is it from?"

Tom looked up at the barman. "Leave the bottle, please. I'll pour." He turned back to Margolis. "It's a Loire wine from vineyards right opposite Chinon. Got a little bit more body than Chinon." He grinned. "And it hasn't been discovered yet—so let's keep this all need-to-know."

Margolis nodded eagerly in agreement. "I'll create a compartment. Only mention"—he picked up the bottle and examined it—"Bourgueil in the bubble." He took a second look at the label and did a double take. "Tom," he exclaimed, "I don't believe it. It's already a classified wine!"

Tom smiled, then steered the younger man back on course. "So it's tough."

"*Can't.* That's the big word around the office. 'Can't do this,' or 'Can't be done.' What they *mean* is they won't do it—or they're incapable." Margolis took a big gulp of wine. "Everything's 'Daddy, may I?' and the answer's always 'No, you can't.'" He snagged a piece of sausage on a toothpick, popped it into his mouth, and washed it down with Bourgueil. "Plus, there's my languages. Like I said, I'm three-plus in Spanish. Frankly, I'd rather have gone to L.A.—do a tour in Buenos Aires, Santiago—even San Salvador. I understand the culture, and there's lots of action these days—except nobody believes me when I tell them."

Margolis leaned forward. "Did'ja know UBL's people are starting to liaise with some of the Salvadoran gangs—paying big bucks to have themselves smuggled into Texas or Arizona? Boy, when I heard that, I thought to myself, That's *something*. But all I got was, 'What's your point?' I'm telling you, so far as the seventh floor is concerned, Latin America doesn't exist. If you want to get ahead these days, you gotta be in DO, you gotta do CT, and you better do it in Europe or take a thirty-day Iraq tour." He shook his head, poured himself more wine, drained the glass, then held it, toast-like, in front of his nose. "Baghdad? *Me?* Fuggedaboudit. So, here I am. Henry J. NOTKINS, Parisian counterterrorist."

24

5:07 P.M. The wine bar had filled up—mostly bureaucrats from the Ministry of the Interior headquarters, which sat directly across the rue des Saussaies. They crowded the bar, drank Sancerre, Juliénas, and Chinon, nibbled on sausage and tartines and gossiped. Tom and Adam were on their second bottle of Bourgueil—most of it inside Adam. Way before 4:30, the kid had pulled his legal pad off the table and sat on it. He'd never made a note.

Tom felt slightly guilty, but only because shaking information out of Margolis was easier than the "spot, assess, develop, recruit" training sessions at the Farm where retired case officers role-played prospective agents. He'd preferred to have spent his afternoon mentoring Adam Margolis—helping him to do what the guy had joined CIA to do in the first place. Indeed, there was probably nothing so wrong with the youngster that a couple of years of intense inculcation, tempering, and trial and error couldn't fix.

Like introducing him to a place like this, where by spending two or three hours just listening to the conversations going on around you, you'd pick up enough decent gossip from the Ministère de l'Intérieur to write a good report. Like making sure he blended in and understood enough French so he could get the job done. Tom caught a glimpse of the oblivious look on Margolis's face. Jeezus—like making sure that the kid had the proper antennae to realize where he was in the first place.

But alchemy wasn't Tom's job anymore. Nor was it in his interest. He was there to elicit and—if the stars aligned—to recruit this naïf as a penetration agent. He wasn't there to teach. And since he'd war-gamed the encounter, he understood that the best way to do so was the 10-90 ploy.

The 10-90 was an elicitation technique used both by case officers and good journalists. You used buzzwords that suggested you knew a lot more than you actually did. Some of the time, if you caught the target off guard, you'd draw them out and fit a few more pieces of the puzzle together.

So Tom began with something he actually did know: "I hear you made an interesting contact recently."

"Oh?" Margolis cocked his head in Tom's direction. "Who?"

"Iranian chap. Short guy. Wispy white hair. Recently deceased."

"Shahram?" Margolis's eyes went wide. "You heard about *that*?"

"It's all over Langley—and beyond."

"You coulda fooled me." Margolis took a gulp of wine and leaned forward conspiratorially. "Harry Z—that's my boss, Harry Z. INCHBALD. Harry Z said they were round-filing my report. The guy's a fabricator, is what Harry told me. No credence whatsoever."

Tom knew exactly who Harry Z. INCHBALD was. His real name was Liam McWhirter. He'd been Tom's boss in Cairo in 1989. At CTC, Tom was McWhirter's superior. INCHBALD's CTC cubicle had been five or six down from Tom's in the warren of cubicles that housed the unit's Islamic section. He was a fat, sloppy burnout of a case officer with a scraggly beard and thinning butterscotch hair styled in an extreme comb-over. A Turkish speaker who'd liaised with MIT during two tours in Ankara, McWhirter had been eased out of CTC after the security guards had twice in three weeks discovered him passed out in his car in the west parking lot at about 8 P.M., an empty liter bottle of Absolut on the seat and the motor idling.

And what had they done with McWhirter? Fired him? Sent him to rehab? Forced him into retirement? No way. They'd promoted him to section chief and posted him to Paris.

That was the whole frigging problem with the panjandrums at Langley. They kept the people like Harry Z around, while they threw away the Sam Watermans.

"Round-filed?" Tom pulled himself back on track and put a dour expression on his face. "Didn't happen."

"Whoa."

Tom refilled Margolis's glass. "In fact, your home office just created a task force based on what the Iranian told you."

Margolis's face went white. "You're kidding."

"Negatory." Tom shook his head. "And it's based right here."

"At my . . . office?"

"On the money."

"Why?"

"I guess because the information that you received from the contact was pretty damn valuable."

Margolis stuck his lower lip out. "That's not what Harry Z told me."

"Maybe headquarters didn't tell Harry Z."

"But it's Harry's section." Margolis leaned forward and whispered. "You know—the AQN stuff."

"Maybe Harry didn't tell you." Tom shrugged. He gave the kid a concerned look. "I'd be worried."

"Why?"

"Office politics. You've seen the leaks from headquarters lately. Everyone on the seventh floor is scrambling to cover their butts."

"What does that have to do with me?"

"They're popping smoke grenades," Tom said. "They're trying to distract from the fact that HQ is incapable of doing just about anything effectively. So maybe they create a mirage—an AQN task force based here in Paris. Except it doesn't exist."

Margolis took a big glug of his wine. "I don't understand."

"I can tell you that on paper, there is now a counterterrorism task force based in Paris, specifically working on the information that the Iranian gave you."

"Who told you?"

"We have our sources, Adam."

"Okay, let's say, for argument's sake, you're correct. But what good does it do if the whole thing's a mirage?"

"It does the DCI a lot of good. He can go up to Capitol Hill and tell the intelligence oversight committees he's recruited a well-placed unilateral source in Paris who has twenty-four-karat information about the AQN's capabilities and intentions."

"But it's a lie."

"The intelligence oversight committees don't know it's a lie. So the short answer to your question is that making up a story about a new, forward-based counterterrorism task force gets Congress off CIA's back."

"But there won't be any results if there's no real task force."

"Results?" Tom snorted. "Congress doesn't care about results. Know what we used to call the members of the oversight committees? Mushrooms. Mushrooms, because we'd feed 'em manure and keep 'em in the dark and they'd grow fat and happy. Congress never gave a damn about results. Neither the House nor the Senate ever cared whether CIA was doing its job."

"Mushrooms." Margolis giggled. "That's funny." He turned serious. "But it's inconceivable to me. I mean, I didn't get any information from the Iranian. All he wanted was money."

That was a surprise. Tom fought to keep his reaction neutral. "The Iranian asked for money?"

"He wanted the whole twenty-five mil reward we've posted. Half a million up front and the rest when he brought him in and we verified the DNA is what he told me."

"Him?"

"The *guy*. The *big* guy."

It was time to let the kid correct him. So Tom went for the obvious choice. "UBL?"

Margolis gave him a negative wag of the head. Tom gave the kid the reaction he wanted. He looked puzzled. He stroked his chin. He scratched his cheek. Then he leaned forward far enough to make sure his lips couldn't be read, and stage-whispered, "Imad?"

"Bingo." Margolis's head bobbed up and down once. "You got it."

"Wow. What else did the Iranian tell you?"

"That was all. That he could lay his hands on the big guy—if we came up with a down payment."

"He didn't talk about anybody else?"

"Not to me."

"Hmm." Tom played with his wineglass. He let the kid watch him think. After about half a minute, he rapped the table with his knuckles. "Adam, sooner or later the story's going to come out."

"What story?"

"The story about your contact."

"Why?"

Tom looked at the kid earnestly and lied through his teeth. "Because it will. Because they leak stories from the seventh floor. Lots of finger-pointing. 'This division screwed up.' 'That case officer screwed up.' It's all smoke screen—to save their own jobs. And you've got a problem because when the *merde* hits the *ventilateur* and it comes out that there is no task force—that it's all been make believe—the fingers are going to start point-ing at you."

"Whose fingers?"

"The head office. Harry Z. The press."

"But I didn't *do* anything," Margolis said, alcohol-motivated anger bubbling to the surface. "I just met with the Iranian."

"You're the junior man." Tom let that thought sink in. "You're the disposable, Adam. Remember what they taught you about disposables at the Farm?"

Tom watched the kid's face metamorphose. Margolis stuck his lower lip out. "That pisses me off."

Showtime. Tom looked at the younger man solicitously. "Maybe I can help."

The youngster spread butter on a slice of baguette, topped it with two slices of sausage, and stuffed the whole thing into his mouth. "How?"

"Look, I have—*we* have—really good contacts back at"—Tom leaned forward—"the home office. You realize that, right?"

Margolis nodded. He looked at Tom. "Y'know, I really think it was the money." He chewed and swallowed. "Now that I think about it, Harry said the home office was very pissed about the money, but they thought the info might turn out to be pretty good."

That was another revelation. Tom checked to see whether Margolis had any awareness of what he was saying. The kid's eyes told him the answer was no. Tom took things up a notch. "Where did you meet the contact?"

"The Iranian? He came to the embassy."

"When?"

"That was the strange thing. He called on Friday the tenth of October."

"You're sure of the date?"

"Positive."

"When did he call?"

"Late in the day."

"*When,* Adam?"

The kid's *in vino veritas* expression displayed confusion. "I told you. Late." He caught the piqued look on Tom's face. "Oh, *when*. After five. I spoke to him for a couple of minutes. He introduced himself. He told me he'd had dealings with us before. He said he had something big that—and he said this right on the open line—that he could lay his hands on . . . you know, the big guy. But it would cost us plenty. I knew I'd have to get back to him, of course. So I did everything by the book. I was noncommittal. I asked for a twenty-four-hour phone number and explained we'd be in touch."

"Then?"

"I took my notes to Harry Z, dropped them off at about five forty-five, then I went home. Harry must have walked it up the ladder back at HQ because he called me Saturday afternoon. Told me to be standing on the front steps of the embassy on Sunday morning at eight forty-five, to have a pad and a tape recorder with me, and to talk to this guy under alias."

"What alias were you to use?"

"Jeff Stone."

The order sounded odd to Tom. CIA's walk-in debriefing room on the embassy's ground floor had audio recording capabilities, and he mentioned that fact to Margolis.

"Seemed strange to me, too. But Harry was very specific. He described the Iranian to me. I was to watch for him—that's easy enough, given the maze of barriers we have out front—wait until he was admitted to the gatehouse, then pick him up, walk him into the embassy, and listen to what he had to say. I was to make absolutely no commitments then write a report and have it on Harry's desk by nine Monday morning."

Something wasn't right. "When Harry called Saturday, what did he tell you about the contact?"

"Tell me?" Margolis blinked. "He described him physically, if that's what you mean."

"No—I mean what he said about who the guy was—his background, his past relationship with . . . where you work."

"Harry?" The kid popped the last chunk of sausage into his mouth. "He didn't say a thing."

"And what checking did you do?"

"None. I told you—he called late on Friday and we close the office promptly at six. I was told to be at the embassy Sunday morning." He looked at Tom. "I was operating blind."

Close the office promptly at six? Clock-punching spies? It was frigging inconceivable. Still, if this drivel was true, and Tom had no reason to believe he was getting a runaround because none of the kid's body language suggested the faintest hint of deception, then Margolis was a bigger schmuck than Tom had thought and Shahram had been totally mishandled.

Even an idiot would have Googled Shahram's name to see if anything came up. But Margolis had done nothing. Tom groaned inwardly but kept a poker face. "How did it play out?"

"Just like Harry said it would. I was a couple of minutes early. I waited. The Iranian was late—he showed up at nine, on the dot. I guess there'd been some misunderstanding about the time. I went down to the gatehouse, walked him in, we talked for about half an hour."

"Did he bring any paper?"

Margolis shrugged. "Nope."

"Nothing? Then how did he substantiate his claim?"

Margolis's expression started to change and he crossed his arms.

Tom eased up. "You know what I'm saying—if a walk-in doesn't offer a piece of paper . . ."

". . . We're always supposed to ask for something. Insist. I know that," Margolis said peevishly. "But he claimed he wasn't carrying any paper. He kept saying that within seventy-two hours after he got a down payment, he'd pass us a twenty-four-karat package."

"Those were his words?"

"Uh-huh."

Tom looked into Margolis's eyes. "What did he tell you, Adam?"

Margolis blinked. "They orange-tabbed what he said, Tom.[28] I don't think I'm supposed to get into that. It would look bad on the polygraph."

"Suppose I tell you, then. The Iranian told you there would be an attack somewhere in the Middle East within the next week to ten days."

The astonished look on the kid's face was confirmation enough. But Adam didn't disappoint. "How did you *know*? Who told you?"

Tom smiled, and deflected. "Remember—I have a lot of friends at your headquarters."

The answer, of course, was that Tom hadn't known. Not exactly. It had been a guess. But an educated guess. He'd gone over all the notes from his lunch with Shahram. Obviously, Shahram had put some of the puzzle pieces together. At lunch, he'd tied the Gaza bombing to the other two blasts. Which told Tom that Shahram had realized before October 15 that Imad Mugniyah and Tariq Ben Said were both in Israel and something nasty was imminent.

The question, of course, was that if CIA had the information, why had Langley not acted? Because it hadn't. There had been no warnings sent to Tel Aviv—or anywhere else. There had been no proactive security mea-sures taken. It was as if Langley hadn't given a damn.

But Tom wasn't sitting at Le Griffonnier to figure out what Langley had or hadn't known—or to decipher the motives behind its negligent behavior. He wanted to know everything about Shahram Shahristani's embassy meeting. Because that meeting was the key to everything that had followed.

[28]An orange tab designates a Top Secret document.

25

IT WAS TIME TO START the cold pitch. Tom looked into Adam's eyes. "I told you I knew what the Iranian said." He paused, his eyes entreating. "I need your help, Adam."

Margolis's voice took on a solicitous tone. "You were right on the money, Tom. He said he could provide the big guy on a platter. His words. Dead or alive. His words. He said he had information on other operations, but they'd cost us more."

"That was all?"

"Like you said, he said one attack was imminent."

"Did he say where?"

"He told me it would occur in Israel within the next week to ten days."

"And what did you do?"

"I put it all on tape, just as I'd been ordered to. I took notes, too."

"And?"

"And then it was finished. I told him we'd get back to him."

"And you escorted him back to the gatehouse?"

"Yes. I'd just picked up my stuff and was ushering the Iranian down the front steps when Harry Z came charging through the lobby and called to us from the portico. That surprised me, because I didn't even know he was in the building."

Tom said nothing.

"Harry introduced himself to the Iranian—under alias, of course." Margolis picked up his wineglass and drained it. "We all walked together down to the gatehouse. Just before we got there, Harry said he'd forgotten something upstairs, but he'd wanted to meet Shahram and thank him for his help. He gave Shahram an envelope. Said it wasn't much, but he hoped it would compensate Shahram for his time, just in case the other thing didn't work out."

"What was the Iranian's reaction?"

Margolis tapped his fingertips together. He cocked his head in Tom's direction. "Reaction?"

"When he got the envelope."

Margolis pondered the question. Tom could see the gears in the kid's head engaging. Margolis's face screwed up. He bit his lower lip. "I dunno, he . . . he just kind of gave me this strange look—he stared at me. And he stared at Harry Z, and then he slipped the envelope into his pocket. Never looked inside. And he said, *'Au revoir,'* and I escorted him down to the gatehouse."

"That was it?"

"Yup. Never said another word." Margolis paused while Tom emptied the last of the Bourgueil into the kid's glass. "But the look on his face. It was . . . strange, Tom."

"Describe his expression if you can."

The kid thought for about half a minute. "He was . . . kaleidoscopic. His face went from, like, bewilderment—no, it was darker than that. Bemusement. To . . . resignation, and then he looked at both of us with this incredible, smoldering contempt. It was amazing, actually."

Of course it was. Shahram had realized at that instant he was a dead man walking. Tom had seen the amount of static surveillance around the embassy. On a Sunday morning the watchers could be anyone: dog walkers, trysting lovers, tourists, joggers, or bored cabdrivers. The French, the Arabs, the Israelis, al-Qa'ida—they'd all be there. Some would have video.

Shahram had probably gone straight back to Cap d'Antibes—until he'd reached Tom and confirmed the lunch at Gourmets des Ternes. No wonder DST had had a team waiting at the airport.

Obviously, Shahram had understood—he was a professional after all—that he'd been set up. He'd had to realize, when Harry handed him the envelope right in front of all that static surveillance, that someone at Langley wanted him targeted.

But why? Maybe because Shahram knew how deaf, dumb, and blind CIA really was. Or maybe because he knew about Imad Mugniyah and the Palestinians running joint ops. Or perhaps just because Shahram had screwed with Langley for two decades and the Langley bureaucracy was sick and tired of losing. And the look on Shahram's face had said it all—except Adam Margolis had been oblivious.

Tom had seen a similar expression on the face of a man about to die once before. It was in a photograph that hung in Rudy's cubicle back at 4627's Washington offices.

One of the paramilitary agents Rudy'd run in the old days was a Cuban-American B-contract named Felix Rodriguez. Felix was a Bay of Pigs veteran who'd been fighting Castro since 1959. In 1967, when he was twenty-six, CIA dispatched him to Bolivia to help capture Ernesto "Che" Guevara.

Felix did his job well. On October 8, 1967, acting largely on information Felix had developed, Bolivian forces captured Che. On the ninth, Felix flew to the tiny village of La Higuera to debrief the legendary Marxist guerrilla and terrorist.

There is only one photograph of Che alive on that day. It was taken with Felix's camera. He and Che are standing, surrounded by Bolivian soldiers. The look on Che's face tells you he knows he's going to die. It is an expression that merges bemusement, resignation, and contempt. Tom had spent a lot of time staring at the photo, wondering what had gone through Che's mind.

Now, remembering Shahram's phone call, he had some idea. *"I have an engaging story to tell you,"* Shahram had said. *"Très provocateur. You will be fascinated. We must meet tomorrow. Must. I will not accept an excuse."*

But it hadn't been Shahram's coaxing words that had made Tom change his schedule. It had been the man's urgent tone. But now that he thought about it, he understood that Shahram hadn't projected urgency at all. He was signaling desperation—*oougah, oougah, dive-dive-dive* desperation. And Tom hadn't caught it. He hadn't. Not until now, goddamnit.

He fought his way back through the memory to focus on Adam Margolis. "Adam," he said, "what did you do . . . with the tape?"

"I transcribed it, checked it, and handed everything to Harry Z."

"Your notes, too?"

Margolis nodded. Tom remained silent, as if he was thinking. Finally, he said, "I think we can help fix things."

"Fix what?"

"Your problem."

"Problem?"

"Merde. Ventilateur."

Margolis's head bobbed up and down once. "Gotcha."

So far so good. The kid hadn't thrown his wine in Tom's face. That meant he was approachable. Now Tom had to set the hook. He had to make sure Margolis thought of this as a team effort. "There are three small snips of information at the embassy. Once we're sure about them, we can protect your back."

"Which are?"

Tom's gut was churning. *Thank you, Jesus. Margolis just bought in.* There'd been no "but-but-but." No reticence. Just "Which are?" Tom knew his foot was in the door, so he wasted no time. "One, we need to know what Harry Z did with the information you passed him. Two, we need to know who got hold of him with the instructions about the Sunday-morning meeting. And three, we need to see a copy of the transcript you gave Harry Z."

The kid emitted a low whistle. But he didn't object to any part of Tom's demands—either in body language or eye movement.

Margolis looked at Tom. "What time frame?"

He'd asked a specific question. The door cracked another inch. "Over the weekend in question. Harry called you on Saturday. Who messaged him?"

Margolis's eyes went wide. "How do I find *that* out?"

"I'd check the message logs," Tom said as matter-of-factly as he could.

"Message logs."

"Right."

"Where are they?"

"They're in the administrator's section of the SIPRNET."

That caused Margolis's first sign of vacillation. "They're on the secure network?"

Reinforce. Support. Bolster. But don't ask him to commit a crime. "It's nothing you're not cleared to do."

"But . . . but it's the *secure* net."

"And you're on it every day, aren't you?"

Margolis shrugged. "Sure. But I'm not an administrator." His eyes narrowed. "Who is the administrator?"

"If things work the same as they did when I was in Paris, Harry Z."

"But he has a password. I don't know it."

"When I was in Paris, the administrator's password was *GUEST*."

"You're kidding."

"All caps, of course."

"Jeezus," Margolis said. "My SIPRNET password is ten characters long and alphanumeric, and if I didn't have it written down on a card in my wallet, I'd never remember the damn thing."

Tom smiled indulgently and made a mental note for Reuven to get hold of Margolis's wallet at some point. Who knew what other jewels the kid kept on his person.

Margolis had no idea what was going on in Tom's head. "Okay, I'll try." The kid's mouth suddenly pruned up—like he'd licked a styptic pencil. "But what if they find out? They box me, you know."

"Nobody's going to ask you how many times you were on the secure network, Adam. You know as well as I do they're more interested in unauthorized meetings with foreign nationals or your sex life."

Margolis snorted. "As if I had one these days."

Tom tried to be avuncular. "The message log is easy, Adam. Piece of cake." He paused. "Now, as to what Harry did, it's all a matter of checking his out-box." He paused. The kid wasn't being balky, so he pressed on. "And as for the transcript, does Harry still take those afternoon breaks?"

"You know about them, too, eh?" Margolis's lips curled disparagingly. "Every damn day."

"As I recall, Harry's habit is to go to lunch, come back to the office, then leave again at about three for an hour or so."

Margolis's slight nod confirmed to Tom that the pattern hadn't changed. Tom winked roguishly at Margolis. "He just about always forgets to lock his safe, y'know." He caught Margolis's sudden smile. "Nuff said?"

"Gotcha." Margolis scrunched his chair closer to the table. The kid nodded and leaned forward conspiratorially. "When do we need the poop?"

Tom kept a straight face. "By the weekend, Adam. You're going to be a busy guy tomorrow. You may even have to work late." He paused and watched the kid drain the wine. "Don't worry—it'll all go smoothly. I'll come out to your place Saturday morning and we'll go over the stuff then." He caught the look on the kid's face. "Don't worry—I'll be clean." He gave Margolis a reassuring smile. "What's your cell-phone number?"

"Zero six, twenty-four, sixty-six, fourteen, eighty-two."

"I'll ring you if there's any kind of hiccup."

"Is there anywhere I can contact you?"

"You can leave me a voice mail at 4627." Tom recited the number.

"Got it." Margolis checked his watch, scraped his chair away from the table, and retrieved his yellow pad. He stood up, brushing crumbs from his suit as he did. "Gotta be going. Got a train to catch."

"Have a safe trip." Tom cocked his head at the younger man. "See you Saturday." He paused, then said, "How's eleven o'clock?"

The kid nodded and backed away from the table.

"You be waiting outside. I'll drive by and pick you up. We'll go someplace nice for lunch." Tom was gratified to receive a circled thumb-and-forefinger okay sign.

6:24 P.M. Tom watched Margolis go, fighting an uncharacteristic inclination to kick the kid's ass into next week. *He just didn't get it.* The meeting had been a setup. Shahram had told them there'd be an attack in Israel sometime in the next week to ten days. That had to be Gaza. Langley had done nothing—and Jim McGee had died. In fact, instead of checking on Shahram's information—which was on tape, according to Margolis—someone at Langley decided to paint a huge target on the Iranian's back, then step back and see what happened next. If nothing happened, then Shahristani was fabricating. And if Shahristani was murdered, then maybe his claims were worth following up.

Jeezus. And Adam Margolis and his boss, Harry Z—disposables who'd take the fall if Shahram was, in fact, murdered and the decision to dangle him was traced back to Langley—were the guys with the cans of Krylon.

It wasn't the first time a potentially valuable source had been screwed in that fashion. Tom remembered a 1988 case in Damascus that was equally appalling. There'd been a walk-in—a Lebanese Shia calling himself Hassan—who came to the embassy gates and asked to speak to an American diplomat.

He'd been met by an energetic young case officer named Bryan V. OFUTT[29] and ushered into the ground-floor debriefing room. Hassan claimed to know where three of the hostages who'd been captured by Islamic Jihad in Beirut were currently imprisoned. When OFUTT pressed for details, it became apparent to the case officer that Hassan was the real thing. Hassan knew, for example, the precise medicines being taken by one of the non-American hostages, an Indian engineer. He described in detail the appearance of Father Lawrence Martin Jenco, an American priest who'd been kidnapped by Imad Mugniyah in January 1985.

Most important, Hassan not only told OFUTT precisely in which building of the Sheikh Abdallah barracks compound in Lebanon's Bekáa Valley the hostages were being held, he also knew that their captors were not Hezbollah guerrillas but, in fact, Iranians. Islamic Revolutionary Guard Corps troops—the Seppah-e Pasdaran.

OFUTT slipped Hassan about twenty dollars in Syrian dinars and told him to wait. He went upstairs to the embassy's second floor, punched a combination into the cipher lock on the heavy door to the CIA station, and reported what the Lebanese had told him to his boss, Martin J. POTTER,[30] the station chief.

POTTER was a wreck of a man. Alcoholic, thrice divorced, and afraid of being up-and-outed, his instinctual reaction was to do nothing. But OFUTT was adamant—American lives might be at stake. And so POTTER used the secure phone and called Langley. The NE desk duty officer put POTTER on hold while he ran the message up the chain of command.

The CIA's director at the time was Judge William H. Webster. Webster was known inside the DO as the Stealth DCI because of his judicially cau-

[29]This is a pseudonym.
[30]This is a pseudonym, too.

tious disinclination to sign off on high-risk recruitments or operations. When asked what to do about Hassan, the DCI delegated the decision to his executive assistant, whom he'd brought from the FBI. The whole operation looked like a risky scheme to the G-man. And so, the seventh floor punted, tossing the decision back to NE Division.

But the NE Division chief and his deputy were both on vacation, and the deputy's deputy was taking two weeks of paternity leave. And so the determination on how to handle Hassan fell to the deputy deputy's assistant, a deskman pseudonymed Alfred F. PARDIGGLE. PARDIGGLE was a former reports officer who had been elevated to the DO under DCI Robert Gates's "cross-fertilization" program. He had no real-world operational experience. But PARDIGGLE did have a long-term fascination with popular espionage fiction.

And so what did PARDIGGLE do? He instructed Damascus station to hold off on any action until it had polygraphed Hassan. That instruction was pretty much by-the-book. But then PARDIGGLE decided to get cute. If the lie detector showed no deception, he cabled POTTER, the station chief was to dangle the Lebanese and see who nibbled at him.

PARDIGGLE had read about the dangle technique. Precisely where, he couldn't quite remember. Was it Clancy? Ludlum? Westlake? Freemantle? Deighton? Whatever. Point was, it had worked. On the page.

OFUTT protested strenuously. Even if Hassan's claims weren't true, Langley was putting the man in harm's way. The first rule of case-officerdom, he told his boss, was that you don't screw your agents. Cable PARDIGGLE, said OFUTT, and tell him to shove it.

POTTER, however, was in no mood to contradict the suits at Langley. The closest polygrapher was in Cairo and he had a day's work left before he could head for Damascus. So Hassan was bundled out the back door but told to return Saturday morning. The polygraph would be held at the Damascus consulate, located a block and a half from the main embassy.

At 9 A.M. on Saturday morning, the polygrapher and his portable polygraph, along with POTTER and OFUTT, who carried yellow legal pads and a tape recorder, all marched hup-two, hup-two from the embassy gates down the street to the consulate—which of course was closed.

POTTER unlocked the door and the Americans disappeared inside.

Half an hour later, Hassan made his way to the thick front door, rapped on it, and was admitted. None of this, of course, was lost on the Syrian Mukhabarat[31] teams that kept both the consulate and the embassy under twenty-four-hour surveillance.

Hassan emerged from the consulate an hour and a half later. Right there, in the doorway, POTTER pulled a white envelope out of his jacket pocket, displayed a thick wad of cash, and handed the envelope to Hassan. The Lebanese self-consciously jammed the money into his trousers then scampered off—right into the waiting arms of the Mukhabarat, who wanted to know why someone was meeting with American diplomats on a day when the embassy was closed.

Given their interrogation methods, it didn't take the Syrians long to discover who Hassan was—and what he'd told CIA. Their reaction—which OFUTT discovered six months later—was to bundle Hassan into the trunk of a car and deliver him bound and gagged to Imad Mugniyah, who tortured the unfortunate Lebanese for three days, then finally dispatched him with a bullet to the brain.

PARDIGGLE's reaction had been . . . sanguine. "Next time, I suggest you interview dangles during business hours," was how he responded to OFUTT's furious cable.

Tom reached inside his jacket, unplugged the microphone concealed behind his lapel, and switched off the digital recorder he'd been running for the past two and a half hours. He drained the last of his wine and stared at the crowded bar, his fingers tapping on the marble tabletop. Something about the meeting with Margolis was gnawing at him, but he couldn't put his finger on it. He called for the check and laid a stack of euros on the saucer.

The bulb went off just as the waiter cleared the plates and glasses. *The recruitment had been too easy.* How had Sam Waterman put it? Sam had defined these sorts of situations as examples of Waterman's First Law of Espionage, which went: "When Something Is Too Good to Be True, It Is in Fact Too Good to Be True."

Langley was setting a trap for him. Why, he had no idea—except for

---

[31]Secret police.

Tony Wyman's cryptic remark earlier in the week that CIA headquarters had refused to fund 4627's Ben Said operations. But reasons didn't matter—not now. Oh, he'd find a way to foil the ambush. But now there was no time to think about devising countermeasures. He had to get home, change clothes, and meet Reuven. They were scheduled to put the bug in Ben Said's safe house tonight.

VII

RUE LAMBERT

26

TOM FROZE, the key to his apartment six inches from the dead bolt. The intrusion device he'd carefully placed before leaving in the morning had been disturbed. That meant someone had tried to gain entry—or was waiting for him inside.

His heart started to thump. Slowly, he backed away from the door so he could gather his thoughts.

He'd been careful—or so he thought. Given the level of static surveillance around the embassy, he'd performed a cleaning route, taking an indirect course from Le Griffonnier to the Miromesnil metro stop. There, instead of heading southwest toward Passy, he went the opposite way, to Gare St. Lazare. He'd left the metro and used the station's multiple exits and entryways to confuse any pursuers, crossed the square against the light, and then walked against the traffic flow up the rue de la Pépinière, turned the corner at Place St. Augustin, and dropped into the metro, switched lines twice, rode to Villiers, then on to Étoile. There, he changed lines again, took the metro two stops to Franklin D. Roosevelt, meandered for six minutes, letting two trains come and go, then caught the third one to Trocadéro. He raced through the passageway, changed lines once more, and rode one stop to the Passy stop—a three-minute walk from his apartment. At no time had he sensed he was being pinged.

And yet the signs were clear. Someone had made surreptitious entry into his apartment. The *minuterie* light went out. Tom reacted. Quickly, he brought himself under control. He slid along the wall to the light button and pressed it. Then he carefully made his way back to his doorway, stopped, and waited until the light went out again.

He dropped to hands and knees, pressed his eye to the threshold, peered through the crack. There were lights on.

Behind him, he heard mechanical grinding. He jumped to his feet. The elevator stopped. He heard the inside being pulled open. The *minuterie* went on, the elevator door was pushed outward, and Tom's neighbor Madame Grenier stepped into the corridor.

She acknowledged his presence with a regal nod. "Good evening, Monsieur Stafford."

"Good evening, Madame Grenier." He waited until she found her own keys, unlocked the door across the corridor from his, and went inside.

He slid the key into the bolt. Turned it. Put pressure on the handle. Pushed downward. Eased the door open slowly.

No reaction. The foyer light was on but the rest of the apartment was dark. Stealthily, Tom made his way into the small kitchen on his left. Pulled the biggest chef's knife he had from the butcher-block holder on the counter, held the weapon point up behind his back, and headed for the living room. That's where the concealed safe was.

But the living room was empty. He stood there for a moment, straining to hear any anomalous sounds. There were none. The pipes gurgled. He could hear the muffled traffic noise from the street. He gnawed on his lower lip for a few seconds, steeled himself, then started for the bedroom.

Halfway across the big Sarouk, he stepped on a loose floorboard that sounded—at least to Tom—as loud as an air horn. He cursed his clumsiness and gripped the knife tighter.

And then, from the bedroom, came MJ's voice. "Tom? Tom, is that you?"

"MJ?" He exhaled a huge, noisy sigh of relief. "My God, what a wonderful surprise," he called out, quickly looking for some place to put the knife down. He set it on the coffee table then went to the bedroom. "What on earth are you doing here?"

She sat up in the bed. She was wearing one of his shirts. Her long hair was all askew. She'd taken off her makeup. She looked absolutely, sleepily, sexily magnificent. "I guess I conked out. Didn't you get my message?"

He took her into his arms. "No—I mean, what are you *doing* here?"

"They suspended me. So I decided—"

"They? Who? What?"

She smiled at him indulgently. "Don't worry. It's the best thing that ever happened." She caressed his cheek. "Mrs. ST. JOHN went ballistic when I told her I'd been in Israel. She thought it had something to do with the photographs. She threatened to revoke my clearance, Tom."

"Can she do that?"

"Who cares."

"I do."

MJ looked at him. "Why?"

"Because you'll need your clearance to work for 4627." He embraced her. "Suspended, huh? Good. You're right. Best thing that ever happened." He stroked her hair. "We'll celebrate." He kissed her gently on the lips. "But we'll celebrate tomorrow."

"Tomorrow?" She pulled him closer. "What about tonight?"

"Tonight I've got a date with a bald Israeli."

27

REUVEN HAD BEEN BUSY. He'd isolated Ben Said's safe house through the process of deduction and through experience—field smarts. Terrorists already understood that safe houses could be identified through the utilities. If you had ten apartments in a building, all of them allegedly occupied full-time, and one had an electric bill that was only 10 percent of the others, it was logical to deduce that either the occupant spent a lot of time on the road or that you'd located a safe house. So the bad guys compensated these days by leaving their lights on.

Reuven also knew that in Paris, no terrorist worth his WMD would ever use the local phone system. Parisian phones both public and private were too damn easy to bug. DST had the capability of eavesdropping on any line in the city within minutes, and unlike the FBI, they didn't need to beg for search warrants or have their FISA paperwork approved by some ACLU-loving judge to get the go-ahead.

So in Paris, terrorists tended to communicate either in person or by e-mail. Or, to make calls these days, the bad guys often used prepaid cell phones, which they'd change on a daily or even twice-daily basis. The phones themselves were cheap, and the prepaid SIM cards, available anywhere in Europe, made it easy to switch numbers and carriers.

Bottom line: the safe house would be the only apartment in the building that either didn't have phone service at all or didn't bill any outgoing calls. So Reuven had used his contacts and checked the building's utility records. As he suspected, the electric bills were all pretty much the same. But the phone bill for the rearmost apartment on the *deuxième étage* was less than half of all the others. Plus, according to a gossipy neighbor, there was seldom anybody home.

Reuven suggested an early-morning insertion because rue Lambert would be deserted after midnight. The construction site adjacent to L'Étrier was locked up tight at 5 P.M. and opened at eight in the morning. The bistro closed down by ten, the café half an hour later. Normally, Reuven said, the street was all tucked in and bedded down by 11 P.M. And the early risers didn't start moving until 6:30 or so. That gave Tom and him a roughly two-hour window to do what they had to do.

Even so, the approach would have to be on foot. Vehicles stick out like sore thumbs on streets like rue Lambert no matter what the hour, and the last thing Tom wanted was to give some bored gendarme pause for concern. So just after one in the morning, they cruised the neighborhood in one of the dinged-up 4627 vans until they finally found a parking spot on the boulevard Barbès, about a block and a half south of the Château Rouge metro stop. It was a bit farther from the target than they wanted to be, but given the parking situation in Paris—which is tight no matter what the hour—it could have been worse.

They sat, lights out, for twenty minutes and noticed nothing untoward. Traffic was light. There were no repeaters cruising. So they climbed out into the damp chill, locked the van, and walked north. They were both in disguise. Reuven wore a chef's baggy checked trousers and carried a leather-wrapped roll of knives inside of which were concealed the silent drill and video cameras. Tom, also in chef's clothes, carried a large cloth shopping bag that bore the logo of the Charles de Gaulle duty-free shops. The bag contained what appeared to be food and wine. Actually, the bottles and packages held dye and plaster, as well as an assortment of other supplies in case of contingencies.

Reuven had spent the past few days walking the neighborhood and he knew it as well as any native. His insertion route took them north along the store-lined boulevard to rue Custine, a two-way street that had light night-time traffic. They'd veer onto rue Custine, make their way to rue Nicolet, then approach the target from the south side of rue Lambert. Once there, they'd head straight for the door and make entry.

Indeed, getting inside was going to be the easiest part of the evening's work. Reuven had managed to make a copy of the outside door key. It hadn't been hard. It took him less than two days of surveillance to get a sense of the street's rhythms. He'd targeted an elderly woman resident of the house—watched as she'd gone shopping, then bumped her as she struggled, her arms filled with groceries, to pull keys out. Of course she'd dropped them and Reuven, hugely apologetic for his clumsiness, had retrieved them for her, found the door key, opened the door, then handed them back.

She'd never noticed him palm her house key and press it into the small tin of modeling clay he held in his hand. He didn't even have to make impressions of both sides. The door lock was a cheap one—he'd be able to fabricate a duplicate out of a blank in a matter of minutes.

1:35 A.M. They'd just passed a shuttered KFC chicken joint and crossed onto rue Custine when a vehicle passed them, moving slowly. Light-colored Citroën. Parisian tags. A single silhouette inside. Neither Tom nor Reuven reacted. They stayed on the eastern side of rue Custine, two slightly intoxicated guys weaving slightly as they walked, after a long night.

They'd just crossed rue Doudeauville when they heard a car approaching from the rear. As it passed, Reuven gave Tom an imperceptible nudge. Same Citroën. Not good. Cops? Maybe. DST? Possible. Bad guys? Not out of the question, either. Whichever one didn't matter. What mattered was they'd been noticed. Not only noticed, but whoever it was had wanted them to know they'd been noticed.

They continued on another block, moving past the insertion point. On the corner of rue Labat they saw a van parked close enough to the intersection so that it almost protruded into the right-of-way. Tom almost didn't give it a second glance—until the vehicle rocked ever so slightly as they crossed the street. There were people inside. More sentinels.

The two men kept moving until they were out of sight of the van. They were now faced with a tough decision. They'd been spotted—twice. And if the opposition was on its toes (and they had no reason to believe it wasn't), they'd been videoed. The question now became whether to proceed or to pack it in and try again another night using another set of identities and prosthetics.

Tom looked at his Israeli colleague. "So?"

"So?" Reuven shrugged. "So, obviously we're blown." He paused. "What do you want to do?"

Tom thought about it. "I think we go provocative."

"Rue Lambert?"

"What other choice do we have? They know we're here. And a hundred euros says that after tonight, he closes this place down and who knows how long it'll take us to find his next safe house. I want to know what he's doing that's so important."

"I agree." The Israeli nodded. "So, *nazuz*—let's move."

1:41 A.M. They walked along the opposite side of rue Lambert, moving north to south, nattering at each other in low tones. Tom glanced across the narrow street toward the target doorway. A homeless man accompanied by a scroungy dog was huddled there, asleep or passed out.

Reuven whispered, "What a coincidence, huh?"

Tom snorted. "Yeah, right." He knew there are no such things as coincidences. There were a lot of doorways in this neighborhood, and this bum was the only vagrant they'd seen. Provocatively, they crossed the street and passed directly in front of the sleeping man.

The dog's ears flattened against its head and it growled as Tom and Reuven approached. The man stirred, as if roused from a deep sleep. He was dressed for the street: three or four layers of old clothes. His hair was matted into dreadlocks. His untied shoes were scuffed raw. The man looked at them through hooded, wary eyes, then lay back down, belching loudly as they drew abreast.

"Goddamn, Jean-Pierre," Reuven muttered as they passed. "I thought you said this was a shortcut."

"Screw you, Philippe," Tom answered.

They continued to the bottom of the street and turned the corner, heading east.

Reuven said, "You saw the watcher behind us?"

Tom nodded. For a fleeting instant there had been a silhouette in a doorway near the corner of where Nicolet dead-ended into rue Bachelet. Tom swung his head around to catch a second look. He saw nothing. He was certain something big was going on. The opposition had the neighborhood sealed off. "Was it like this yesterday?"

"No."

So the development was recent. The implications were troubling—a leak, or a penetration of 4627. But he couldn't worry about those possibilities now. He had to concentrate on the current situation. "The guy down the street from us. Did you see his hands?"

"Hands were at his sides," Reuven said.

"Agreed. That tells me he doesn't have night vision."

The Israeli slowed down. "So, *nu*?"

"That means," Tom said, "we go to Plan C."

"You're a funny fellow."

Tom paused just long enough to look at the Israeli. "What do you think?"

"One: I've never seen a street person in six days of surveilling this neighborhood. Now we see one—two if you count the guy behind us. Two: the guy we passed looked pretty authentic, but he smelled clean. I caught a whiff of soap. Three: you saw how his shoes were all scuffed up? But the soles were brand-new rubber." He looked at Tom. "You?"

"Agreed. I missed the soap. But I caught the shoes."

"So?"

"Tells me there's activity up there—important enough for them to set both static and mobile security. I want a look-see." He stared at the Israeli. "Possible?"

"Of course. There's an alley near the top of rue Ramey," Reuven said in response. "It's right at the sight-line periphery of the van on rue Labat. But it's overcast tonight and I think if you're careful you'll be able to get over the wall without them seeing you. You go in and you head south. You climb three more walls and cross three tiny yards. There are no dogs, so you shouldn't be bothered. The yard after the third wall backs up against the target house. There's two exterior drainpipes running from the ground to the roof. The one on the left-hand side takes you past the safe-house window—two floors aboveground. If you pull a good Spider-Man and hang on one-handed, you might even be able to get video."

Tom said, "Hmm."

"It all depends whether or not they've left the shades up—and how you feel about whatchamacallit shinnying up drainpipes these days." He looked at Tom. "I hope you still remember your rock-climbing skills from Dartmouth."

Tom suppressed a double take and answered the Israeli matter-of-factly. "It's kind of like riding a bicycle, Reuven—you don't forget." But he couldn't stop himself from asking, "How the hell did you know about rock-climbing?"

Reuven allowed himself to crack a hint of a grin. "What, you don't think I ran a thorough profile on you back when you and I were butting heads?"

28

1:45 A.M. They continued walking east on rue Nicolet, crossing midblock onto the south side of the street. The move was relatively secure because Reuven knew the single streetlamp between the foot of rue Lambert and rue Ramey wasn't working. He knew it wasn't working because he'd shattered it the previous night with a ball bearing fired from a small slingshot. When no one had reacted to the sound, he'd taken the time to sweep up the glass shards and get rid of them. The ploy had worked: the lamp hadn't been replaced yet.

The third house from the corner had a large recessed portico. "Go there." Reuven nudged Tom into the doorway. The Israeli checked over his shoulder, then followed. He knew the watcher down the street couldn't see them without exposing himself.

1:46:14. Tom ripped his long web belt out, shed the gray-and-white-checked chef's trousers, turned them inside out, pulled them back on over his black running shoes, then rethreaded the belt. He did the same with the red-and-blue Paris Ste. Germaine anorak he wore over a set of black thermals. The anorak reversed into solid black.

1:46:17. Reuven unrolled the package of chef's knives. He paused, then handed Tom one of the pencil-like miniature video cameras. "Use the high-resolution night-vision lens."

"Good idea." Tom slipped the camera into the fanny pack he'd carried inside the shopping bag of food. Then Tom worked a radio earpiece into his ear, attached the mike to the collar of his jersey, ran the wire down to his waist, clipped a secure radio receiver to the fanny-pack belt, turned the unit on, tugged on it to make sure it was securely seated, then plugged the earpiece in.

The radios were for emergency use only. In Hollywood, they jabber on their radios during black ops the way teenagers use cell phones in shopping malls. In reality, you never speak unless it's a life-and-death situation. Radio transmissions—even secure ones—can bleed into other frequencies. Indeed, terrorists in hiding often keep TV sets turned on. If the screen starts picking up snow or other interference, it is a sure sign that there are folks talking on UHF or VHF radios in the vicinity.

1:46:27. Reuven attached his own radio, which also had a throat mike, then watched as Tom took off the long-billed baseball hat he'd been wearing, pulled a black knit watch cap from the shopping bag, and jammed it onto his head. The American affixed a fake mustache onto his upper lip and allowed Reuven to adjust it.

1:46:33. Reuven pulled a hat out of the shopping bag, exchanged hairpieces, and reversed his jacket and trousers, altering his shape and his silhouette.

1:46:44. Tom handed Reuven the shopping bag. He pulled on the pair of thin, black Kevlar-lined leather duty gloves he'd bought out of a law enforcement catalog. "Go—see you later."

In response, Reuven gave his colleague an upturned thumb.

"Very funny."

"I'll give you one tap on the radio when I'm clear of rue Nicolet. Only move then."

"Understood. See you at the rendezvous."

1:46:51 A.M. The Israeli slung the long handles of the shopping bag over his right shoulder and strode boldly down the three steps, turned left, and marched up the street. He'd constructed his cleaning route so as to make things as difficult as possible for the opposition. It wouldn't be hard, either. First of all, they appeared to be using single watchers. Bad tactics. When Reuven had set up the hit on Palestinian intelligence chief Atif B'sisou in Montparnasse, he'd used four three-man teams to seal the area. No matter how the Palestinians might have reacted, Reuven had been confident there'd be at least one Israeli team on them every second.

Reuven pulled the cap down on his head and headed straight for rue Bachelet. It was a rule of combat: when ambushed, counterambush. When attacked, counterattack. Do not shy away. Get in your adversary's face—which is exactly what he was doing now. There were only two possibilities: the watcher would go passive, in which case he'd shift his position to keep Reuven from seeing him. If he did that, Reuven would lose him on the cleaning route. Or he'd go provocative and aggressive, in which case Reuven would deal with him using the suppressed Glock he'd carried in the small of his back, but which now rested in his right hand, concealed by the shopping bag's big outer pocket.

In either case, Reuven would turn right onto rue Bachelet and follow the one-way street with the traffic flow, then veer west and scamper up the long stairway at the end of rue Becquerel. Any pursuers would immediately become obvious. Moreover, they'd have to really scramble to cut him off at the stairway's top end on rue Lamarck.

Rue Lamarck was a scythe-shaped, one-way street. The long handle of which extended as far west as the avenue de St. Ouen. The scythe's blade ran around the eastern base of the Sacré Coeur cathedral compound. And running off that section of rue Lamarck were a bunch of the tiny, narrow, no-more-than-alley-wide streets common to the Montmartre district. Reuven would use those passageways to lose any pursuers. He'd complete his cleaning route by circling clear around Sacré Coeur, then move east and south once more, waiting for Tom near the Château Rouge metro stop. It was a piece of cake. Maybe.

1:47:33. Careful to stay on the outer part of the narrow sidewalk, Reuven came abreast of the doorway where he'd spotted the watcher. He glanced left. The doorway was empty. The guy had obviously shifted position while he and Tom were doing their fast change. That was good news/bad news. Good news was that he'd gone passive. Bad news was he was out there somewhere, prowling and potentially dangerous. Either way, it was time for Tom to get moving. Reuven reached down with his left hand and tapped the transmit button on the radio once.

1:47:39. As Reuven made his way around half a dozen parked motorcycles at the end of rue Nicolet and turned onto rue Bachelet he realized the opposition had been doing some contingency planning, too. The two streetlights, which less than twenty-four hours earlier had given the street of antique houses the postcard look of Toulouse-Lautrec's nineteenth-century Montmartre, were now both extinguished. The entire length of the 170-meter-long street was plunged into ominous, murky darkness. Things had gone from Le Lapin Agile to *Rififi*.

1:47:42. Reuven's mind and body both reacted to his surroundings, but his physical appearance never changed. Combat was mental. That's what they taught you in the *Mat'kal*. It required training, discipline, and confidence.

1:47:43. Reuven crossed the narrow street. *Scan and breathe. Scan and breathe.* That was what the firearms instructors drilled into you day after day on the range. Do not succumb to tunnel vision. Take in oxygen. Keep every instinct keened. Ears open. Nose open. Miss nothing. Become a sponge. Anticipate.

1:47:45. Reuven's radar sensed movement behind him. Then his ears caught the faint but nonetheless distinct scrape of running shoes against asphalt, moving in quick, potentially violent fashion. The motion in itself was eloquent. It told the Israeli his opposition was armed with a knife or a garrote, not a gun. And then the smells hit him: garlic, tobacco, and sweat—even in the chill, there was sweat.

1:47:46. Reuven feinted right but moved left, rolling over the low hood of a car and dropping into a crouch as a body came hurtling past the spot where his left shoulder had been. He heard the whoosh of the blade as it slashed air.

He caught a glimpse of the man wielding it. Dressed in *banlieue* hip-hop and carrying a big folding knife with a curved blade. *An amateur.* Only amateurs use knives that big. Maybe. But maybe also a professional—a gangsta paid a hundred euros to make this look like a street robbery.

1:47:48. Reuven tucked the shopping bag tightly under his right arm. He brought the Glock up, parallel to the pavement.

1:47:49. His left hand racked the slide, loading a round into the pistol's chamber. Simultaneously, Reuven swung the suppressor's muzzle across his assailant's sweatshirt-covered chest, almost as if he were swinging a paintbrush, and as the muzzle crossed center mass, he pulled the trigger twice in rapid succession—*thwop-thwop.*

The target went down. But instead of dying, he groaned loudly, cursed in guttural Arabic, rolled away from Reuven, and tried to pull himself to his feet. He'd never even let go of the big knife.

The son of a whore's wearing a vest. Reuven shifted the Glock into a two-handed grip, stepped up, and using the car to steady himself, put a carefully aimed third round into the side of the hip-hop's head.

1:47:52. The hip-hop dropped heavily, splayed out on the sidewalk facedown, thrashing like he'd been jolted with a Taser. He bucked half a dozen times then went still. A puddle of dark blood began to drain from the head wound.

1:47:57. Reuven backed away from the car, breathing through his mouth to make sure he took in a lot of oxygen. He pointed the muzzle of the Glock slightly downward—the stance they called low ready at the range— swinging the weapon left/right, right/left, his eyes searching the darkened street for anomalies. He thought he heard the faint sound of shoe leather on concrete moving away from him, but he couldn't be absolutely sure.

1:48:03. Reuven looked up and scanned the windows. Thank God it was all quiet. There were no lights; no nosy neighbors. He dropped to his knees and crawled around until he'd retrieved his three 9mm shell casings from the street and shoved them in his pocket. Then he approached the dead hip-hop and rolled the corpse with his toe, careful to stay away from the large puddle of blood leaking from the side of the man's shattered temple. He'd been right: the hip-hop had the look of an Algerian or Moroccan *banlieue* gangbanger—right down to the jailhouse tattoo on the back of his hand.

1:48:29. The Israeli patted the dead man down. There was a wallet, a pager, and a cell phone. Reuven stuffed them into the shopping bag. Gingerly, he pulled the hip-hop's sweatshirt up. There were five hundred-euro bills secured in the Velcro straps of the bulletproof vest. He took them, too. The money was folded around a small piece of yellow paper—one of those silly Post-it sticky notes.

Reuven held the paper up and squinted in the darkness. On the Post-it was written *Raynouard* ١٧. The numerals were Arabic—17. The address was Tom's.

The Israeli started up the street at a dead run, heading for the long flight of stairs. He knew there was an all-night taxi stand near the intersection of rue Lamarck and rue Caulaincourt.

29

1:47:39 A.M. When he heard the single *tsk* in his ear, Tom slipped out of the doorway, kept close to the building, and made his way slowly up the street. The key was to do everything slowly and evenly. No jerky movement. Nothing that would attract attention. At night, sudden movement normally causes people to shift their eyes—change focus, use peripheral vision. And Tom didn't want anybody doing that. He wanted his adversaries staring straight at him because that way they were likely to miss him. Of course, if they had night-vision equipment, it wouldn't matter. But better safe than stupid.

1:47:52. Tom crossed the foot of rue Nicolet. He'd started to ease around the corner onto rue Ramey when he saw headlights coming in his direction. He stopped, stepped back, and retreated into a doorway.

The car—it was a small convertible—continued south on rue Ramey. As soon as its taillights had disappeared, Tom stepped out, made his way to the corner, and turned north. He was about halfway up the block when the intersection of rue Labat came into view. He continued cautiously until he dared to look across the street and saw the van was gone. That struck Tom as strange. Static surveillance units seldom shifted their positions because doing so drew attention to them.

Tom had once spent thirty-eight hours straight on a two-man static surveillance. It had been in Cairo, in the summer. After about twenty-six hours in hundred-plus-degree heat, he'd come down with a horrible case of turista. All the Imodium, of course, was stored safely in the medicine cabinet back at his apartment, and so the last half day had been without question the most uncomfortable twelve hours in his entire life. He didn't want to think how nasty it had been for his unfortunate partner.

1:48 A.M. The mouth of the alley was sealed by a two-and-a-half-meter wall—just over eight feet—topped with an occasional shard of glass. There was no gate. The wall was smooth—there were no dogs' teeth to help him gain any purchase.

He paused, took a deep breath, then sprang, catching the exposed cap of the brick wall with his fingertips. He pulled himself straight up vertically, as if he were chinning on a bar. In truth, he hadn't done any rock-climbing since college. He ran, of course, and when he'd been at Langley, he'd occasionally lifted some free weights down in the clandestine personnel gym. But since he'd moved to Paris, his exercise sessions had been sporadic at best—and now he was going to suffer the painful consequences.

But he kept going. When Tom's nose was level with the top of the wall, he threw his arm up and over, careful not to impale himself on the pieces of broken bottle. Then, inch by inch, Tom struggled until he'd pulled himself over the top of the wall. It was no fun.

Exhausted, he rolled and dropped into the first of the three yards. He was careful to land evenly. He didn't need a sprained ankle. Not tonight.

1:50. He caught his breath and scanned his surroundings. It was just as Reuven had described: a postage stamp of a yard. A tree, bare in the November chill, stood in the center of the four-by-four-meter plot. Laundry was hung out. Tom picked his way past the rear of the house, trod carefully in the darkness up to the far wall, and jumped tippy-toe like a six-year-old at a candy counter to see if he could make out what was on top. This wall came topped with a single strand of what appeared to be rusty barbed wire. More fun and games. He shook his head and sprang for the lip of the wall.

1:53 A.M. Tom stood, head tilted back, looking up toward the second floor, his gloved right hand resting on the shiny black-painted cast-iron drainpipe. It was perhaps four inches in diameter—about the size of a healthy hickory sapling. But a lot smoother. The good news was that pipe joints protruded every four feet or so, and they'd give him something to catch on in case he lost his grip and started to slide. Tom exhaled, reached up, grabbed the first joint, wrapped his legs around the pipe, and pulled. By the time he was eight feet off the ground, he was sweating.

He remembered, in the way ironic memories sometimes intrude, that Sam Waterman had once told him, "Kiddo, pain is simply weakness leaving the body." The thought brought a grim smile to his face. If what Sam said was true, Tom would be left completely without weakness by the end of his night's work.

1:58. He was almost at the halfway point—which meant his nose was almost level with the first-floor windows. He looked down. It had taken him more than five minutes to climb less than eighteen feet.

2:02. Three-quarters of the way home. He'd developed a rhythm. He used his upper-body strength (what there was of it) to pull himself up a few precious inches. His legs were wrapped around the pipe, his feet jammed against the rough brick wall. He'd pull, and squeeze, pull and squeeze, and rise a few inches with each painful repetition.

2:06. Tom's head came level with the sill of the target window. Exhausted, he reached up to the next pipe joint and, using the last of his strength, wrestled himself the final half foot into position. Rivulets of sweat running into his eyes, he hung there totally spent, his weight supported by the half an inch of pipe joint his sneakered insteps rested on. After about fifteen seconds, he rubbed his face against his sleeve, breathed deeply, and then set to work.

First, he slid his right hand around the drainpipe to keep himself from slipping. With his left hand he loosened the inch-and-a-half-wide web belt around his waist, pulled it out through the trouser loops, ran it behind the pipe, cinched the pressure buckle tight, and then took hold of the belt with his left hand and wrapped the strap three times around his hand and wrist. Now, by using the belt, he could swing himself back and forth, giving himself the reach he needed to see inside the window.

2:07. Using his right hand, Tom retrieved the camera from his fanny pack. He said a silent prayer to the gods of video transmission and activated the device. Holding it securely in his hand, he swung himself to his right, sidling up to the window.

It was shut tight. He brought himself back, feet clamped on the pipe joint and left hand holding firmly on to the webbing, while he considered his next moves.

He shoved the camera back into the fanny pack and—taking no chances—zipped the compartment shut. Then he swung back toward the window as far as he could. It took him two tries, but he finally was able to touch the cracked paint of the outer sash with his fingertips.

That wasn't enough. He swung back to the drainpipe. Now he took his right foot off the pipe joint altogether, skidded his left instep around the lip of the joint, unwrapped the web belt to give himself another five inches of reach, then pushed off once more.

This time he swung low enough so that his right hand was actually able to grasp the wooden sill. Not daring to breathe, he held himself there, fully extended for some seconds, the unwilling hero of his own Harold Lloyd cinema verité feature film.

When he'd finally convinced himself he wasn't going to fall, he gripped the sill and pulled his body as low as possible. Carefully, he brought his face close to the dirty glass.

2:09:21. The shade had been pulled down. Of course it had—he'd seen no light emanating from the window from the yard below. But now, with his nose just inches from the glass, he saw roughly an inch, maybe an inch and a half, of open space at the bottom of the window shade.

Using every bit of his strength, Tom unwrapped the belt one more wind and extended himself another two inches. Now he was at the very end of his tether, and his left toe on the pipe joint was all that kept him from falling. Still, he strained to peer inside. It was impossible.

He let go of the sill and swung back, heaving a huge sigh when he had both hands and both feet firmly on the drainpipe. He fiddled with the web belt until he had it wrapped exactly the way he'd need it. Tom extracted the camera from the fanny pack. Then he slipped his right foot off the pipe joint, leaned out, and swung back toward the window.

He eased his right hand past the sill, held the camera lens up to the glass, and moved the pencil-size instrument, oh so slowly, from left to right, hoping that Murphy's Law would, this one time, not be in effect, and that the camera's low-light-capable lens would capture whatever was in the room—and even perhaps, some images of what lay beyond.

2:13 A.M. He'd counted to a hundred and eighty—roughly three minutes of video. If the gods were indeed smiling on him tonight, the camera's transmissions were secure on the battery-powered recorder in the 4627 van. Well, he'd know everything there was to know in a few minutes.

Gently, Tom set the camera into the fanny pack and zipped the pouch closed. He pendulumed back to the drainpipe, where he hung for some seconds, the sweat pouring off his face and neck. His feet were so numb he couldn't feel his toes.

He unwrapped the web belt from his hand, pulled it around the pipe, and buckled it around his waist. He tightened the Velcro tabs on the backs of his gloves so his wet hands wouldn't slip on the painted cast iron.

He slipped his hands around the drainpipe as if it were a firehouse pole, eased his feet off the joint, and slid down until his running shoes caught on the next lowest protrusion. He stopped momentarily, then repeated the action, faster each time, dropping another four feet, then another, then another.

2:19. Tom peered over the wall at the end of the alley. The intersection was deserted. He jumped, pulled, scrambled, rolled over the top, dropped onto the pavement, and headed south toward the rendezvous point at a slow jog.

He'd just reached the foot of rue Ramey when Reuven's voice exploded in his ear. "Change of plans." It took Tom an instant to realize Reuven was speaking in Arabic.

Tom answered in kind. "Go."

"I'm at your flat."

"What?"

"MJ's all right—nothing happened. No time to talk. Grab the truck. Meet us out front. I'll explain."

"Us? But—"

"Just move—move *now*." Reuven's belligerent attitude didn't brook any opposition.

"On my way."

30

2:48 A.M. They were waiting in the vestibule. Reuven ushered MJ into the front seat of the truck, slammed the door shut, then went around to the side, opened the cargo bay, loaded her suitcase, and hoisted himself inside. "Office, Tom. Go to the office—now. I called Tony Wyman. He'll meet us there."

Tom wanted answers before they moved. He looked at the confused, frightened expression on his fiancée's face and enveloped her in his arms. "It's all right, sweetie. Everything's going to be just fine."

Then he turned toward the Israeli. "What the hell's up?"

"That fellow on the street had your address on him," Reuven machine-gunned in rapid French. "Since you told me this wonderful woman had shown up unexpectedly, I thought it prudent to get over here."

"Why in God's name didn't you get hold of me?"

"Because you had a job to do, my friend—something I couldn't do. And because I was on the case." Reuven smacked his fist into his palm. "The sons of bitches are onto you. I don't know how, but they are."

Tom had more than an inkling how. They were onto him because Tom had been the last person to talk to Shahram Shahristani. They were onto him because they were keeping the American embassy under constant surveillance and he'd turned up there and left with a known CIA case officer. The same case officer they'd seen talking to Shahram Shahristani. They'd known because they were competent adversaries and they could put two and two together.

Reuven broke into Tom's train of thought. "Did you see anything up there?"

"The shades were down and the lights were out. I saw nothing. But there was a gap between the shade and the sill and I used the camera."

Reuven lifted the painter's tarp to reveal the rack of video equipment. "While you head for the office I want to see what you got."

3:19 A.M. Reuven had scrambled the staff and 4627's offices were in condition red. A pair of security cars sealed off the front and rear exits. The entrance to the five-story building was manned by an armed guard. Inside, roving two-man teams patrolled the corridors.

Tom had never seen Tony Wyman without a tie. Now Wyman, in a pressed pair of jeans and a thick cashmere turtleneck, monocle screwed into his right eye, squinted intently at the high-resolution plasma screen in Tom's office. A police scanner played softly in the background as Reuven explained what Wyman was looking at.

"Tom—freeze the picture. Those are detonators," the Israeli said, pointing at a slightly fuzzy image of objects roughly the size of tongue depressors. "Ben Said disassembles the backpacks piece by piece. He inserts several thin sheets of explosive to replace the layer of padding between the inner and outer linings at the bottom and back side of the bag. Then he removes one of the stiffeners they use where the backpack straps connect to the body of the rucksack, and replaces it with the detonator."

Reuven pointed at the half dozen detonators lying on a kitchen towel—kitchen because the words *Cuisine et Tradition* in dark lettering were visible on the portion of the towel that was draped over the edge of the table. "I can't be sure, but it seems pretty straightforward. The bottom end—the business end if you will—is pressed into the plastic explosive. It follows that the middle section is probably the battery that sends the electric charge into the explosive and detonates it. And the top is actually a small receiver and antenna—similar to what's inside a cell phone."

Tony Wyman nodded.

"Then he reassembles everything carefully."

Wyman said: "Where does he get the thread?"

Reuven's eyes brightened. "Good point."

MJ looked at the Israeli. "Huh?"

"He has to sew the backpacks using the original needle holes and a thread that looks exactly like this—" Reuven reached across MJ, pulled her own Vuitton backpack from where she'd hung it over the arm of her chair, and tilted it. "Look at the stitching. The thread is unique. He had to have an inside source." The Israeli returned the backpack and scratched himself a note. "I'll check it out."

"Good." Wyman nodded. "How many bombs, Reuven?"

"If I could count the detonators, I'd know better," the Israeli said.

"There are eight backpacks, Tony," Tom said. "But there may be more."

"Makes sense." Wyman looked at Tom. "Do we have the place covered? I don't want Ben Said disappearing on us."

"Reuven took care of it."

"I called some friends from the old days," Reuven said. "Corsicans. Trustworthy. Nothing happens without us knowing."

MJ pointed at the screen. "Why not just alert the French? Let them take care of everything?"

"They'd get the bombs and that's all," Tom said. "I want Ben Said."

She crossed her arms. "The bombs are better than nothing."

"They're nothing without the bomb maker, MJ," Wyman said. "He shifts locations, identities, whatever, and starts all over again. Now that he's perfected the detonator design, we're talking a matter of what—weeks?"

Reuven nodded. "Maximum."

"So?"

"This time it's high-fashion backpacks," Wyman said. "And we have a real leg up because we know that. Next time it could be anything. Attaché cases. Carry-ons. Shaving kits. Makeup bags."

MJ cocked her head in Wyman's direction. "But won't he shift his base of operation anyway if he knows you're onto him?"

"It's possible," Wyman said, looking at her.

"But harder to do than it might appear," Reuven said.

She looked at the Israeli. "Why?"

"Because," Tom interrupted, "of two factors. The first is that, from everything Shahram Shahristani told me the day he was killed, Ben Said's IED designs are unique. That's how he makes his money. He doesn't sell his know-how. He sells finished products. Also, he tends to oversee the jobs himself. He was in Gaza. Now he's here, because this is where the bombs are going to be used. My guess is some of that is ego, but it's also to ensure that whoever buys his designs doesn't reverse-engineer them and steal the proprietary stuff."

"Second," Reuven broke in, "we're not talking about making Molotov cocktails or homemade mortars," Reuven said. "Those you can put together anyplace. These devices are precision IEDs. Moreover, it's amazing what can be traced these days. You need a more or less sterile environment. No dust, no dander, because you have to be meticulous about the postexplosion forensics. A microscopic bit of soil that's unique to a certain place. Or a tiny fragment of a towel—they can trace those things nowadays. So the environment can't contain anything that forensics sniffers or the latest generation of airport screening devices might detect."

The Israeli noted the skeptical expression on MJ's face. "Look for yourself, MJ." Reuven tapped the screen. "Run it from the beginning, Tom."

"Huh?" Tom was distracted by the police scanner. "Listen."

Tony Wyman turned toward the radio and the four of them fell silent. The police were responding to a possible homicide on rue Bachelet.

Tom turned toward the Israeli. "Reuven?"

"Later," the Israeli said in Arabic, his eyes flicking toward MJ. "I'll fill you in on the details later." He switched back to English. "Run from the beginning, please."

Tom dutifully clicked the mouse on the screen. The DVD began with out-of-focus moving images followed by a lot of black. "That's from when I stowed the camera in the fanny pack." He fast-forwarded until he saw the image of the safe-house wall. "Okay. Here's where it gets interesting."

He clicked on *speed* then *slow*. The jerkiness decreased and the camera started to pan smoothly across the room. In the foreground, the green-tinged video showed a folding picnic table draped with plastic sheeting on which sat several Vuitton backpacks in various stages of disassembly. To its left, at an oblique angle, was another, smaller picnic table, also draped in dark plastic, which held the detonators. In the gap behind those two tables sat a third. It was more substantial than the other two—more like a drop-leaf dining table. In its center Tom could make out a large sewing machine sitting atop a small crate. The right-hand side of the table was visible through the backpacks, revealing what appeared to be a pasta roller bolted to the end of the drop leaf.

The camera moved on, its autofocusing lens now concentrating on the back wall of the room. Some sort of plastic sheeting had been hung. As the camera panned, Tom saw that every one of the walls was covered in plastic sheeting.

Tom slowed the DVD's speed so he could look more closely and waited until the camera moved from right to left. The plastic over the window made it harder to see, but the objects on the tables were still identifiable.

"Okay," Reuven said. "Now . . . stop."

Tom froze the image.

Reuven used his pen to point at the bomb-making materials on the tables. "Breaking this down won't be easy. This isn't the kind of thing you throw in a garbage bag and move. The backpacks have to be handled carefully. After all, they have to look new." He looked at Tom. "Show the pasta maker, Tom."

Tom double-clicked and the image of the long table with the sewing machine popped onto the screen.

Reuven waited until the camera panned between the backpacks to the end of the table that held the pasta maker. Just visible next to the machine were a trio of cookie racks on which sat six-inch strips of what looked like fresh-made lasagna. "Okay, stop."

Tony Wyman squinted, then said, "Yes?"

"That's the explosive," Reuven said.

MJ said, "Just lying there? Isn't that dangerous?"

"No." Tom's hand caressed her shoulder. "The explosive itself is inert—it's not dangerous until the detonator's inserted. But look at how thin it has to be."

"You're right." Reuven pointed to the racks. "Looks to me like it's what—two, three millimeters at most."

Wyman looked at the Israeli. "Is that significant?"

"For sure. Plastique isn't elastic the same way pasta dough is. It's more like modeling clay, or Silly Putty. It's easy to cut, and roll, and form into shaped charges. But it's damned hard to roll into thin, delicate sheets unless you happen to have the right equipment. Obviously, all Ben Said was able to get was this pasta roller. Once the son of a bitch has rolled out the explosive, it becomes very, very fragile. From what we can see here, my guess is he's rolled about three, maybe four knapsacks' worth." Reuven looked at Wyman. "Believe me, he's not going to want to do the job twice."

Tony Wyman shook his head. "He's using a goddamn everyday pasta roller."

"Can you think of something less likely to attract attention?" Reuven tapped the plasma screen. "With the exception of the explosives and the detonators, there's nothing in this room that can't be bought off the shelf."

The Israeli tapped the screen then turned back toward Tony Wyman. "Look—these guys are smart. You were able to destroy Abu Nidal's organization because it was hierarchical. You cut the head off, and the beast dies. These guys work out of anonymous, self-supporting cells. Or they're loners like Ben Said. They also study their targets. They probe for weaknesses. They bide their time. They're patient, experienced, dangerous, well disciplined, and above all they're resourceful. So while the FBI or Shabak or DST double-checks every building-supply or fertilizer manufacturer looking for fancy-schmancy, our boy goes to Monoprix or BHV, pays cash, and walks away with everything he needs right off the housewares and small-electronics shelves."

"Makes one wonder." MJ played with her hair.

Tom said, "Wonder what?"

"Where he got the explosives. Where did they come from? Did he make them in the next room? Where's his laboratory? Did he bring them into this place in a shopping bag or in his briefcase? How did they get from wherever they were manufactured to that table?"

The three men looked at one another and realized no one had an answer.

Tony Wyman's monocle dropped onto his chest. "Roll the video again, Tom. From the top."

Tom clicked on the play button, then the slow button, and the camera panned slowly left to right. The four of them watched for more than two and a half minutes in silence.

Finally, Wyman said, "Hold on the backpacks, will you?"

Tom ran the disk fast-forward until the table with the backpacks was centered on the screen. He paused the DVD and looked over at his boss.

Tony Wyman said, "Can you give me a print of the table with the backpacks? I don't care about the packs, but I want to see the whole table, legs and all."

"Sure." Tom cropped the image just as his boss had asked and clicked the printer icon. Thirty seconds later, he handed tony Tony a borderless eight-by-ten-inch photograph.

Wyman plugged the monocle into his right eye and studied the picture intently. After a quarter of a minute, he said, "Hmm."

Then he gave Tom an intense look. "Can you do the same thing for me with the table holding the detonators?"

"Sure." Tom had no idea at all where tony Tony was heading.

31

3:38 A.M. Tony Wyman held the photographs side by side directly in front of his long nose and examined them closely, one then the other. He said "Hmm" again. He looked at Tom, swiveled his chair, and said, "Come see."

Tom came around and peered over Wyman's shoulder, squinted, then shrugged. "What am I looking for?"

Wyman used his right pinkie to summon Reuven. "Now you. What do you see?"

The Israeli leaned over Wyman's other shoulder. "Tables. Backpacks. Detonators. A kitchen towel."

Wyman peered over at MJ. "You're the professional here, m'dear."

MJ took the two photos from Wyman, laid them on Tom's desk, then rummaged through her purse but came up empty. "I guess I left my glasses back at Tom's. Tony, can I borrow your monocle?"

Wyman dropped the gold-rimmed glass into her palm. She put the black silk ribbon around her neck, then affixed the lens in her right eye. "Whoa, this is way too strong for me." She tried to use the monocle as a magnifying glass, but that technique didn't work, either. A frustrated MJ handed the monocle back to Wyman. "I can't see anything worth a damn, Tony."

Wyman's fingers drummed on the desktop. Then he stood up. "Aha. Follow me."

The three of them traipsed after him, followed by the two security guards Wyman had stationed outside Tom's door. They took the elevator down one level, then padded on an Oriental rug down an L-shaped corridor to the back of the town house and through sliding pocket doors into 4627's research room.

In many ways the place resembled a law library: dark wood bookcases and file cabinets, and a quartet of leather club chairs, each with its own reading lamp. In one corner, MJ saw a computer whose 4627 Company screen saver bounced back and forth across the width of the flat screen. There were also a pair of long tables. On one of them sat a stack of reference books—thesauruses and dictionaries in a dozen languages. The other, which sat adjacent to a five-drawer, legal-size file cabinet of city and country maps, held 4627's world atlases. And attached to the end of the map table was a hinged, black metal, twelve-power magnifying lamp.

Wyman laid the photos on the table, flipped the protective cover from the thick magnifying glass, turned the light on, and stepped back. *"Mademoiselle, s'il vous plaît?"*

Using the lamp's handle, MJ played the eight-inch glass over the photographs, working systematically left to right and then back again. When she'd finished with the first picture, she repeated her actions with the second. The three men stood quietly, Wyman rocking back and forth on his heels, his right hand playing with the change in his trouser pocket.

Finally, MJ looked over at tony Tony. "I see anomalies in these photographs," she said.

Wyman flashed her a wicked grin and spoke in a Long John Silver accent. "And they be what sorts of anomalies, Marilyn Jean?"

"Why would Ben Said have two containers of olive oil in what you've told me is a room he's trying to keep as sterile as possible."

Reuven Ayalon cocked his head in MJ's direction. "Olive oil. You're sure?"

"Either olive oil or a bulk container of imported olives." MJ stood aside. "Take a look, Reuven."

The Israeli played the magnifying glass over the photograph. Finally, he looked up. "She's right—but I think it's a barrel of olives, not the oil." He backed away so Tom could take a peek.

Tom peered at the photo. Then he gave MJ an anxious look. When she nodded at him, he said, "Give MJ a couple of minutes to play with these. I think she can make things a lot clearer than I did."

3:56 A.M. Tom waved the eight-by-ten at Tony Wyman. "She got it," he said proudly. "She's a genius."

MJ blushed. "Not according to Mrs. Sin-Gin."

Tony Wyman took the photo. "My Arabic's rusty," he said. "But I think it reads *Boissons Maghreb Exports*." He looked at Tom. "The name sounds familiar. What's the significance?"

"It's an import-export company. Belongs to a Moroccan named Yahia Hamzi. He's the third man in Shahram's surveillance photos. Shahram described him as Ben Said's banker.

"Dianne Lamb, our little bomber girl in Israel, met Hamzi here in Paris," Tom said. "At a Lebanese restaurant in the seventeenth."

"I found the place," Reuven interrupted. "It's called Rimal. It's on boulevard Malesherbes."

"Lamb was told his name was Talal Massoud," Tom interrupted. "And that he was the editor of *Al Arabia,* the magazine that employed Malik Suleiman—the Tel Aviv disco bomber."

Reuven picked up: "Hamzi's a regular."

Wyman cocked his head in Tom's direction. "Does two plus two equal four here, gentlemen?"

"If you're thinking what I am, the answer's yes." Tom turned to Reuven. "What do you think?"

"I agree."

MJ gave Tom a puzzled look. "What in God's name are you talking about?"

"That last day when I had lunch with Shahram," Tom said. "He told me

Ben Said's new explosive was terribly difficult to make. Said it had to be cooked in small batches. Said that Ben Said used up his entire stock of the new stuff in the Gaza explosion."

"So?"

So, one: we can extrapolate that he's running short. Aside from what's been rolled out and is sitting on the drying racks, I don't see any plastique in the room—no bricks, or mounds of anything to be rolled out." He scanned the room. "Does anybody?"

"No," said MJ, "but I don't know what to look for."

"There's nothing there," Reuven said authoritatively.

Tony Wyman gave the Israeli a probing stare. "So everything's on the drying racks?"

Reuven didn't back down. "That's what I think."

"Next," Tom said. "Reuven's earlier surveillance indicated no activity on rue Lambert. That tells me Ben Said wasn't on scene." He looked at Tony Wyman. "But last night—there were hostiles."

"So?"

"Indicates one of two things: either DST's got something working or Ben Said's getting close." Tom put his arm around MJ's shoulder. "Here's my two-plus-two: you asked how Ben Said moves the explosive once it's been fabricated. How does he get it to the safe house. Obvious answer, given the photo: the explosive gets shipped in a container of Maghreb's imported olives. Maghreb is Yahia Hamzi's firm. Shahram told me Hamzi was Ben Said's banker. But was Shahram being literal or figurative? Maybe he was saying Hamzi moves stuff around for Ben Said—launders the goods, or the cash, or whatever, if you will. Okay. Now, let's posit the explosives are fabricated in Morocco in small batches—just as Shahram said. Then they're shipped to Paris—or wherever—in Maghreb olive containers."

MJ played with Tom's fingers. "Wouldn't the oil affect the plastique?"

"Not at all," Reuven said. "And getting rid of the oil coating would be as simple as using soap and water."

MJ's eyes went wide. "Holy cow."

"Tom," Tony Wyman said, "I think we need to speak with Mr. Hamzi about these matters." He swiveled toward the Israeli. "In private, of course. Is there some way you might arrange that, Reuven?"

"Are there time constraints?"

"Obviously, the sooner the better. Sometime in the next twenty-four hours would be optimum." Wyman looked at Tom. "You look dubious, Tom. Am I asking the impossible?"

"Nothing's impossible, Tony." Tom found it significant that Wyman had directed the initial question to Reuven. That was because Reuven had done these kinds of ops before and Tom hadn't. Besides, Wyman had worked with Mossad in the past—when he'd targeted Abu Nidal.

Many of the CIA's Arabists—Charlie Hoskinson was one—tended to keep the Israelis at arm's length. They distrusted Mossad's motives. Wyman, it was said, had liaised with Mossad off the books on some European operations during the Gates and Webster era, when Langley was institutionally opposed to any sort of risky or audacious operation.

But talk about risky. Snatching Hamzi was way beyond risky. It was dangerous. The French tended to frown on kidnapping in their capital. But there had to be a way.

Tom looked at Tony Wyman. Wyman expected results, not excuses. And he was obviously waiting for Tom to say something—Tom could almost hear the ticking of the clock in Wyman's brain.

He let his mind go free—float with the white sound of the police scanner. *Wheelbarrows, Tom. Think wheelbarrows.* And then the answer came to him in a sudden epiphany—*create dread*. It was so simple it had to work. "We question Hamzi in Israel," Tom exclaimed.

Tony Wyman gave him a skeptical look. "Isn't that a bit complicated, Tom? Planes. Unwilling passengers." He looked at Tom. "Remember when Mubarak tried to smuggle that dissident out of Frankfurt in the trunk?"

He turned to MJ as Reuven and Tom stifled guffaws. They knew the story. "Once upon a time, the Mukhabarat el-Aama—that's Egypt's intelligence service—kidnapped a bothersome anti-Mubarak dissident in Germany. They snatched him from Freiburg where he was teaching political science and preaching revolution. They drugged him, stuffed him in a trunk, and tried to ship him back to Cairo as diplomatic mail. Problem was, the son of a bitch woke up just as the Germans were loading the trunk on the plane. There was one hell of a diplomatic flap and the incident caused Mubarak all sorts of political embarrassment in the Western press." Wyman looked at Tom and Reuven. "We don't need any flaps, guys."

"And we won't have any because I'm not being literal," Tom interjected. "We use the warehouse. We build a cell, a hallway, an interrogation room. We snatch Hamzi. We put him to sleep. He wakes up in a cell. He hears Hebrew being spoken outside the door. He hears other prisoners talking in Arabic. The guards—what he sees of them—are wearing Israeli uniforms. What's he going to think? He'll swear he's been kidnapped by Mossad and flown to Israel."

Tom looked at the smile spreading across Reuven's face. "We re-create Qadima. We squeeze Hamzi. After he gives us what we want, he goes to sleep again—and *badda bing,* he wakes up in Paris."

"I like it," Wyman said. "Because if we succeed, Tel Aviv will get all the blame." He cast a quizzical look at Reuven. "And how are you with that outcome?"

"I'm retired, remember." Reuven shrugged. "Besides, the people at Gelilot are big boys. They've been blamed for a lot worse things than kidnapping."

"Good," Wyman said. "The question is, can we accomplish this within a workable time frame?"

"For what you want, twenty-four hours is tight. So perhaps things will take slightly longer," Reuven said. "The construction alone will take almost a day, I think."

Tom said, "If we keep an eye on Hamzi, we should be all right."

Reuven said: "I'd like to use one of my former networks."

"Which one?" Wyman played with his monocle.

"The Corsicans. They're already involved—running the surveillance on rue Lambert. They're expensive, of course. But they're good, they're quick—and they're very discreet."

"Corsicans." Wyman's head bobbed in agreement. "Works for me." Tony had employed Corsicans before and they were everything Reuven said they were.

"Reuven." Tom cocked his head in the Israeli's direction. "Is there any chance we might snag Salah for this?"

The Israeli reacted. "Y'know," he said, "that's an interesting idea."

Wyman looked over at Tom. "Who's Salah?"

"He runs the interrogation center where I interviewed Dianne Lamb."

Wyman played with the monocle's silk ribbon. "I'm not sure I like it."

"Why?"

"I don't like the possibility of competing agendas," Wyman said. "Salah isn't our unilateral or our employee. He's liaison. That means he'll be doing Gelilot's work as well as ours."

"Sometimes, Tony," Reuven broke in, "that's not so bad. Besides, I think in this particular case, Gelilot's agenda and ours will run parallel—at least in the short term." He gave the American time to think about what he'd said. "And Salah's one of the best in the world at wringing information out of these people."

"Can we trust him?"

"Look." The Israeli crossed his arms. "Say you're right. Say he'll report to Gelilot everything he learns. Okay, sooner or later, they'll use it—to their advantage and maybe not to ours, or to Langley's. But Salah won't hold back on us—and neither will Mossad."

Wyman gave the Israeli a penetrating stare. "Why, Reuven?"

"First of all because we're giving Mossad access to someone who might give up something useful. And second because in a sense, we're carrying Gelilot's water on this whole Ben Said business."

"How so?"

"Gelilot screwed up on Ben Said. They didn't catch the pattern. We— through Tom's good work and Shahram's instincts—did."

"And?"

"And, let's say we snag Ben Said. Do we—the 4627 Company—take the credit? Of course not. Because what is 4627? It's a private risk-assessment firm. Operationally, we don't exist. Operationally, we are entirely in the black. So who takes credit when we succeed, eh?" The Israeli paused, then quickly answered his own question. "Nobody does—and everybody does."

The Israeli looked around the room. "My old boss at Gelilot, Shamir, was a tough bird. A real prick—let me tell you, when the son of a bitch became prime minister, he was just as tough and unyielding. And whenever something fatal happened to one of our enemies—like the Black September murderers who planned and perpetrated the 1972 Olympics assassinations being tracked down and killed one by one, or the Fatah terrorists who bombed Israeli diplomats and then subsequently disappeared off the face of the earth—Israel, of course, would get the blame. And the government always denied, denied, denied. No comment. But Shamir always used to tell those of us who worked in the embassies, 'Never, never, never,' he'd insist, 'deny the stories too loudly. Leave the sons of bitches guessing. Whether or not it was us, always leave them guessing.'"

The Israeli's palms came together. "So, like I said: let's say we snag Ben Said. Make him disappear. The putzes who write for *The Guardian* and *The Independent* will scream accusations at Mossad. And Mossad? Mossad won't deny it too loudly. The left-wing American press and the left-wing French press, they'll accuse CIA. And guess what: CIA won't deny it too loudly, either. Why? Because CIA is in such bad shape that any suggestion at all that Langley might have pulled off a successful operation against a bin Laden–level terrorist will make the seventh floor happy."

Reuven looked at Tony Wyman. "So, I say we bring Salah on, and we do what we do, and who says what afterward, or what their long-term agendas might be, none of that matters. Not one bit."

Tom said, "I think Reuven's right, Tony."

Wyman said, "I'm inclined to agree." He rapped the table and nodded. "Do it."

"Done." Tom started to leave, then turned back toward his boss. "Tony, can you set MJ up in a secure place for a couple of days?"

"Good point." Wyman smiled at MJ. "I'll put you at the Sofitel Faubourg, mademoiselle. That's where I'm staying. The room service is good, and because it's on the same block as the American embassy, there are hundreds of SWAT cops around to make sure no one from the *banlieues* gets anywhere close."

MJ frowned. "What am I—under some kind of house arrest?"

Tom took her by the shoulders. "These people play rough. I think you should lay low—at least for a couple of days."

"I think you just want me out of the way while you guys play cops and robbers." She looked at him critically. "And where will *you* be staying?"

"Staying?" Tom gave her a reassuring smile, trying to hide the fact that she'd hit the nail on the head. Tom *did* want her out of the way in case events turned sour. He fell back on tradecraft: *charm, deflect, redirect.* "Sweetheart, I don't think I'm going to be getting much rest in the next forty-eight hours."

32

BY 7:30, REUVEN'S CORSICAN IN CHIEF, who identified himself to Tom simply as Milo, had assembled a twenty-five-man crew of carpenters, bricklayers, electricians, and painters in the 4627 warehouse. Milo was built like a whiskey barrel. He stood about five-foot-nine and his upper arms were as big as most men's thighs. His plaid flannel shirt was open halfway down his hairy chest, revealing a jewel-encrusted crucifix suspended from heavy gold links wrought in the style of an anchor chain. The links were as thick as a baby's fingers.

Milo smelled of tobacco, garlic, and brandy. Under what Tom took to be his perpetual five-o'clock shadow, a long, nasty scar ran from just behind his right ear, across his cheek and lower lip, all the way to the upper left corner of his mouth. The upward thrust of the scar gave the Corsican a decidedly sinister yet slightly goofy look—Tom was reminded of the ludicrous expression frozen on Jack Nicholson's face when he played the Joker in one of the Batman movies.

At 7:55, Tom gave Milo a rough floor plan of what he wanted. The Corsican asked half a dozen brusque questions, then summoned his people—most of whom looked like his relatives—into a scrum. Milo made a short speech, then barked a series of orders in a dialect Tom found completely impenetrable.

Just after noon, Tom's cell phone rang. "Game on," Reuven's voice boomed. "Arrival this evening."

"Bon." Tom tried to shield the phone from the noise of the air hammers and circular saws and continued in Arabic. "Is our friend bringing the perfume and the CD?"

"Both," Reuven said. "No problem."

"What about the other place?" Tom was talking about rue Lambert.

"No movement. No developments."

"When do I see you?"

"Later. I have errands to run. Bye." The phone went dead in Tom's ear. He turned and looked with satisfaction at the progress being made. The warehouse now resembled a movie set. Lights, some of them big scoops covered with colored gel, others with barn doors to limit and focus the throw of the light, hung from scaffolding. There were walls joined together by oversize clamps and ramps covered with padding to mask any sound of footsteps. The vehicles had all been moved to one side of the place so there was ample room around the perimeter of the set. As Tom watched, two Corsicans strung speaker wire for the two amplified subbass speakers that from above could create a cornucopia of wall-vibrating sounds running the gamut from the window-rattling noise of about-to-land military aircraft to the ominous rumble of close-by thunder. Another pair of laborers were uncoiling flexible plastic air-conditioning conduit, which Salah would use both to create heat and cold in the cell and interrogation room and to pump in the manipulative odor of *parfum pénitentiaire* that would create the requisite feeling of dread in Yahia Hamzi.

7 P.M. The interrogation center was ready for painting. Tom did a walk-through. It was quite remarkable—as if a little piece of Qadima prison had been flown from Israel and enclosed in a well-insulated outer shell here on the St. Denis–Aubervilliers border. From the outside, you were obviously looking at a stage set. But from the inside, the place was totally, frighteningly, realistically convincing. It was built around a corridor about twenty feet long. The corridor walls were real masonry—except the cinder blocks were a half-inch-thick facade. The floor was covered with thick rubber pads.

At each end, the corridor took a ninety-degree left turn—which ended after only four feet. But Hamzi wouldn't ever be allowed to discover the ruse. On the right side of the corridor were four scarred steel doors, each one with a peephole five feet above the ground, and a food slot at waist level. Three of the doors were dummies—there was nothing behind them. The fourth led to the cell they'd keep Hamzi in.

Seven feet from the end of the corridor on the left-hand side was the doorway to the ten-foot-square interrogation room. They'd poured quick-setting concrete over inch-thick plywood to make the flooring. The door was made of solid steel and clanged like a prison door should when it was slammed shut. The furnishings were as close to Qadima as Milo's crew could get their big hairy hands on. There was a utilitarian gray metal desk and two olive-drab straight-backed metal frame chairs. The legs of the in-terrogatee's chair had been cut down before the chair itself was bolted into the floor so that Hamzi would sit three inches lower than Salah.

There were three video cameras hidden in the walls. Concealed in the center desk drawer was a voice stress recorder, whose remote readout screen Salah could see simply by glancing down. The temperature of the interroga-tion room could be adjusted within minutes to whatever Salah wanted.

Down the hall was Hamzi's eight-by-six-foot cell. The cell was designed and furnished to Reuven's specifications, which he'd phoned in at about two. There was a steel bed frame, on which rested a one-inch-thick mattress made of cheap foam covered in itchy, urine-stained canvas, a threadbare blanket the size of a bath towel, and a pillow that reeked of old vomit.

The cell's floor, like the interrogation room's, was concrete. And the bed, which sat jammed against the sidewall, was bolted into it. Four air vents played directly into the small space so that no matter where its occupant might try to hide, there would be an unending flow of cold or hot air. Directly under the bed was another small vent, camouflaged to look like an unused drain built into the floor. It was connected to the plastic conduit they'd use to pump the dread-causing odor into the cell.

The ceiling, which held three clusters of lights encased in dirty, thick, protective covers, was nine feet off the ground. Across from the bed was a single, perpetually dripping spigot that emptied into a six-inch open drain in the floor. The drain was rigged to clog on command. Next to the drain was a metal pail—the cell's toilet. High on the wall above the spigot was a single frosted windowpane covered by bars and grime-covered wire mesh. The outside lighting could be adjusted—evening, morning, nighttime.

Then there were the speakers. They were positioned behind the walls and above the corridor. From a sound console in the control room that was being built in the warehouse office, every sound, from hobnail-boot steps, to the sounds of torture, to the traffic noise outside the "prison," could be controlled.

The painting was critical. The cell had been finished in rough plaster that resembled the stuccolike material common to prisons all over the Middle East. Now it had to be "aged," then covered with Arabic graffiti that had to appear as if it had been encrusted many times over with paint to remove the offending marks. The subtext of the cell was "Abandon hope, all ye who enter here."

For its part, the interrogation room had to evoke a grungy, penal-institutional reaction that would—on sight alone—convince Hamzi that the only way he'd survive his ordeal was to tell everything he knew. To help achieve this, Salah had sent instructions to have the room painted in a drab, phlegmlike green.

As a further inducement, on Salah's instructions, one of Milo's Corsicans visited a butcher shop where he bought a kilo of fresh beef liver. The liver was perforated with a fork, then the bloody offal was sponged onto the floor adjacent to the chair. The resulting blood puddles were dried with a hair dryer to darken and age them, and then swiped with a towel, as if someone had tried to clean up the mess but hadn't quite succeeded.

Tom spent a few minutes sitting in the interrogatee's chair looking at the liver stains. They were subtle but evocative. Talk about performance art. You had to really work at the visual problem for a while before you finally comprehended what you were looking at. Which, of course, is why it was all so intimidating.

Sitting in the cut-down chair, Tom had to admit to himself that Salah's trompe l'oeil mind game was terrifyingly effective. Painstaking attention to detail, he concluded, was everything in these circumstances.

7:15 P.M. Reuven arrived to create the cell's graffiti. Tom watched as the Israeli scratched messages, curses, and random numbers into the stucco with his fingernails, raking the walls so hard he drew blood. He was working like a man possessed. Less than twenty-four hours ago, Reuven had taken a life. And yet the effects of that violent act seemed not to show at all. Not outwardly, at least.

By 7:40, Reuven had finished and was ready for the painters. He pronounced his work satisfactory, washed his lacerated fingers with hydrogen peroxide, and headed out for de Gaulle to pick up Salah from the Air France flight.

Tom watched him slip out the door. He was an impenetrable, unreadable man, the Israeli was. He was to be sure a valuable ally. Indeed, 4627 was lucky to have found him because in the business of intelligence gathering, where personal connections and wide access were everything, Reuven had what seemed to be an endless supply of both. But once in a while over the last week and a half, Tom had found himself wondering what really drove Reuven Ayalon. What made the man tick?

The answer was, Tom Stafford had no idea. Reuven was as compartmentalized an individual as he'd ever met. There were circles within circles within circles. Which was why Tom now felt a hiccup of . . . unease. Being a street guy, a fisher of men, Tom had an unshakable instinct that there was something covert in play here—some hidden element to the Reuven Ayalon equation—that he didn't yet comprehend, and perhaps never would. There was no logical rationale for this reaction. Except . . . whenever he started to think deeply about Reuven Ayalon—tried to get inside the man's character and analyze his motivations—Sam Waterman's old catchphrase "retirement is just another form of cover" always seemed to slip into Tom's consciousness. Except . . . except . . . Reuven detested the current head of Mossad. He'd said as much—more than once. "He's worse than Tenet," is how the Israeli had put it. "Believe me—I didn't have to leave my job. I wanted to. It was impossible to work anymore."

11:30 P.M. Salah came through the narrow warehouse doorway, bringing a sudden chill into the big space where Tom was pacing. He appeared smaller than Tom remembered him—but then, the last time he'd seen Salah, the man had been dressed in olive-drab coveralls. Now he wore a long black double-breasted overcoat that dwarfed his small frame. He carried a worn brown leather briefcase. Reuven followed behind with Salah's luggage, a bright green soft-sided suitcase.

Tom's face lit up. He waved off the Corsican security guard and jogged to the door. *"Ahlan,"* he said, taking Salah by the shoulders and embracing him in the Middle Eastern fashion. "Welcome."

The little man's eyes sparkled. "I am glad to be here. Glad to be of help," he said in Kurdish-accented Arabic.

Salah let the briefcase fall to the floor and shrugged out of his coat, revealing a worn black wool sport jacket whose left arm was pinned to the shoulder. The Israeli dropped to one knee and opened the scarred briefcase flap, rummaged inside, and handed Tom a package wrapped in brown paper and butcher's twine.

"For you and your fiancée," Salah said. "From my wife, Hannah."

Tom was genuinely touched. He unwrapped the paper. Inside was a plastic baggie holding perhaps a dozen small rectangular pieces of dark brown candy dusted with powdered sugar.

Salah said, "This is called *loozina*. It is very sweet, and very good. In our part of Iraq—Kurdistan—it is supposed to bring good luck to a marriage."

"I am honored. We are honored."

"You are welcome." Salah stepped back and looked around. "This is immense," he said. "Very large. Very impressive."

"It works for us," Tom responded, not knowing quite what to say. He looked at the little man, who was rubbing at his mustache with the back of his right index finger. "Can I get you something? Coffee? Perhaps you would like to rest."

Salah dropped his hand, closed the briefcase, and stood up. "Reuven has brought me up to speed," he said. "I would like a small glass of whiskey—Scotch. J&B, if you have it, without ice or water. And then"— the Israeli pointed at the outer shell of the interrogation center—"I would like to see what you have built in there." He looked at Tom. "We have much to prepare for."

33

TOM CHECKED FOR PURSUIT VEHICLES in his rearview mirror. He saw nothing, but even so, he downshifted and hit the BMW's throttle, kicking the black motorcycle upward of 180 kilometers an hour through the highway's soft curves.

He'd come out of St. Denis and headed due north, then turned northwest, then south, then north again on the A15 superhighway, driving almost all the way to Pontoise. Then he'd reversed course, wheeled the big bike around, and taken back roads, running the perimeter of the denuded trees and evergreens of the Forêt de Montmorency. At Domont, he turned south onto Route 309 and drove through the forest, to Sannois. From there, Tom headed north and east, taking the back roads to Cormeilles-en-Parisis.

10:21 A.M. Tom slipped into the town from the southeast. Dressed in reinforced black leather from head to toe, a shiny black helmet with reflective visor covering his face, he looked like a character out of *Star Wars*. Underneath the leather he wore jeans and a turtleneck. And in the left-hand saddlebag was a tweed sport coat.

Because he was following Waterman's First Law of Espionage, Tom wasn't taking any chances. Expect the unexpected was the watchword of his particular faith. So, beneath the visor, he wore a prosthetic that altered his appearance just in case Margolis had set him up to appear on candid camera. In his saddlebags were magnetized license plates that could be slapped on at a moment's notice. And by peeling off the appliqué that covered the front fender, rear fender, and the gas tank, the BMW could metamorphose from bright cobalt blue to black in a matter of seconds. He'd punched up a map of Cormeilles-en-Parisis on the computer, highlighted the streets he'd have to travel, and taped it to the gas tank so he wouldn't have to hesitate or ask directions.

10:23. He drove slowly past the garages on rue Joffre, then turned east and cruised the residential neighborhoods. Like many of Paris's bedroom suburbs, the center of Cormeilles-en-Parisis had block after block of cookie-cutter apartment buildings. As you approached the outskirts, there were single-family dwellings that, except for their architectural style and their lack of SUVs in the driveways, could have been bedroom communities in Reston, or Yonkers, or Evanston.

10:30. He turned down rue Marceau, checking the map as he banked left. Margolis's apartment house would be on rue General de Gaulle, which would be a left turn from rue Marceau about a hundred and fifty meters down the block. Tom eased up on the throttle and pulled to the curb to allow a delivery van to pass him.

That was strange. It was Saturday. In union-run France, deliveries were customarily done Monday through Friday, between eight and four. Tom sat at the curb and watched.

Just past rue Charles de Gaulle, the van U-turned and set up so that its back window faced the intersection. As it did, Tom gunned the BMW and drove past, noting and memorizing the license-plate number—another anomaly because the *département d'immatriculation* numeral on the plate was 64—which meant the van was registered in the Pyrenees, on the Spanish border. Strange for a delivery van with a Parisian address stenciled on its side. So Tom didn't turn onto rue General de Gaulle. He went to the next block and turned right. Then he drove two blocks, turned right again, drove four blocks, and turned right again on a residential street named rue Baudin and continued on until he crossed rue Marceau.

Two blocks past rue Marceau, at Place Marie, he turned right again, veering onto avenue Parmentier, which ran more or less north–south from the edge of town to the railroad station. He pulled to the curb. Something was just not right. Tom reached for his cell phone. Then he shoved it back in his black leather jacket. Too easy to intercept calls. He'd handle this by himself.

He checked his six, then merged into the light traffic and steered the Beemer down avenue Parmentier. The street actually had some character. There were mature oaks and poplars lining the broad sidewalks. There were a couple of decent-looking restaurants, some nice cafés—and not a Starbucks or McDonald's in sight, which is more than the Champs-Élysées could claim.

10:42. Tom drove until he came to rue General de Gaulle, turned right, drove half a block, found six feet of empty curb between cars, and pulled over. Motor idling, he reached into the right-hand saddlebag and withdrew a small pair of range-finding binoculars, which he trained down the street.

Two blocks ahead on the right-hand side stood Margolis's apartment house—a four-story redbrick shoe box of a place. From the look of it, it had probably been built in the early seventies. If he stretched, Tom could just make out the van on rue Marceau. Now he refocused the binocs, panning them back and forth on rue General de Gaulle.

God damn. There were two surveillance teams on the street. Eight guys, evenly divided in a pair of black Citroën sedans with Paris-issued private plates parked on opposite sides of the street. The cars were facing each other so the men could chase down either end of rue General de Gaulle.

There was a second van, too. It was gray, and despite the Paris address on its side, the van had a license plate ending in 23, which meant it had been issued in Creuse. Van Two sat at the near intersection on . . . Tom checked his map . . . rue Roosevelt. It was a trap. And frigging Adam Margolis was the bait.

Tom ran his field glasses over the setup. How obvious could you get? They'd prepositioned for a by-the-numbers traffic stop. The vans would seal the street off, the sedans would block the car, and the bad guy would be toast. At least that's the way it looked on paper. In real life, however, it was the eight dumbshits in the two Citroëns who'd be toast. Because they'd made a very basic error in their operational planning.

From the way the trap was set, it was obvious to Tom they'd assumed he'd be driving a car. Why? Because Henry J. NOTKINS and his boss, Harry Z. INCHBALD, were idiots.

In fact, Tom could make out INCHBALD in the front seat of the Citroën facing him. It was Liam McWhirter, all right, even though he was wearing a Harpo Marx wig, fake eyeglasses, and a light disguise prosthetic: still the same red-faced, porcine drunk. Tom adjusted the binoculars. Jeezus, McWhirter was even wearing his trademark wrinkled blue button-down Brooks Brothers shirt under the tan Nautica golf jacket.

Tom panned the other seven, but found no familiar faces. He went back to McWhirter, who was holding his radio upside down, speaking into the mike out of the side of his mouth. Nothing like being obvious. What the hell were these guys trying to do?

Tom had told Margolis he'd be driving. He hadn't said *what* he'd be driving. But Margolis assumed it would be a car—and that, no doubt, is what he'd told Harry Z.

Too bad. Tom shut the engine off, raised his visor, and adjusted the prosthetic. Then he pulled a detailed road map of *Paris et environs* out of his saddlebag. He sat sideways on the BMW's saddle, arms crossed, studying the map, and worked out two alternate evasion and escape plans, just in case he'd need them.

10:55. Adam Margolis, CIA bait boy, appeared on the front steps of the apartment house. He was carrying a legal-size brown envelope. Tom adjusted the focus on his binoculars and looked into the windshield of the Citroën facing him. Harry Z. INCHBALD pointed at Margolis, smacked the driver's arm, and spoke into the radio. The driver reached down and forward with his right hand. Turning the ignition key, no doubt. Tom watched the big sedan vibrate slightly as the driver gunned the engine. He focused on the other Citroën, and the two vans. All the drivers were revving engines. They were good to go.

So was Tom. But he didn't go anywhere near Henry J. NOTKINS or Harry Z. INCHBALD. That move would have been pure Hollywood bull puckey. Sure, if Tom were being played by Brad Pitt in a Jerry Bruck-heimer movie directed by Michael Ritchie, he'd gun the bike, roar down the street, veering at the last minute onto the sidewalk, where he'd knock a couple of fruit stands into next week, slalom past terrified knots of pedes-trians, snatch the envelope out of Margolis's hand, and thread the needle at the end of the blocked-off street (missing the blocking van by microns). Then, after using a parked car as a ski jump for the motorcycle, he'd skedaddle. The two Citroëns and two vans would careen after him, and there'd be a wild, six-minute *wham-bam-slam* jump-cut chase against on-coming traffic that would end with all the bad guys' vehicles wrecked, Tom in the clear, and moviegoers on the edge of their seats.

So much for fantasy. Tom, who had once rear-ended his Agency vehi-cle and spent thirteen hours on the damn postaction paperwork justifying the expense, backed the bike around the corner, shut the motor off, then wrestled the Beemer onto its stand. Then he went back and surreptitiously observed McWhirter's wannabe trap for another half minute. He made brief mental notes.

Then he pulled one of the two untraceable 4627 prepaid cell phones he was carrying out of his leather jacket, dialed 17, which is the two-digit toll-free number for the Paris region Gendarmerie Nationale, and, using a Mar-seillaise accent, told the police operator there was a kidnapping of an American diplomat in progress on rue General de Gaulle in Cormeilles-en-Parisis and that four vehicles were involved. Tom recited the license-plate numbers, described the positions of the Citroëns and the vans on the street, and hung up. Quickly, he pulled the battery out of the cell phone and stomped it with his boot heel. Without a battery, the phone's position could not be tracked—even by DST.

He strolled back to the BMW, straddled the bike, rolled it off the stand, and turned the ignition key.

11:03. From six blocks away, Tom heard the approaching hee-haw of police cars before the four cars of Americans did. When he saw the two black SWAT vans heading toward rue General de Gaulle, he knew the gen-darmes weren't taking any chances. Before Harry Z. INCHBALD's team knew what was happening, they'd be swarmed by submachine-gun–toting cops in black fatigues, pulled out of the vehicles, and proned on the ground.

11:04. Tom raised the visor of his helmet, removed the prosthetic, peeled all the remaining cement off his skin, and dropped everything into a plastic baggie, which got stored in one of the saddlebags. Then he backed up the bike, turned it around, and rode to avenue Parmentier. There, he found a café, parked, pulled off his helmet, secured it to the saddle, went to the bar, and ordered a double *café crème* and a *pain au chocolat.*

11:58 A.M. Tom paid for the food, returned to the bike, and drove at a leisurely pace back to rue General de Gaulle. He circled the area so he could observe the street from both ends. There was no sign of the Americans—or the police. He drove a couple of blocks farther east, then pulled to the curb and dialed the cell-phone number Adam Margolis had given him.

It was answered after three rings. "This is Adam."

"Hi, Adam. Guess who."

There was a pause. "You son of a bitch."

"What in heaven's name are you talking about?" Tom played the innocent. "I'm running about an hour late, and I'd—" The phone went dead in Tom's ear.

Too bad. The kid obviously had no sense of humor. Well, the problem was endemic at Langley these days. They'd all forgotten how to laugh at themselves.

Tom kicked the bike into gear and headed back to St. Denis. At least one thing was clear from the morning's exercise: 4627 was now officially persona non grata at Paris station.

34

TOM FLIPPED HIS CELL PHONE CLOSED. "Two containers addressed to Yahia Hamzi's Boissons Maghreb cleared customs at Orly this morning. He sent his truck to the *zone de fret*. Our guy at Orly says the bill of lading lists wine and olives. The containers came via Air France cargo. Five pallets."

"Good." Reuven Ayalon drummed his fingers on the desk. "Now we wait to see what Hamzi does." He punched a number into his cell phone. "Let's see where he is now." Reuven waited, then spoke in rapid Arabic. He listened, then flipped the phone shut. "He's still at lunch—he drove to Rimal and he's eating alone. But he just took a phone call."

Antony Wyman looked over at Tom. "We're set, right?"

Tom tapped his cell phone. "Ready and waiting." Reuven had engineered a false-flag op. He'd decided that the Corsicans would stick out in Pantin. And so, as Reuven explained it to Tom and Tony Wyman, he'd had Milo's Corsican Mafia contacts recruit a couple of gangbangers from an Algerian drug gang to do the snatch. It was a straight cash deal. The Algerians were told Hamzi was behind in his vig payments and the Corsicans wanted him. Payment was two thousand euros in used banknotes: a grand in advance and the rest on the safe delivery of Hamzi and his Mercedes to a prearranged location in Malakoff, a southern suburb of Paris convenient to the *périphérique*.

From there, the Corsicans would drive Hamzi to a location in Bagnolet, where Reuven and Tom would meet them. Reuven would set the hook—tell Hamzi he was being flown to Israel for interrogation—then administer a dose of ketamine potent enough to knock the Moroccan out for a couple of hours. The rest would be up to Salah.

Who didn't have a lot of time to break the Moroccan. If the explosives were indeed in the Orly shipment, then Ben Said was almost certainly in Paris. And he'd want to get his hands on the goods so he could finish rigging the bombs. The interrogation process had to be completed in a matter of hours.

2:52. Tony Wyman paced the research room like a caged animal. He was uncharacteristically nervous. He'd spent the weekend working to unravel the Adam Margolis fiasco—and he didn't like what he'd discovered. The order to lure Tom Stafford into a compromising situation had come straight from the seventh floor. That actually made sense in a perverted sort of way. If the seventh floor could prove Tom had acted improperly, it could arbitrarily yank his clearance. That would, in turn, put 4627's entire CIA contract in jeopardy—a loss of more than $30 million over the next twenty months.

But why jettison 4627? It was one of the few sources of accurate and actionable intelligence product coming to Langley these days. Tony debriefed Tom, of course—but without concrete results. They'd even done a chronology and created a time line, starting when Shahram said he'd taken the surveillance pictures of Imad Mugniyah and Tariq Ben Said on rue Lambert and ending with the Iranian's murder. But nothing made sense.

Oh, they were being gamed. Instinctively, Wyman understood that. But he had no real idea what the game was, or why it was being played. He marched over to the long walnut table and looked down at the chronology again. *There was something missing from this puzzle.* But what?

Tom had set up an operations center in the 4627 research room over the weekend. They'd had secure phone terminals, three computers, video equipment, and a color laser printer brought in from upstairs. The room itself was pretty secure. There were no windows, the outer walls were well insulated and had white sound running through conduits, and 4627's technicians swept the place twice a day. He looked across the room to where MJ was Googling something or other on one of the computers.

She'd insisted on accompanying Tony Wyman to the office. "I'm going crazy in that damn hotel room," is how she'd put it. Wyman agreed readily. She'd already proven herself to be an asset. When she and Tom married, Wyman had already decided, they'd become 4627's first tandem.

Wyman looked over at her. "MJ?"

She swiveled her chair to face him. "Tony?"

"Do me a favor, will you?" He tapped the folder containing the chronology. "Take a look at this and tell me what's missing."

"No problem."

She logged off the computer, went to the sideboard, and made herself a mug of hot chocolate, which she carried to the side table sitting next to one of the leather club chairs. Then she retrieved the two-page chronology, took a yellow legal pad and a pencil from the long walnut table, dropped into the chair, pulled her reading glasses out of her hair, and stuck them on the end of her nose.

Tom watched her settle in, thinking she was the most beautiful woman on the face of the earth.

3:11 P.M. "Tony," MJ said, "what about me?"

Wyman's monocle dropped onto his vest. "What about you what?"

"I'm not in the chronology."

Wyman gave her a quizzical look. "So?"

"October tenth: Shahram calls Paris station. October twelfth: Shahram visits the embassy. October twelfth: Shahram goes into hiding. October fifteenth: Gaza." She paused. "Okay, now I add myself into the time line. Five P.M., October sixteenth: I send the name Imad Mugniyah to Mrs. ST.

JOHN. Very early October seventeenth: Mrs. ST. JOHN calls the seventh floor about my Imad Mugniyah photo. Before I get in, she's already rejected the picture and she's looking for a way to get rid of me." She looked at Tony Wyman. "But the seventh floor has already heard about Imad Mugniyah—a week before."

"Hmm." Wyman scratched his chin.

"Then," MJ continued, "roughly the same time as Mrs. Sin-Gin is telling me to go to hell, Tom is having lunch with Shahram. Shahram gives Tom pictures of Imad Mugniyah and Tariq Ben Said. Shahram knew he'd been set up the previous Sunday. Giving Tom those pictures and the information about Ben Said was his . . . I don't know, his insurance, his . . . something."

"Not insurance," Tom broke in. "Look, Shahram had his own agenda with Langley. Maybe he was running a scam, maybe not. It's possible Shahram wanted to see if he could still put the squeeze on the Agency. It's also possible he felt justified about asking twenty-five mil if he facilitated Imad's capture. But then Langley slammed him—didn't just turn him down but painted a big target on his back." Tom paused. "Look, Tony, I think Shahram truly believed he'd developed valid information, and he hated these people enough to want to get it out. So he called me."

"Hoping we'd put it to good use," Reuven said.

"Good use?" Tony Wyman pulled a vermeil Montblanc rollerball out of his vest and played with it.

"Actionable intelligence. We'd get our hands on Ben Said," Tom said.

Tony Wyman twirled the Montblanc. "And then what?"

"Turn him over."

"To whom?"

Tom shrugged. "Ultimately that's your call, Tony. But if Ben Said was responsible for Jim McGee's death, we should have him extradited to the U.S."

"That means a trial. It means a media circus."

"What about the French?"

"There's no death penalty in Europe," Reuven said.

"Which is why the French will never let him be extradited," Tom added.

Tony Wyman slid the pen back into his vest. "This is all very preliminary," he said. "It's a distraction. Right now I'd like to know Langley's motivation for throwing a wrench at us." He looked at the others. "That affects our bottom line, lady and gentlemen."

"Protection of the status quo," Tom said. "Everybody keeps their jobs." He tapped the photos MJ had printed from the video he'd shot in Ben Said's bomb lab. "Can you imagine how long anybody on the seventh floor would be employed if you took these pictures and showed them to Porter Goss. Goss wants George Tenet's job bad."

Tony Wyman gave Tom a wary look. "Porter and I were in the same training class—and we've stayed in touch." Wyman scratched his chin. "As I recall, he was an adequate operator." He paused. "I agree—he wants Tenet's job, and having one of our own as DCI could improve the situation at DO. But I'm not in favor of a coup—at least for the present."

"Why?"

"It's not in our interests." Wyman's voice took on an edginess. "Because we have no resolution, Tom. No bad guys in handcuffs. No bombs for show-and-tell."

Wyman was deflecting. Tom couldn't believe it. "Tony, I'm serious. Look at what's happening in the press. Langley is leaking like a sieve these days. It's goddamn unprecedented. All sorts of stories about how the White House cooked the books on Iraq. Stories about how CIA tried to warn the president that there were no WMDs." Tom slapped the table with the flat of his hand. "It's all chaff, Tony. Disinformation. What the Sovs used to call active measures. You know it as well as I do. The president asks the DCI whether or not there are WMDs, and the DCI tells him, 'It's a slam dunk,' even though anyone at Langley worth their salt had doubts about the depth of the program. And now the seventh floor is trying to weasel out of the responsibility for giving everyone—everyone from the White House to the Pentagon to State—either bad intelligence or no intelligence at all. This whole rotten situation is about job security, Tony. No more, no less. We should take what we know to Porter Goss and let him run with it."

"The answer is no," Wyman snapped. "Let me be blunt here, Tom: 4627 is not in the business of staging coups at CIA."

"Maybe we should be."

"Perhaps you and Reuven should worry more about refining the details of the current operation to ensure we don't have any flaps and less about the machinations of Washington politics." There was about thirty seconds of dead air. Then Tony Wyman said, "Thank you, MJ. Your contributions have been enormously valuable." He picked up the two sheets of time line and the yellow legal pad on which MJ had written her notes, and tucked them under his arm. "You guys keep at it," he said. "I'm going to make some phone calls."

When Wyman had left the room, Tom turned to Reuven and spoke in Arabic. "What do you think?"

The Israeli shrugged. "I think he's a boss. Bosses do what bosses do." Reuven's cell phone chirped. He flicked it open and said, *"Parle-moi."* Fifteen seconds later, he snapped the instrument shut. "The shipment just left Orly. Our guy's headed for Boissons Maghreb," he said. "If he loads any containers of olives into his car, we'll snatch him." He looked at Tom. "Let's get to the warehouse."

RUE DU CONGO, PANTIN
4:54 P.M.

They were using the small EUREC truck. Reuven, in repairman's coveralls, a black knit cap, and a bushy mustache attached to his upper lip sat behind the wheel, a cell phone clapped to his ear and a cigarette dangling from the corner of his mouth. Tom was set up in the rear of the blue ÉCLAIRAGE & SIGNALIZATION truck behind a black gauze sniper's screen that made him invisible to anyone staring through the windshield but didn't impede the vision of his light-gathering Steiner binoculars or the telephoto lens of the digital Nikon single-lens reflex he'd set up on a tripod. Behind Tom, Milo stretched out, eyes closed, on a dirty cot mattress.

Tom turned toward Milo. "Where are the Algerians?"

"Around," Milo grunted.

"Not obvious, I hope."

Milo propped himself up on an elbow. "Did *you* see them?"

"Not yet."

"You won't." The Corsican lay back down and rested an arm across his eyes.

They'd set up on the south side of rue du Congo, just past the intersection of rue Auger, giving themselves an unobstructed view of the block-square commercial zone of small warehouses, contractors' storage sheds, and light-industrial companies. They were roughly 175 yards from Boissons Maghreb, well within the range of Tom's 500mm telephoto lens. Hamzi's facility was, in fact, not a proper warehouse at all, but a deep, moderately wide storefront with basement storage. The place sat between an electrical contractor and a restaurant-supply house. The heavy steel trapdoors to the basement were propped open and the hydraulic lift was level with the sidewalk. Obviously, they were waiting for a shipment.

5:19. The truck from Orly eased up onto the curb and blocked the sidewalk to make unloading easier. Two burly Arabs unbuckled the rubberized canvas sides of the truck, revealing three plastic-wrapped pallets holding what appeared to be cases of wine and two pallets on which were stacked dozens of two-foot-high yellow plastic barrels of olives. Tom shot a dozen or so photos.

5:22. It was growing dark rapidly. As Tom affixed the night-vision device to the camera lens, the truck crew stopped work and lit up cigarettes. That, too, was captured on the Nikon's memory stick.

5:47. Hamzi arrived in a champagne-colored Mercedes 500-series coupe with Paris plates whose grille and bumpers had been gold-plated. The Moroccan drove up onto the sidewalk and parked.

Reuven heard Tom say, "Pimp your ride much, Yahia?" As the Moroccan exited the car, Tom muttered to himself and shot more pictures.

5:48. Hamzi took a look around—a wary coyote sniffing the wind. He looked much the same as he had in Shahram's surveillance photo: clean-shaven, a round, dark face set off by thick-framed eyeglasses with tinted lenses, and a full head of curly black hair. He was dressed in a dark raglan-sleeved wool overcoat, under which he wore his customary light-colored suit and open-necked shirt. The Moroccan's body language betrayed nothing untoward. He turned his attention to the cargo and gesticulated, berating the crew, who ground out their cigarettes on the pavement and resumed unloading.

5:53. It had gone completely dark. The first load of wine cartons descended into the Maghreb cellar. The pallets of olives were still untouched. Tom increased the power of the lens, focusing on Hamzi's head, watching as the Moroccan watched the elevator disappear. Suddenly Hamzi whirled, looking straight into Tom's lens, as if he sensed the American's presence.

Rattled, Tom hit the shutter and captured the expression on Hamzi's face. As he did, it occurred to him that the Moroccan might have heard the shutter, even though the Nikon's shutter was digital not mechanical. Even though Tom was more than a hundred and fifty yards away and the truck was just one shadow among many.

Tom was nervous. He edged forward and whispered, "Time to make the adjustment, Reuven?"

He had no evidence that they'd been compromised. But there was something about Hamzi's actions that made Tom uneasy. It was almost as if the Moroccan knew he was being watched. Was it them? Was it the Algerians? Had there been a slip somewhere? Ops like this were risky and hugely prone to compromise. You could never be sure what was what. Tom said, "Reuven?"

"Your op," the Israeli said. "Your call."

Tom chewed his upper lip for several seconds, watching Hamzi. The Moroccan was talking to his crew. Then he turned away and looked into the darkness, staring straight into Tom's eyes once again. Tom almost dropped the camera onto his lap. "We move, Reuven."

5:55:14 P.M. Tom slapped the Israeli's shoulder. "Go."

Reuven turned the ignition key, eased the truck off the curb, drove fifty feet, and without signaling made a quick right turn into a narrow passageway heading south. Once they were out of sight of rue du Congo, the Israeli floored the truck and sped eighty yards to where the passageway spilled into a narrow, crooked street that ran east to west. Before Reuven had started the engine, Tom had already collapsed the tripod. Once the truck was moving, he ripped the sniper screen down and stuffed it, along with the tripod, camera, NV, and binoculars, into a black canvas satchel.

5:55:47. At the end of the passageway, Reuven brought the truck to a stop and jumped onto the pavement. Tom followed him. The Israeli rapped the side of the truck with his knuckles. "Milo—back to the warehouse, please."

"My pleasure." The Corsican slid behind the wheel and drove off.

5:55:56. They'd prepositioned a black Audi sedan. Reuven used a remote control to unlock the door of the big car and switch the ignition on.

The car's side and rear windows were heavily tinted and its interior lights had been turned off.

5:56:11. Tom climbed into the passenger seat. He clutched the satchel on his lap, unzipped the top flap, and retrieved the sniper's gauze veil. "Go."

5:56:25. Reuven edged the car into the street. All lights out, he drove about sixty yards and stopped.

5:56:36. Tom handed the Israeli one side of the sniper's veil.

5:56:38. Reuven took it and pressed the corner up against the far upper left-hand side of the windshield, attaching the gauze with a small tab of Velcro. Then he attached the bottom to a Velcro patch on the lower edge of the dashboard. Tom mirror-imaged Reuven's actions on the right-hand side of the windshield.

5:56:43. They were perhaps sixty feet south of the rue du Congo intersection. As Tom retrieved the camera, Reuven edged the Audi forward crawling foot by foot until they were able to see the Boissons Maghreb storefront.

5:57:30. The truck was still there all right—complete with the pallets of wine and olives just as they'd been less than three minutes before. But the sidewalk in front of the storefront was deserted. And Yahia Hamzi and his gold-plated Mercedes were nowhere to be seen.

35

"MERDE." Tom ripped the gauze off and slammed the dash.

"Got an idea." Reuven gunned the Audi, swerved right at the corner, then took his first right again. "If he's going back into town, this is the shortest way."

"And if he's not?"

"Then we're screwed. But he's not carrying any olives. The two pallets were still wrapped securely. I don't think he's making the drop."

"Are you sure?"

The Israeli snorted. "I'm a trained observer, remember?"

Tom was in no mood for jokes and said so.

"Take it easy, boychik." Reuven took a reassuring tone. He handled the big car smoothly. Reuven swung left onto a busy avenue, chockablock with brightly lit stores and sidewalks crowded now that the Ramadan fast had ended. Tom caught a glimpse of the street sign. It read Av. J. LOLIVE.

"There!" Reuven said. "Look. That's him." Quickly, the Israeli pulled the car over to the curb. "About half a block ahead—he double-parked on the right."

Tom rummaged for his binoculars. The car was Hamzi's all right. Stopped on a block of cafés, newspaper stands, and small supermarkets. The Moroccan had double-parked outside a greasy spoon, leaving his flashers on.

Tom started to lift the field glasses to his eyes but Reuven slapped them back onto his lap. "No," the Israeli said in Arabic. "Don't."

"Sorry." Tom had gotten so excited he'd forgotten his tradecraft. He checked the pedestrian traffic. Pairs of bearded men in skullcaps walked arm in arm, their wives in burkas trailing behind carrying the grocery bags. The refrigerated display window of a halal butcher opposite Tom flaunted whole goats and half lambs, their entrails hanging from the partially skinned corpses. Somewhere close by, *banlieue* gangbangers were playing Rai rap on a boom box. Reuven was right: they'd crossed into an alternative Islamic universe.

Tom squinted at the steamy window and read the Arabic aloud. "Abu Ali Café." He started to exit the Audi, but Reuven grabbed his arm. "Stay put."

Tom shook off the Israeli's hand. "I want to see what he's doing," he said in French.

Reuven shook his head and continued in Arabic. "It doesn't matter what he's doing—he'll get back in the car in a minute—the flashers are going." The Israeli's tone was rebuking. "C'mon, man—take a look at the people in the street. It's like we turned the corner and suddenly we're in Beirut, or Oran. Look at yourself. You put your gringo ass anywhere near that place, you'll blow us."

"What if he's meeting Ben Said there? Or phoning him?"

"If he is," Reuven said, "we'll find out about it soon enough." The Israeli rubbed his hands together. "Wait him out, Tom. Time is on our side—not his."

Tom wasn't entirely convinced. Then he saw Hamzi come out the door of the café juggling a pair of oversize brown plastic bags. The Moroccan opened the car door, leaned inside, and dropped his cargo on the floor of the front passenger seat. Then he climbed in, closed the door on the driver's side, checked his side mirror, pulled into the rush-hour traffic, and accelerated away.

"Food for the troops." Reuven let Hamzi get past the metro sign at avenue Hoche, two hundred meters ahead, only then nosing the Audi forward. "He'll veer left before the *périphérique*. That'll take him back to rue du Congo." He followed Hamzi's trail but turned right at the metro stop, paused long enough to allow a burka-clad woman to cross against the light, then steered onto a one-way street. "This'll take us back where we began this little diversion." He looked at Tom's worried expression and spoke in English. "We'll get there before he does. Trust me."

7:22 P.M. Tom stared through the night-vision device and watched the last of the wine disappear into the cellar. All that remained now were the two pallets of olives. The heavy traffic flow on rue du Congo had dwindled to a trickle—a vehicle only every seventy, eighty seconds. Hamzi's Mercedes sat on the sidewalk behind the truck. Hamzi himself had disappeared inside his storefront with the two bags of takeout and hadn't reappeared in more than an hour.

"So?" His eyes still on Boissons Maghreb, Tom nudged Reuven. "How do we activate the Algerians?"

Reuven tapped the cell phone in his hand. "One call."

"Are they close?"

Reuven remained silent.

"How does it all work, Reuven? What happens if there's a hitch?"

"If there's a hitch we work around it."

"And?"

"And what? We take this one step at a time, Tom. One step at a time." He looked analytically at the American. "This is your first, isn't it?"

"My first."

"What you people call direct action."

Tom swallowed hard. Then his head bobbed up and down once. "Affirmative."

"Listen to me: it's all right to be nervous. You're jumpy. That's natural, too—so long as it's just the two of us. But you can't ever show it. Not to outsiders."

"I know, Reuven."

"Listen to me," the Israeli continued. "Direct action is different from everything else you've ever done. It's more than mind games, or exploiting vulnerabilities, or spot, assess, develop, recruit, and run—all the agent stuff you're so very good at." He paused. "Direct action is full contact, Tom. It's life-and-death. It's the soldiering part of what we do."

"But . . ."

The Israeli looked at Tom. "You're ambivalent."

Tom shrugged, his hand inadvertently brushing the black gauze affixed between them and the windshield.

"You were never in the Army."

"No."

"Me, I'm a big believer in universal service. It's a great leveler. In Israel, we form friendships in the Army that last a lifetime. One reason is that we stay in the same reserve unit for years and years. Train with the same people. Fight with the same people."

"What's your point?"

"My particular unit," Reuven said, "honed very special skills. We were trained to observe our enemies for long periods of time without attracting attention, and then kill them quickly. Not by the hundreds, either. But by ones and twos, or sixes and sevens. Sometimes during hostage rescue situations—up close, with great speed, surprise, and violence of action. Sometimes looking them in the eyes as they died. Sometimes sniping them from great distances, and sometimes executing them asleep in their beds."

He gave Tom a quick glance, gauging his reaction. "Killing," Reuven said, "is a skill—a craft, if you will. Your man McGee had it. He was no murderer, no sociopath. But he understood what had to be done—and when it was necessary he took the proper action."

He gave Tom another fleeting look, and Tom saw the sadness in the Israeli's eyes. Then he realized it wasn't sadness at all. It was weariness. It was the bone-tiring fatigue that came from so many years of shadow warfare, so many years of intensity, passion, and rage.

Reuven continued: "There is no joy in taking life. But there are people in this world who need to be killed. Removed permanently, because of the threat they present."

The Israeli paused. "That may sound cold. But Israel has been at war a long time, Tom. Every day is life-and-death for us. And so we are used to making hard decisions about taking human lives. You can use any term you like: *direct action, lethal finding, targeted killing, assassination.* The nomenclature is simply a bureaucratic determination. The goal is the same: to forever remove a specific threat; a threat so severe that if we let that threat persist, our citizens will die. So we do what we have to do—and we suffer the consequences on the world stage with our eyes open."

He paused. "Y'know, for years, America thought of terror as a law enforcement problem. We in Israel never did. We always knew it was war. Call it what you will—warfare on the cheap, asymmetrical warfare, warfare by other means, insurgency—terrorism is war. Dirty war, but war nonetheless. And the object of war is to kill more of the enemy than they kill of you."

"I know."

"Well, for years, you Americans allowed terrorists to kill more of your people than you killed terrorists without suffering consequences. All those planes hijacked. All those Americans murdered in Beirut, in Khartoum, in Mogadishu, in Pakistan, in Kenya, in Jordan, in Tanzania, in Saudi—and in Israel. Now, after 9/11, you finally began to see some light. To deal with terrorism as what it is: unrestricted warfare."

"But the cycle of violence, Reuven."

The Israeli made a dismissive gesture. "*Ach,* the so-called cycle of violence is a lie. If the cycle-of-violence argument were true, then the Germans would still be suicide-bombing Brits and Americans for the tens of thousands of German civilians who were slaughtered during World War Two's firebombing raids." He looked at the American. "Here is the truth, Tom. This man, Ben Said, has to be stopped."

"I agree. So why not turn him over to the French—do what MJ suggested?"

"My reaction? Bottom line? Because of what he knows," Reuven said. "Look, this guy is a specialist. A genius who has managed a quantum leap in the construction of small, deadly, explosive devices." The Israeli paused. "That's why I say it's important—imperative—that he takes his secrets to his grave." Something external caught Reuven's attention and he peered through the Audi's windshield. "I don't think Tony Wyman or Charlie Hoskinson would disagree, either. Already, this animal has done quite enough damage. Quite enough for a lifetime."

The hard expression on Reuven's face calcified. "Believe me—I know the extent of the damage the Ben Saids of the world can cause."

That was when Tom really got what Sam Waterman had been talking about when he'd told Tom that retirement was just another form of cover. Understood why Reuven had agreed so readily to run 4627's Tel Aviv operation. Why the Israeli had been working so feverishly for the past couple of weeks. Why he'd pulled strings to get Tom access at Qadima. Why he'd been able to arrange in a matter of minutes for Salah to come to Paris. Why he'd scratched his hands bloody creating the graffiti on the cell wall at the warehouse. *It was personal.*

Tom shifted on the leather seat so he could see Reuven's reaction. "You think it was one of Ben Said's suicide vests that killed Leah."

If Tom had expected a visible epiphany, he didn't get one. The Israeli's face showed no reaction—not a quiver. No lump in throat. No sigh of angst. No deeply evocative moan. It was Reuven's absolute silence that was so damned eloquent. All Tom heard were the ambient noises of the street and his own measured breathing.

After about a minute, Reuven shattered the vacuum. "If you display anything but steely resolve, you'll lose control of the op, Tom. And you know as well as I do that control is everything, especially when you're working false flag or through an access agent."

The reason behind Reuven's penchant for deflection, Tom understood, was that there were some doors, some compartments, some hidden emotional and operational caches that the practitioners of their particular trade refused to open for anyone—even the best of friends. Especially the best of friends. Tom nodded. "Gotcha, Reuven."

"I hope so." Reuven turned toward the American. "Now, when we grab Hamzi, you'll get behind the wheel of this car. Don't let anyone see your face—even with a prosthetic. Don't say anything. Don't freeze. And for God's sake, don't react."

"React to what?"

"Remember." Once again, the Israeli deflected Tom's question. "Whatever happens, your job tonight is to get *this car* back to the warehouse. Full stop. My responsibilities lie with Hamzi and the barrels." He looked at Tom. "Got it?"

"We'll meet back at the warehouse, then." Tom nodded. And although he was uncomfortable with the subtext of whatever Reuven's operational decision with regard to Ben Said might turn out to be, he decided he could live with that part of it. "Got it, Reuven."

9:04 P.M. The last load of olives disappeared belowground. Tom watched as the two steel doors were dropped and a heavy lock was run through the hasp that protruded at sidewalk level. One of the cargo loaders swung into the cab of the truck, started the ignition, eased into the deserted street, and drove off. Thirty seconds later, two of Hamzi's employees came out the front door carrying eight-foot metal poles with handles on one end and hooks on the other. They reached up, snagged the outer edges of the corrugated steel security curtain, and yanked it downward.

From their vantage point eighty yards away, Tom and Reuven could hear the dissonant sound of metal on metal. As the Maghreb workers locked the curtain in place, Reuven retrieved a hands-free unit from the Audi's console. He stuck the plug into the top of his cell phone and screwed the foam earpiece into his right ear. The microphone rested against his clavicle.

9:17. Hamzi came through Boissons Maghreb's front door. He was carrying two bottles of wine. He unlocked the Mercedes, laid the bottles on the front passenger seat, slammed the door, and locked the car again. Then he went back inside.

9:23. Hamzi appeared again. This time he was wearing his overcoat. He wore it cape-style, thrown over his shoulders collar up, in the affected European fashion. Hamzi went to the rear of his car. He hit his remote. The running lights flashed three times and the trunk popped open. The Moroccan reached in and adjusted something. Then he signaled the doorway. Two of his helpers appeared. Each was carrying a pair of two-foot-high blue plastic barrels. Hamzi took them one at a time and placed them in the Mercedes' trunk. He reached down, produced a long bungee cord, and secured the barrels together to prevent them from tipping over. He stared for an instant, and then, satisfied with his work, slammed the trunk door closed.

Reuven pressed the transmit button on his cell phone. There were about five seconds of silence, and then he said in Arabic, "Go shopping."

36

HAMZI TURNED AND, GESTICULATING, obviously gave instructions to his people. Then he climbed into the car and turned the ignition switch.

Showtime. Reuven allowed the Mercedes to drive off. Tom reacted, but the Israeli said, "Not to worry, boychik, he's covered. We let the work get done, then we do our jobs."

9:27. Reuven retrieved a pair of thin leather driving gloves from the console and pulled them on. Then he turned the ignition key and put the car in gear, accelerating smoothly onto rue du Congo then immediately swinging left, to head north on a narrow one-way street.

Reuven steered with his left hand, his right index finger pressing against the cell-phone earpiece, his expression one of intense concentration. "Gotcha," he said. "On my way."

There was a blinking traffic light ahead. Reuven ran it then immediately swung right, onto the quai that ran parallel to the Canal de l'Orecq. Tom looked over at the Israeli, his face a mask of concern. "Jeezus—what about Hamzi's cell phone?"

"The intercept vehicles have frequency jammers." Reuven floored the big sedan, flattening Tom against the passenger seat. "Hold on."

"They have *what*?" Algerian gangbangers didn't have access to frequency jammers.

Reuven ignored Tom's question. He accelerated past one of the canal locks then drifted left, onto a narrow bridge that spanned the canal. Tom took a quick glance as Reuven sped north, then west. Jeezus H. Keerist, they were less than half a block from the Pantin Garde Nationale barracks.

Tires squealing, Reuven four-wheel-drifted around a corner. He sped east until he reached the chain-link perimeter fence that marked the big commuter rail storage and maintenance facility. He turned south, then east again, finally threading the needle past a set of steel-and-concrete barriers into a narrow, dark street that looked as if it had been flattened by bombs. Reuven looked at Tom. "Everything demolished," he said disparagingly, "to make way for a branch of IKEA. Progress, eh?"

There, in the Audi's headlights, was Hamzi's Mercedes. The Moroccan's car was trapped in a pincer by two dark-colored late-model sedans with Paris license plates. Behind the Mercedes were a pair of motorcycles. As Reuven pulled up, Tom could see the motorcycle riders. They wore black leather and visored helmets that covered their faces. The drivers, dressed in dark jeans and leather jackets, had balaclavas. All four were armed: two pointed long, dark semiautomatic pistols at the Mercedes. The other pair held miniature submachine guns with suppressors fixed onto their stubby barrels.

The Mercedes had stalled out. Inside, the Moroccan was looking wildly around, screaming into what was obviously a useless cell phone.

"Goddamnit—what are they waiting for, the Messiah?" The Israeli slammed to a screeching stop, smashed his palm into the dash and extinguished the headlights, jumped out of the car, and ran to the door of the Mercedes.

With a gloved hand he smashed the window, reached inside, switched the car's lights off, yanked the door open, jerked Hamzi out onto the street, pulled the cell phone out of the Moroccan's hand, body-slammed him onto the ground, and dropped onto his back. Hamzi's thick-framed glasses skittered across the macadam.

For an instant, Hamzi froze. Then he must have realized he was struggling for his life, and he tried to roll out of Reuven's grasp. But Reuven wasn't going anywhere. Tom could sense the man's desperation as he bucked and kicked.

Reuven must have caught sight of Tom because suddenly he whirled, looked back toward the Audi, and shouted, "Go-go-go!"

Tom heard. But he couldn't move. Everything was wrong. The snatch wasn't going according to plan. Not even close. He and Reuven were scheduled to take control of Hamzi in Bagnolet. Not here. Not so close to Boissons Maghreb.

The Moroccan screamed. Reuven grabbed Hamzi by the hair and yanked his head backward. He twisted the Moroccan's neck. Hamzi struggled even more wildly. He kicked and screamed and tried to pull himself off the ground. Reuven smashed the side of the Moroccan's head into the pavement and Hamzi crumpled. He still struggled, but the fight had gone out of him.

Finally, the others piled on. The subgun-toting motorcycle riders slung their weapons and held Hamzi down. Another assaulter clapped a gloved hand over the Moroccan's mouth. The second balaclava wearer handed Reuven a large black canvas satchel. The Israeli unzipped the bag and rummaged through until he found what he was looking for: a small leather case. He opened the case, extracted a syringe-looking device, pulled the needle protector off, and plunged the syrette right through Hamzi's overcoat into the man's hip.

The Moroccan went limp. Reuven stood up. He replaced the syringe in its case and dropped the case into the satchel. He looked at one of the leather-clad figures and pointed at his submachine gun. It, too, was placed in the bag.

Then Reuven produced a roll of tape and bound Hamzi's legs together at the ankles. The Moroccan's arms were also quickly pinioned. Then Reuven grabbed Hamzi under his arms and dragged him back to the Mercedes. Reuven let Hamzi's body slip to the ground. He opened the Mercedes' rear door and, with the help of one of the black-clad men, pulled the Moroccan onto the rear seat. The black satchel was tossed in next. Finally,

Hamzi's body was covered with a dark blanket that one of the black-clad figures handed to Reuven. Someone handed Hamzi's glasses to the Israeli, who dropped them into the breast pocket of his coveralls.

Tom still sat transfixed. Dumbstruck. The whole sequence hadn't taken more than half a minute. They'd rehearsed this. They'd had to.

That was when Reuven looked over to where he was sitting frozen in the passenger seat of the Audi. "Why in God's name are you sitting like a statue?" he shouted at Tom in Arabic. "Remember what I told you? Get the hell out of here."

Reuven flicked his cell phone open, punched a number, and spoke rapid Hebrew. Then he whistled once sharply and circled an index finger in the air next to his head. The four others jumped on the bikes, wheelied, and sped off into the night.

Only Reuven and Tom remained. Reuven slid behind the wheel of the Mercedes and slammed the door shut. He looked back. "Damnit, Tom—"

"I'm going." Tom pulled himself out of the Audi, went around the hood of the car, dropped into the driver's seat, adjusted it, snapped the door shut, and slammed the car into gear. His head was spinning. These weren't Algerians. Gangbangers. Drug enforcers. The whole thing was too slick, too professional. Corsicans, maybe. Who knew who they were. Who knew what the hell was going on.

And then Tom realized exactly what the hell was going on.

Because Reuven had told him, *"Control is everything, especially when you're working false flag or through an access agent."* And like some frigging greenhorn he'd nodded dumbly and said, *"Gotcha, Reuven."*

This was a false-flag op, all right. A goddamn *Mossad* false-flag op. Reuven was in control. Hadn't Shahram been trained by Israelis? They'd no doubt recruited him years ago. And Reuven? His portfolio in Paris had included Iran. Tom's mind flashed back to Herzlyia. The retired Shin Bet man Amos Aricha had known Ben Said was formulating the new explosive in small batches. Only Shahram had known that factoid.

Reuven had known about Ben Said all along. He'd recruited Tom as the access agent. And if anything went wrong, 4627 were the patsies who'd take the fall. Tom slammed the steering wheel with such force that he bent it. "Reuven, you goddamn son of a bitch."

He stomped the brakes, threw the car into reverse, and backed up violently, smacking the rear bumper of the Audi into the Mercedes, jamming it into the intercept cars.

He set the parking brake, jumped out, ran to the Mercedes, and pounded on the roof of the car with his fist. "Goddamnit, Reuven—open up."

Reuven swiveled around, threw the Mercedes into reverse, powered up the big sedan . . . and accelerated. The smell of burning rubber rose into the night air. But the Audi didn't budge.

"Goddamnit to hell, Reuven—" Tom's pounding put a dimple, then a crease, in the roof of the German car. "Let me in or you go nowhere."

The Israeli lowered the passenger-side window. "Move the Audi, Tom."

"Then what?"

The Israeli thought about it. "Then you can come with me."

"All the way?"

Reuven scratched under his hairpiece. "To the end," he finally said. "We'll play it out together." He looked at Tom and his voice softened just a bit. "You've earned it."

Tom pondered the offer. "Keys, Reuven."

The Israeli blinked. "What?"

"Give me the keys first."

Reuven examined Tom's face. Then he grimaced, and with a sigh pulled the keys out of the ignition and handed them to the American. "Happy now?"

"No, I'm royally pissed—at me more than at you." Tom shoved the keys in his pocket, strode back to the Audi, and moved it out of the way, handling the vehicle roughly. He turned off the ignition and was just about to lock the doors when Reuven exited the Mercedes.

Tom pulled himself out of the Audi and went around to the opposite side of the car to put distance between himself and Reuven. He was both disappointed and disgusted with himself. He was as blind as Tenet's CIA. He'd had no idea what the man's actual intentions were. He'd relied on a liaison relationship and that relationship had screwed him. Tom stood, fists clenched, as the Israeli approached.

Reuven reacted to Tom's body language and raised his hands in mock surrender. "Relax, boychik," he said. "Since you're coming with me, we'd better wipe this car down and get everything out of it. Then I'll torch it."

"But the cops'll track the registration."

"Not this one—unless they keep track of Audis stolen in Turkey." He gestured toward Tom's hands. "Believe me, there's no records." He paused. "When you get into Hamzi's car, touch nothing, or use your handkerchief. You're not wearing gloves and I'm not carrying an extra pair. I don't think leaving fingerprints or evidence is a good idea."

37

10:19 P.M. Reuven collapsed onto the steering wheel of Hamzi's Mercedes and wiped sweat off his face with a handkerchief. It was cold in the car because there was no driver's-side front window. They'd brushed the broken glass off the seat and removed as much of it as they could, but there were still shards on the floor by Tom's feet. Even in the chill, Reuven's collar was wet with perspiration. It was the only outward sign of the stress he'd been under.

They'd driven in silence for about eighteen minutes through northeast Paris, Reuven carefully observing all the traffic laws while Tom sat, arms crossed, fuming. At 10:17, they pulled up to a deserted garage just off the rue Simplon, about six blocks from the Gare du Nord.

Reuven obviously had a remote device in his pocket because the big roll-up door raised as they cruised up the street and drove straight inside.

The door descended behind them now, sealing them inside with an ominous thud that echoed inside the cavernous, empty space.

Reuven opened his door and rolled out onto the concrete. "Quick, Tom. Help me pull him out—but touch nothing except Hamzi."

"He called you, didn't he? Before he called me." The two of them eased Hamzi's inert form onto the ground.

"Pull off his coat and toss it in the car."

"He called you, goddamnit. Shahram. He was your agent."

"Not now, not now." Reuven yanked the black satchel out of the Mercedes. "On the front wall, Tom—lights. Just at the left-hand side of the door. Turn them on."

"Wasn't he, Reuven?" Tom held fast. "Tell me."

The Israeli gave Tom a long, forlorn stare. "Not my agent," he said. "It was closer to a peer relationship—we shared information. Kaplan, my old boss at Gelilot, was his instructor in the 1960s. Kaplan introduced us. I never formally recruited Shahram. But we dealt with one another for twenty years. Almost twenty-one."

"He contacted you. He had to. Because you told Amos Aricha about Ben Said's explosives—how he made them in small batches."

"Amos is a bigmouth." The Israeli sighed. "Shahram called right after he'd come from your embassy—he realized he'd been targeted. He couldn't talk on the open line, of course. But he said just enough to make me very anxious for him. I told him to call you."

"Oh God." Tom heaved a huge groan. He made his way across the smooth concrete and found the switch. He flipped it up and two sodium work lights came on, flooding the garage interior with sallow, greenish yellow light. Tom stood by the door, welcoming the draft chilling his ankles. He felt dizzy, light-headed, nauseated. Circles within circles. Jeezus H. Keerist. *What if, what if, what if . . .*

Tom's mind muddle was interrupted by Reuven's voice. "Tom—come help me." Reuven had rolled Hamzi onto his chest. "Here." The Israeli slit the Moroccan's bonds. "First, we take his jacket off."

Tom complied on autopilot. "How long will he be out?"

"Depends. If he has a weak heart, forever. If not, maybe six, seven hours."

"You never intended to interrogate him."

"Not true, boychik. But the majority of the interrogation will be done . . . elsewhere." They shifted Hamzi's position. Reuven looked down at the inert Moroccan with disdain. "This guy needs to go on a diet." He was right: moving Hamzi around was like trying to manipulate a sack of potatoes.

They struggled with the Moroccan's arms. Tom pulled on a sleeve and heard the sound of ripping cloth.

"Careful, boychik," Reuven said. "We're going to need these clothes."

"Sorry." Tom adjusted his grip. Finally, they eased Hamzi out of his suit coat.

Reuven took it and began a methodical search. He checked each of the pockets carefully. One held a gold and tortoiseshell enamel Dupont lighter. Reuven opened the top and flicked it on to make sure it worked. Then he removed the fill plug to make sure nothing was concealed inside. The lighter went onto the floor. There was a glasses case in Hamzi's breast pocket. That, too, was scrutinized without results. Then Reuven turned the suit coat inside out. He worked his hands up and down the sleeves inch by inch, his fingers probing for secret compartments or foreign materials sewn into the lining. He ran his hands around the shoulder pads. "Nothing."

He looked over at Tom, who was watching. "Pull off his shoes."

Tom eased the brown loafers off Hamzi's feet. Reuven dropped the suit coat to the floor, undid the Moroccan's belt, and began to pull Hamzi's trousers off.

"Check the soles and heels. See if anything is stored there."

Tom ran his finger around the edge of the thin sole on the right shoe. There was nothing untoward about the shoe's construction. He checked the shank. It was flexible. He played with the heel. It was attached solidly. He repeated his actions with the left shoe. "Nothing."

"Check the lining."

"What are we looking for?" Tom held the shoe up to the light and peered inside. It looked normal. He examined the right shoe. "Nothing, Reuven."

"Stuff. Anything. Everything." The Israeli went over Hamzi's belt inch by inch. He found nothing. The belt was dropped onto the floor and Reuven started unfastening Hamzi's trousers. "Pull the linings out of his shoes."

Tom used his fingernail to peel the faux leather back from the heel, then stripped the lining away from the last. The damn thing was cemented securely, and it took Tom some effort, but he finally removed it. There was nothing underneath. No secret compartment, no writing. He picked up the left shoe and began again.

Except this time the lining peeled back easily. It had been secured with rubber cement. And on the back side was a small yellow Post-it, on which were written numerals in Arabic: ٣٠٦٧٩ —30679.

"Reuven!" Tom held the lining up. "Safe combination?"

"Doubt it." The Israeli was examining the contents of Hamzi's wallet. "He'd know his safe combination by heart. I think it's the punch code for the safe house. Ben Said's a professional. He'd change the code weekly at a minimum—probably daily when he's around."

"And he's around."

Reuven jerked his thumb at the trunk of Hamzi's car. "What do you think?"

Tom started to answer, but the big garage door jerked upward noisily. "Reuven?"

"Reinforcements." Even so, the Israeli moved behind the Mercedes and Tom noticed that he'd picked up the black satchel and thrown it over his shoulder, and that his hand was inside the bag—probably holding the submachine gun.

A graphite-gray Citroën saloon with opaquely tinted windows eased into the garage. The heavy door dropped as soon as the car cleared the threshold.

Tom squinted, trying to see through the dark glass. The driver was uniformed—a chauffeur. Then he saw Salah pull himself out of the front seat of the car.

The Israeli smiled—obviously delighted—when he saw Tom. He gestured graciously with his good arm. *"Salaam wallahkum,* Tom," he said in Arabic. "I am glad Reuven brought you. As it is written in the Koran, 'God will bless the true believers.'"

Tom didn't feel like a true anything.

"Salah," he said. "What's this all about?"

"Tawil balak—give it time." The little man rushed past him and scampered behind the Mercedes, where he drew Reuven off to the side.

The trunk of the Citroën popped open. Then Salah's driver stepped out of the big car. It was Milo. "Good evening," he said to Tom.

Milo removed his chauffeur's cap and laid it on top of the dash. "You will excuse me?"

The Corsican walked to the rear, extracted a big screwdriver and two white-and-black diplomatic license plates from the trunk, exchanged the car's plates, and dropped the old ones into a garbage container. He pulled a pair of heavyweight black nylon satchels out of the Citroën's trunk and set them on the garage floor. Then he walked to where Salah and Reuven were speaking and interrupted them long enough to ask a quick question.

Tom saw Reuven nod and toss Milo something from the bag that still hung from his shoulder. Then Milo went over to where Hamzi lay, rebound the Moroccan's arms and legs, taped his mouth, then flipped him up onto his shoulder, carried him to the Citroën, eased him into the vehicle's trunk, slammed the lid shut, and double-locked it.

Tom watched as Milo retrieved his chauffeur's cap. "Where's he going? Back to our warehouse?"

"For a few hours," Salah said. "Your boss wants to know about several matters. And there are a few loose ends we'd like to tie up on our end."

"And then?"

"And then? We'll drop him off at the Moroccan embassy. The Mukhabarat will want to talk to Monsieur Hamzi, even though he hasn't been to Morocco in years himself. We've alerted them to his . . . connections."

"Rabat." Milo smiled. "King Mohamad—he pay good, you know, right, Reuven?"

Tom was listening just hard enough to hear the sound of the second shoe dropping. He looked at Salah, then at Reuven, then back at Salah. "You're retired, aren't you?"

"Sometimes," Salah said obliquely. "I work on contract basis for my old employers. Sometimes Reuven and I and some others do projects together. Like your 4627 Company." He smiled slyly at Tom's reaction. "What—you think CIA is the only agency that has to farm out what it can't do itself?"

Reuven walked up. "Money, money, money is all these guys ever talk about. Nothing but the bottom line." He tapped Milo's chest. "Did you find me one?"

Milo said, "Yes, but there's no time to make it work."

"Just put it in," Reuven said. "It doesn't have to move."

"It? What?" Tom looked at Milo, confused.

"New window," Reuven said, jerking a thumb at Hamzi's Mercedes as

Milo put on a pair of work gloves and eased a curved piece of auto glass out of the rear of the Citroën. "Car needs a new window."

The Israeli looked at Tom. "Salah brought you a change of clothes," he said, switching into English. "And something for your head. But before that, we have to deal with the olive barrels. I don't want to risk the explosive falling into the wrong hands."

11:34 P.M. The trousers were about two inches too short for the Israeli and the waist was at least three inches too big. But at any distance more than six feet away, even in daylight, Tom had to admit Reuven Ayalon would pass for Yahia Hamzi's twin.

That was because the Israeli understood two of the basic principles of disguise. First, he understood that the object of disguise is to play a trompe l'oeil with the mind of the observer by allowing the observer's mind to think it sees what it is seeing. Reuven had studied enough psychology to understand that the human mind views the world in patterns; patterns that allow every one of us to make the scores of intuitive shortcuts we make on a daily basis. These patterns are because one particular memory section of the brain has the ability to draw a firm conclusion based on experience and patterns without having to go through endless comparisons. Thus, when someone is asked to identify a photograph of a mustached man in a bowler hat and striped baggy trousers who is holding a cane, the brain skips the intermediate steps of trying to identify every single person with a mustache we've ever seen because the memory section remembers watching *The Gold Rush* and tells the mouth to say "Charlie Chaplin."

Why? Because that's the pattern the mind has been programmed to accept. The pattern is preconditioned by prior experience, prior exposure.

Reuven understood that if a disguise reinforces the key elements of appearance, it will fool the brain into jumping to the right—which will be the wrong—conclusion. Two and two will equal four. In Hamzi's case, the key elements were the Moroccan's curly, pseudo-Afro hairstyle, his heavy-framed, rose-tinted eyeglasses, and his habitual light-colored suit. All three of those elements had stuck, Tom remembered, in Dianne Lamb's memory.

So even if Reuven was a few centimeters taller than Hamzi and twelve kilos lighter, if he built his disguise around that basic trio of key elements, the brains of anyone who knew Hamzi would instantaneously fill in the blanks and send the Yahia Hamzi recognition signal into that person's consciousness.

Second, Reuven understood the quacks-like-a-duck rule. If he looked like Yahia Hamzi, and he drove Yahia Hamzi's car, and he was schlepping barrels of Yahia Hamzi's Boissons Maghreb olives, then he had to be— *quack-quack*—Yahia Hamzi.

Tom watched as the Israeli squatted and arranged the hairpiece's ringlets in the Citroën's rearview mirror. Then Reuven stood up and theatrically whipped Hamzi's overcoat around his shoulders just the way the Moroccan did. Reuven struck a pose. "Not bad for quick-and-dirty, eh?"

He pulled two pairs of flesh-colored latex gloves out of the satchel Milo had brought, pulled one pair on, and handed the other to Tom. "You'll need these." Reuven put two fingers into his mouth and gave a shrill whistle. "Time to move, boys."

38

REUVEN PULLED THE MERCEDES up onto the curb in front of L'Étrier. The bistro was shut down for the night. The street was empty—no watchers visible, although both men understood they were probably being surveilled. The Israeli switched the headlights off and popped the trunk. He swiveled toward Tom and spoke in soft French. "You remember the number?"

"Three zero six seven nine."

"Justement." He cracked his door, turned to Tom, and snapped his fingers. *"Nazuz, habibi."*

Tom nodded and exited, went to the rear of the car, which was directly opposite the front door of the safe-house building, undid the bungee cord, retrieved two of the blue plastic barrels, and hefted them into his arms.

They were cumbersome, not to mention the fact that they weighed fifteen kilos each. Salah had given Tom a short black leather jacket, a black mock T-neck sweater, a pair of dark trousers that almost fit around the waist, and a light prosthetic that altered Tom's appearance and hairstyle. Since it was one of those one-size-fits-all apparatuses, Tom felt conspicuous wearing it. But Reuven had insisted.

They'd discussed the plan on the way over. Tom would help carry the barrels upstairs. Then he'd leave, drive Hamzi's car away, stash it close by but out of sight, and return to the safe house by clambering up the damnable water pipe. Only this time Reuven would have dropped a climbing rope to make the ascent easier.

Reuven slammed the driver's-side door. The Israeli had all of Hamzi's pocket litter—including his fist-size clump of keys. He followed Tom to the trunk, picked up one of the barrels and his black satchel, then slammed the trunk shut and hit the remote. The Mercedes's lights blinked twice. With his head, Reuven signaled Tom to follow him. The Israeli cradled the barrel in his left arm. In his right was Hamzi's key chain.

There were two dozen keys on the big ring. But Reuven had decided that only three could be the safe-house front-door key. Because the building was being renovated, the original wood door had been removed. In its place was a utilitarian steel slab with sprung hinges, wide enough for wheelbarrows to move through, and a big, industrial-strength latch-bolt lock.

Since Ben Said would have the safe house under surveillance, everything Reuven did had to be self-assured. No fumbling, no awkwardness. He'd rearranged the keys so that the three prime candidates were right on top of the pile.

With Tom in tow, Reuven went up the two steps to the door and inserted a key. It didn't fit. He cursed in Arabic, hefted the barrel, shook the key ring in obvious frustration, selected a second key, and slid it into the lock.

The cylinder ratcheted as it turned, making more noise than Tom would have liked. Reuven scowled, pulled the door open, held it while Tom went through into the entryway, then followed, pulling the metal-reinforced wood shut firmly behind him. "Mahmoud, you wait," Reuven said in Moroccan-accented Arabic. "I'll get the *minuterie*." He fumbled slightly, then found the button and pressed it. "Come," he growled. "Follow me."

The building was a wreck. The ground-floor walls had been demolished. There was plaster and dust everywhere. Bare bulbs hanging from exposed wires provided the illumination. The hallway smelled of stale cigarette smoke and old cooking oil. "The French," Reuven said, continuing his Arabic monologue. "They live like dogs."

He led the way to a narrow stairway, the marble treads concave with age and thick with plaster and wood shavings. "Up," he said, reverting into French, *"deuxième étage."*

12:13. Tom's shoulders were burning by the time they reached the third floor, but happy to be past the construction that clogged the ground and first floors. At the landing, Reuven stopped long enough to let the lights go out. Then he pressed the *minuterie.*

Reuven peered down the hallway. It was deserted. He scanned the black-and-white tile flooring, saw something, tapped Tom's arm, and pointed. There were footprints in the fine dust.

Reuven's hand instructed Tom to stay where he was. The Israeli crept forward. Then he straightened up and signaled for Tom to follow.

12:14. They stood in front of the safe-house door. Tom leaned against the wall, eased into a squatting position, and let the olive barrels slide down gently onto the corridor's tiled surface. "Heavy, Yahia," he said, wiping at his face with the patterned handkerchief that Salah had pre-positioned in his right-hand trouser pocket.

Reuven grunted. He'd placed the blue barrel on the floor next to his leg, although the black satchel still hung over his shoulder.

Now he produced a tiny LED flashlight in his left hand. Where it had come from Tom had no idea. The Israeli cast his eye down at the keys in his hand, looked at the single lock on the door, and selected the one he hoped would fit.

Tom watched as the Israeli shone the red light on the door lock. The door itself was nothing special—solid wood, with a brass escutcheon and a single-cylinder dead-bolt lock of the most common type. He glanced up and down the door frame. There was no keypad for the security device. And then he took a quick glimpse up and down the hallway and understood Ben Said's thinking. Every door had only one lock. And there were no burglar alarms visible anywhere.

So the security device would be inside. The question was, where had Ben Said put it—and if they didn't get to the damn thing in time, where would the alarm go off?

Well, they'd find out soon enough.

12:14:41. Reuven turned the key. Tom heard the dead bolt click three times. That was unusual. Most dead bolts opened on two turns of the key.

Reuven pressed the handle down and pushed the door inward.

Tom heard a muted but unmistakable electronic squeal from inside the safe house—as if an infrared beam had tripped an alarm box.

12:14:50. Reuven stepped across the threshold. Tom followed. The Israeli closed the door behind them and panned the light, moving it quickly but evenly left to right, right to left.

Tom followed the light as it played back and forth. In the corners of the foyer, he glimpsed an infrared beam projector. The receiver base would be just opposite. If the door was even cracked, the beam would be interrupted.

They were in a narrow foyer perhaps eight feet square. To Tom's left was a short corridor. Straight ahead was a long, narrow room, the entrance to which was blocked by a sheet of clear plastic attached to the wall by wide, dark tape. It didn't take Tom more than a millisecond to get his bearings. The drainpipe he'd climbed was straight ahead and to his right. Beyond the plastic sheeting were the tables with the backpacks, detonators, and the pasta machine that Ben Said used to roll out his explosives.

12:14:53. Reuven hissed, breaking Tom's concentration. The Israeli was shining his light on the floor molding to their right. Taped to it was a four-inch block of plastic explosive. Wires from the explosive led to what looked like a cell phone.

The beam from Reuven's light played on the left-hand floor molding, revealing a second, identical IED.

12:14:55. Reuven shifted the light. Straight ahead, on a small wood table—the kind that flanks sofas and holds a lamp—sat a rectangular dark box about the size and thickness of a paperback book. There was a calculator keypad embedded into the top of the box.

12:14:57. Reuven went to the box, picked it up, and punched the five-number code onto the keypad. The wailing, which was coming from somewhere beyond the plastic sheeting, stopped, and Tom reveled in the sudden silence. He inhaled deeply—realizing at that instant that he hadn't taken a breath since they'd crossed the threshold.

12:15:02. Reuven flipped Tom the keys to Hamzi's Mercedes. Using his hands, the Israeli signaled Tom to go back downstairs, get the last of the olive containers, and bring them all into the safe house, but not to close the door until he'd finished.

12:15:44. Reuven examined the box. The keypad indeed belonged to a cheap calculator—the kind you could find at any office-supply store for less than five euros. The box itself weighed about half a pound. It was made of some sort of injection-molded carbon fiber or preformed Kydex-like material. The seams were bonded—invisible. Reuven guessed that there was either a self-destruct or a doomsday device inside, which would go off if any attempt was made to get inside.

He dropped the box into the pocket of Hamzi's suit coat and went to the explosive charge, dropped to one knee, checked it, and removed the detonator, rendering the IED safe.

Next, Reuven took a look at the safe-house door. He focused his light on the bolt hole and peered inside. The hole had been chiseled out much deeper than usual. At its rearmost point, Reuven could see a metal contact plate to which a pair of black wires had been soldered.

Obviously, when the dead bolt was turned three times a contact was made and the keypad box armed itself.

Reuven closed the door then searched the short corridor, his LED probing the floor and walls inch by inch. There was a bathroom on the right-hand side. He entered it and found nothing untoward. Next to the bathroom was another door. Carefully, the Israeli opened it. When he shone the light down, he discovered another infrared-triggered IED, which he disarmed.

When Reuven was confident there were no more active booby traps, he returned to the foyer and focused his attention on the plastic sheeting. Carefully, he went to the left-hand corner of the arch leading to the next room, pried the end of the tape that sealed the sheeting to the floor, and gently pulled it free. Carefully, he worked his way across the six-foot opening until the entire bottom flap of plastic had been unfastened.

He repeated his action with the left-hand-side vertical strip, pulling just over four feet of tape free of the wall, turning when he heard Tom's shoes scrape across the floor as the American carried the first of the blue olive barrels into the safe house.

Reuven stood. "Bring that second barrel at once, Mahmoud," he said. "Don't dawdle like an Egyptian."

Tom gave the Israeli a dirty look.

12:22 A.M. Tom stacked the last of the barrels in the foyer. He nodded at the plastic where Reuven had removed the tape. Reuven nodded and shone the red LED around the seam, then, tucking the big black satchel under his arm like a football, led the way into the room with the tables of detonators and knapsack bomb components.

12:27:16. Obviously, they were in what had been the *salon*. To the right was a small kitchen. Straight ahead was the window adjacent to the drain-pipe Tom had climbed. Reuven pointed the light at the far wall next to the windows. Flanking each windowsill, hidden from outside view and undisturbed by the plastic sheet that covered the window, were more infrared sensors and receptor units. Taped six inches below the bottom edge of the sill apron were small explosive charges hardwired to the receptors.

Reuven pulled a small monocular from his trouser pocket, examined the right-hand-window booby trap, quickly established that it, too, was inert, and pulled the detonator out. Then he repeated his action on the left-window unit.

Before Tom had time to think about the nasty possibilities had he broken into the safe house the other night, Reuven tapped his shoulder. The Israeli pointed at the sidewall.

Tom shrugged, asking, "What the hell do you want now?"

Reuven demonstrated by pulling up one of the strips of tape that held the plastic sheeting to the wall. He motioned for Tom to do the same on the opposite side.

Tom complied. They removed the roughly eight-by-twelve-foot section of plastic from the wall. Then, under Reuven's direction, they laid it on the floor and retaped it securely. They repeated the sequence with a second piece of plastic sheeting, covering most of the *salon* and about half the foyer flooring.

12:40 A.M. They examined the detonators on the kitchen towel. *"Merde."* Reuven frowned. He didn't like what he saw. There were five detonators and components of eight knapsacks—perhaps even nine. The numbers didn't add up. Well, there was no way to deal with the problem now.

Reuven scooped up the detonators, produced a handkerchief, and carefully folded them into it. He pulled Tom close, stuffed the package into the American's pocket, and whispered into his ear, "Handle carefully. We'll want to dissect one of these and see how he designed them."

12:42. Reuven went to the long table that held the sewing machine and the pasta maker. He removed all of Ben Said's carefully rolled-out explosives, wadded them up, wrapped them in the plastic sheeting he'd removed from the window, and handed them to Tom, who took one of the empty olive barrels from under the picnic table and dropped the package into it.

The Israeli pulled a pocket secretary and a pen from his breast pocket and wrote a short note, which he showed to Tom. Tom's expression told Reuven that he'd received the message loud and clear.

The Israeli reached into the waistband of his trousers, retrieved the Glock with its stubby suppressor. He demonstrated to Tom that the weapon was loaded by easing the slide back about half an inch and displaying the 9mm round in the pistol's chamber. Then he closed the slide and handed the pistol to Tom, who somewhat self-consciously stuck the gun inside his waistband, positioning it in the small of his back, just as Reuven had done.

12:44. Tom played with the weapon's position until he found the most comfortable one. Then he tightened his belt one notch and jiggled his body. The gun was secure. He pulled Hamzi's keys out of his trouser pocket and showed them to Reuven.

In Arabic, Reuven said, "You take the car, Mahmoud. Leave it in the usual spot. I'll find my own way home."

"Yes, Yahia." Tom turned to go. Reuven pointed at the barrel that held Ben Said's explosives. Tom picked it up and tucked it under his arm. Then Reuven handed him the plastic box with its security keypad. Tom squeezed through the flap of plastic sheeting, resecured the tape in position, placed the box on its table, then headed for the door.

"Lock the door securely closed behind you, boy," Reuven's voice commanded.

12:47:15 A.M. Tom was just below the first-floor landing when he heard someone turn the front door lock noisily. He'd been making his way foot by foot in the darkness, picking his way over the construction detritus, counting the steps to monitor his progress. It was easier than he'd thought: his night vision was sharp enough that he could make out more or less where he was going.

Now all of a sudden the *minuterie* below came on and for an instant he was blinded. He heard voices stage-whispering in Arabic and French. There was a bump—as if a suitcase had been dropped—and then he thought he heard a voice mutter, "*Khara alaay*—well, shit on me." The words were indistinct. But they told him there was more than one person down there.

My God. Ben Said. And he's not alone. Holding tight to the barrel under his arm, Tom raced up eight steps to the first-floor landing, trying to remember where the obstacles were. At the top he adjusted his load, then dashed tippy-toe thirteen paces to the stairwell leading to the second floor, praying that he wouldn't trip. As he went, he worked Hamzi's keys out of his trouser pocket, trying desperately to keep them from jingling, fighting to make no sound whatsoever—not even daring to breathe.

12:47:21. There were twenty-two steps between the first and second floors. His heart pounding so loudly he felt they must have heard it below, Tom found the safe-house key on step nineteen—just as the *minuterie* light went out. He kept climbing, his arm around the barrel, his fingers resting lightly in the banister. Twenty. Twenty-one. Twenty-two. He reached for the newel cap that signified the landing. Turned left in the darkness toward the safe-house door.

12:47:40. The lights came on. *Oh God, oh, damn, oh Christ. They were coming up the stairs.* He wondered how many of them there were. They sounded like a herd of goddamn rogue elephants, a frigging buffalo stampede.

12:47:42. Tom stood in front of the safe-house door, telling himself it was going to be all right. *Don't drop the barrel. Don't drop the key. Take the key in your hand. Hold the damn thing securely. Put it into the lock. Turn once. Turn again. Turn once more. Open the damn door.*

12:47:45. Tom yanked the key out of the lock and pressed the door handle downward. From inside he could hear the muted sound of the alarm as the door broke the plane of the infrared beam.

He stepped inside and closed the door behind him. "It's me," he whispered. "Ben Said and others. They're right behind me."

Without waiting for a response, Tom ran for the table. *Oh Christ oh God what's the number?* It had suddenly evaporated from his consciousness. He found the box, squinted in the dim light, and desperately punched 3-0-6-7-9 into the keypad.

The wailing stopped. He ran back to the door and, careful not to disrupt the infrared beam, inserted the key into the lock and turned the bolt once-twice-thrice. Only then did he dare suck air into his lungs.

"Bedroom." Reuven hissed at him from the darkness beyond the plastic curtain. "Keep low—don't let them see a silhouette. Use the pistol. Stay until I call you."

Tom started to set the olive barrel down then realized it was a bad idea. He shifted his weight to balance the load, reached into his waistband, pulled out the Glock, and started to tighten his finger around the trigger. He jerked his finger out of the trigger guard as if he'd touched a live wire. *I'd probably shoot myself in the foot.*

He indexed his trigger finger along the frame and pointed the Glock's muzzle downward. Behind the stubby suppressor he could make out three greenish spots. The gun had night sights. As Tom moved, he held the weapon up so the front dot was even with the two rear dots. That would be his whatchamacallit sight picture. That's how the instructors at the Farm had referred to it.

Desperately, he tried to remember what they'd taught him about pistol shooting. He couldn't recall much. In fact, Tom couldn't remember the last time he'd fired a gun.

12:48:08. He'd just reached the bedroom door when the alarm went off. Instinctively, his finger dropped onto the trigger. He backed just inside the door, dropped to one knee, eased the barrel onto the floor, concealed himself behind the jamb, put the weapon up, held it securely in a two-handed grip, and trained it down the eight-foot corridor. Christ, this was close quarters.

39

12:48:11 A.M. Tom heard the sound of a key in the front door lock. The bolt turned. He jumped at the sound and then cursed himself. The bolt turned twice more. Tom heard the door handle move. Then the alarm squealed and he started again.

The door eased open. Tom held his breath as the ambient light from the *minuterie* outside washed into the tiny foyer.

As if in slow motion, a wraithlike figure in a long, flowing overcoat moved through the doorway, heading for the table. Tom counted the seconds off: *a thousand one, a thousand two, a thousand three.*

The alarm shut off. Now a second, then a third shadow came through the door. The third shadow was carrying a big case—like a three-suiter or a wheeled garment bag. For an instant, Tom thought he saw weapons in their hands. Then the door closed behind them and it went dark again. He held the Glock up high, his eyes completely focused on the three green dots that told him where he was aiming.

The third man—the one with the suitcase—turned to face the corridor. Did he have something in his free hand?

Tom followed suitcase man with the sights on the pistol. His lungs were bursting for oxygen, but he couldn't bring himself to breathe.

The shadow moved slightly. Now he was partially obscured. But Tom could almost smell him, he was so close.

Tom could hear his heart pounding. He froze, trying to become invisible.

From the part of the foyer Tom couldn't see came a voice, speaking accent-free Arabic. "Yahia? Yahia? C'mon out, old friend. We have to talk." The voice was smooth, coaxing, almost feminine in tone. Suddenly Tom's nostrils flared and he caught the sweet citrus scent of aftershave or cologne. He refocused his eyes and realized that Suitcase Man had moved closer—he was less than two yards away.

And then came six rapid shots—no louder than a hammer striking nails. *Thruup-ruup-ruup, thruup-ruup-ruup.*

The shadow in the corridor jumped—turned toward the sound of the shots.

Panicked, Tom jerked the Glock's trigger twice. The pistol surprised him. There was no *boom-boom,* only a pair of *thwoks.*

Suddenly the doorjamb next to his head splintered. Tom froze, blinded by the bright orange muzzle blast of the weapon that was *oh-my-God* pointed right at him. He tried to disappear—to become a puddle on the floor. But he found himself completely unable to move. He was helpless. Incapable of motion. It was like being in the middle of a nightmare.

The doorknob just behind Tom's head shattered. He felt something slice into his scalp. And still there was no discernible gunshot sound—only muffled bursts. *Thruup-ruup-ruup.*

Tom tried to control the pistol in his hands. But the gun took on a life of its own, firing one-two-three-four-five-six-seven shots before he could bring the trigger under control.

He tried to focus on his sights. But all he could see was the muzzle flash as his adversary came closer-closer-closer moving in stop-time slow motion, now just over an arm's length away.

Tom forced himself to lower the Glock's muzzle until he could see over the top of it.

He saw the green dot—that was the front sight. Beyond it was the looming outline of the man trying to kill him.

Frantically, he pulled the trigger.

The pistol fired once and then the slide locked back. Tom tried to force it forward, but the goddamn thing was stuck—it wouldn't move.

He was a dead man. Heart pumping, he closed his eyes, anticipating the bullet that would kill him.

And then there was only silence.

Tom opened his eyes. He could feel the pulse racing in his wrists. He dropped the Glock onto the floor. Scrambled onto his hands and knees and crawled past the corpse. His hand landed in a puddle and he stifled a gasp. "Reuven?"

Suddenly the lights in the foyer came on. Tom was blinded. When he looked up, Reuven was staring down at him.

"C'mon," the Israeli said hoarsely. "No time to waste, boychik."

Tom tried to focus. "What?"

"No time. Get up, Tom. On your feet."

Dumbly, Tom did as he was told. He stepped over the man he'd just killed. There was blood—a lot of it—and brain matter splattered on the floor.

Reuven rolled the corpse with his foot. "You hit *him* more than once," he said. "Good shooting."

"It was luck," Tom protested. "Dumb stupid luck."

"Remember what Shamir said: never deny too loudly."

Tom stared at what he'd done and his knees buckled.

Reuven caught him. "Easy, boy."

Tom felt really queasy. He began to see spots and the room started to turn.

"Breathe, Tom," Reuven instructed him. "Take in oxygen."

Tom sucked air into his nose and mouth and thought he could smell blood. He opened his mouth wide in a silent, panicked yawn. Maybe that would help stifle the sickness he was feeling.

It didn't. He took a deep breath and felt a little better. Took a second and third and the spots disappeared. Tom shook the Israeli's hand off. "I'm okay. Okay."

"Sure you are."

Tom reached for the handkerchief in his pocket and blew his nose.

Sucked oxygen into his lungs. Wiped at his eyes. He returned his gaze to the corpse at his feet and a new wave of nausea almost swept him off his feet.

Reuven took him by the arm and led him into the foyer.

As he approached the other corpses, a second wave of panic amplified by doubt washed over Tom—they'd killed the wrong people. And then he bent down and forced himself to examine the corpse of the man who'd silenced the alarm. It was the same individual who was in Shahram's surveillance photo and MJ's picture from Gaza. It was Tariq Ben Said—or whatever his name really was. Tom heaved a huge sigh of relief.

Ben Said and a second man lay atop the plastic sheeting, arms and legs splayed out. Reuven had head-shot them—a neat triangle of bullet holes between the bridge of their noses and their upper lips. The realization that the Israeli had sucker-punched them caused another emotional tsunami to wash over Tom. They'd actually murdered these men. Killed them in cold blood.

Reuven must have read his thoughts. "What? You thought I'd tell them, 'Go for your guns,' like this was some old Western movie?" He bent down and started to rifle through Ben Said's pockets. "This isn't the Marquis of Queensbury, Tom. This is real life."

The Israeli pulled a German passport from Ben Said's jacket. "Let's see who he is this week." Reuven opened the document and squinted. "Lothar Abdat, born twenty-seven March 1956 in Hamburg."

He flipped through the pages. There was a credit-card receipt and Reuven peered at it. "Air France—the main office on Champs-Élysées." He patted Ben Said down. "But no ticket." He reached into the bomb maker's trouser pockets and turned them inside out, spilling coins and keys onto the plastic, and pawed through them. Reuven gave Tom an encouraging look. "Take the other one. See what he's carrying."

1:14 A.M. They'd stowed almost everything they could in the wheeled duffel bag. They'd pulled the clothes off the three bodies. As Tom packed Ben Said's explosives and the detonators, Reuven used a kit in his satchel to take the corpses' fingerprints, as well as saliva and hair samples for DNA testing. Now he picked up the Vuitton knapsacks one by one, counting the various components on the folding table as he lifted them up and dropped them into the duffel.

Tom had regained his composure. It actually hadn't taken him long, something that surprised him because he, like most Americans, was both unaccustomed and unprepared to deal with the sorts of lethal encounters that typified this brutal new form of warfare.

Reuven looked over at him. "Double-check for shell casings, okay? We're still missing one nine-millimeter and one twenty-two-caliber."

"Okay." Tom went to the foyer and dropped to his knees, his fingers searching along the floor molding of the short corridor. Reuven had fired six times. He'd fired ten shots. The man he'd killed had shot three times. So far they'd recovered only seventeen casings.

He found the missing 9mm shell just behind the bedroom door frame. He still disagreed with Reuven's "kill them all and let Allah sort it out" approach to terrorism. But in one respect, the Israeli was absolutely on the mark: America's unpreparedness and its inability to deal on a societal level with this new kind of war were indeed things that had to change.

The Marquis of Queensbury and his book *were* out the window. Bin Laden and al-Qa'ida certainly didn't play by any rules. And it was a rough game that was getting rougher by the day. The bad guys had beheaded Danny Pearl in Pakistan. Now insurgents were taking hostages in Iraq and beheading them, too. It wouldn't be too long before it happened closer to home.

The world was turning upside down. *Was?* Tom snorted loud enough to make Reuven look up. Hell—the world had already turned upside down. It used to be so damn uncomplicated. Terrorist groups were hierarchical. Cut off the head and the rest of the organization died. That was true of all the old-line groups: the Red Army Faction; Brigate Rosse, Baader Meinhoff; PLO, PFLP, Japanese Red Army, Sendero Luminoso. All of them were hierarchical.

He finally came up with the missing .22-caliber casing, which had wedged behind a loose piece of floor molding. Those neat and tidy days were gone forever. If Task Force 121 got lucky in Afghanistan or Pakistan and grabbed Usama today, al-Qa'ida would still continue to wage war on the West. Because it wasn't a terrorist organization in the conventional sense. It was a cell-based politico-military organization with stand-alone guerrilla and terror operations like Ben Said's running concurrently in a score of countries. The same thing was true of Islamist terror groups in Indonesia, the Philippines, Egypt, Algeria, and Morocco.

The old terrorists tended to be Marxist or Communist inspired and supported—so-called people's liberation movements. Al-Qa'ida and other Islamist movements were more insidious. They exploited local nationalism and Islamic fervor, transmogrifying terror into a particularly effective—and deadly—fusion of politics, ideology, and religion. And it was going to be a protracted series of battles. If the current situation were overlaid on a World War II time line, the U.S. was still in the first months after Pearl Harbor. Moreover, CIA was almost entirely ill-equipped to deal with Islamists.

But then, so was 4627. Tom broke his thought train and looked over at Reuven. "What about the bodies?"

"Milo will handle them in the morning. This place will be totally *sanitaire* by tomorrow night. The cars we give to him, too—Ben Said had car keys in his jacket. We'll find it and drive to the warehouse. They'll go to the grinder—with these three."

Reuven caught the horrified expression on Tom's face and ignored it. "My guess? Your fiancée was right and I was wrong. Ben Said was about to tie up loose ends. Get rid of Hamzi. Shift the operation. Cover his tracks." The Israeli paused. "But that's not the problem."

"What is?"

Reuven jerked a thumb toward the knapsack parts. "There were four detonators and six whole knapsacks, right?"

"Yup." Tom nodded.

"Well, there were enough parts to make three more knapsacks on the table."

"So?"

"How many Montsouris packs did Hamzi order?"

Tom thought about it for a few seconds "Twelve."

"One for Dianne Lamb," Reuven said, "six on the table, and three in parts. That leaves two unaccounted for." The Israeli paused. "And then there's the Air France receipt." He looked at Tom, his expression grave. "We're behind the curve. Ben Said's operation is already in play."

40

THEY'D LAID EVERYTHING from the safe house out on the long library table. Tony Wyman picked up one of the wads of explosive and sniffed. "No odor at all." He shook his head. "How in God's name did he do it?"

"We'll know in a couple of days." Reuven rubbed his shaved head. He looked exhausted—emotionally wrung dry. The Israeli looked at his watch. "When's your IED guy getting here?"

Reflexively, Wyman checked his own wrist. "Any minute now."

Tom slapped the telephone receiver down. "Got it. Thanks."

Reuven cocked his head in Tom's direction. "So?"

"He had tickets on the Air France Flight 068 to Los Angeles. Business class, departing Wednesday November twenty-sixth, returning Friday the twenty-eighth on Air France Flight 069. Second trip: Air France 070, departing Wednesday the tenth December, returning the twelfth on Air France Flight 071." He checked his notes. "That's a lot of flying in a short time."

"Scouting trip," Tony Wyman said. "Has to be. It's a common AQN tactic. They're known to do thorough target assessments." Tom knew Wyman was correct. He had friends in the Federal Air Marshals Service who, for a period of months, had noted an increase in provocative behavior on domestic flights all over the United States. Subsequent investigations had determined that al-Qa'ida was probing for weaknesses in the system.

Still, Tom was dubious. "Ben Said wouldn't travel just to scope out the plane—check for marshals on the flight or evaluate the security. It wasn't his style." Indeed, the bomber had put himself at considerable risk by taking an Air France flight in the past. But there'd been a deeper purpose when he'd flown to Israel: to test the detonators.

"There's more," Tom insisted. "There has to be." He frowned at Reuven. "It might have been helpful for us to be able to ask the man himself."

Reuven's expression grew cold. "Don't go there."

"Why not? It's a valid question. Why kill him in cold blood? Why did we have to kill them all before we'd had a chance to learn anything?"

"It was necessary." Reuven turned away.

"C'mon, Reuven—why?"

The Israeli answered him with silence.

"You can't squeeze water from a stone, Reuven. You can't get answers from a corpse."

"Maybe"—the Israeli whirled around—"you'd have preferred to spend two or three months double-checking everything he told us so we can separate the fabrications from the truth. If, that is, he'd even given us a grain of truth in the first place?"

"You don't know unless you try."

"I know he won't make any more bombs," Reuven growled. "I know he won't blow up any more women and children. I know he won't kill any more 4627 people. Maybe for you that's not good enough, boychik. For me, it is." Fists clenched, he advanced on Tom.

Who wasn't about to give an inch. "He doesn't have to make more bombs, Reuven. By your own count, there are two of them still out there— and no way to find them now that he's dead."

"Enough." Wyman stepped between the two. "This bickering is getting us nowhere." He looked at Tom. "What's done is done. I'll—"

He was interrupted by urgent knocking on the library door. One of the 4627 security people opened it. "Mr. Wyman? There's a Roger Semerad downstairs asking to see you."

Wyman's face lit up. "Please—escort him up here right away." He turned toward the others. "Roger's retired FBI. He was their top explosive forensics guy until he contracted multiple sclerosis just over six years ago. He'd always been something of a maverick—and his wisecracking got on Director Freeh's nerves. So Freeh eased him out—right into the arms of Deutsche Telecom. Now he's based in Bonn as DT's head of technical security. I called him last night—asked him to make the drive over, just in case."

"Isn't it a long way to come on spec?"

"Not for Roger. He drives a Bentley turbo. Believe me—he looks for just about any excuse to make a road trip."

9:28 A.M. Roger Semerad was a big guy with a voice to match, a face full of salt-and-pepper beard, and a bone-crushing handshake. He got around in a small black electric cart equipped with a clip-on headlight, an old-fashioned bulb-powered bicycle horn clamped to the handlebars, and a bumper sticker that read EVEN MY DOG IS A CONSERVATIVE.

He high-fived Tony Wyman then gave Tom and Reuven, whom he'd caught staring at him out of his peripheral vision, a penetrating second glance. "Here's the story in a nutshell, fellas," he said. "I'm Roger. I got MS. Can't hardly feel my legs anymore, so I need the scooter, and which is also why I'm driving an automatic Bentley instead of a Ferrari. And just in case you wanted to know, frigging MS screws with you worse than a cheap gin hangover."

There was a moment of self-conscious silence as Tom and Reuven suddenly found the pattern on the rug hugely fascinating.

Semerad cocked his head at Tony Wyman. "Think they got it, Tonio?"

"Hope so."

"Me, too," Semerad growled. "That said, let's get to the problem solving."

He scootered across the room to eyeball the display on the library table. "You guys gonna compete with the Cameroonians at the *marché puces*?"

"Something like that."

"Well, you ain't gonna go very far on that slim inventory, Tonio. Kinda meager."

"All depends how it's used," Tom said. "We think it's enough to bring down a couple of planes, maybe more."

"Tell you what." Semerad took a quick turn around the library then parked himself in front of Wyman. "I'm gonna set up in that there corner." He pointed toward the map table and its magnifying light. "Alls I need is for someone to unstrap the case off the back of this contraption and I'm happy to go to work."

Tom gave him a skeptical glance. "Don't you want to know what we're looking for?"

"Nope. I kinda like to find out for myself." He steered the cart over to the table and plucked a detonator off the green felt, hefted it, then looked it up and down. "Nice," he said. "Whose work?"

Tom stood with his arms crossed. "We'll let you tell us, since you like to find things out on your own."

Semerad laughed. "Touché, kiddo." He tooted his horn twice and wriggled his eyebrows in a passable Harpo Marx. "Gangway, gents. The cavalry has arrive-ed."

11:55 A.M. "Frigging incredible." Roger Semerad raised the jeweler's loupe on its headband and wiped perspiration out of the corners of his eyes with a huge blue-and-white handkerchief. "This guy's a genius—if he weren't a frigging criminal, I'd hire him." When his remark was greeted by silence he waited until the others had gathered around him. "He's managed to miniaturize a SIM card and a PDA processor and use 'em to create his detonator package."

Wyman said, "SIM card like in a cell phone?"

"You got it, Tony. A Subscriber Identity Module. In technical language it's the thingy that stores all your subscriber info like your account number and your phonebook. Can't use a phone without a SIM card these days."

"So basically what we've got here is a cell phone without the phone."

Semerad nodded. "In a way."

"So how does it become a detonator? Don't you need a ringer to trigger the explosion?"

"That's how it's commonly done. Like the car bombs and IEDs we're seeing in Iraq now. ETA—the Basque separatists—and the IRA have been using cell phones for years. They wire cell-phone ringers to detonating caps. Place a call or send an instant message to the doctored phone and ka-blooey. Believe me, it's not rocket science. But there's no ringer here. That's the creative part. He's replaced the ringer with a computer chip."

Tom shook his head. "I don't get it."

"This guy, he pulled the processor out of a PDA—like my Palm Tungsten over there, but a much older model. You know that all computer chips create heat, right?"

Tom nodded.

"Most of the newer chips have what you might call a throttle control on them. They're programmed to shut down if they get too hot."

"Understood."

Semerad held up the detonator. "Well, there's no governor on the chip in this doohickey."

Wyman popped the monocle out of his eye. "Which means . . ."

"Which means when the cell-phone component responds to a call and a specific code is keyed in, it sets the chip running. And the chip keeps getting hotter and hotter. And I mean hot. Red-hot. Fire-in-the-hole hot."

Wyman shook his head. "But heat alone doesn't set plastic explosive off, does it, Roger?"

"You need something that produces energy to set off your explosive—like a percussion cap or even the cell-phone ringer. In this case, your bomb-maker has been real inventive. First he slipped some explosive into the body of the detonator—that way, when the bomb goes off the detonator itself is destroyed, leaving very little in the way of forensic evidence. And then he's managed to create a brief but powerful electrical charge by combining the technologies in the SIM card and the PDA chip." He shook his head in amazement. "This guy is incredible. He's transferred all the elements—even the carbon fiber antenna—onto some sort of flexible membrane to cut down on weight and signature. He's miniaturized the equivalent of an electric blasting cap, a remotely operated blasting machine, and a self-destruction device and fit everything into a package that weighs, what? I'd venture less than fifty grams." He gestured toward the Vuitton knapsacks, then looked over at Wyman. "Tonio, I'd wager a big pile of *dinero* that this damned thing is completely undetectable passing through airport security."

Reuven looked at the detonator components. "Time frame?"

"To explosion from the time the sequence is initiated? Maybe five seconds."

The Israeli frowned. "Range?"

"Worldwide. You could place the call from anywhere—even do it online."

"Jeezus H." Tom shook his head. "Can you tell us what telephone number has been assigned to this particular SIM card?"

"Sure—if I had the right equipment."

"Which is where?"

"Well, they'd have it at Verizon, or Sprint."

Tom's eyes widened. "The U.S. cellular companies?"

"Yup. This isn't a European SIM. All the local SIM cards are GSMs. This one is CDMA. Which means it's Verizon or Sprint." Semerad backed his scooter up. "You guys got broadband?"

Tom nodded. "Sure."

"You let me plug my laptop into your connection and I'll pull down what you need in a matter of minutes."

1:21 P.M. Roger Semerad squinted at the computer's screen. "The detonator SIMs are all for Los Angeles–area numbers."

Tony Wyman looked at Tom. "What were the dates of those flights?"

Tom checked his notes. "Outbound Wednesday, November twenty-sixth; returning Friday, November twenty-eighth. Outbound Wednesday, December tenth; returning Friday the twelfth."

"I think," Wyman said, "we can rule out an attack over Thanksgiving."

"Why?" Tom asked. "He's scheduled himself to be in Los Angeles over Thanksgiving. What better time for an attack than during the peak holiday travel time."

"No," Reuven said. "The al-Qa'ida model is to stage simultaneous attacks, not a series. They carried out the operations against your embassies in Kenya and Tanzania within minutes of each other. On 9/11, they hijacked four aircraft almost simultaneously. It's the AQN pattern."

Wyman played with his monocle. "You read it as attacks on Flights 068 and 070, and attacks on Flights 069 and 071 all on one day."

"Two days," Tom said. "All of Ben Said's tickets were for a Wednesday and a Friday," Tom said. And then he clapped his hand over his mouth. "Oh, my God—it's Christmas. It has to be Christmas."

Wyman pulled a pocket secretary out of his jacket pocket and flipped through it. "Tom's right. This year, Thanksgiving and Christmas both fall on Thursdays."

He paused. "Fits the al-Qa'ida pattern of scoping out the flights firsthand. Satisfies the simultaneous-attack criterion, too."

"But that's not enough."

Wyman turned toward Tom. "Why not?"

Tom looked at his boss. "Wheelbarrows, Tony."

"What?"

"Roger said the SIMs all came from phones registered in the Los Angeles area. Now, you can make a call from anywhere to anywhere on a cell phone. What this tells me is that Ben Said bought his cell phones in Los Angeles because that's where he's going to use them."

Wyman frowned. "That's awfully thin, Tom."

"Maybe. But it's what I think."

Roger Semerad wheeled his scooter next to Tom and said, "Wasn't al-Qa'ida going to strike at LAX during the Y2K New Year celebration?"

Wyman nodded. "The guy coming from Canada with the explosives in his car, right?"

"That's the one." Semerad played with the handlebar of his scooter. "Isn't one of AQN's benchmarks that they like to hit targets more than once?"

Wyman spent half a minute in silence. "If we go ahead, we're doing so on very circumstantial evidence."

Tom said, "That doesn't make it any less valid."

Finally, Wyman turned to Reuven. "You head back to Tel Aviv and get the DNA work done."

The Israeli saluted.

"And make sure your man Salah gets us copies of everything he pulls out of Hamzi."

The Israeli nodded in agreement. "Will do."

Wyman cocked his head in Reuven's direction. "By the way, what do you guys call your company?"

Reuven didn't hesitate. "Hawkeye."

"Well, next time—if there is one—we operate jointly, Hawkeye's going to split the expenses. I can't afford to float you people."

"What about seventy–thirty," Reuven said. "You're established. We're just starting out."

"Half and half, Reuven, it's the American way." He paused. "But you get to use our facilities here and in Washington—not that you haven't been doing that already." Wyman turned to Tom. "Write this up. You know what to leave out and what to include. I'll check it over. Then we'll head for Washington. I want you and MJ with me when I present this package to CTC." He caught Tom's look of amazement. "Your fiancée had a lot to do with this," he said. "If she hadn't had the grit to bring the Gaza material to Paris in the first place, we probably wouldn't be standing here."

Tom beamed.

"You work with her."

"I'm on it."

"Good. We're handing them twenty-four-karat material, Tom. And I can assure you they don't get twenty-four-karat very often these days."

CHANTILLY, VIRGINIA

41

THEY WERE EARLY for the 4 P.M. appointment with representatives from CTC because Tony Wyman always liked to be early, and besides, like all good case officers, he preferred never to go anywhere he hadn't scoped out in advance.

They'd driven out from the 4627 corporate offices in Rosslyn in Wyman's big, gray Suburban. Tom found the venue bothersome. A proposed meeting at CIA headquarters had been summarily rejected by the CTC chief, who hinted that Wyman and Tom were unwelcome presences at Langley. Wyman had suggested as an alternative one of CIA's Rosslyn satellite offices because of their proximity to 4627. That, too, had been rejected. Instead, CTC had dictated the Chantilly site, just short of an hour's commute west of Rosslyn through the crowded Dulles corridor and along the perpetually gridlocked Route 28.

14528-C Flint Lee Road turned out to be an anonymous shoe box of a one-story building set among scores of identical one-story shoe-box buildings that lined both sides of a potholed, four-lane road that ran on an east–west axis half a mile south of Route 50 and six-tenths of a mile due south of Dulles Airport's barbed-wire-topped outer perimeter fence.

As they turned onto Flint Lee Road, Tom, who was riding shotgun, said, "I don't like it, Tony."

"Why?" Wyman flicked a glance in the rearview mirror then turned toward Tom.

"Just gives me bad vibes. And why the hell did they make us drive an hour? You know as well as I do they have plenty of suitable sites in McLean or Vienna." He stared through the windshield. "Plus, there's only one way in and out."

"Amen." Wyman drove past the turnoff to 14528, turned left into a cul-de-sac warren of warehouses, and pulled over. He turned to MJ, who was riding behind him. "What about you?"

She shrugged. "You guys are the operators. You tell me."

Tom said, "I think we position ourselves in a standoff position and see who arrives."

Wyman nodded. "I agree."

"What are you concerned about, an ambush of some sort?"

Tom thought about Jim McGee riding in the front seat of the armored State Department FAV and said, "Nothing's out of the question these days."

"Oh, for heaven's sake," MJ said. "Aren't you two being just a little bit too much cloak-and-dagger?"

Tom turned to face her. "Didn't you see the T-shirt I put on this morning?"

"T-shirt?"

"It's the one that reads PARANOIA: IT'S MORE THAN A FEELING, IT'S A WAY OF LIFE."

"Very funny."

"A little paranoia every now and then," Wyman said, "can be a good thing."

MJ gave him a skeptical look. "Are we talking about now-now, or then-now, Tony?"

"Both." He swiveled toward her and deflected. "So, when's the wedding?"

MJ's hand dropped onto Tom's shoulder. "Day after Christmas." She saw the crestfallen look flash across Wyman's face. "It's just us and my family, Tony—the ceremony at the local parish and a reception at my parents' house in Great Neck."

"I understand." He nodded. "Not to worry."

At 3:17 P.M., Wyman's cell phone rang. He turned the radio down and plucked it out of the utility tray. *"Pronto?"*

He listened for a quarter of a minute, his expression darkening by the second. "You told them they could shove it up their asses, right?" he growled. "Good. We're on our way back."

Wyman slapped the clamshell phone shut, put the Chevy in gear, and wheeled roughly out of the cul-de-sac.

"What's up?"

"This appointment was a ruse to get us out of the office. At three sharp, two Agency security types showed up in Rosslyn demanding all our files on Ben Said, as well as the transcript of your conversation with young Adam Margolis. Said we were in possession of illegally obtained classified materials and were obliged to turn everything over to them immediately." He looked at Tom. "Oh, and by the way, your security clearance has been revoked."

"Oh?"

"The reason given was that you compromised an Agency operation."

"What?"

"Liam McWhirter's setup in Cormeilles-en-Parisis."

"When he was trying to compromise *me*." Tom rolled his eyes. "You've got to be kidding."

"Dead serious." He looked at Tom. "Don't worry—we'll deal with it."

Tom bit his lower lip. "What about the office?"

"And Bronco asked them for their warrant. They told him they didn't have one—this was just a friendly call. Bronco told them to get stuffed and they backed off." He looked at MJ. "It was a bluff—for now."

"For now?"

"Look," Wyman said. "The seventh floor has a staff of lawyers and security investigators who just love to make things tough for certain people."

"They dress like the guys in *Men in Black*," Tom said. "We used to call them the DCI's gestapo."

"We still do," Wyman snorted.

Tom looked at his boss. "So, what's the plan, Tony?"

"It's time to put a stop to all this crap." Wyman flipped the cell phone open, punched up his phone book, scrolled down until he found the number he wanted, hit the transmit button, and waited for the connection.

Then he said, "Porter? It's Tony Wyman. I'd like to bring two of my colleagues for a meeting with you in the committee's bubble room." He paused. "I'm talking CRITICOM." There was another pause. "Uh-huh. An hour and three-quarters." Wyman checked the dashboard clock. "We can do that. I don't want to talk on an open line, but let me say we have information relating to certain operations that would have resulted positively in the CT area, but which were blocked by the seventh floor. And we can document the fact that DO is so dysfunctional that private companies like mine have to perform CIA's core missions and thus affect the national security of the nation with no oversight over our operations whatsoever."

Wyman listened. "Yes, I know there are no recruitments anymore. No risk taking. I know he said five years. But it's been more than eight already—and there's been no improvement since I pulled the plug. The DO is dead, Porter. A shell. Remember the nimble, flexible, core-mission-oriented enterprise where we used to work? Well, it's a fleeting memory." He listened some more, then nodded. "Yes, I'm convinced they have to go, Porter. It's time to muck out the stables." There was another pause. "We'll be there. Thanks."

As Wyman snapped the phone shut, Tom said, "I thought you told me 4627 wasn't in the business of staging coups at the CIA."

Wyman looked at his young protégé long and hard. "You were the one who told me we should be. You were right. This country's been deaf, dumb, and blind for more than a decade now, and that's too goddamn long. Porter may not be the perfect choice—but he's our guy. He's all we've got these days. It's time for them to go. All of them. Every last piece of dead-wood." He looked at Tom. "We owe that much to Jim McGee." He paused. "And to Shahram."

MJ's eyes filled up. "When Tom and I marry, I expect you to fly in and stand up for him, Tony."

"Fly? *Moi?* Not on the twenty-sixth of December, m'dear." Wyman caught her worried look in the rearview mirror and laughed. "It's not so far to Great Neck. I'll drive, if you don't mind."

EPILOGUE

IN THE EARLY EVENING of November 18, 2003, the chairman of the House Permanent Select Committee on Intelligence and his chief counsel held a two-and-a-half-hour off-the-record meeting with three unidentified individuals in HPSCI's bubble room, which is located in a secure area on an upper floor of the U.S. Capitol building. Left behind after the session was a thick folder of materials, which were secured in the chairman's personal document safe. The meeting was never logged in any of HPSCI's formal records, and HPSCI's chief counsel requested that the U.S. Capitol Police officer manning the security checkpoint directly outside the hallway refrain from checking the identities of the visitors and entering their names in the committee's sign-in book.

Precisely what was said at that meeting is still unknown. But a string of subsequent events—virtually all of them covered in the media—might serve as an accurate indicator.

• On December 24, 2003, Air France canceled the December 24 Air France Flights 068 and 070, and December 25's Air France Flight 068—all to Los Angeles. The return flights to Paris, Wednesday's Flight 069, and Thursday's 069 and 071, were also canceled.

• That same day, French prime minister Jean-Pierre Raffarin issued a statement explaining that the preemptive measure had been taken "on the basis of information, currently being checked, which was gathered in the framework of Franco-American cooperation in the fight against terrorism." According to a report on French television and sourced to unnamed security officials, the flights were aborted because intelligence information suggested al-Qa'ida was to bring down multiple civilian aircraft somewhere between Paris and Los Angeles during the Christmas holidays. Some newspapers reported that thirteen passengers were detained for questioning. According to press reports, all thirteen were released.

• A short article in the December 26 *Le Matin* reported that in an unintended consequence of the increased security at Charles de Gaulle airport, three expensive Louis Vuitton Montsouris knapsacks—one carried by a passenger on Flight 068, another by someone traveling on Flight 070, and a third on Thursday's Flight 068—were confiscated when French customs inspectors discovered the bags were counterfeits. The passengers, according to the story, were interrogated, and after it had been established that they believed they'd bought genuine Vuitton merchandise, the knapsacks were replaced on the spot by the French authorities with real Montsouris.

• Beginning in early January, Washington reporters who covered the intelligence beat found themselves the recipients of an unexpected trickle of leaks from Capitol Hill sources detailing the sorry state of CIA in general and the Directorate of Operations in particular. By the beginning of March, the trickle had become a torrent, and DCI George Tenet began to realize that someone up on Capitol Hill had painted a huge target on his back.

• On January 19, 2004, Al Jazeera reported in a short tell-story that Moroccan authorities, acting on what was described by Mukhabarat sources as the fruits of a successful interrogation, discovered an Islamist bomb factory in a residential villa on the outskirts of the city of Safi, a hotbed of Islamist activity 250 kilometers southwest of the capital city of

Rabat. Six Salafist radicals were killed during the assault. Two Moroccan Special Forces soldiers were wounded.

• At 2:24 P.M. on Wednesday, May 26, 2004, the CIA's congressional liaison was summoned to the HPSCI offices, where he was handed a single page of language that would be included in the Intelligence Authorization Act for fiscal year 2005. The officer was instructed to show it to CIA's top leadership. The page read as follows:

All is not well in the world of clandestine human intelligence collection (HUMINT). The DCI himself has stated that five more years will be needed to build a viable HUMINT capability. The Committee, in the strongest of possible terms, asserts that the Directorate of Operations (DO) needs fixing. For too long the CIA has been ignoring its core mission activities. There is a dysfunctional denial of any need for corrective action . . . If the CIA continues to ignore the experience of many of its best, brightest, and most experienced officers, and continues to equate criticism from within and without—especially from the oversight committees—as commentary unworthy even of consideration, no matter how constructive, informed and well-meaning that criticism may be, they do so at their peril. The DO will become nothing more than a stilted bureaucracy incapable of even the slightest bit of success. The nimble, flexible, core-mission oriented enterprise the DO once was, is becoming a fleeting memory. With each day it becomes harder to resurrect. The Committee highlights, with concern, the fact that it took only a year or two in the mid-1990s to decimate the capabilities of the CIA, that we are now in the 8th year of rebuild, and still we are 5 years away from being healthy. This is tragic. It should never happen again.

• It has been rumored but not confirmed by CIA sources that shortly after the congressional liaison faxed the page to Langley's seventh floor, someone in the DCI's office suite was heard to shout, "I don't care what you say. That goddamn son of a bitch Tony Wyman wrote that crap."

• On Wednesday evening, June 2, 2004, George John Tenet called President George W. Bush and informed him he would be resigning as DCI the next morning.

• On Thursday, June 3, 2004, Tenet resigned, effective July 11.

• On Tuesday, August 10, 2004, President George W. Bush nominated Congressman Porter J. Goss of Florida as the new director of central intelligence. Goss would be the second member of Congress to hold the title. Goss was confirmed by the Senate and took office on the twenty-fourth of September, 2004.